# WHO'S THAT GIRL

# BLAIR THORNBURGH

# Who's that GIRL

HARPER TEEN
An Imprint of HarperCollinsPublishers

HarperTeen is an imprint of HarperCollins Publishers.

ISBN 978-0-06-244777-7

Typography by Ray Shappell
17 18 19 20 21   PC/LSCH   10 9 8 7 6 5 4 3 2 1
❖
First Edition

*For Mom and Dad,*
*who rock*

# CHAPTER ONE

Everything weird started the day my dad brought home the yurt.

"Robert?"

Anne McCullough, alias Mom, was peering through the windows of our back door, cup of coffee in hand, and frowning. Robert Schwartz, alias Dad, had taken the station wagon somewhere early that morning and was now puttering around in the yard. But since puttering was one of those activities Dad did to relax, like separating the recycling or buying dress shoes on eBay, I wasn't exactly concerned.

"Nattie?"

Natalie McCullough-Schwartz, alias Nattie, alias me, was sitting at the kitchen table, chomping through a noontime bowl of granola. It was Saturday, after all, so I was entitled to loaf around for a bit, reading and eating cereal to the soundtrack of the college radio station that my parents had playing 24-7.

"Whuh?" I responded without looking up from my phone, where I was completing my normal Saturday-morning Pixstagram catch-up session.

"Where did your dad go this morning?"

"I dunno." I shrugged. "Groceries or something? I was asleep."

My mom was still frowning. She had her grayish auburn hair piled up on top of her head in a knot, which could have been either an intentional artistic look or just the result of not having brushed her hair yet. I was sporting a similar style, but for the latter reason.

"Sam? Did you see my husband go anywhere?"

Huang Xueyang, alias Sam Huang, was sitting at the desk in the kitchen, eating breakfast and probably checking his email from his family in China, and shook his head. Perhaps to assuage parental guilt over their blatant negligence of every school-related activity from signing permission slips on time to "not forgetting the date of the parent potluck for the third year in a row," the McCullough-Schwartzes had been first to volunteer when the Owen Wister Preparatory Academy needed host families for foreign exchange students. So, since the beginning of the last school year, Sam Huang had been part of the clan. It was like suddenly having a fifteen-year-old brother, which I liked because it meant I always had someone to split a microwave lasagna with, my mom liked because it meant we were putting the spare bedroom to good use, and my dad liked because Sam played classical guitar and was "the son I never had," which made Sam and me feel kind of equally uncomfortable.

My mom looked out the door again.

"Robert?"

Even though it was October, we still had the screen door up, because procrastination is a McCullough-Schwartz family value. So my dad should have been able to hear her, but she wasn't getting a response.

*"Robert?"*

There was a definite tone now. Sam poured another bowl of Cocoa Puffs. I scrolled down my phone. At the top of my feed was an artsy shot of the Donut, the front-lawn sculpture at Owen Wister Preparatory Academy that was actually called something like *Concentricity of Knowledge*, a photo that was intriguing because one, it was a Saturday, so no one was at school and two, it was posted by user *sebdel*, alias Sebastian Delacroix, who had left Wister forever when he graduated. Or so I had thought.

"I think he's . . . Is he *unloading* something from the car? Sam? Nattie?"

Sam smiled but shook his head. I wasn't going to move, but Mom clearly wanted someone involved and I, as her flesh and blood, was beholden to her will.

"Nattie. Come here."

Reluctantly, I tore myself away from creeping on Sebastian Delacroix's Pixstagram feed and stood up. She took a pull from her coffee and narrowed her eyes, pointing out into the backyard.

Dad was definitely out there, wearing his weekend polar fleece and covering his balding head with one of his grimy bandannas. Next to him, on top of the maple leaves that no one had raked yet, was a stack of various pieces of wood, a beat-up red toolbox, and what seemed to be a heap of fabric.

"Looks like it," I said.

"I can't believe this," Mom said. "And neither of you knew anything?"

She cast a hard look back at the room, where Sam Huang was now kind of cowering.

"Sam," Mom said slowly and a little too nicely, "you know you can tell us anything. I mean, tell me. Especially about my husband's whereabouts."

"I . . ." Sam Huang darted a glance at the door. "I wasn't supposed to say."

Mom was not having it. "Come on, Sam. Where did he go?"

Sam Huang fidgeted again. "He said he was going to pick up something for the lawn. And that it was a surprise."

"Aha." Triumphant, and indignant, Mom swung open the screen door and started off across the yard. I unrolled my sleeves and followed, because it was chilly and I was curious. The ground was cold and a little mushy under my bare feet, but not cold enough to make me go back for shoes.

"Robert? What's going on here?"

Mom marched right up to the edge of the little clearing Dad had made with his supplies in the corner of the yard,

4

and folded her arms. Around us, the air was thick with mystery, and also fog. I tried to put it together: we already had a toolshed, and both Sam and I were way too old for a swing set. I *had* begged for a trampoline for my last birthday, but Mom insisted they were death traps, and she was probably right, given the way Dad tended to construct things. The McCullough-Schwartz basement was a graveyard of splintered IKEA dressers and oblong birdhouses no self-respecting blue jay would nest in.

"Oh, there you are!" Dad said, as if he'd completely missed her entreaties from the kitchen. He straightened up and mopped his face with the bandanna. He was beaming. "Looking good, isn't it?"

"*What* is?"

My dad's grin faltered just slightly.

"The yurt. Of course."

"Nattie?" Sam Huang appeared, holding my phone, which I'd left on the kitchen table. "You have a message."

I took my phone and unlocked it to discover not one message, but three.

From: Tess Kozlowski

JAMBA ALERT

where are you

it's important!!!

"What's a *Jamba alert?*" asked Sam Huang. "Is it an emergency?"

I considered. Last May, Tess had found herself mysteriously subscribed to text alerts about smoothie deals from Jamba Juice, which we both thought was hilarious, and so, naturally, ever since then, we have referred to every text message, whether smoothie-related or not, as a *Jamba alert*. I knew our role as a host family was to be ambassadors for the American people, or something, but this was a weirdness that went beyond national cultural differences and into the weirdness of my particular group of friends.

"No." I locked my phone again. Tess was my best friend and the person I trusted most in the world, but she was also the most liberal person I knew, both in her politics and her definition of *important*. So I knew whatever her deal was could wait until after the yurt. Whatever that was.

"The *what*?" Mom was saying.

"Yurt," Dad repeated, like this was a word people used every day. "The traditional dwelling of the nomadic peoples of the steppes of Central Asia. It's a sanctuary."

"Robert," Mom said slowly. "We don't dwell in the steppes of Central Asia. We dwell in the suburbs of eastern Pennsylvania."

"Right, but that's just the beauty of it. It's like an escape, for the family, right here in our backyard." Noticing me, he wiggled his eyebrows. "Whaddya think, Nattie Gann?"

Natty Gann was the name of a plucky Depression-era orphan from a 1980s Disney movie that no one except my dad seemed to remember. It was also his favorite, dadliest nickname for me.

"I thought you said you were going to build a hot tub one day," I said.

Actually, the putative yurt was taking over the exact space where I'd envisioned having our spa. I'd always wanted to have a cool place to put my friends—Tess, Tall Zach, and Zach the Anarchist, alias the Acronymphomaniacs, which we called ourselves not because of any actual nymphomania, but because we were fond of abbreviations and also belonged to a club with an uncommonly unwieldy acronym. It had just sort of stuck.

"He said he'd *think* about it," Mom corrected.

*Bzz. Bzz.*

I thumbed my phone unlocked again.

From: Tess Kozlowski

nattieeeeee come hang out

"A yurt," Dad said soberly, "is much *better* than a hot tub."

This I took issue with. Because while I knew that, as a teenager teetering on the verge of adulthood and also the college process, I should have capital-G goals like "achieving purposefully," "actionizing change," and "not failing the math portion of the SATs," my number one *actual* goal in life was just not to be weird. A hot tub was different, sure, but in a cool way. (Well, literally in a hot way, but the point stands.) A yurt, though, would just be a monument to strangeness and eccentricity—and for what? I couldn't put it on a college application unless maybe I was applying to something like architectural school. And even *then* they'd probably flunk me for being too weird.

"Now, just a second, Robert," Mom said. "We haven't even discussed this."

"Right, I know. But I was browsing the online yesterday night, and someone in the city was getting rid of this yurt kit for practically nothing because he had nowhere to put it, but I had to act fast or else he was just going to donate it to charity. I picked it up this morning."

Dad looked proud, but Mom looked positively pained.

"What on earth are we going to *do* with a yurt?" she asked.

"What on earth would a *charity* do with a yurt?" I asked.

It took Dad a minute to come up with an answer. "Hang out," he said. "Do some art projects. Or just get some nice peace and quiet, you know? The guy told me the yurt is intentionally built with a low ceiling and door, so you can't get in without *humbling* yourself—"

"It's built that way to keep the heat in," I pointed out, vaguely recalling a social studies class.

Dad wasn't listening. "We'll get some cushions out here, a couple of candles, maybe a cast-iron stove to burn up some logs. . . ." He got a dreamy look in his eyes.

Mom looked like she'd rather burn the raw yurt materials than any logs. Even though she is, professionally, a creative person, Mom is not a big fan of Dad's weekend projects. Maybe it's because she gets to build frames for beautiful paintings all day and he's cooped up in an office doing whatever it is executive directors of nonprofit voting-rights advocacy groups do all day, or maybe it's because he's left one half-dug koi pond too many in our front yard, but either way, the McCullough-Schwartzes do not have a good track record with home improvements.

"You can't just start building a yurt in our backyard, Robert," Mom said. "It looks . . . ugly."

"Well, sure, it looks ugly *now*," Dad said. "But soon it'll be a circular canvas tent!"

This did not placate Mom. "What will the neighbors think?"

"It's not *for* the *neighbors*," Dad said. "It's for us. Look, Sam Huang loves it."

Sam Huang did not look like he wanted to get involved in an altercation between his host parents. I briefly wondered what would happen to him if they got divorced. Or to me, for that matter.

"We need to have a place to relax," Dad said. "It'll be good for us."

Mom pursed her lips. "Does the place to relax have to be so . . . visible?"

In my pocket, my phone buzzed for the billionth time.

From: Tess Kozlowski

NATTIE JAMBA ALERT GET HERE OR ELSE WE
WILL ALL BE VERY SAD

:'( :'( :'(

I decided it was probably time to indulge Tess. And also get dressed, because it was twelve fifteen and I should probably do something more with my day than Pixstagram stalking. I was curious about the outcome of the whole yurt-stravaganza, but knowing my parents, the odds of a swift resolution were about as good as me applying to architectural school.

"I'm . . . gonna go see Tess," I said, and backed away slowly.

"Great," Mom said, in a tone of voice that was anything *but* great.

"Have fun!" Dad said brightly.

"Bye, Nattie," said Sam Huang.

The screen door slapped behind me as I crossed the threshold back to the warmth of the kitchen and the bowl of mush that had once been my breakfast. When I stomped down the back stairs ten minutes later, Mom and Dad were at the counter, Dad gesticulating wildly and Mom laughing over a fresh cup of coffee, Sam Huang was set up at his computer watching guitar videos on YouTube, and beneath everything else, as always, the radio was softly playing an unfamiliar song.

# CHAPTER TWO

"*There* you are." Tess took a dramatic slurp of her frozen cappuccino and thunked the cup back on the table. She was wearing a lace-up black shirt, purple eyeliner, and an accusatory expression. "Took you long enough."

"It took me five minutes," I said, and checked my phone just to be sure. Moonpenny's Coffee Shop was six blocks, if that, from the McCullough-Schwartz enclave. Plus, as the only halfway-interesting place to hang out in the neighborhood, it was usually twice as full as anywhere else on the half mile of scented-candle shops and pet boutiques that constituted the business district in Wister. The squishy armchairs up front were colonized, as always, by shiny-haired Wister moms, and the tables by the windows were the exclusive property of plugged-in college students surrounded by psychology textbooks and looking stressed-out. We the Acronymphomaniacs—meaning me, Tess, and the Zachs— had one semiregular table that was usually reliably empty because it was around the corner from the bathroom, which was convenient, given that Moonpenny's offered unlimited free refills, but also gross.

"I sent you like ninety Jamba alerts," Tess went on.

"I *know*," I said. "I'm sorry. There was a yurt-related disaster going on at home."

"A *what?*"

"Nothing," I said quickly. Tess narrowed her eyes and swatted me on the arm.

*"Je frappe toi."*

That was Tess's bad French for *I hit you*, which paradoxically meant that she was glad to see me. I hit her back, gently, as was customary.

*"Je frappe toi* more." You do weird things to the people you survived French 1a with. I did my best to squeeze in with my iced tea, knocking into all six knees in the process. "Why, did I miss anything?"

Zach West, alias Zach the Anarchist, looked up from a notebook. "Pretty much nothing."

And then he looked right back down again. Zach West was actually pretty quiet, but he did have a lot of politically charged T-shirts (including one that said "Suck the Fystem" that he'd had to turn inside out when he wore it to school), *and* he was a vegetarian, so, because of the aforementioned two-Zach situation in our friend group, we'd somehow communally decided that he was an anarchist. Zach had said characteristically nothing in protest, and the name stuck.

"Nattie!" Zach Bitterman, alias Tall Zach, beamed and waved. "You almost missed Other Zach's cookies."

Tall Zach was Tall Zach because he was tall. He was also quite possibly the most beautiful person at Owen Wister Preparatory Academy, at least since Sebastian had graduated, with full lips and dark eyes shown off by what Mom would call "good bone structure." Since Tess appointed him events chair of the Owen Wister Preparatory Academy Lesbian, Gay, Bisexual, Transgender, Queer, Intersex, and Asexual alliance, Tall Zach's magnetic good looks, combined with his positive energy and his SPCA-like tendency to adopt kids without a fixed social group, had single-handedly doubled our membership. (Granted, after all the seniors had graduated in the spring, our membership had only been about five. But still.)

"I can't take any credit for these, of course." Tall Zach pushed forward a waxed-paper-lined shoe box filled with tiny jam-filled thumbprint cookies. "But Other Zach did a great job."

"Are you even allowed to bring your own snacks here?" I asked.

"Who cares?" Tess said, and dunked a cookie into her cappuccino-slush. "Would you rather eat a Moonpenny's muffin?"

I glanced back to the little glass case by the cash register, where the baked goods looked suspiciously unchanged from the last time we'd all hung out here.

"Fine." I grabbed two cookies out of the box, but stopped before I ate any. The jam in the middle was red, and I'd left my EpiPen at home. I was pretty sure that I could sprint the six blocks back to the McCullough-Schwartz residence and stab myself before histamine overload had fully set in. I was *also* sure that Mom would kill me even if I survived for being so irresponsible. I had been very, very allergic to strawberries since birth, but ever since we switched pediatricians and got a stern talking-to about the severity of anaphylaxis, Mom had been really paranoid about making sure I always went out armed for combat against berry-induced death.

"They're raspberry." Zach the Anarchist looked up from his notebook a second time, which startled me, partially because it was out of character and partially because his eyes were this crazy, ice-bright blue. With his blond hair, the effect was intensely Scandinavian. "Those are okay, right?"

"Oh," I said. "Um, yup. As far as I know strawberries are the only berries that can kill. Thanks."

Zach the Anarchist shrugged and broke his gaze to look very intently at his notebook. Today he was wearing a red T-shirt, only instead of that revolutionary guy's face on it, there was Bart Simpson. The cookies, like most of his baking experiments, were very good.

Tall Zach took the last three out and popped one into his mouth whole. "Whuf?" he said, when Tess gave him a reproachful look. "I'm carb-loading for my meet on Tuesday."

As the only one of the Acronymphomaniacs with any kind of athletic ability, Tall Zach routinely justified lunches of sour gummy worms and chocolate doughnuts with his cross-country running. Tess opened her mouth to retort but was cut off by a woman in bright-pink pants whacking her with the bathroom door.

"Do you ever get the sense that no one notices us?" Tess said, as soon as the woman was out of earshot. "Or is it just that hanging out here sucks?"

"Agree on both counts," Tall Zach said. "But it's convenient. Except if you're Other Zach, I guess."

Zach the Anarchist lived all the way in downtown Philadelphia, although he did have a car.

"I don't mind," he said to his notebook.

I gave my iced tea a shake—too much ice, not enough tea—and set it down. "So is there a reason this was an emergency, or—"

"Well, one, we just needed you here," Tess said, chewing industriously, "because otherwise we're lacking our token heterosexual female, and without it the Acronympho quadrangle of orientations is not fully complete."

"Yeah." Tall Zach swallowed. "And I was getting sick of scoping out all the guys by myself."

He swept a glance around our corner of the café, but the only male person in the vicinity was the small kid with the immense laptop setup, who had big puffy headphones on over a tangle of brown hair and who blushed and looked away when Tall Zach smiled at him.

"Two," Tess went on, "because my parents are driving me absolutely batshit and I had to get out of the house."

"What was it this time?" I fished out a tea-flavored ice cube and crunched it.

"Wister Prep sent home flyers about the Winter Formal thing, and my mom wanted to know if I had a *young man* I wanted to ask." Tess fluttered her eyes briefly shut before snapping back to attention. "I told them I was taking Tall Zach."

"Ew, cooties." Tall Zach made a face, then softened. "Tess, you should really just tell them."

He gave her shoulder a squeeze, but she ignored him.

"Three, and finally," she said briskly, "because Zach the Anarchist is being morose, and he needs help with his Latin homework, and because you, Nattie, are a Latin genius."

"Not really," I said, although it was kind of true. All four Acronymphomaniacs had added Latin as a second language in eighth grade, but after Tess had discovered that declining nouns wasn't going to help her with the SATs and Tall Zach had switched to Spanish 1b so he could go on the exchange to Mexico in ninth grade, only Zach the Anarchist and I were still taking it.

"Whatever. You probably get all As. Dr. Frobisher loves you," Tess said. "And Zach the Anarchist could really use your help."

"Not really," Zach the Anarchist said. His cheeks were very pink.

Tess rolled her eyes. "Why is everyone being so contradictory today? Look, Natalie—"

"Ugh, don't call me Natalie," I interrupted. "It sounds so formal. Like I'm being desposisted in a court of law or something."

"Depositioned." There was a teeny smile on Zach the Anarchist's lips. "But nice try."

Now it was my turn to go pink. "Whatever. Go back to being morose about Mia."

Everything went silent. Well, as silent as it could be with the clanging of the espresso machine and the gurgling of the babies and the thumps of music leaking out of the laptop kid's headphones. Mia, Zach the Anarchist's girlfriend who he'd met at math camp, had broken up with him nearly two weeks ago, and we'd all sort of tacitly agreed not to mention it.

"Sorry," I said quickly. "I mean, um, or don't. She's not even worth being morose over." I'd only met her once, because she went to a public school in the city, closer to Zach's house, but beyond her alleged abilities in math, she hadn't really struck me as worthy of Zach the Anarchist. "She just had, like, big boobs."

"*Nattie.*" Tess gave me a billion-watt glare, but whatever she was going to say was blessedly cut off by Tall Zach leaping up in the direction of the counter.

"Anyone want anything? Anyone? Anything?" He looked at each of us in turn, clearly trying to siphon away some of the awkward. None of us budged. "Okay. I'll just . . . Bye!"

I could still feel the nuclear heat of Tess's stare, and even worse, the low-grade warmth of embarrassment coming from Zach the Anarchist. I had meant to make him feel better, but naturally, me being me, I had done it completely wrong and it backfired. Yes, Mia had been well-endowed, and yes, maybe I was a little mad that when Zach the Anarchist finally got a girlfriend it was someone with actual curves and the ability to wear red lipstick without looking like a clown after drinking fruit punch, but still. What on *earth* possessed me to say that? I wanted to melt.

So I did what I always do in uncomfortable situations, which is pull out my phone and pretend to be invisible. Sebastian's Pixstagram post was still at the top of my feed, and I held my phone to my chest and idly clicked on his profile, acting like I was busy typing something important as Tess slurped her cappuccino ominously. Besides the picture of the Wister Prep Donut, there was one of a Wawa sandwich next to a can of grape-flavored Hypr, one of the lit-up gingerbread houses of Boathouse Row along the Schuylkill, and a selfie in front of the big angel statue at 30th Street Station. Whatever Sebastian was doing these days, he was doing it in Philadelphia.

"What are you looking at?" Tess pushed herself to my shoulder.

"Nothing," I said, but she'd already seen.

"Are you Pixstagram-stalking Sebastian Delacroix?"

"No," I said, even though the selfie was very obviously him. "I was just browsing."

"Dude, you love him," Tess said. "*Love.*"

"Do not."

"Oh yeah? I seem to recall you following him to Meredith White's end-of-school party back in June *expressly* so that you could make out with him."

There was a loud clatter.

"'Scuse me." Zach the Anarchist left his notebook at his seat and stepped around where Tess had crouched next to me. "Refill."

"Sure, sure," Tess said distractedly, and waved him on.

"We didn't . . ." I started, then paused to scooch so Zach the Anarchist could get up, and then to scooch again so Tall Zach could sit back down. "Sebastian and I didn't make out," I said, as loud as I could without attracting attention.

Tess squinted at me like I was going out of focus. "What do you mean? What were you *doing* all night?"

"Just . . . stuff," I said to Tess. "Who cares?"

"Come on, dude!" Tess grinned at me. Well, she *smiled*, anyway. Her lips were firmly together, but that didn't mean she wasn't happy. Tess Kozlowski does not, as a rule, grin. Ever since Dr. Kozlowski, Tess's dad, had used a huge, braces-wearing picture of a twelve-year-old Tess for a billboard to advertise his practice, Tess had stoutly refused to reveal her teeth when smiling, even postorthodontia. "Even I, a five point five on the Kinsey scale, will concede that Sebastian Delacroix is sex on two legs, if dudes are your thing. Right, Tall Zach?"

"Huh?" Tall Zach had been ripping open his fourth sugar packet to pour into his strawberry frappé.

"Sebastian Delacroix," Tess said. "Right?"

"Oof." Tall Zach winced, then breathed out hard. "Yeah. Yeah, *totally.*"

I picked at a corner of waxed paper in the cookie shoe box. "Even after the Talent Show Incident?"

Tall Zach recoiled slightly. "Eurgh. I still can't believe that happened."

"I can't believe Nattie *filmed* it," Tess said.

My face got hot. "I didn't know he was going to do . . . *that.* I just . . . I don't know, wanted to have video of him." It sounded a lot creepier when I said it out loud.

"Anyway, that was like a million years ago." She started industriously flicking through my phone. "Ooh, it looks like he's still playing music, though. Does he have a band?"

"Give me that." I snatched it out of her hand.

Tess pouted. "I'm just saying, if he's in town, you should totally call him up."

"Nobody uses phones as phones, Tess," I said.

"It's an expression. *Text* him up, or whatever." She flounced back over to her seat in the booth. "Even if you almost kissed him, he's still the hottest guy you've *almost* kissed."

It was then that I noticed Zach the Anarchist had left his mug on the table when he'd gotten up for a refill.

"Well . . . yeah," I lied. "Yeah."

At seventeen, I had almost kissed two people.

The first one had actually been Zach the Anarchist, at the end of freshman year, which I didn't even like remembering because of how dumb I'd been about the whole thing. Granted, we were ninth graders, so we were *all* kind of dumb, but I went above and beyond. That particular night, we were in the middle of an Acronympho marathon of Lifetime movies, which we watched not because they were good but because we could all at least agree that they were terrifically bad, and we had just finished one about a courageous group of suburban moms crusading to save their daughters from a predatory group of internet drug dealers in sinister-looking denim jackets when Tall Zach leaped up for the bathroom and Tess went to make more popcorn. This left Zach the Anarchist and me alone. Together. Kind of close. Because despite the huge basement TV room Zach had because his moms both work in high-powered executive positions, he and I had skipped the squishy comfort and good viewing angle of the leather couches and sat on the floor. Together. And since I'd spent that whole year getting this warm fluttery feeling when I was around him, like I didn't just like boys, but one boy in particular, this felt—to my ninth-grade mind, anyway—very major.

So the credits were rolling, and I was messing with one of the nubs in the carpet, because the carpet in the Wests' basement is kind of nubbly in this way that's fun to run your fingers over absent-mindedly. And Zach the Anarchist was doing the same thing, close to where I was sitting. And then our hands kind of brushed. And then I noticed that Zach was close enough for me to smell the root beer on his breath, which was kind of gross but also kind of exciting. Basically, everything would've gone fine, except that I completely and totally ruined it.

"Can I kiss you, Nattie?"

"Uh . . ."

Five-second pause.

"I don't know?"

I know. I *know*. If Tess hadn't started yelling that the microwave was on fire (it wasn't) I might have evaporated from my own stupidity. So ever since then, I got nervous when there was even the slightest chance that Zach and I would be alone together. Which, weirdly, was almost like still having a crush on him. Almost.

Anyway, I recovered from that enough to almost-kiss a second boy a year later, and that boy was incredibly, impossibly, Sebastian Delacroix. Last June, I'd found myself standing alone at the end of Meredith White's annual pool party, watching people fall into the pool, pretend to know how to break-dance, and try to make a drinking game out of badminton. To Meredith's horror, some seniors had showed up with beer, which Tess had insisted all of us get some of—her to drink, and me and Zach the Anarchist to use as a prop in our defense of "Why don't you have a beer, man?" The thing was, even with my friends there, I secretly hated parties, and I hated how much I hated them, because how dumb is it to wish you were home watching *Law & Order* with your mom instead of being a normal, not-weird teenager?

Also, having taken a tiny exploratory sip, I discovered I did not like beer. It tasted like rotten straw.

It was while trying to find a covert patch of weeds in which to dump my nasty straw-tasting beer that I ran into Sebastian Delacroix.

"Oh," I said. "Um, hey."

"Hello," said Sebastian Delacroix.

Sebastian Delacroix had one of those ridiculous names that could go to one of two extremes. A Sebastian is either the creepy kid who spent most of elementary school eating paste, or a guy who owns his weird name and makes it mysterious and sexy. Sebastian Delacroix was definitely the latter. He was tall, tan, and was rumored to have a tattoo. He played guitar and wore blazers that showed off his broad shoulders. He wrote poetry in a notebook he kept in his back pocket. He was funny.

So, obviously, everyone was in love with him. Myself included.

At the time of Meredith's party, Sebastian was no longer the hottest guy in school because he was no longer, technically speaking, a guy in our school. He had graduated a year ago and headed off to NYU to start a degree in photography, but really, that only served to amplify his natural attractiveness into some kind of mythical hotness.

"Natalie, right?" he said. "Weren't we in French together?"

We were, but only because I was taking two languages at once and because Sebastian was not *très bien* at languages and had had to add French 3 his senior year in order to graduate. Still, I was shocked he remembered. Of course, *I* remembered, because I had spent every other day that year getting up at six to blow-dry and straighten my hair just so it would look not-weird for the forty-five minutes Sebastian might catch it in his peripheral vision.

"Uh, *oui?*" I cringed so hard I almost pulled a muscle. Sebastian didn't seem to notice.

"Not a drinker?"

I realized I was still, stupidly, holding my Solo cup over the fence.

"Not really," I said, because there was no way to deny that I was not about to drink the beer that was already half splattered onto what I now realized were not weeds, but Mr. or Mrs. White's hostas. "I'm, uh . . . just trying to get the plants drunk."

Sebastian stared at me for a minute and then chuckled. In my shock, I accidentally emptied the cup onto my feet.

"Shoot," I said. My mind was still reeling: *Is he laughing with me, or at me?* I felt glowy, terrified, and sticky-footed all at once.

"You okay?"

"Fine," I said. My plastic Target flip-flops were the only part of my outfit that was actually mine—well, the flip-flops and my underwear with the ducklings on it. I'd had to borrow a green halter dress (and some red lipstick) from Tess because apparently none of my clothes were suited to a party situation.

"How's, uh, New York?" I said, just as Sebastian said, "You look good, Natalie."

"Thanks," I said.

Sebastian bit his lip. "New York is good, I guess. New. Yorky. My new band's recording some stuff for an EP, so I actually have to get back tonight."

"Ah," I said, not sure how to react and not exactly sure what an EP was. Not that bands weren't cool, just that *I* wasn't cool enough to know about them. My favorite record happened to be Joni Mitchell's *Blue*, which was strummy and sad and thoughtful and was last on the charts when my mom was two years old. I was, to say the least, behind the times.

"Yeah," Sebastian said. "The Young Lungs. It's me and a couple of guys from school, but I write most of the songs."

Unable to meet his eyes because of my congenital

awkwardness, I took an instinctive look away from him and back at the party. People were screaming in the water, a girl in the corner was crying incomprehensibly into her cell phone, and the music was loud enough to rattle your brain in your skull. Nearer to the backyard gate, Meredith White was looking at me with laser-heated anger. Well, not me; me *and* Sebastian. Meredith wasn't an Acronympho, but she did do the literary magazine, which was only a few degrees separate. She was one of those girls who wore turtlenecks and worried too much about homework.

Something in the way she looked at us made me feel a few shades less weird. If I was making Meredith jealous, I must be doing something not-wrong. I flicked my head around and smiled.

"So I'm gonna go," Sebastian was saying. "Unless . . . you want a ride?"

I considered for all of two seconds. Tess would understand, Tall Zach was out of town, and I wasn't sure if Zach the Anarchist was even still here.

"Yeah."

Sebastian's car was a beat-up Crown Vic sedan with a broken radio and crummy upholstery, the bottom littered with cans of Hypr energy drink and actual CD cases, like this was the past or something, all from bands I'd never heard of. He blasted some singer-songwriter he liked and told me about his plans for crafting the Young Lungs' sound and how he was considering dropping out of NYU altogether just to focus on music because school was a waste of time. I mostly nodded, because saying something out loud would increase my chance of sounding dumb by at least 50 percent.

After about half an hour, I realized we weren't driving anywhere in particular.

"So, Natalie," Sebastian said, drumming his fingers on the wheel. "That's a beautiful name, by the way."

"Thanks," I said. "I mean, I didn't pick it or anything, but thanks." Make that 100 percent. I balled up the hem of Tess's dress in my fist.

"Well." Sebastian's face was half in shadow, so I couldn't see his reaction. "Do I take you home?"

"Uh," I said, "I probably shouldn't stay out *too* late. My parents will think I've been murdered."

But Sebastian just chuckled this time and then pulled the car to a stop.

"Hah," he said. "You're great to talk to, Natalie."

I knew for a fact that the only reason I'd been good to talk to was that I had successfully managed to say as little as possible, but I at least had the good sense not to say that out loud. So I just nodded. Mysteriously.

"Thanks."

And then Sebastian Delacroix reached out and touched my face.

Everything in my inexperienced body freaked out. All at

once, my hands started to tremble, my feet felt stickier than ever before, and my mind blazed with a giant neon sign that said "This Is It" and also "Why Did You Wear the Duckling-Print Underpants."

But then he let go. No kiss, nothing. Just ten seconds of his fingers on the space between my chin and my ear. Six silent blocks later, I was dropped off without so much as a wave.

And that was the last I'd heard of Sebastian Delacroix. Or so I thought.

# CHAPTER THREE

"Where are the spoons?"

Mornings in the McCullough-Schwartz household had never been an organized affair, but the following Friday was especially bad. Sam Huang was standing, confused, at the kitchen cabinet, with a bowl of cereal in one hand. Mom, who was pouring a mug of coffee, leaned back and frowned.

"They're not in the silverware drawer?"

Sam Huang shook his head.

"Nattie?" Mom said. "Why don't we have any spoons?"

"I don't know," I said without looking up, because I didn't, and I was also preoccupied with doing my Latin homework, which I definitely hadn't left for the last minute. For the beginning of the fall semester, Dr. Frobisher had started us off reading Catullus, a Roman poet who wrote a lot of really sexy stuff, a lot of really angry stuff, and a lot of really sexy, really angry stuff, to this woman named Lesbia—well, *nicknamed*, anyway, because we don't know who she really was. Catullus just thought she was as smart as the lady poets of Lesbos, like

Sappho, so he called her that. I usually just looked up some words and winged it in class, but now Dr. Frobisher was making us do these worksheets about *theme* and *poetic devices* to prove that we actually understood the mechanics of the poetry and weren't just copying English translations from the internet.

I turned to my worksheet and wrote *Natalie McCullough-Schwartz* across the top—or tried to, anyway. The pen died by the second *u*.

"Shoot." Mom was stooped over by the dishwasher. "Someone forgot to run it last night."

"It wasn't me," said Sam Huang.

"It wasn't me, either. My day's Tuesday." I scribbled a few million times in my notebook to no avail. "Where are all the pens?"

"Probably with the spoons," Mom said. She dumped two packets of fake sugar and a glug of half-and-half into the mug. "Nattie, eat something. Your father's going to be down any minute. Sam, just use a—oh, okay."

Sam Huang had started to eat his cereal with a ladle.

"Normal people," I said, "keep pens in the house."

"Okay!" Dad strode in, briefcase in hand and tie hanging around his neck. "I'm here. What time have we got?" He kissed Mom on the cheek and she started doing his tie.

"It's—oh." She dropped his tie and frowned. "I have no idea. Why isn't that right?"

The radio next to the coffeemaker was blinking out 3:43,

the inaccurate result of all of us forgetting to reset the clock a few power outages ago.

"Well, we've got to leave soon. Probably." Dad rummaged around for a travel mug as Mom jabbed at the front of the radio, presumably attempting to reset the clock but only succeeding in turning up the volume.

"Excuse me!" I yelled from my notebook. "Some of us are doing homework."

"Nattie? Doing homework the morning it's due?" Dad acted shocked.

"Sounds like your daughter, all right," Mom murmured. "Do you want me to make you some oatmeal, Nattie?"

"Yes, please." I ignored both of them and focused on my Catullus, where I had made some almost useless notes. Across the counter, the microwave chimed in tune with the song on the radio. The music was kind of catchy, I guessed, the kind of upbeat song that didn't risk its indie cred by getting *too* exuberant, with lots of flourishing guitar riffs and synthesizer sounds. Not terrible. I looked around for something to stir my oatmeal with as the lady DJ with the sultry voice came back on.

"—that's a new group from Brooklyn called the Young Lungs. Pretty catchy stuff—"

I froze, and then immediately unfroze, because the oatmeal bowl in my hand was very hot.

"Shoot!" I dropped the bowl on the counter. The DJ was still talking.

"And if you're up for being on the cutting edge, they're playing *tonight*, an all-ages show in downtown Philadelphia at Ruby's, so—"

"Are you okay, Nattie?" Sam Huang peered over at me from across the counter.

"I'm fine," I said, rubbing my hand. "Just, um, surprised." The radio had switched to something piano-y and soft. I drummed my pen against the notebook. Sebastian wasn't just in Philadelphia for fun—he was here to play a *show*. With his *band*. That *actually existed*. Either it would be awesome and cool and kind of sexy, or it would be the Talent Show Incident all over again. Either way, I was solidly intrigued.

"Can I go to a concert tonight?" The words flew out of my mouth without even having taken full shape in my brain.

Dad frowned. "A concert?"

"Yeah." I shut my notebook, Latin homework having been officially abandoned. "It's this one band, and, um, Tess says that they rock, so we were thinking we might go. . . ."

Dad and Mom exchanged a look.

"They rock?" Mom said. "Do you even *like* rock music? I thought all you listened to was my Joni Mitchell album."

"I like rock," I said, thinking back to the thirty seconds of rhythmic guitar I'd just heard on WPHL. "It's great. And I promise to be safe and responsible and everything. I just want to go listen to music."

Mom lifted an eyebrow. "Where is this concert?"

"Ruby's," I said. "It's in Center City." Somewhere.

"Oh yeah," Dad said. "I went there to see a Steely Dan tribute act a while back. Called themselves Deely Stan."

"Is it an acceptable place for our daughter?"

"*Stan.*" Dad chuckled. "What? Oh, sure. She'll be fine. Hey, maybe Sam can go with her, too."

Sam Huang shook his head. "Can't. A Cappella."

A Cappella at Owen Wister Prep was like the football team, in that it was competitive, obsessed with its own importance as the wellspring of school spirit, and involved matching outfits. The fact that Sam had made the cut at the end of last year despite being only a sophomore was kind of a big deal and a responsibility he took very seriously, which came down to attending thrice-weekly top secret evening rehearsals and hanging out with only A Cappella kids at school.

Mom didn't look convinced. "Well, I don't want her going *alone*. You say Tess is going, Nattie?"

"Sure," I said. "I mean, yes." I made a mental note to ask or bribe or threaten Tess into coming with me. Mom looked at Dad.

"I feel like we should have rules in place," she said. "For concerts and that sort of thing."

"Like a curfew?" Dad asked.

"No drinking," Mom said. "Do not drink any alcohol."

"That's a good one," Dad said. "No getting anyone pregnant."

I rolled my eyes. "Dad."

"Don't take any wooden nickels." Dad was on a roll

now. "Stay away from the brown acid."

"*Robert.*" Mom sighed. "Nattie. We just want to be sure you're going to use good judgment—which includes keeping your phone on, by the way. We gave you that phone as a privilege, but if something happens and we need to get ahold of you—"

I was only half listening, partially because I'd heard Mom's speech about Phone Responsibility and the Privilege of the Family Plan about once per billing cycle, and partially because Dad was looking at me funny, like he was going to sneeze, or cry.

"Wow," he said. "Our little girl's all grown up."

"*Dad*," I said. "I'm just going to a concert, not getting married."

"I know," Dad said with a sniff. "But still. I feel like I blink and suddenly you're a whole new Natalie."

"Is he crying?" Sam Huang asked, peering over with his backpack on.

"So . . . does this mean I can go?" I said. Dad was too busy dabbing at his eyes to answer. Mom took a long, deep breath and handed me a fork.

"Just eat your oatmeal, Nattie."


Sam Huang and I made it to school only a cool six minutes late for homeroom, not late enough to warrant a demerit but not early enough for me to find Tess before first period. If I was going to convince her to come to a last-minute rock concert with me, I'd have to do it after our normal OWPALGBTQIA meeting at lunch. Well, if OWPALGBTQIA meetings could ever be described as *normal*, anyway.

"Humans! People! Everyone!"

Tess was sitting on the edge of a desk in Alumni Building Room 104, alias Dr. Frobisher's Latin classroom, alias base camp for OWPALGBTQIA meetings, which we had picked only because it was so far away from the rest of campus that none of the bigger, more populous clubs would ever challenge us for it. Since the fall, when we'd basically started from scratch after all the seniors left last year, the club consisted of mostly underclassmen, who were sporting a variety of creative haircuts and colors, picking at food brought in from the cafeteria, and not paying attention.

Tess, understandably, was not happy being ignored. She rapped her knuckles on the edge of her desk, to little effect, and then jumped off onto the floor and put her hands on her hips, which, combined with her serious-business combo of vest, studded jeans, and red lipstick, made her look downright intimidating.

"*Hello?*" It barely cut through the murmur. To my right, Tall Zach had stretched out his long legs and was languidly unwrapping a Fruit by the Foot. Behind him, crouched against the wall with his laptop on his knees and his headphones plugged in, was the tiny kid I recognized from Moonpenny's. Zach the Anarchist was probably somewhere toward the back of the room, eating a hummus sandwich or something.

Personally, I was just trying not to get pizza drippings on the budget stuff that I had somehow ended up in charge of.

In front of us, our fearless leader's eyes were narrowing, and I was just beginning to steel myself for some kind of bigger explosion when one came.

"Hey, *shut up!*"

I jolted in my seat, and everyone obeyed. The command wasn't from Tess, but from across the room, where, of all people, Zach the Anarchist had jumped to attention. Tess beamed, and I watched as Zach sat back down with a look of mild surprise on his face, like he couldn't believe he had yelled at everyone *either*.

"*Thank* you," Tess said. "Now. We have actual business to discuss today. Treasurer, if you would."

No one moved.

"Nattie!"

I froze in my seat, a bite of pepperoni halfway to my mouth. "Sorry. If I would what?"

"The budget stuff," Tess said. "The only actual responsibility you have as an officer of this club?"

"Oh. Right." I got up, shuffling the pages of the spreadsheet I'd printed out last night. "So, after a thorough analysis of our finances, it looks like the OWPALGBTQIA is not, at this point in time, fully solvent."

"We're broke," Tess said flatly.

"We are, pretty much, broke," I agreed. It was true: even

though our main expense for the last school year had been tie-dyeing supplies for the end of pride week in the spring, we hadn't exactly made any money since then.

"Right now, our assets stand at"—I looked down at my printouts—"about thirty dollars and a box of extra-extra-small white T-shirts."

"This is a problem," Tess said.

"Yeah," Tall Zach said. "Those things would only fit a baby."

Tess rolled her eyes. A girl with pink bangs raised her hand.

"Yes?" Tess said. "You don't have to raise your hand, uh—"

"Chihiro," the girl said. "And, um, why does it matter if we don't have money? What do we need the money for?"

"Well," Tess said, "for one thing, we have to maintain a balance of at least two hundred dollars to stay officially registered as an extracurricular student organization. Right, treasurer?"

"Uh, right." This was about all I knew about our club's money: we had to have some, or else no more club. I tried to look officially nonplussed.

Tess nodded her approval. "And *also*, according to the Wister Prep bylaws, or whatever, all registered student organizations must maintain a membership of at least fifteen students, or else we are considered ineligible for meeting space and they can give our room away."

The room went silent as we all mentally tallied heads and realized that there were only eleven of us.

"Without a meeting place, we're nothing!" Tess cried.

"Trust me, there are groups that would *love* to have this room. The knitting club is *breathing down our neck* to get at this space."

"Boo, knitting club," Tall Zach said, and hissed supportively. Everyone else glanced around at the peeling posters of the Acropolis and the scarred actual-chalk-and-wood chalkboard in a way that suggested they wouldn't be too broken up if they never had to come back to Alumni Building Room 104 again.

"This is serious!" Tess thumped the desk. "People, we have a problem. And that problem is that nobody knows who we are."

There were murmurs of assent. Or murmurs, anyway.

"Look at this!" Tess held up a copy of last year's yearbook, Wister Remembers, which everyone but the yearbook kids called Wister Wemembers, for obvious reasons. "*This* is the recognition A Cappella group got in last year's yearbook."

She opened it up to a two-page spread crammed with clipart music notes and color photos of A Cappella kids frozen midbounce, belting out some *ba-* and *da-*inflected song, the guys in matching ties and the girls in matching headbands.

"Hero worship!" Tess cried. "And for what? They're the most exclusive, insular, and elitist club in school!"

More murmuring, a little more animated this time. Tess did have a point: being in A Cappella had given Sam Huang more popularity and name recognition in a year and two months at Wister Prep than I had gotten in my entire life (well, my entire life from kindergarten onward). His tenor-section status meant that random people in the hall were more likely to think of me as "Sam Huang's host sister" than the other way around. Not that I really minded, of course—anonymity was fine by me.

But it was not, apparently, fine with Tess, who was now flipping to a spot farther on in her Wister Wemembers.

"And *this*"—she held it open a second time—"is what *we* got."

Over a caption that said *Lesbian, Gay, Bisexual, Transgender, Queer, Intersex, and Asexual alliance* (on two lines, because it was kind of a long caption), there was a giant gray box that said "Photo to Come." That was it.

"That doesn't mean anything," said Tall Zach. "Wister Wemembers gets tons of stuff wrong."

"Yeah," Zach the Anarchist agreed. "Remember how last year every sports team had *captians* instead of captains?"

"No," I said. "But they did call me *Natasha* on our class page."

Across the room, Zach the Anarchist laughed.

"*Anyway.*" Tess closed the Wister Wemembers with a snap. "A public profile is important. We graduated half our membership last year and we're in danger of nonexistence. We can't get money without people, and we can't get people without some awareness. So. Let's brainstorm. What can we do to get people to know who we are? How can we get public attention? How can we *swell our ranks?*"

Silence.

"Don't everyone speak at once." Tess rolled her eyes.

"Think, people! I know that traditionally we've done our one event—"

"*What* event?" A girl with an elaborate nose ring whispered not very quietly in the equally decorated ear of the guy next to her.

He shrugged sleepily. "Uh, pride week?"

"We have a pride week?" nose-ring girl asked.

"You can't change pride week!" cried Chihiro of the pink bangs.

"No one is changing pride week!" Tess said.

"Good," said Chihiro.

"I think pride week should go on for longer," said nose-ring girl. "Like for maybe ten days, or something, so that people actually know it exists."

"Then it wouldn't be a *week*, Alison," sleepy guy explained. "They'd have to change the name." Alison looked pissed. Zach the Anarchist snorted into his cup of tea and tried to regain a straight face by looking in my direction, but that almost made *me* crack up, which made Tess sigh.

"Guys, listen. Pride week remains as is, for now. It's not until May, anyway. I'm talking about something *new*. I want us, the beautiful humans of the OWPALGBTQIA, to stage a revolution."

"I can play all of *Ultramix 4* on heavy mode," came a voice from the corner by Tall Zach.

"What?"

It took a few seconds for the laptop kid to realize that he

and Tess were not talking about the same thing, since he'd spent most of his time clicking around and making weird sounds on his keyboard.

"*Dance Dance Revolution?*" he said. "Video games. Never mind."

Tall Zach sat up in his seat. "Oh, sorry, I'm the worst at introductions. Everyone, this is Endsignal. He's a freshman, and his real name is Eric Something, but Endsignal's his handle for the internet and stuff and that's what he says everyone calls him."

"Hi. Um, hi." Endsignal pushed his glasses up and looked with trepidation at the collected OWPALGBTQIA-ers. "Yup. Hi."

Zach the Anarchist and I waved. Tess looked torn between the duty of welcoming a new member and her desperate need to retain order in the meeting, but she managed to smile.

"Excuse me?" Alison waved her hand. "Why are we doing this again?"

"Because it's *important*," Tess said. "We need to make our voices heard."

"Isn't that what pride week is for?" Alison said.

"You didn't even know what pride week *was* until a minute ago," said Chihiro.

"We could have a car wash," Tall Zach said. "That's what the team did to raise money for cross-country camp."

Alison whirled around and stared at him. "What, with all the girls in bikinis? I bet you'd like that."

Tall Zach made a face. "Uggo. You wish."

"It could be equal-opportunity swimwear," Tess said. "We could mess with gender norms and put *everyone* in bikinis."

"In October?" I said. I pictured myself in a swimsuit, teeth chattering and gripping an icy hose. "No thanks."

"Okay, *not* a car wash," Tess agreed. "Yeah, you, in the blue."

"Um, raffle?" squeaked a voice from underneath a sweatshirt hood. Some freshperson.

"We'd have to get a prize first," I said. "Which we can't afford, unless someone will barter for T-shirts."

"Or . . ." Bryce spoke slowly, like he was hatching a brilliant scheme. "The T-shirts *themselves* are the prize." He settled back triumphantly as Zach the Anarchist let out an actual, audible laugh. I wanted to laugh, too, but Bryce already looked confused.

"We can't have a raffle, anyway," Tess said. "They're against school policy. Something something gambling something."

The room went silent, except for another stray laugh that I *think* came from Zach the Anarchist. Tess sighed.

"Okay, well, if no one has any ideas, I guess the meeting is adjourned—but!" She jabbed a finger at the poster of the ruins of Pompeii, which, under the circumstances, was not the most encouraging image. "Think big, everyone. Be bold. Be fearless."

The OWPALGBTQIA got to its collective feet, hefting backpacks and throwing out the greasy paper boats once filled with cafeteria tater tots. Tall Zach bounded out of the door, heading to his next class at almost a sprint like only a tracklete could. Endsignal began rolling up his various cords and wires, and Zach the Anarchist slipped out without saying good-bye.

Meeting over, I swallowed, ready to ask Tess my favor.

"Hey," I said. "Can I tell you something?"

"What? Oh, okay. Walk with me." Tess stuffed an arm into her coat and grabbed her backpack. "I'm going to the computer room to print out flyers. At least those are free to advertise."

"Right," I said, and led the way down the hall to the first door on the right. The computer lab was mostly deserted at the tail end of lunch, save some kids surreptitiously checking their Tumblrs and Meredith White with her giant rolly backpack, probably doing something for the literary magazine. Tess logged into her email, opened up a Word doc, and began typing furiously.

"Which of these clip-art rainbows do you like the best?" she said, eyes glued to the screen.

I shrugged. "Whichever. They're just going to print in black and white, you know."

"Oh." Tess paused her typing, then kept on. "Whatever. Something's better than nothing."

I frowned. Even for someone as intense as Tess, she seemed extra plugged-in. "Are you sure you need to do this now?" I asked. "We could just take a break. I'm sure we'll still find recruits somehow."

Tess stopped typing. "*Somehow* is not good enough."

"Okay. Um, sorry." I squinted at her. "Is there a reason you're having a membership drive all of a sudden?"

"Besides the fact that our very existence as a club hangs in the balance?"

I thought of my spreadsheets. "Ugh, God, don't say *balance.* I just meant, like . . . we have *some* new members. Endsignal. Those three sophomores." Alison and Chihiro I was pretty sure I'd never seen before the beginning of this school year, but I at least knew *of* Bryce, since he'd come out as transgender last year, which was pretty cool.

"I guess. It's just . . ." Tess's jaw tightened, the screen with the "Join the Best Club Ever in the Whole School!!!" document glowing softly on the side of her face.

"It's my parents," she said at last.

"Your parents think the club doesn't have enough people in it?"

"No!" Tess looked up and flicked me in the forehead.

"Ow!"

"Sorry. You were asking for it." She blew her bangs out of her eyes. "It's just . . . you know."

Tess stared intently at her folded hands. I swallowed.

"Yeah."

"It's not like—God, it's not like I think they'll *judge* me or anything, you know?"

"They are registered Democrats," I agreed.

"Right. But they're just . . . I don't know. My mom's always asking me about the boys in my class. My dad still talks about *gay marriage* even though it's just *marriage* now." Tess's voice was totally unloud. "So I want to rally our people up. Make the OWPALGBTQIA the cool club to join. Just . . . be normal. But still be us."

She stared at the opposite wall, where a flyer for the Winter Formal fluttered over a fire extinguisher.

"Anyway. Whatever." She cleared her throat. "Is that what you wanted to talk about? How your poor lesbian friend needs to uncloset herself to her family already?"

"Um," I said. "Actually, no."

"Ugh, thank *God*. Because no offense, as a straight person, your opinion is completely invalid." Tess swiveled back to the computer. "A hundred and fifty flyers is probably enough, right?"

"Maybe we should just get a billboard."

Tess spun back around. "Do *not* joke with me about billboards. That was seriously traumatic." She rubbed her closed lips and returned to the screen.

"Sorry."

"If that orthodontia money wasn't going to put me through college, I'd have sued my parents for emotional damages." She hit Print, then wheeled on me again. "So *what* is so urgent?

Some kind of drama? Oh my God, wait. Did you call Sebastian Delacroix?"

"No!" I whispered, kind of loudly. "I mean, not exactly." I snuck a look over my shoulder to make sure we were out of Meredith's earshot and took a deep breath.

"I heard them on the radio," I said. "Sebastian's band."

"The *radio*?" Tess screeched.

"Yeah," I said, a few thousand decibels quieter. "On the WPHL morning show."

"Ooh, the one with that sexy lady DJ?"

"Yeah."

Tess's eyes widened.

"Dude, I'm pretty sure that station is *syndicated*."

"What does that even mean? Is that a good thing? You're looking like it's a good thing."

"No. I mean, yes. Sebastian might end up *famous*. Sebastian and whatever his band is called."

"The Young Lungs," I said. "Anyway, the thing is, they're coming to town, and—"

"Hey! Tess, Nattie."

Meredith White appeared in our corner of the lab, her arms full of printouts.

"Hey," I said, smiling and attempting to affect the disposition of someone who was definitely not going to a rock show that night, which, seeing as that was my typical demeanor, was not that difficult. Meredith smiled, which, in combination with her clear blue eyes and wavy French braid, gave her a look that was nothing but pleasant.

"I think these are yours," she said, and handed Tess a stack of papers.

"Oh," Tess said. "Yup. Thanks."

Meredith beamed. She was the kind of person who beamed.

"Can I interest you ladies in Wister Writers?" She handed me and Tess each a flyer without waiting for a response. "We're always looking for new fiction and poetry submissions."

"Thanks," Tess said, holding the flyer gingerly by a corner like it was coated in snot.

"Yeah, thanks." I smiled back at Meredith to show that I wasn't entirely opposed to the concept of poetry, even though the closest I'd come to writing poetry was my terrible Catullus translations.

"No problem," Meredith said. "Hey, we should hang out sometime. I feel like I haven't seen you guys since the summer."

"Yeah, totally," I said, willing myself not to blush as I remembered exactly the circumstances under which I had last seen Meredith.

"Actually, I was kind of eavesdropping," Meredith said, "and I was just wondering if you guys were talking about Sebastian Delacroix's band?"

"Nope," I said, panicking.

"Yeah," Tess said, loud enough to drown me out.

"Oh, cool!" Meredith smiled and looked at her shoes.

"Because, um, I heard that they're playing some club down-town tonight? And I kind of want to see them, but I can't go by myself, because my parents won't let me."

Tess's perfect eyebrows were nearly touching her hairline, but her face was mercifully expressionless otherwise.

"Of course." She chanced a tiny glance in my direction, but fortunately, Meredith rushed in with more words before I had to say anything.

"I've heard they're actually pretty good, and I used to hang out with Sebastian a lot, so it seems like a nice thing to do. Go out and support them, I mean."

As far as I was aware, Sebastian would never hang out with someone like Meredith White. Not that there was any-thing wrong with Meredith, exactly. She just was a little too much—her big smile, her giant backpack, her pool party invi-tation list that included literally everybody at Wister Prep and their brother. (Sam Huang, though invited, had been at home in China at the time, or else he probably would've been there, too.) Besides, of everyone in this room, *I* was the one Sebas-tian had actually Almost Kissed. *I* was the one who'd actually been in his car. *I* was the one he'd said had a beautiful name. I was nothing like Meredith White, fussing with the end of her braid and practically radiating desperation.

I'm not proud of this, but right then, I actually felt pretty proud.

"We should all go together," I heard myself say.

"Really?" Meredith said.

"Really?" Tess said, with a good deal more incredulity than Meredith.

I shrugged, the picture of casualness. "Why not? I kind of want to hear them, too."

"Cool!" Meredith's face lit up. That poor girl. "I have to stay after school for Wister Writers, but I could drive down afterward and meet you guys there?"

The bell rang, exactly on time.

"Sounds perfect," I said. "Gotta go!"

I stuffed my Wister Writers flyer in my pocket and swept out of the room with Tess in tow.

"Dude," Tess said. "Look at you."

"What?"

"Little Miss Cool Concertgoer. You're practically strutting."

For some reason, I thought about Meredith, twisting her braid and bumping into people with her backpack on wheels.

"Yeah," I said.

Tess nodded sagely. "Nothing wrong with indulging in some full-on lusting now and again."

"It's not full-on lusting!" I said. "It's . . . aloof consideration of a possibility."

"A *lusty* possibility," Tess said. I shot her a look and she quickly retreated into a palms-up.

"Okay, okay. Well, *whatever* it is, in its own weird, totally hetero way, this is actually kind of awesome. Nattie finally kissing a boy at last." Tess arched an eyebrow at me. "So what are we wearing tonight?"

# CHAPTER FOUR

My bedroom was a mess, but even if I cleaned it, it wouldn't be cool. I'd begged to paint the walls Blushing Blossom Pink when I was six, and it had been so much work to prime the walls and tape the molding and throw down drop cloths that my parents made me promise I'd never change my mind. And I didn't, for about six months. Now, it looked like stale cotton candy—horrible, especially with Mom's weird homemade lace curtains and my sagging inflatable chair covered in stuffed animals and the paper lanterns covered in dust. If I ever ended up on one of those shows where a prospective date rummages through your room and tries to decide if you're normal enough to go out with, I'd flunk. Right now, I felt awkward enough with Zach the Anarchist sitting cross-legged against the wall of my bedroom, watching Tess drag all my hangers from one end of my closet to the other with a grating sound.

"Why am *I* here, again?" Zach said.

"Because Tall Zach had cross-country after school, and we need someone to evaluate the efficacy of our outfits," Tess said. "Also, to drive. You wouldn't want us to take the *train* to the city, would you?"

After some quick Google mapping, Tess and I had discovered that Ruby's Rock Club was just a few blocks away from Zach the Anarchist's house in Center City, so we (meaning Tess) decided to convince him to come over to my house after school—with his car, of course—so that we could all go downtown together.

"I think you'd survive," Zach said, stretching his arms overhead. Today he was wearing a black T-shirt with "Club Sandwiches, Not Seals" on it under a flannel shirt he'd rolled up to his elbows.

"Does anyone have any opinions on either of these?" I asked. "Because otherwise I'm going to put them down."

Tess squinted at the top in my left hand, which had a bunch of buckles and zippers dangling off of it, and then at the one in my right hand, which was made of something fluffy and white. Zach the Anarchist had become occupied with the stuffed-animal pile.

"Zippers," she said. "Definitely."

I examined the top. "It's from, like, fifth grade. It doesn't fit."

"Okay, so the white one. It's"—Tess paused, searching for the most convincing adjective—"different."

"It's weird," I said. "I'm pretty sure my mom bought this for me to play a sheep in *Charlotte's Web*. It's not actually cool."

"It's pretty *baa-aad*," Zach said, holding up a tiny stuffed sheep.

"Stop!" Mortified, I grabbed Lamby from an amused Zach and threw the fuzzy top on the ground for emphasis, which was kind of hard because it was too light to throw properly.

"You'll find something." Tess rattled the hangers again and yanked out a peasanty-looking top. "What about this? It's got this cool abstract design on the front—"

"That's a mustard stain." I took it from her and put it back.

By the wall, Zach had picked up two teddy bears and was making them dance.

"Stop?" I said again, and snatched them out of his hands. "Please?"

Seeing Zach play with all my stuffed animals reminded me just how weird it was that a phrase like *all my stuffed animals* could still apply to me. I needed to burn them on a ceremonial pyre. Plus, something about having him here, in my actual bedroom, where he had never been before, was making me second-guess the whole concert plan. There was no way this was a thing I could actually do.

I flung the teddies at my bed. "So dumb."

"*I* think they're nice." Zach got up and stretched. "Do you have any snacks?"

"Probably?" I said. "Ask Sam Huang."

"Cool. Call me when you're ready."

The stairs creaked across the hallway as Zach left. Tess craned her neck out the door, her red lips a tight line.

"So cranky."

"He's got stuff to be morose about," I said, trying not to cringe. "And you did kind of trick him into driving us, *Tessica*."

"Ugh." Tess hated it when I called her that. "Still not my real name, Nattie. Now, do you have any other clothes? Your outfit says a lot about you."

I eyed my closet. "That's about it."

"Really? You don't own, like, a leather skirt or a halter top or anything?"

"Nope." Unlike Tess, who used clothing to express her personality and looked good while doing it, I had cultivated a personal fashion aesthetic around the idea of just not looking too strange. Normal T-shirts, ordinary jeans. One unfortunate occasion in freshman year, I'd been bold enough to wear a pair of fingerless lace gloves to school, and everyone asked if it was a costume. Mr. Sentman, the ninth-grade physics teacher, even called me "Lacey."

Tess groaned. "This is not going to work. How are you ever going to make an impression on anyone, let alone Sebastian, in something like this?" She held up a "Wister Runs 5K and Walk" T-shirt, which I snatched away.

"I didn't even run in that," I said. "I think it's my mom's."

Tess wasn't listening. "Take off your shirt."

"Um." I glanced back at the doorway—no Zach the Anarchist lurking. Tess grabbed the hem of my T-shirt and yanked up.

"Hey!"

"Relax, Nattie," Tess said from somewhere outside the shirt stuck on my head. "I get why you're nervous. I mean, *I* would never want to date Sebastian—"

"I don't want to date him." I disposed of my shirt in my laundry hamper, by which I mean the floor, and hugged my arms around myself. "I mean, I don't think I do. I just want to . . . figure out what happened between us. If anything *did* happen. Or something."

"He stayed up all night with you and touched you on the face," Tess said. "I think that is definitely *something* that *happened*."

"Yeah, but . . ." I sighed. It was supposed to be the Kiss and not the Almost Kiss. It was not supposed to be dumb Nattie and another *I don't know?* situation.

"Look, all I know is, you, Nattie McCullough-Schwartz, are incredibly sexy and have once upon a time attracted the attention of an indie-rock-star guy who is also, I assume, sexy."

"I'm not sexy," I said, looking down at my bra, which was hot pink and had a weird pucker between the boobs where there used to be a bow. "This is from the kids' section."

"Well, it's working for you." Tess arched an eyebrow. "Sebastian wouldn't have spent time with you if he didn't think you were special. And that's why you need to *look* special. Here."

She threw me a tank top made of lace—the same lace top I'd worn with my gloves.

"No," I said. "I need to wear something underneath it."

"You have a bra on."

"But then everyone can *see* my bra!"

"Exactly." She grabbed me by the shoulders and steered me to the mirror. "Wah-lah."

"It's *voilà*," I said to no one. "And I look—"

"Hot," she said. "You look hot. You look like you're going to a rock show. You look like you need a little lipstick."

Tess tugged at my chin until my mouth sat in an obedient O, then started to color me in.

"Why does it matter what color my lips are?" I said. "It's probably going to be dark in there." I assumed. I'd never been to a club, or a bar, or whatever these places were.

"Because when you make out with Sebastian, I want you to leave a mark." Tess capped her lipstick. "Now mush your lips together."

But I didn't. "Make out? Nobody said anything about making out."

"I figured it was implied." Tess rubbed her thumb against the edge of my mouth. "A logical endgame."

Instead of saying anything, I hit Tess on the shoulder.

"Yeah, yeah, *je frappe toi* more," she said, and gave me

a soft smack in return. "Look, Nattie, I get why you'd be nervous. Everyone thinks their first kiss should be this big, huge, world-changing, heart-stopping kind of thing. But it never is."

"It isn't?"

"No. Trust me. Look what happened with Zach the—"

"Shhzp!" I squeaked, even though there was no one in the hallway.

"Sorry," Tess said at a whisper, which for her was more like a normal speaking voice. "My theory is that first kisses are inherently doomed, because you always want them to be more meaningful than they end up being. But this one could work out. First, Sebastian is experienced, so it'll be a *good* kiss. Second, he's only here for a while, so if it *isn't* a good kiss, you never have to see him again."

"Third?" I asked.

"How many more reasons do you *need*, Nattie?"

"A couple, okay?" I mushed my lips together. Having lipstick on just seemed to make me super conscious of my lips. "I mean, I'm not like the rest of the girls he's been attached to, however briefly. I'm not sophisticated and, like . . . experienced. I'm not ready to have rumors circulate about me."

Tess tapped a painted fingernail against her chin, pensively.

"That's the beauty of it, though," she said at last. "He's gone. He's an NYU man now. He's not going to be following you around the hallways or publishing poems about you in

56

the literary magazine. There is almost zero risk of anything reputation-damaging."

"And he's pretty cute."

"*Hot*, Nattie. Sebastian is *hot*." Tess shook her head. "He's not a puppy, he's a guy you want to bang."

"Right," I said, even though *banging* felt like an awfully percussive verb to apply to my feelings for Sebastian.

She closed-mouth grinned at me and adjusted the tank top over my shoulders. "Perfect."

Twenty minutes later, the two of us were buckled into the backseat of Zach's station wagon and cruising down Lincoln Drive as Zach messed with the radio. He glanced back at us.

"Can you put on WPHL?" I asked.

"Yeah," Tess said. "This stuff is too loud. And eyes front, Captain."

"No." Zach flicked his iPod to something fast and power chord–y, but obeyed and kept his gaze dead ahead. Tess pouted.

"Look, if you're going to strong-arm me into chauffeuring, I at least get to play my own music."

"We didn't *strong-arm* you," Tess said. "You just happened to accept an invitation to hang out in the 'burbs with us and then, by complete coincidence, the two of us needed a ride to a concert that is literally blocks from your house. Right, Nattie?"

"Sure," I said. There was a weird feeling in my chest, and I couldn't tell if it was anxiety about the concert, the fact that Zach the Anarchist had yet to look me in the eye since the unfortunate Mia-mentioning slip the other day, or the cold air that was breezing through the holes in my top. It was all very unnerving.

"We're keeping you company," Tess said.

"You're distracting me from the road," Zach said. I was sitting on the opposite side of the car as he was, and each streetlight we zipped past threw his silhouette onto my lap. "And if you're keeping me company, why are you both sitting in the backseat?"

"Safety?" Tess tried.

"It's a Volvo," Zach said.

"And?"

"And Volvos are like safest family vehicles on the road," Zach said. "The Swedish are master engineers."

"Tell that to all the IKEA dressers my dad has tried to build," I said. "Or ABBA, for that matter."

Tess looked put out. It was hard to tell in the dark, but I think Zach smiled a little. I felt a wash of relief.

"I *like* ABBA," grumbled Tess.

"I hope you're not going to see a tribute act tonight," Zach said. "Because if I had known there was bad pop music, I would have made you *walk*."

"Okay, *one*," Tess said, "ABBA is not bad pop music—"

"They're pretty bad," I said, but Tess ignored me.

58

"—and *two*, the band we are seeing is positively *oozing* hipster cred."

"In that case," Zach said, "I'll let you off up here." He gestured at the on-ramp to Kelly Drive.

"They're not *that* hipstery," I said. "They're more . . . I don't know. They rock, I think."

"You think?" Zach was smiling.

"I mean, my baseline is Joni Mitchell, so I don't have a good barometer for what's hipstery."

"Excuse me," Tess interrupted, "but the Young Lungs are *way* hipstery."

Zach had trained his attention back on the road. The Volvo's turn signal clicked and swept us onto Kelly Drive. Outside my window, the Schuylkill River looked deceptively sparkly and pleasant in the moonlight instead of like the brown line of sludge it was in the daytime.

"But that doesn't preclude them from being good," Tess was going on. "I mean, if nothing else, Sebastian Delacroix is proof that hipsters can rock."

Zach stiffened a little in his seat, but maybe it was my imagination.

"I guess," I said. "I've only heard like part of one song."

"Well, one hipstery song sounds like a solid reason for tricking someone into playing chauffeur," Zach said.

Tess leaned forward and smacked him on the back of the head.

"Watch it!" Zach said. "Distracted driving!"

"Don't be so sarcastic," she said. "For your information, we go to concerts like this all the time."

"Wasn't the last concert you went to at the Academy of Music?" Zach said.

"That was me," I said. "And it was the Kimmel Center." It had also been "An Evening of Spanish Guitar" with my mom and Sam Huang, but I knew better than to bring that up now.

Zach smiled. "Dang. Please teach me to be hard-core like you."

"Okay, *anyway*," Tess interrupted. "We're your friends, remember? Acronymphos forever."

"Yeah," he said, his eyes flicking briefly into the rearview mirror. "I know."

I shifted under my seat belt, uncomfortably awake. The energy of the night was starting to get to me, and again I was full of doubts. Maybe Zach was right. What was I *doing*, showing up at this concert? What was even going to happen? I wasn't fully sure what you *did* at a cool concert, whether you were supposed to dance or just stand there and absorb the music, and what you were supposed to do when you had to go to the bathroom. I tried to envision it, tried to picture Ruby's Rock Club in my mind, but I just drew a blank. I wanted to tell Zach to slow down, even though he was right at the speed limit, just so we wouldn't get to the show so fast.

But I didn't, and he didn't, and after fifteen minutes of

silence—well, as silent as the car could be with Zach's tinny speakers blasting angry antiestablishment music—we pulled up to the corner I recognized as being a few streets over from Zach's town house.

"Is this it?" Tess said.

"You tell me," Zach said. "You're the one who's always going to concerts."

"Shut up," Tess answered. I craned my neck out the window to see if any of the dark, skulking figures on the sidewalk were recognizable. One of them, vaguely female with one hand pulling something suspiciously rolly, squinted into the Volvo's headlights, then waved and came over to the car.

"Hey!" It was Meredith. "I'm so glad you guys are here. I felt like such a loser hanging out outside of this club with all my school stuff."

Tess clambered out and rolled her eyes. "It's an all-ages show. Let them judge."

"Door, please?" Zach called from inside the Volvo. Meredith bent down and shaded her eyes with her hand.

"Zach West? Is that you?"

"No," Zach said. "Just a chauffeur."

Meredith laughed and waved, and Tess shut the door behind her.

"Thanks, dude!"

"You're welcome," Zach said.

"Yeah, thanks, Zach," I said. My stomach clenched, and

I felt the inexplicable urge to open the door, climb back in, and tag along to the safety of Zach the Anarchist's house, where we could have an Acronympho movie night and where at the very least I knew how to find the bathroom. In the front seat, Zach was poking at the radio again, for no real reason. I hugged my arms around myself.

"I look ridiculous, right?" I said, kind of quietly. Zach tipped the rearview mirror a little, so that the reflection of his eyes was right on mine.

Maybe it was just a kind of postpubescent physical evening out, or maybe it was just my own postpubescent hormones making me see things, but somewhere in the last few months, Zach the Anarchist had changed. It wasn't that he was taller, exactly—I mean, he *was* taller, though thankfully still not as tall as Tall Zach, which would have thrown our nicknaming schema into chaos. He just looked . . . older. Bigger. Not huge or anything, but just slightly broader, grown-up in the way that you grow when your diet is 75 percent tofu lo mein. In the low light, his cheekbones really stuck out, and his mouth . . . well, it had always been a pretty nice mouth, but now it seemed . . . pouty, I guess. Not in a supermodel-duck-face way, but more in the way that all the punk guys on his bedroom posters looked. Thoughtful. Boy-like. The kind of mouth that wouldn't have been so bad for a first kiss.

"You look a little . . . cold," he said at last. As if on cue, I shivered. Had I just been checking Zach the Anarchist out?

"Nattie!" yelled Tess from the sidewalk. "While we're still young?"

"Yeah, well." I tugged at the Volvo's door latch and started to climb out. "Tess has some idea that this is going to make me blend in with hipsters, but—"

Something soft hit me in the back. Zach's plaid shirt.

"What?" I scooped it up off the sidewalk. Zach, now just in his T-shirt, only shrugged.

"Camouflage," he said. "And I'm trusting you not to lose it."

I didn't even have time to say thank you before he pulled away.

# CHAPTER FIVE

Inside, Ruby's Rock Club was far from a blank. Actually, it was kind of a dump.

We'd each paid our ten bucks at the door and gotten our hand stamped by a bouncer who was about as wide as he was tall, and he was *really* tall. Inside, the space was dark, warm, and smelled vaguely of beer. There was a bar with a couple stools crammed around it in the far corner, but the rest of the club was just a long, narrow room with brick walls and a barely elevated stage at one end. Strings of lights with bulbs shaped like giant lips scalloped the walls, and something rhythmic and unidentifiable was pumping over the PA system.

"Follow me."

As soon as we were fully inside, Tess charged forth to secure us a good spot in the back left corner of the room. Zach's shirt was a little too hot in the stuffy air, but something about the red light on the red stripes of plaid made me feel intriguingly alien and different. Cool, even.

We got a couple stares from college-aged-looking kids in

vests and knit hats as we settled into place, but I imitated Tess's ultraconfident posture and ignored them. Besides, most of them were staring at Meredith's backpack (which, I noticed, had her initials stitched on it and everything). If Meredith saw them staring, she at least had enough sense not to deploy the wheely part.

I couldn't say that I was feeling quite as relaxed as Tess. My senses seemed supercharged, even as everything was reduced to a dull roar of voices competing with music competing with one scruffy-looking guy shuffling around the stage area and tapping his finger on the microphones.

"When do you think they'll go on?" I asked no one in particular, my voice hardly cutting through the landscape of bar sounds.

Tess checked her watch. "It's ten of nine, so . . ." She shrugged. "I guess it depends on if there are any opening bands or not."

"There are," Meredith said. "I looked on their website. The Young Lungs are up second."

"Second out of how many?" I asked.

Meredith frowned. "I think four?"

"So technically speaking, the Young Lungs *are* the opening band," I said.

"*An* opening band," Tess corrected. "The first band is bound to be the worst, so comparatively I'm sure they'll be much better."

More people were coming in now, in groups of three or

65

four that brought little gasps of cool air from the outside and began to fill up the clear view of the stage I'd had before. Beside me, Meredith scooched her backpack behind her legs, so that it was between us and the wall, more or less concealed from public access.

Tess glanced back at the bar. "Do you think they would serve me if I tried to order something?"

"Sooner you than me," I said. Tess could probably pass for at least twenty-five, if you squinted.

"Um, sooner *both* of you than me," Meredith said, her eyes lingering on the gap in Zach's shirt where my bra was still clearly visible. "I didn't realize I should have gotten dressed up. No wonder the guy at the door was giving me weird looks."

"Mm," Tess said, craning her neck toward the bar. "Maybe I'll just get a Diet Coke for fortification."

She ducked between us and disappeared toward the bar, leaving me standing kind of awkwardly with Meredith. A few people over, I could see one of the guys in the knit hats dart a glance our way and whisper to his friend, a blond girl with a bull ring through her nose. I brushed my hair forward to cover my shoulders and reminded myself to stand up straight. Meredith was looking toward the stage and kind of rubbing her hands together, like she was nervous.

"So do you have a lot of homework this weekend?" she asked after a brief moment of relative silence. "Because I have this bio project—"

"Not really," I said shortly, because for some reason Meredith didn't get that talking loudly about *homework* at a rock show was the equivalent of wearing a sign that said "We Are Just Dumb Children." The bull-ring girl was snickering behind her hand.

"Oh. Lucky you." Meredith gave the Backpack™ a little thump with her heel. "I wonder where the bands are."

"I would guess backstage," I said, "but then again, I'm not sure this stage has enough room to *have* a back."

"Yeah," Meredith agreed. "I figured they'd be here hanging out."

I looked around at the collective coolness that was the crowd around us and shrugged.

"Maybe they are," I said. "I feel like any one of these people could be in a band."

Bull-ring girl was gone, but the guys in the hats were looking at us again.

"Dude." Tess reappeared at my elbow, clutching a glass of soda with a little straw in it. "Nattie. That guy is totally checking you out."

"Er," I said. "No thanks."

"Come on. You've still got"—she checked her watch—"two minutes before the first band goes on. Assuming they'll be on time, which I guess they probably won't. That gives you, what, at least half an hour before Sebastian's onstage? Might as well practice."

I glared at Tess to make her stop, not exactly wanting Meredith to overhear.

"What I *meant* was," Tess said, "his friend is kind of cute. Think she's into girls?" She sipped her Diet Coke.

"Your guess is better than mine," I said.

"Are you a big fan of the Young Lungs, Nattie?" Meredith said suddenly.

"Sure," I said. "They're pretty good." It wasn't an outright lie. I didn't really know from indie rock, but the half-minute snatch I'd heard of the Young Lungs' oeuvre was decently catchy.

"I just sort of realized they existed," Meredith said. "I mean, I had always really liked Sebastian's poetry, and I knew he was good on the guitar, but I didn't know he had started a band. But he started posting videos of it on Pixstagram and so eventually I was like, okay, fine, I guess I should go to the concert and support a . . . um, a friend of mine."

Meredith took a breath. She was talking at the brisk clip of the perennially overcaffeinated, and I couldn't tell if her face was actually flushed or just basking in the glow of the lip lights like everything else.

"But I haven't listened to any of their songs yet," she finished. "Do you think that's weird? Are any of them good?"

"Yeah," I said. "I mean, no, it's not weird. You'll hear them now, right? So that's good enough." At least, I *hoped* that was how these things worked.

Meredith nodded, as if she had any idea what happened at rock shows. "Yup."

Onstage, a girl with a shiny black bob of hair and precariously tall platform shoes was clomping up to the microphone. Behind her, the scruffy guy who'd been shuffling around the stage earlier was settling in, a single drumstick in his hand, behind a keyboard that had a tambourine mounted on one corner. Meredith got really quiet, and Tess raised her eyebrows.

"Is that the first band?" Meredith asked.

"Is that even an instrument?" I asked.

Tess did a palms-up. "Don't look at me. Maybe that's what's cool now."

"Hello, everyone," she said. The microphone gave a little squeal, and the lights dimmed just enough to turn the sequins on her dress into little winks of green light.

"We're Ultimate Trajectory and these are some damn good songs. One! Two! Three! Four!"

# CHAPTER SIX

Half an hour later, I'd come to the conclusion that Ms. Trajectory and I had different ideas about what "damn good" meant, at least vis-à-vis *music*. Maybe someone, somewhere enjoyed distorted, unintelligible songs with laser-zap sound effects and seemingly random bursts of tambourine, but that person was not in evidence at Ruby's Rock Club and was certainly not me. The crowd remained as shiftless and noisy with Ultimate Trajectory thrashing and shrieking onstage as they had before the lights had gone down. In fact, most people seemed to be talking *louder* to overcome the music. Meredith and Tess were both quiet, Meredith from politeness and Tess from trying to get a better look at the girl with the nose ring.

Ms. Trajectory wailed one last time into the microphone and raised it above her head for a dramatic finish. It must have been hot under all those sequins, because her sleek hair was now stuck to her cheeks.

"Thank you, Philadelphia!" She bowed her head to a smattering of applause. Some guy in the crowd yelled out, "You're welcome!" which set his friends laughing. The girl onstage looked a little confused and picked her way offstage slowly but clompingly, her male partner slumping along after her.

"Well," Tess said brightly. "That was refreshing."

"I think I finally see why adults hate rock music." I pushed Zach's shirt's too-big sleeves up to my elbows for what felt like the zillionth time. "It's bad for the youth."

"What?" Meredith said. Frowning, she snapped a finger next to her head. "I think my ears are ringing."

Tess yawned and looked at her watch. "Jeez. It's not even ten. I feel like such an old lady."

I wasn't really listening, watching instead as two guys in black T-shirts came onstage and replaced the keyboard with a few amplifiers and a rack of guitars. One of them started fiddling with the knobs while the other stepped up to each microphone, giving it a "check, one two" and flipping hand signals up at an invisible sound booth. Behind them, I could just make out a big *YL* on the drum kit.

Two letters, just like that, and I was literally trembling with anticipation. I hadn't seen Sebastian in months, hadn't even talked to him since he drove away from my house, and now I was about to watch him come onstage and sing a song to a room full of people. In my conscious mind, I knew I should be freaking out. But the stammering, clammy-handed nervousness I had expected wasn't coming. I just felt energized, like someone had jump-started my pulse.

The hum in the room grew and swelled. Meredith was snapping her fingers some more, trying to get her hearing back. Tess turned to me and started to say something about getting another Diet Coke or the girl or something else, but I didn't hear it, because the lights were going down again and the band was coming onstage. All skinny guys in tight pants with varying degrees of beard, and then Sebastian.

"Hey." He leaned into the microphone, and then back a bit, and then he smiled. Somewhere in the crowd, a cheer rose up, and his smile got a little wider. He stooped to sling on his guitar and then stepped back to the mic.

"We're the Young Lungs, and these songs are just okay."

"Woo!" Tess heaved her hands into the air, her exhaustion apparently forgotten, and immediately began to dance. The song was upbeat and syncopated and sounded worlds better than Ultimate Trajectory.

And Sebastian looked better than anything I'd seen all night.

He had this relaxed, liquid way of moving onstage, like he knew he was being watched but wasn't trying to do anything too dancey and ridiculous—just play his music and maybe look good at the same time. His hair was cut at a new angle so that it just barely flipped into his eyes when he strummed, and his arms looked extra tan against the white edges of his T-shirt. He sang with his eyes darting all around the room and an angular smile, his face lightly stubbled like it was when it had been close to mine.

I was transfixed, and the song whirled forward into its second chorus. Before I knew it, the band was crunching into the final chord and the crowd was clapping, a few people even cheering.

"Not bad," Tess said, catching her breath from her little fit of dancing.

"They're pretty good!" Meredith yelled, a huge smile on her face. I restrained myself from doing the same and just nodded.

"Yeah." I'd been so focused on watching Sebastian that I hadn't listened so much to what the song sounded like, but then again, I didn't really need to. The visuals were just as good.

"So I guess you guys like music," Sebastian said. "Here's some more of that." He began a quick, high-pitched strum and nodded his head as the bass thumped in after him, and then they were off. More cheers, and a few people sprang forward to dance.

"I could get used to this," Tess called out over the noise. "Nattie?"

I gave her a smile and shrugged. She shoved me in the shoulder.

"Look at you, trying to be all casual."

"I'm not trying to be all *anything*." I adjusted the collar of Zach's shirt around my neck. "I'm just out to enjoy a promising up-and-coming band."

"Sure," Tess said, but the look on her face said she knew better. She flung out an arm to pull us onto the dance floor, and Meredith shook her head, but, to my surprise, I accepted. Everyone seemed to be kind of twisting and swaying rather than full-on bump-and-grinding, and I found myself moving without feeling weird or self-conscious. Tess even twirled me, and we danced for the whole song, and kept going as the Young Lungs launched straight into the next one. Sebastian's voice was all around me, singing something about fairy tales and second chances, and I let it flow over me. Tess danced me closer to the stage, but I hung back, just for safety's sake. Not that anyone was judging me: for all anyone knew, I was a genuine hipster who actually owned this plaid shirt and went to dingy bars all the time. And whether anyone could tell or not, some part of me had once, however briefly, caught Sebastian's eye. I didn't know if he would notice me now and I realized I didn't care. All I knew was that dancing was great and thinking about him made me practically glow.

The song died. I fell back toward a side wall, trying to catch my breath, but before I could get in so much as a second inhale they were off again with another, and then another, and soon I was literally panting with the effort to keep up. Finally, after a crisp rattle of drums, the band took a break.

"Wow." Sebastian stood at the microphone, wiping a hand over his forehead. "Sucks that you guys hate to dance."

The crowd yelled back something unintelligible and affirmative. He grinned.

"Yeah, okay. And I imagine no one's ever had their heart broken?"

A mixed chorus of boos and cheers rose up. My heart leaped to my throat.

"Thought so. This one's about that."

He leaned back, strumming out the chords I recognized from this morning. Somewhere on the edge of my vision, I was aware of Tess swiveling around to me, but all I could see was Sebastian.

*"Well, there's curves like madness in her hips*
*And red like sin painted on her lips."*

It was beyond strange, watching the boy I'd Almost Kissed four months ago stand on a stage and sing about some other girl. It wasn't like the initial shock of hearing his voice on the radio, and it wasn't like anything he'd said to me for the short time we'd spent together. It was different, bigger, better.

*"Got heat like wildfire in her eyes*
*A short short skirt riding up those thighs*
*Can't keep myself thinking straight*
*'Cause she's speaking a language I can't translate."*

"I bet it's French," I called to Tess. "He sucked at French."

"What?" She frowned, clearly not getting my stupid joke. I was about to try again, but that's when I heard it.

*"Oh, Natalie . . ."*

I froze.

*"Hair like a burning flame."*

A bolt of panic ricocheted through me. Had I just heard what I thought I'd heard?

*"Natalie*
*I can't forget her name."*

Tess widened her eyes at me and screamed. I grabbed her and shook my head furiously. Knowing Tess, she would think the appropriate reaction would be to gesture wildly at me and yell, "That's her! He can't forget *her!*"

*"Natalie*
*Sets herself apart."*

Zach's shirt was slipping off one shoulder. I shoved it back in place in a way that hopefully looked like a cool dance move and kept dancing like nothing was happening. What if

Sebastian looked out and saw me? I wasn't sure if I wanted him to know I was here, and now he was singing about me. Hell, he could practically be singing *to* me.

Then again, Sebastian probably couldn't see me with lights in his eyes, and nobody except the bouncer outside knew what my name was. I moved from swaying to actual dancing again, back on the dance floor, shaking my head like I was anyone else. Like I actually *was* fiery.

*"Natalie,*
*Why'd you break my heart, heart, heart?"*

Tess did a big, closed-mouth smile as she whirled around me. "Yeah, what do you have to say for yourself?" she yelled.

My heart was throbbing.

"Um," I called back. "My bad?"

"You!" She screamed with laughter and twisted around behind me. "This is insane! You are insane! Sebastian is totally in love with you!"

"Yeah, well . . . so?" I called back. He launched into the second verse, but I could barely hear the lyrics. Our encounter had been so . . . brief, and kind of awkward. And maybe it was just that "Natalie" fit into the song.

But everything about this moment had gone wiggly around the edges—surreal. The song was pumping, we were dancing, and just for the tiniest flash of a second, I was totally careless, totally cool.

It couldn't be about me, except that it could. I wanted it to be. And then, just like that, it was over.

"Thank you, Philly!" Sebastian said into the microphone. His face was a little flushed. "If you want to hear more of us, you can buy our album out front. Or you can wait for the guy who buys our album out front to put it on the internet."

The crowd laughed, but Sebastian just shrugged.

"Good to come home. You've been awesome. Get hype for the Forty Thieves!"

He flashed a final grin, then slung off his guitar and walked away to some dark and invisible area to the side of the stage. The lights came up, the roadies reappeared to cart stuff off, and the bar began to hum again. The spell was broken, and yet my heart was going like I was still dancing.

Tess said something, but I completely missed it, watching as Sebastian's lanky form disappeared in the darkness.

"What?" I turned back to her.

"I said, I have not danced that much in at least two days."

"I haven't danced that much in *ever*," I said.

"Whatever. NATALIE!" She practically screamed it. Quick as a reflex, I jabbed my heel onto her toes.

"Shut up," I said.

"Nattie," she said again, her voice lower. "You are the woman of Sebastian's dreams."

"I'm not," I said, but even I had to admit, the evidence was pretty convincing.

"You have to go find him! You have to."

"I . . . don't know," I confessed. "The next band's going to be on soon. Where would I even find him now?"

Tess had no time to waste.

"Who cares about the next band? Just find Sebastian."

"Shouldn't I be . . . aloof?"

"Okay, one, who even says *aloof*, and two, *no*." Tess punched my shoulder. "*Je* am *frappe*-ing some sense into you."

I rubbed where she'd hit me. Sebastian already thought I was cool. And I definitely thought he was attractive. I could just keep being the mysterious girl he seemed to think I was. Say a quick hello, do a deep-voiced laugh, maybe find someone to give me a cigarette so I'd seem reckless enough to endanger the health of my lungs.

"You're totally blushing," Tess said.

"Shut up. It's just the lights," I said. I glanced around the bar.

"What about Meredith?"

"I'll tell her you went to the bathroom or something. Besides, we have to split soon anyway. It's eleven already, and it'll take us at least half an hour to get home. I love you and want to indulge your Sebastian lust as much as reasonably possible, but I am *not* risking getting grounded." For all her tendency toward hedonism, Tess was no-nonsense when it came to her midnight curfew.

I reached my hand into my pocket and gingerly pulled out my phone, like it was a grenade.

"Okay." I was cool. I was calm. I could do this. "How do I look?"

Tess skimmed an appraising glance over me. "Hot. Very hot."

"Thanks."

"No, I mean—you're all red. Here." Tess sidestepped to my back and shucked Zach's shirt off my shoulders, leaving me bare-armed and bra-exposed.

"There." She wadded up the shirt under her arms. "Much better."

"Is it?" I folded my arms. Even the humid club air felt cold on my skin.

"Abso-freaking-lutely." Tess grabbed a wrist and yanked my arms apart. "I'll go get Meredith and our stuff. *You* have fun."

"Yeah." I swallowed hard, swiped open my phone, and pulled up a new Pixstagram message. I didn't have Sebastian's number, but he seemed like the type who'd be checking his inbox a lot.

*Don't overthink it,* I reminded myself. *Keep it simple. Just go find him, and then—*

"Hey."

I whirled around and found not Sebastian, but the guy with the hat from before. He was a little shorter than me, with a leather jacket on that was a size or two too big for him. I slid my phone locked and tucked it back into my pocket.

"Hi," I said, folding my arms.

"You're a good dancer."

"Thanks," I said. I tucked a strand of hair behind my ear and sized him up. He wasn't bad looking, but then again, he was no Sebastian. And he smelled kind of like beer.

"What's your name?" He was practically yelling over the din of the crowd.

I jumped again, but this time, it was from the buzzing of my phone. I could barely make my fingers move fast enough to get it open.

From: Tess Kozlowski

Meredith is getting her car. Meet outside in TEN

MINUTES, WOMAN!!!

The guy in the hat was saying something else, drowned out by the throb of some gnarly punk song that was crunching out over the PA.

"What?" I yelled back at him.

"I said, you do *have* a name, right?"

"Natalie."

It was my name, spoken so softly in my ear that I jumped a third time. And I definitely recognized the voice. I turned, and there he was.

"Sebastian," I said. I blinked once, wordless. He was standing close to me, forced closer by the crush of the crowd as more people poured in to see the Forty Thieves, and he looked . . . nervous. Or maybe surprised. But he was still smiling, and still, obviously, attractive.

"Hey," I said.

The energy of before was flooding my body, making me move without a second thought, and I had no choice but to make an apologetic face at the hat guy.

"Sorry, I have to go."

Hat guy shrugged, but I could tell he was a little miffed for being thrown over. But honestly, the choice was down to him and Sebastian. What did he expect?

I turned back to Sebastian and smiled again.

"Nice set."

It was all I could do not to fist-pump in victory over saying something normal. But I resisted, and instead tipped my head at him as if to say, *your move.*

"You're here," he said.

My brain immediately launched into a quicksilver mono-logue of dumb thoughts. *Of course I'm here. Do you not remember when we shared an incredibly intimate face-touching moment in the front seat of your Crown Vic?!* "Yup."

"You wanna get some air?"

*Wait, of course you remember it, because you wrote a song about me. You wrote a song about parts of my body that you didn't even see except under poor-visibility conditions, and definitely not without clothes.*

*Also, wait, yes, air. Good.* "Sure."

I trailed out after him, up the tiny set of steps at the side of the stage and then out a back door to a grimy alleyway bathed in orange fluorescent light. A few paces away, Sebastian's car was parked on an angle, trunk open and full of a jumble of amps, instruments, and cords. Sebastian grabbed an already-open can of something energizing from off the back bumper. I leaned against the wall of the club as he took a long pull, staring at me the entire time.

"Nice set," I said, not wanting to waste a moment of my now-nine-minute time span.

"You said that already."

*Shoot—abort. Recover. Think of something.* I instinctively went to push up a sagging plaid sleeve that was no longer there. "Well, it was . . . really nice."

"We try."

"You, uh, succeed."

Sebastian drained the can and crumpled it into a nearby Dumpster. I looked at the heap of equipment in his car, which seemed like it had been thrown in rather than carefully loaded.

"The guys are off getting beers," he said, answering my unasked question. "Said they'd finish the gear stuff later."

"Ah," I said. "Well, it . . . looks like they pay better than they plack. I mean, um"—*shoot*—"play better. Than packing."

"Thanks, I think." Sebastian looked at his shoes for a second, then came over next to me and leaned against the wall, too. His eyes were intensely dark, in a probing kind of way, and I realized that, excepting some oral presentations in

French, this was the longest uninterrupted stretch he'd ever spent looking at me.

"You're welcome, I think," I said. My heart was pulsing in the weird space between chest and stomach, but in an exciting way, like we were back in the car during the the Almost Kiss. If I could just keep my cool, I could have a legitimate, prelude-to-an-Actual-Kiss conversation. But that felt like a big *if.*

"How's Newy—New York?" My tongue felt huge. *Newy New York?* I wasn't making sense. I clenched my jaw and tried to articulate better. "And *umschool?*"

*Umschool.* Because that's a thing.

"Dropped out," Sebastian said. "It just . . . didn't make sense anymore. Not like it ever did."

"Oh," I said. "Um. Hm." My heartbeat had migrated to my throat, which was making it hard to make actual sentences. Did people just . . . drop out of school like that? No, duh, of course they did—musicians, writers, the guy who invented Facebook, it totally made sense for a certain kind of—

*Okay, focus, Nattie. Ask about the song or—*

"You didn't tell me you were coming to the show," Sebastian said suddenly.

*You didn't tell me there was a show.* But all I could say was, "Um . . . well, surprise?"

*Yes, good, act like you've just jumped out from behind a couch at a birthday party, you genius.* I dug my fingernails into my palms.

Sebastian said nothing, just flicked a gaze at the ground and then back at me.

"Did you like it?"

I swallow-shrugged. "I did say, 'Nice set,' didn't I?"

Finally. Yes. A complete, articulate, sort of bantering sentence. I resisted the urge to press my hand to my heart in relief. Sebastian was looking right at me, and I was suddenly very aware of him being taller than me, and his arm being so close to my waist, and his face being so close to mine that I could see his eyes from underneath his hair and the stubble on his cheek and the way he was biting his lip.

"So you're, like, cool?"

"I mean, I guess I am," I said. "My friends think I'm okay."

Sebastian smirked. "I mean, you're cool with . . . this."

This. This. What was *this*? The alleyway? The concert? The song? I opened my mouth to ask, then shut it again, hard. *Don't do that*, my brain screamed at my dumb body. *Just be cool. Act like you know what he's talking about.*

"Oh," I said. My head felt hollow and floaty, and I could barely pry my lips apart. "Oh! Yeah! Of course. Yeah, like, no big deal. At all. Hahaha!"

No cool person had ever laughed the way I had just laughed. I fluttered my eyes shut and prayed for instant, improbable death. But Sebastian didn't seem to notice.

"Cool." He nodded. "Cool."

He took a step toward me, and I sucked in a breath that I hoped was not too disgusting-smelling. I'd done it. I'd played it cool, and this was it. This was Sebastian finally kissing me. This was—

—something buzzing.

"Is that yours?"

My phone. Ten minutes were up.

"Oh." Shoot. Shoot! I fumbled it out of my pocket and slid it unlocked.

"Is that . . . important?"

"Um, sort of. Yes." I swiped away a message from Tess that said WE NEED TO LEAVE ARE YOU KISSING HIM YET.

"Okay," Sebastian said. He didn't move for a second, like he was trying to make up his mind, and then spoke again. "You know, I really didn't expect this."

"Yeah!" I chirped, and instantly regretted it. *This* again. What did he *mean*? Me at the concert, me hearing the song, me, period? Why couldn't I just act natural about things? I tried again. "I mean, no"—*ugh, God.* I winced—"I mean, *I* know. Life's . . . full of surprises!"

That was something *Dad* liked to say. I sounded like a forty-eight-year-old yurt enthusiast. Sebastian scratched the back of his head.

"Yeah."

"Sorry," I said, and I really was. If there was a time to ask about the song, about anything regarding Sebastian's feelings

86

for me, it had totally passed. I had done my Nattie-iest and completely blown the moment. "That was . . . I'm just a fount of aphorisms today."

Sebastian blinked, then laughed uneasily. "A what?"

"Um, never mind." *Just something dumb.* A second buzz from my phone: JAMBA ALERT NATTIE MAKE OUT AND LET'S GO. But Sebastian's eyes were intense on me again.

"I really have to go," I said, thinking maybe that would prompt him to sweep me into his arms.

He shrugged. "No worries."

"See you later?"

God knows why I phrased it as a question. But Sebastian gave a little laugh.

"Yeah. Life's full of surprises."

And then he reached for me, or, actually, for my face, and—not kissed me, but kind of pressed his thumb into my lower lip.

I had no idea what to do. I couldn't say *uh, bye* or anything, because my lip was being pressed hard into my teeth. I could probably, like, *lick* him, or something, or just mush my mouth into his hand. But then he dropped his hand, and chuckled, and ran a hand through his hair.

"Bye, Natalie."

Face and especially lower lip burning, I felt my way through the dark backstage, pushed my way through the chaos of the Forty Thieves' set, and ejected myself out onto the sidewalk.

"There you are," Tess said from the window of Meredith's minivan. "That was *at least* twelve minutes. It's almost eleven thirty."

"Sorry," I said, clambering into the backseat. "Had to powder my nose."

"Mm-hm." Tess chucked Zach's shirt at me as Meredith eased the car back into traffic.

"Everyone have a good time? Make out okay?" Tess flashed a devilish, tight-lipped smile back at me, which I returned with a simple Mona Lisa–style look of mystery. Okay, maybe I hadn't kissed Sebastian in the technical mouth-on-mouth sense of the word. But we'd kind of had a Moment. A moment with physical contact.

"They were pretty good, I thought," Meredith said. Her voice was as loud as if we were still inside Ruby's instead of her much quieter car. "I kind of thought there would be more O-Dubs people there, though. Did *you* guys see anyone from school?"

Tess shrugged and twisted her bangs between her fingers. "It's college-visiting weekend for the seniors. Everyone's probably off underage drinking in Ivy League dorms. And I'm pretty sure we're the only juniors keeping tabs on Sebastian Delacroix."

"I just wish that first band hadn't been so *loud*," Meredith went on, as if she hadn't even heard Tess—which, given the apparent state of her eardrums, she might not have. "It would have been nice to actually hear the lyrics, you know?"

Tess opened her mouth to reply, but I rushed in first.

"I don't think you missed anything," I said.

"And I wish Sebastian had come out with the rest of the band. I wanted to tell him he did a good job." Meredith clicked a turn signal and swung us back toward the highway that would carry us home. Wister seemed like it was a universe away as I watched the patches of light whoosh by, almost matching the rhythm of the poppy, upbeat song on the radio. "God, he's so *cute.*"

Poor, poor Meredith.

"He's not cute," I said at last. "He's hot."

# CHAPTER SEVEN

"Something is definitely different. I can see it in the whites of your eyes."

Tess jabbed at me with her fork, chewing emphatically through her leftover meatloaf. I just aimed the whites of my eyes down toward my sandwich and tried not to smile.

"I admit nothing."

When I looked back up, Tess had leveled a stare at me. "Sure you don't," she said. "Look at you. You can't even *eat*."

"I can't even eat because it's 10:32 in the morning." Since Upper School lunch at Owen Wister Preparatory Academy started at the ungodly hour of 10:50, we club officials often ended up scarfing down food at the end of third period, which we all had free. I gave my sandwich a valedictory poke and put it away for good. "Are you going to tell me why you called this emergency Monday meeting?"

Sunday night, Tess had sent me an all-caps Jamba alert that we of the OWPALGBTQIA were to assemble the following day at lunch for a MANDATORY SPECIAL MONDAY

MEETING, but why it was special—or mandatory—she had not yet said.

"One, all in good time, and two, don't try to change the subject," Tess said. "Have you listened to it yet? I mean, yet again?"

"Maybe," I said. *Definitely.* "Once or twice." *I lost count after twenty.*

"We're listening to something?" Tall Zach bounded into Dr. Frobisher's room from the hallway, with Endsignal and his music apparatuses trailing. "What are we listening to?"

"Oh, just a little group called the Young Lungs." Tess smiled wolfishly. "They're Nattie's new favorite band."

"Ooh, isn't that Sebastian Delacroix's music thing?" Tall Zach stuffed his legs under the desk by the window and unwrapped two glazed doughnuts from a cafeteria napkin.

"Absolutely," Tess said.

"Um, yeah," I said.

"Hey, one of their songs is even called 'Natalie.'" Endsignal's voice chirped from somewhere behind his screen. "Did you know that?"

A dead silence fell in Dr. Frobisher's room, except for the faint bleeping of the Endsignal battle station.

"I . . . had an idea," I said.

A slow look of realization spread over Tall Zach's face. "Oh my God," he said, grinning his giant grin. "Nattie, Sebastian *totally* loves you!"

"He does not," I retorted.

"Does too," Tess said, and rapped her pencil against the cover of my Catullus book. "Why *else* would a straight guy write about a girl?"

"Catullus wrote to boys, too," I said to Tess. "He wasn't *totally* straight." But that wasn't the point. "But that's not the point. And that's a terrible lunch, Tall Zach. Especially for an athlete."

"But I *like* doughnuts," Tall Zach said, and ate one.

"Um, Natalie?" said Endsignal.

"Everyone just calls me Nattie," I said, unsure if I had made this distinction clear to him.

"Oh." He sat still for a moment. "I was actually just reading about the Young Lungs on this website, if you want to see."

I followed his motions, crouched above his laptop, which was scabbed over with layers of weird stickers and decals, and squinted at the screen, where he had about a billion tabs open.

"*Beatmaxing and timestretching in the Audacity beta release?*" I read. "I only know, like, two of those words."

"Oh, sorry. Wrong tab. That's some random DJing stuff." Endsignal skittered his fingers over the keys and swapped out the black-and-white wall of text for a candy-colored website with a giant cartoon turntable on the top.

Vivian Violet: Putting the *die* in indie rock since Kurt Cobain.

"Is that a person's *name?*"

"Yeah. She's this awesome DJ from New York who does

all this crazy stuff," Endsignal said. "And a music blogger. She wrote a thing about the Young Lungs the other day."

"Um, excuse me? I haven't even heard the song yet!" Tall Zach said. "Guys, I just want to be cool!"

"Oh man, you *have* to. It's great." Tess thunked her can of Diet Coke next to Endsignal's computer and punched in a search for "Young Lungs website Sebastian Delacraw."

"That's not how you spell it," I said.

"Whatever." Tess clicked, and a grainy black-and-white photo of the band greeted us, the same one I'd looked at every hour on the hour for the last two days.

"Ugh, he is so good-looking," Tall Zach said. "And that's such a good picture. So artsy."

It looked like the kind of picture Sebastian would take, but he was right in front, looking intense and mysterious as always, and even though I knew I shouldn't let it, my heart kind of skipped a beat looking at him. I wanted to be like, "Hey, he touched my face once! I mean twice! That cool guy with the haircut and the guitar! Me, Nattie!" but fortunately, I had better sense than to yell this kind of sensitive information out in the middle of school. Tess clicked a little Play button, and suddenly Endsignal's speakers were pumping out a rhythmic, distorted strum of a guitar.

"I like it," Tall Zach said.

"Got a sick drum part," Endsignal said.

"Do we have to do this now?" I said.

"Shut up, all of you," Tess said. "Listen to the lyrics."

A few bars later, the words started, in a singing voice that I now recognized as Sebastian's.

> *"Well, there's curves like madness in her hips*
> *And red like sin painted on her lips*
> *Got heat like wildfire in her eyes*
> *A short short skirt riding up those thighs."*

I squirmed a little. It was one thing for the song to get played on college radio or at a concert full of strangers, but having it played for my actual friends was completely different. I didn't exactly want Tall Zach and Endsignal, for example, to be thinking about my thighs.

> *"Oh, Natalie*
> *Hair like a burning flame*
> *Natalie*
> *I can't forget her name*
> *Natalie*
> *Sets herself apart*
> *Natalie*
> *Why'd you break my heart, heart, heart?"*

"That could be anyone," I said. "By the way."

"Shush," Tall Zach said.

"Just wait," Tess said as the chords shifted and sped ahead into the second verse.

> *"Too cool to leave, too tough to tease*
> *And she won't give in if you don't say please*
> *With just one look she can make you burn*
> *Oh, Natalie, when will I ever learn?"*

"Oh my God, Nattie!" Tall Zach couldn't handle it. "Do you love this song? It's so . . . indie rock."

"Is it? I mean, it's . . . the coolest song I've heard lately," I hedged.

Tess rolled her eyes. "Zach, you're forgetting that this is the girl who thinks the only thing worth listening to is dead folk singers."

"Hey," I said. "Joni Mitchell isn't *dead*."

Tess waved a hand. "She's old. Same difference. And *this*"—she paused for heightened drama—"is definitely about you. Do you actually think Sebastian even *knows* another red-headed Natalie?" She gave the end of my ponytail a gentle yank in punctuation.

I could *feel* my face go hot pink. Tall Zach wiggled his eyebrows, and Endsignal quietly edged his laptop out of the blast radius of Tess's Diet Coke.

"Well?" Tess said.

"Did he tell you he was going to write you a song, Nattie?"

Tall Zach practically had to fold in half to look me in the eyes.

"Guys." Panic was starting to crawl up my throat, sharp and unswallowable. "It's not like we even know that it's *definitely* about me. He never said anything about it."

"But it's called 'Natalie'!" Tall Zach exclaimed. "Who *else* could it be about?"

I chewed on my lip. I knew I definitely wasn't the only girl Sebastian had ever . . . ever what? Touched the face of? "I don't know, plenty of people," I said. "It's not exactly an uncommon name. No one even calls me Natalie."

"Wait, wait," Tess said. "You spent twelve minutes with him and you didn't even definitively discuss this song?"

The heat went back into my cheeks. "Um, not exactly, no."

"Then what else were you *doing*?" Tess yelped.

"We were . . . I don't know. Talking. And stuff."

"Well, I'm declaring the song is about you," Tess said. "It has to be."

"Nattie! You're so special," Tall Zach cried, stooping down to give me a squeeze on the shoulder. "That song is totally about you."

"Thanks. I mean, sort of," I said. "Sebastian wrote poetry for, like, every other girl at this school. Right?" I turned around and found myself looking at Endsignal, who just shrugged.

"But this is a *song*," Tall Zach said. "And wasn't it on the *radio*? That's different."

"It was on *college* radio. That's not *that* different."

"So, congrats and everything, but . . . ," Endsignal piped up from below me. He was staring at Tess in an unmistakable *get away from my computer* kind of way, but she ignored him and flicked back to the search results.

"Look at this. They're all over the blogosphere."

"There's only six pages of results," Tall Zach said.

"And no one says *blogosophere*," Endsignal said.

Now it was my turn to laugh. Tess looked indignant.

"I'm just trying to celebrate my best friend's newfound fame, if that's all right with you?"

"I'm not famous," I said flatly. "There are *cats* that have more internet fame than I do."

"On the internet, no one knows you're a cat," mused Endsignal.

"Guys!" I said, more sharply than I meant to. There were definitely more than a few pages of results, though. I swallowed hard. "Sorry. But can we just . . . not talk about it? Especially not at school? I don't really want it to be, like, a thing."

"Sure, of course," Tall Zach said immediately, then frowned. "Wait. Won't Wister people figure it out, though?"

"Oh . . . I doubt it," I said, more to convince myself than anyone else. Tall Zach looked intrigued, or possibly incredulous, so I kept talking. "When Sebastian was here, he and I were, like, polar social opposites, right? And, um, he's two years ahead of us. I mean, if you hadn't heard this song, would you even think someone like me had ever even *spoken* to Sebastian?"

Tall Zach considered, chewing. "Would you be mad if I said no?" He flashed a grin before I could answer. "No, no, I promise. Sworn to silence. As long as everyone *else* is."

Tess slumped her shoulders. "Fine. Sorry." She relinquished the computer, to Endsignal's visible relief, and went back to her lunch. "I just thought it was flattering."

"What's flattering?"

Zach the Anarchist, in a T-shirt with an upside-down American flag, swung through the double doors to Dr. Frobisher's room, right under the big sign that said "Procul O Procul Este Profani." Mercifully, before anyone and especially Tess could answer, the post-third-period rush flooded into the hallway and OWPALGBTQIA kids started to push their way in.

"Nattie was just—" Tess started.

"—nothing," I interrupted. "No one has ever paid me a compliment of any form in, uh, ever."

I gave Tess an unmistakable *I'll send you a Jamba alert about it later* kind of look. I felt sort of bad about keeping a secret from Zach the Anarchist, especially when he'd been the one to drive us, but if I was being honest with myself, I was scared of what he would do *if* he knew. Not that I knew *what* his reaction to knowing about the song would be or anything. But maybe that was what made me so nervous.

Ten or so minutes later, after all the underclasspeople whose names no one could remember had arrived and taken their seats, Tess strode to the front of the room.

"Okay, everyone, *shut up*! For reasons that will become apparent in due time, this meeting will require utter silence."

The room went silent, ish.

"Now, I know that last time, basically none of you had any ideas for awareness raising. But I've figured out a solution." Tess was pacing the front of the room, holding a sheet of paper.

A freshperson in a hoodie raised a hand. "Um . . ."

"I said *in due time*!" Tess thundered, and the freshperson with their hand up shrank back into their hoodie.

"Okay, *anyway*." Tess snatched up some chalk from the tray. "I've found our solution. It's going to give us a higher profile in the school at large, it will drive people to our membership ranks in droves, and it will also be very, very fun."

It was clear that the last part was an order. Satisfied, Tess wrote "Operation BGDP" on the board—except, because she had started too far to the right, it came out more like

O P E R A t i o

n

B G D P

"We're taking over the Winter Formal," Tess announced. "It's going to be different. It's not going to be a Sadie Hawkins thing anymore, which is, by the way, ridicul—"

"I thought Sadie Hawkins was a feminist," interrupted

Alison, whose name I had remembered from the previous meeting because she was very loud.

"Sadie Hawkins was a *person*?" said Bryce. He looked, as always, very sleepy under all his ear piercings.

"Are you *stupid*, Bryce?" said Chihiro of the pink bangs.

"Don't say *stupid*, Chihiro," said Alison. "What I don't get is why Sadie Hawkins is suddenly ridicul—"

"I always thought it was a made-up name," Bryce said, sleepily. "Like when you call a smart person *Einstein*."

Across the room, Zach the Anarchist was silently losing it behind his hands. I laughed a little, too.

"Can you all just shut up again?" Tess said, her fearless-leader composure wavering just a bit. "Okay, yes, so a Sadie Hawkins dance is technically feminist, but what we *really* need is a Winter Formal that's gender-blind. A dance with no expectation of bringing any kind of date unless you want to."

There were murmurs throughout the room. I had no one in the immediate vicinity to murmur to, but I mentally agreed, because Tess really made it sound awesome. I'd never really liked all the pressure that a Sadie Hawkins dance put on me. Not, of course, that I'd ever actually asked someone. I was dumb, but not *that* dumb.

"What we *need*," Tess went on, "is a dance that doesn't presume anything. A dance that invites people to be their true selves. A dance"—she paused and took a dramatic inhale through the nose—"that celebrates who *we* are, exactly, specifically, and for real."

The murmuring stopped. Tess swiveled her head from one side of the club to the other, waiting for a standing ovation or tears of joy or something, but it was clearly taking most of us a little too long to get there.

Tall Zach craned his neck at the board, raising a tentative hand. "What does that acr—"

"Operation Big Gay Dance Party," Tess answered. "OBGDP for short. It's like . . . like one of those old-fashioned debut balls, where everyone officially enters society or whatever. But with no mandatory gender performativity."

"You mean"—Zach the Anarchist paused, like he wasn't sure if he was actually going to say what he was about to say—"a coming-out party?"

Apparently Tess *did* mean, because no sooner had he said it than Tess, clearly delighted, beamed—or, well, beamed with her mouth clamped firmly shut so we couldn't see her teeth—and pointed right at the stripes and stars on Zach the Anarchist's T-shirt.

"Ding ding ding!" she cried. "We have a winner!"

The murmuring started again, but it sounded like a generally *positive* murmuring. Tess licked her lips and raised her hands for quiet.

"Now, of course, no one *has* to do or say anything they're not comfortable with," she said. "But if you want to say something, and especially if you feel like the announcement is long overdue, particularly to your irritatingly inquisitive family, as some of us do . . ." She gave a tiny shrug. "This is it. Your big, sparkly, celebratory chance."

"Hmmm." Next to me, Tall Zach was considering, which for him meant literally rubbing his chin pensively. But then he nodded. "I like it! I wish I'd had a big dance party when *I* came out."

"It was seventh grade," I pointed out.

"And you did make the announcement at your bar mitzvah," Zach the Anarchist said. "So you kind of *did* get a party."

Tall Zach considered. "I guess. But telling everyone I liked boys was a last-minute addition. Otherwise the DJ wouldn't have looked so surprised when I grabbed the microphone."

"Right. See, this is *different*," Tess said. "This is about creating an occasion with a specific intention. Taking something that can be terrible and ugly and hard and making sure that it's *joyful*." Now she pointed at me. "Nattie. Remember the Menarche Madness party I threw you in middle school?"

Of course I did. After my first period had ruined an otherwise enjoyable McCullough-Schwartz camping trip, the only reason my seventh-grade spring break didn't totally suck was because Tess threw me a surprise transition-to-womanhood party. There had been a game of pin the tail on the tampon. But now was not the time to revisit that particular block of memory lane.

"*Tess*," I hissed. Hopefully she wouldn't bring up the red velvet cupcakes. I glanced around nervously—and right at, of all people, Zach the Anarchist.

But he just shrugged. "Two moms and a sister, remember? Girls bleed, I get it."

"*Some* girls bleed," corrected Alison. "Not all." I held my breath, waiting for her to say something about how terrible Tess's idea was, but she didn't. She actually kind of smiled, kind of. "Anyway, *I* think the dance sounds fun."

Next to her, Chihiro nodded vigorously, her bangs falling in and out of her eyes. Next to *her*, Bryce yawned and gave a thumbs-up.

"Yeah," he said. "Samesies."

"Great," said Tess. "Perfect. Excellent. Because the *good* news is I already floated it with a student council member and they said I can make a case at their meeting today, which I have to be at in"—she glanced at the clock—"ten minutes."

"*Good* news?" said Zach the Anarchist. "What's the *bad* news?"

"Hang on." Tall Zach put down his Capri Sun, crestfallen. "You asked them without asking us first?"

"Sorry, events chair. I had to go over your head for the sake of expediency," Tess said. Tall Zach slurped his Capri Sun and said nothing. "And it's not exactly *bad* bad news," she went on. "The problem is, if we want to cosponsor the dance, we actually have to *sponsor* it. In a monetary sense," she said.

"Student council has asked us to put up a third of the budget for the formal, which is"—she glanced at a printout—"two thousand bucks."

The room went dead quiet.

"Two *thousand*?" I said.

"That has to be wrong," Zach the Anarchist said.

"Okay, one, don't second-guess me," Tess said. "And two, it's not." She thrust her printout into Zach's hands, and I got up to peer over his shoulder. Whoever had kept the accounts for student council last year was freakishly obsessive, putting in cost breakdowns right down to which color of paper streamer cost more. And after decorations, refreshments, and rental of the elegant multipurpose event space in the Wister Racquet Club, the total cost was just over six thousand dollars.

"You aren't going to make *us* chip in, are you?" Across the room Alison narrowed her eyes. "Because—"

"Of course not." Tess nodded crisply at me. "We're going to fund-raise. Right, treasurer?"

"Uh . . ." Suddenly, I could see the whites of everyone's eyes, especially Alison's and very especially Zach the Anarchist's, which made me feel very hot and uncomfortable. Public speaking was probably my number one fear, right after private speaking. Especially private speaking behind rock clubs with guys who play guitar.

"Uh," I said again. "Yeah. Yes. We're going to have . . . a bake sale?"

It was an obvious answer, and kind of a stupid one. But it was better than frozen car washes or auctioning off our supply of white T-shirts or everyone staring at me for any longer.

"A bake sale," Alison repeated. "To make two thousand dollars."

"Sure," Zach the Anarchist answered, blessedly. "I can make something. And so can anyone else who wants to. I mean, we've all got flour and eggs and stuff at home."

"Yeah. That could work." Tess looked at me with an expression that was something like, *Right, treasurer?*

"To make two thousand dollars in the next month and a half . . . ," I said slowly, taking a deep breath. Doing math on my feet was not my strong suit. Actually, doing math on *any* part of my body was not my strong suit, but when Zach the Anarchist abdicated the treasurer's office because he was too busy being Mia's boyfriend, I'd been a good sport. "Assuming we had one bake sale a week, which seems reasonable, and there are eight weeks left until break—"

"Nine," Zach the Anarchist said.

"*Approximately* eight weeks," I continued, "we'd have to take in . . ." Two thousand divided by two was one thousand, and half of nine was four and a half, so a thousand dollars over four and a half weeks was something like . . .

"Four hundred dollars a week," I said, and frowned. "That sounds like a lot."

"Two hundred and fifty," Zach the Anarchist said.

"That doesn't sound *that* bad," Tess said. "I mean, the Upper School is, what, like four hundred kids? I bet we can convince half of them to pony up a buck for a cookie."

"Or brownie," I said.

"I'm *vegan*," Alison said, as if that had anything to do with anything.

"Can you bake for us, Zach?" Tess said.

"Sort of?" said Tall Zach. "I mean, I guess I can try."

"Other Zach."

"Sure," said Zach the Anarchist.

"And a couple other people?"

Hands went up. Tess turned to me.

"I'll supervise," I said. I could cook about as well as I could do math.

"Then it's official. Operation Bake Sale will officially fund Operation Big Gay Dance Party." Tess smacked her hand against the desk like a makeshift gavel. "Someone get on the school intranet and sign up for tabling space in the cafeteria before it gets taken by something useless like animal rights."

"On it," peeped Endsignal. A few keyboard clicks later, he frowned. "Um, the only slot available is on Tuesdays."

"Tuesday is tomorrow," Alison pointed out.

"Yes, duh. Glad you know the days of the week." Tess rolled her eyes. "That's why I called this meeting *today*. Everyone needs to bring in stuff to sell *tomorrow*. Also, two people have to be staffing the table at all times because it's school policy so that no one makes off with the cashbox."

She flourished a sheet of paper and wrote down "Loyal Conscripted OWPALGBTQIA Baked-Goods Purveyors" on the top, then set it on Dr. Frobisher's desk. No one moved.

"So sign up!"

Everyone looked paralyzed. Tess wilted.

"Events chair?" She looked desperately at Tall Zach. "Back me up, here."

Tall Zach leaped up, scrawled his name on the sheet, and then settled back into the desk next to mine.

"Come on, guys," he said. "Do it for the team."

"Do you, ah, know *how* to bake, Zach?" asked Zach the Anarchist.

"I'll have you know, Other Zach, that I make really good Rice Krispies treats, because *I* use Fruity Pebbles."

"Well, I'll have *you* know that technically, there is no actual baking involved in making Rice Krispies treats," Zach the Anarchist said. "Just melting and mixing."

"Technically, there are also *Rice Krispies*," I said. "I mean, not to split hairs or anything."

"But Fruity Pebbles Treats are all rainbowy. Hey, wait, that's perfect for us!" Tall Zach laughed, and I giggled a little, too. From behind us, Endsignal popped up without a word and neatly printed his name next to Zach's. He was halfway back to his laptop when Tess wheeled on him.

"You. What are you contributing?" Tess said.

"I was just going to volunteer," Endsignal said, but Tess shook her head.

"Nope. Nope. I need everyone to pull their full weight and bring something in."

"He's helping me with the fruity treats," Tall Zach offered. He threw a look back at Endsignal, who blushed furiously, but didn't stop him.

"Okay. Fine. Work in teams if you have to." Tess nodded smartly. "So we've got fruity treats. What else?"

"Me and Chihiro are going to be a team so that there's actually something *vegan* we can eat," Alison declared.

"I'm not a vegan," Chihiro mumbled.

"Whatever. You don't eat gluten," Alison said.

"That's not the same thing!"

"Great," Tess said. "No animal products or wheat. I'm sure it'll be a runaway success."

"I'll make lemon squares," Bryce said. "I mean, my mom will, but whatever."

"I can do cheesecake," piped up a girl from the back row.

"I'll make brownies!"

"I can bring a box of Oreos!"

"Great, great, whatever," Tess said, glancing at the clock and brandishing the pen. "Look, I have to run to convince the student council to stop being heteronormative, so Nattie is hereby in charge of making sure you all get signed up. Meeting adjourned!"

She plunked down the sign-up sheet and scooped up her

bag from the desk at my right as the room came to life again, everyone filing forward to scribble down names of various baked offerings.

"Uh?" I said to Tess's back as she strode out into the hall. Then again, I could probably handle a sign-up sheet. I waited as the room slowly emptied out, until no one was left but me, the Zachs, and a few underclasspeople. Tall Zach grabbed the sign-up sheet and studied it.

"Ooh, someone's making baklava?"

"That's ambitious," Zach the Anarchist said, taking the sheet from him.

"That's *mine*," I said, taking the sheet from him. I wrote my name down beneath all the other contributors and paused.

"What are *you* making, Nattie?" Tall Zach said.

"Uh," I said. I wasn't sure what I was going to make, nor was I fully confident in my baking ability. "To be decided."

I folded the sheet in half and turned to unzip my backpack.

"Hang on," Zach the Anarchist said, taking the sheet back. "I haven't put on my contribution yet."

He flattened the piece of paper onto his desk and wrote out something in all caps, angular and slanting to the right, then pushed the paper back to me.

### ZACH WEST—COOKIES.

"Well, it's always nice to see couple of straight kids working a queer bake sale," Tall Zach said, and then laughed. "I mean, not like a *couple* couple. You know what I meant."

"Excuse *us*." Alison and Chihiro paused their quickly

escalating argument over the relative cruelty of honey as a sweetener for banana bread to shove past us. Zach the Anarchist smiled and shook his head, and I felt myself start to smile again.

"Don't start," he said, eyes flashing. "Vegans are vicious."

"To me?" I put a hand on my chest like I was going to swoon. "Humans are animals, too."

"Doesn't matter."

I fake-groaned, folded the student-council-budget spreadsheets in half, and chucked them toward the recycling bin. Zach looked from the bin to me and shook his head again.

"You keep careful records."

"I have them saved, somewhere," I said. "Whatever."

"*How* did you become treasurer again?"

"Abdication," I answered, "of our resident math genius, to canoodle with his girlfriend."

Zach stiffened.

"I mean, um, ex-girlfriend," I said quickly. "I mean . . . never mind."

*Shoot.* I had totally forgotten about my dumb, mean, not-at-all-reassuring comment about Mia and her boobs at Moonpenny's. A glob of guilt stuck in my gut, and I got even guiltier when I realized I'd totally forgotten to bring Zach's flannel in for him.

"Zach," I said, but he was already out the door, leaving me alone with Endsignal and the bake sale sign-ups and the terrible ache of knowing I had just used a stupid word like *canoodle* to describe the author of Zach the Anarchist's heartbreak. Why couldn't I stop being so mean about this?

I stared down hard at the list of names, then looked back up just in time to see Endsignal unplug his laptop. The purple website was still on its screen. Somehow, crazily, I'd actually forgotten about the whole Sebastian thing for almost twenty straight minutes. But now that I'd remembered, I wasn't exactly going to forget.

"Uh, Endsignal?"

Endsignal stopped, power cord in hand.

"Can you email me that music blog thing?" I said. "Just to . . . um, just to see."

"Sure." Endsignal pushed the screen back into place and copy-pasted into an email.

"Thanks." I took a step toward the door, but couldn't quite leave. The sound of the opening guitar lick was still ringing in my head, and I got the feeling it wasn't going anywhere. "Is that site a big deal?"

"Um, not really? I mean, mostly for music geeks and stuff." Endsignal pushed his hair out of his eyes. "Are you okay? You look kind of . . . different. From before."

"Fine!" I said. "Just . . . thinking about the bake sale. Thanks for the link! See you tomorrow!"

But it was totally a lie, especially the part where I was acting cheerful and casual about the whole thing. Because whether I looked it or not, something inside me was definitely, definitely different.

# CHAPTER EIGHT

I didn't see Tess for the rest of the day, which was kind of a relief. I could almost forget we'd listened to the song at all. By the time I got out of my last-period European history class, the hot lava of panic inside my chest had cooled into attractive stalactites of repression. An afternoon spent baking would probably prove even more therapeutic. If I were the kind of person who knew how to bake, anyway. But I did know someone who did. And I definitely owed him a favor.

Outside, it was surprisingly warm for almost November. The leaves on the ground were still cheerful shades of gold and red and not yet the depressing brown gunk that would inevitably get stuck on my shoes. I was a few minutes early, since Mr. Ross could never remember that class ended at three fifteen and not three on the dot, but a few kids were already starting to trickle toward freedom, and so I hung out by the Donut, waiting until I saw a form that was unmistakably Zach the Anarchist–shaped heading out of the science building.

"Hey," I called, waving my hand so Zach would see me. "Zach!"

Zach waved back, and a few shuffling steps later he stopped right in front of the Donut.

"Uh, hey," he said. "What's up?"

"You tell me," I said. "What . . . is up?"

I braced myself for something really bad, something really upset about the dumb thing I'd said after the meeting, but it never came. Zach just shrugged.

"Great!" I said. "Because, um, I was wondering if you maybe needed help. With the cookies."

"From you?" Zach lifted an eyebrow. "Weren't you saying you don't know how to bake?"

"Well . . ." I looked at my shoes. "Yeah."

That was the other part of the problem. Besides my residual guilt over the Mia thing, I hadn't actually signed up to provide anything for the sale tomorrow. Baking with Zach would be a two-birds, one-stone kind of situation.

Zach sighed. "Tell you what. How about you help me with my Latin? If you want to," he added. "I could just . . . use it."

"Oh," I said. "Uh, sure." So maybe three birds, one stone. Zach just stood there.

"So . . . my place, then," he said, after a minute.

"Yeah," I said. "I mean, I guess. It makes the most sense. If that's okay."

"As long as it's okay with you."

"Yeah, totally." I nodded, probably a few times too many. If I'd still had my freshman-year crush on Zach the Anarchist, this would have been when I started panicking. But I didn't, and besides, there were more important things at stake, like baked goods and accurate analysis of classical literature. "Let me just text my dad."

We headed to where Zach's Volvo was waiting like a noble steed. Zach the Anarchist was the only one of the Acronymphomaniacs who had a car, but he was also the only one who needed it. Most Wister Prep students were sourced from in and around the actual suburb of Wister, but the Wests had decided to ship their son all the way out here from downtown Philadelphia for high school, just like they had done with his older sister before him. Fortunately for him, he got his license midway through sophomore year and was saved from the inconvenience of the suburban trains, which treated arrival times as a fun suggestion instead of a schedule to be adhered to.

We sped down Kelly Drive by the river, the foliage-fringed scenery of the Schuylkill whipping past and the art museum rising grandly in the distance like a temple, to the little side street where Zach lived. His family had this cool old row house with green shutters and an authentically old-fashioned plaque on the front from Benjamin Franklin's fire company from back in the days of revolution and liberty and yellow fever. It was all charming, like it could have belonged to Betsy

Ross once upon a time. Less charming was the fact that the little brick driveway was barely big enough for a carriage, let alone a Volvo, and that Zach had pulled in about six inches from the wall on my side.

I sucked it in and maneuvered my way out of the car while Zach went around and unlocked the gate. The Wests are one of those families who never use the front door, except maybe for special occasions, but coming in through their kitchen is practically just as imposing: all stainless steel and pots and pans hanging around. Zach's mom Trish was a federal prosecutor, and I was pretty sure his mom Pat did something at one of the drug companies, so there was definitely money. Which made it kind of ironic that their son ended up so antimaterialistic. Or maybe kind of inevitable.

A squat, brown form whammed itself into my shins as I came up the back steps.

"Watch it!" Zach called from inside the kitchen.

"I'm fine," I said.

"I meant the dog."

I ignored him and bent down to give an ear scratch hello.

"Hey, Bacon! Aren't you a little nugget of energy today?"

Bacon wiggled his butt appreciatively, his tongue lolling out of his mouth like he'd forgotten it was there. Allegedly, Zach's dog was a mix of Boston terrier and boxer, but from his curled-up tail and the way he snorted, I wouldn't be surprised if he had a little of his namesake in him.

Zach came back from the depths of inside and scooped Bacon up like a sack of potatoes.

"Not that bacon comes in nuggets," I said. "That would be gross."

"*All* bacon is gross," Zach said. He nodded inside, and I followed, setting my bag by the shoe rack inside the door.

"Hey, wait a second," I said. "I never thought of that. Why did you name your dog after a meat product?"

"I didn't," Zach said, plopping Bacon back down on top of his stocking feet. "'Knowledge is power.'"

"I mean, I guess," I said.

"No. I mean yeah. Francis Bacon. Philosopher. That's who he's named for." Zach shrugged. "That, and I guess it was kind of a statement. Like, I would just as soon eat actual bacon as I would eat this guy."

Bacon made a snuffly sound of gratitude and started licking the floor. I laughed.

"So . . . ," Zach said.

"So?"

I looked up to find him with his hands in his pockets. He looked a little like he wasn't sure what to do, which wasn't really fair, considering *he* was the one who knew how to bake stuff. He also had this one piece of hair in the front of his forehead that was sticking off to one side, which made him look extra quizzical, and I had this weird impulse to smooth it down for him.

"So what do you want to do?" he finished.

I blinked, suddenly aware of how big Zach's kitchen seemed without the other Acronymphomaniacs there, making a racket and looking around for snacks. The gleaming stainless steel of the counters and stove seemed shinily infinite, like they could reflect into anything. I thought about what it must be like to come home to this kitchen at night with Bacon on the leash, all sleekness and shadows like a polished cave.

Also, we were alone, if that kind of thing mattered. Not that being alone with Zach the Anarchist was really like being *alone with a boy* in the parental-advisory sense of the phrase, but still. I quickly shrugged off the feeling.

"You're in charge of the baking here," I said. "I'm just in charge of the Latin."

"Yeah," Zach said, and then again: "Yeah."

He wasn't moving, so I did. I swung around the kitchen island, peering into the fruit bowl by the sink and sweeping a gaze over the magnets on the fridge.

"Whenever you're ready," I said. "What kind of cookies can you make?"

Zach kind of sprang back to life, like he'd been stalling before.

"Pretty much any." He started ticking things off, one long finger at a time. "Snickerdoodles, oatmeal raisin, shortbread, sandwich, blondies, brownies—"

"Okay, okay." I cut him off, even though I was half tempted

to see how far he could go without running out of ideas. "So what kind of cookies do you *like*?"

"Pretty much any," Zach said again. "What about you?"

"Anything but strawberry," I said.

"That doesn't narrow it down much," Zach said, and then smiled. "Also, no one puts strawberries in cookies, anyway."

"They'd better not," I said, apparently kind of aggressively, because Zach looked startled and held up a hand. He really did have nice hands, which was an extremely weird thing to think. What was my problem?

"Not on my watch," he said. "Scout's honor."

"You were a Boy Scout?" I couldn't picture Zach the Anarchist in shorts, let alone a neckerchief or a sash with little badges sewn on.

Zach narrowed his eyes. "I don't want to talk about it."

I wanted to laugh, but I didn't want Zach to think I was impugning the dignity of his troop or anything. "Never mind. Anyway, it's probably less important what *we* want and more important what our customers want."

"Spoken like a true capitalist," Zach said. There was a pause, in which I was probably supposed to dramatically reveal my crowd-pleasing cookie idea. I still had to think.

"And our customers want *what*?" Zach asked.

I pictured Alison and Chihiro proffering something crumbly and vegan.

"Butter," I said finally. "And actual chocolate."

"So, like . . . chocolate chip cookies?"

I raised my eyebrows. "Now you're talking."

Zach nodded. "All right if I put on music?"

"Sure," I said, and I pulled out my Latin notebook as Zach plugged his phone into the countertop stereo and started rummaging around for baking stuff.

"Okay." I gave my book an emphatic thump that I immediately regretted as extremely weird. What kind of person gives homework affectionate smacks?

"Okay what?" Zach put down a sack of organic unbleached flour. The music he had chosen was, of course, very angry and very loud, like someone had found a way to get a melody out of a jackhammer.

"*Okay*," I said a second time, a little louder. "Catullus Eighty-Seven. Let's see what you've got. Before you get flour everywhere."

After digging in his backpack, Zach flipped open his own notebook, which was already fraying away from the coiled metal spine, and read.

"No can woman such himself to say loved truly so much from me Lesbia loved my is." His mouth had this twisty way of moving when he read, like he was pronouncing everything extra-carefully, which I'd never really seen up close.

"That's . . . no." I took a long pause. "Did you just translate all the words directly from the dictionary?"

Zach pressed his lips together. "It's pretty close."

"Dude, you write that down on Dr. Frobisher's test and she'll flunk you so hard. She'll flunk you and tell your English teacher to flunk you, too, for being so bad at words."

"I word really good, okay?"

I pushed my notebook around so he could see it. "Figure out the subject of the sentence first."

"Nulla."

"Are you just saying that because it's the first word in the sentence, or because you can tell from its grammatical form?"

"I refuse to answer on the grounds that it may incriminate me."

After twenty minutes of underlining, arrow-drawing, and dictionary-flipping, we had more or less wrangled meaning out of Catullus's poetry.

| | |
|---|---|
| *Nulla potest mulier tantum se dicere amatam* | *No woman can say that she was loved* |
| *Vere, quantum a me Lesbia amata mea est:* | *Truly, as much as by me Lesbia was loved.* |
| *Nulla fides ullo fuit umquam foedere tanta* | *No ugly faith was there at any time with so much trust* |
| *Quanta in amore tuo ex parte reperta mea est.* | *As much as was found in my love for you.* |

Zach also contributed some doodles.

"So he's telling her he loves her more than any other woman." I wrote *faithfulness* and *being in love a lot* in the Themes section of our worksheet. "And that's why he trusts her."

"Sure." Zach had given up drawing on his homework and had moved on to spooning flour into a bowl on a metal scale. "Something like that."

He clamped the lid back on the flour tub and started measuring the sugar the same way, one spoonful at a time. Apparently, the secret to baking is just being really, really obsessive about everything.

"Something like that," I mimicked. "Says the guy measuring sugar to the ounce."

Zach shrugged, his T-shirt tightening over his shoulders.

"I'm just saying," I went on. "It's not like you *lack* the analytical capacity for translation. It's just that you don't use it."

"You mess up ratios, the cookies taste bad. You mess up Latin"—Zach ducked to where a little thermometer was clipped inside the oven—"and Catullus is still dead."

I wrinkled my nose. He sort of had a point, but I didn't want to agree with him.

"Anyway, it's not about how he loves her." Zach stood up. "Not exactly."

"What?" My nose stayed wrinkled.

"No woman can say that she was loved more than Lesbia."

Zach got a stick of butter from the fridge. "She's only the best because she's above the other girls?"

"I guess." I added *bragging* to Themes, and then, after consideration, put a question mark to the end of *being in love a lot.*

"And he doesn't even address Lesbia until the end, with that *tuo,*" Zach went on. "Like none of his poems are actually *to* her. They're *about* her. It's kind of creepy."

"It's not *creepy,*" I said. "What about all that kissing he wanted to do to her?"

Zach stared at me, mid-unwrap on the stick of butter, and my face went instantly hot.

"Um," I said. *Brilliant.* "Is there a reason that pan is on the stove? It's just . . . it's hot in here." I fanned myself theatrically and tried to look at a part of Zach's face that was not his mouth.

Instead of answering, Zach dropped the butter into the saucepan.

"So you're just melting it," I said. "Why not use the microwave?"

"I am not just melting it," Zach said. He jiggled the handle and sent the yellow stick sliding around in a little snail's trail of butteriness. "I'm toasting the milk solids so that it gets a caramelized flavor."

"But you have to melt it *first,*" I pointed out.

Zach gave a barely perceptible eye roll.

"Yeah, if you want to get *technical.*"

"You measured flour to an eighth of an ounce! How is that *not* 'getting technical'?"

The corner of Zach's mouth went up, but he didn't fully smile.

"You know what I mean."

He stirred the now-puddled contents of the pan with a rubber spatula shaped like a guitar. I shut my Catullus book and squirmed on my tall stool, suddenly antsy.

"Can I melt the butter?" I asked.

"Brown."

I groaned. "Can I *brown* the butter?"

"You can burn it, probably."

"Ugh." I threw up my hands and retreated to the bag of chocolate bits. They were the good kind, dark and cocoa-y little chunks from a fancy downtown supermarket. Zach flicked a gaze back at me just as I bit into one, and I crossed my arms.

"Quality control," I said.

Zach turned back to the stove and snapped off the burner. The kitchen smelled really good, like a whiff of vanilla extract, and despite my utter disinclination toward anything culinary, it felt much more relaxed and natural now that we were making something.

"Hot, coming through." Zach nudged me out of the way and scraped the mahogany-colored butter into the bowl of sugar, then reached across the counter for a wooden spoon and handed it to me.

"Here. You can be the muscle."

"Participation at last," I said. I took the spoon and stirred the butter and sugar, which began to feel like stirring concrete after about three turns. Across the room, Bacon stretched out of his doggie bed and took an enviably long yawn.

"You all right?" Zach looked up from weighing out a portion of chocolate chips. His face was neutral, but I could tell he was making fun of me. Only this time, I didn't mind so much.

"I'm fine," I gritted out. Every turn of the spoon nearly wrenched the bowl from my hands. "Has this always been so hard?"

"How can you not know how to bake?" Zach said. "Aren't your parents super creative?"

"I mean, I *guess*," I said, leaning into the dough to get it to budge. "My mom is, anyway. But she's so busy making frames and stuff all day that she doesn't really have time to cook."

"What about your dad?"

"He's making a yurt," I said.

"A yurt," Zach said.

"Yeah. The traditional dwelling of the nomadic peoples of Central Asia."

"I know what a yurt is," Zach said. "That's pretty cool."

"It is?" I shoved the spoon back and forth in the bowl.

Zach shrugged.

"Well, right now it's just a heap of boards in the backyard," I said.

"Here." Zach pushed the carton of eggs at me. "Two."

Relieved, I dropped the spoon and plucked an egg out of the carton. I had put one hand on the bowl to steady it when Zach leaped up behind me.

"No," he said, and I froze.

His hand was on mine, his long fingers reaching around my wrist. Warm.

"Um," Zach said, and dropped my hand just as quickly as he had taken it. "I mean, don't hit the egg on the bowl. Could get shell in the dough."

"Right," I said, my heart plodding into the front of my chest. "Maybe you should just . . ."

I jumped away from the bowl like it was electrified and held out the egg. Zach took it, barely brushing my fingers, and cracked it deftly on the counter. I watched him turn the spoon around, considerably faster than I had, his shoulders moving under his T-shirt, and then repeat with the second egg.

I swallowed. There was a weird vibratey feeling in my stomach, and I couldn't tell if it was because things were getting extremely weird or because the stereo had an especially robust bass system.

"Can I pick something to listen to?"

"What?" Zach said.

I grabbed the volume knob and twisted it down a bit. I didn't want to be rude, but after fifteen minutes of ear-shattering screams and guitar sounds, I also didn't want to suffer a punk-rock-induced migraine.

"Oh, sure," Zach said. "Go crazy."

"Thanks." I started clicking through the selection on Zach's phone, which was chipped and scarred and had to be at least fifty years old. All of his music seemed to be bands with misspelled or otherwise incomprehensible names, not one of which I recognized.

"Ew," I said out loud. "Butthole Surfers."

Zach shrugged. "It's punk."

I tried again.

"Dead Kennedys."

"Punk."

"The Exploited."

"Punk."

"Operation Ivy?"

"Ska punk."

"Nofficks?"

"NOFX," Zach said, pronouncing it "no ef ex." "It's punk."

I groaned. "Do you have *anything* I would like?"

Zach shrugged again.

"Nothing by the Young Guns, sorry."

Young *Lungs*, I almost said, but then didn't. The kitchen went silent, except for Bacon's wheezy breathing.

"How was that show, by the way?" Zach darted a glance at me, but I couldn't quite tell what he meant. So I just nodded.

"Tess made me dance, but I survived."

Zach laughed, a single syllable. "Yeah, I've heard those indie mosh pits can get brutal. All that standing and swaying."

"People were dancing," I said. "I don't think it was a mosh pit."

"If you're not getting kicked in the chest, it's not a mosh pit. Trust me."

"Has that ever happened to you?"

"Once."

"Really?"

"I survived."

"Thanks for your shirt," I said suddenly. "I'll, um, get it back to you soon. And for driving us."

Zach said nothing at first, then shrugged.

"You're welcome." Zach gave the dough another turn, then stopped. "Did Sebastian live up to all his hype?"

"Uh," I said. "Why do you ask?"

Perfect. That was a totally unsuspicious thing to say.

Zach was very intently scraping the spoon on the side of the bowl. "Because, like . . . didn't you have a crush on him or something?"

Pause. Silence. Except for the thrashing sound of guitars.

"Or not," Zach said at last. "Never mind. Sorry."

"Uh," I said. "Uh, yes. I mean, yes, it's a no. I mean, I kind of . . ." *Don't say I don't know. Don't say I don't know.* "Nope. Never. Not at all."

"Okay." Zach glanced at me for a whole millisecond before going back to cookie dough. "Okay, cool. I mean, not to imply that anything happened, or anything."

"Yeah." Had I just lied? Did face-touching and thumb-lip-mushing count as . . . anything? I hadn't even spoken to Sebastian since the show. But we didn't normally talk. Well, we did when we were in the same place, but not otherwise. Or did we? Suddenly nothing about any part of human interaction made any sense, at least as it pertained to Sebastian.

Surreptitiously, as Zach hunted for cinnamon, I propped my phone under my Catullus notebook, and, after a meditative breath and some quick mental calculus, opened my Pixstagram inbox.

"I'm not that into the band in particular or anything," I said. True. "I mean, I barely even know them." Sort of. "It was Tess's idea." Not really. "I'm actually just trying to . . . get into music a little bit. Um, more." Not at all even remotely true until the moment I said it.

Zach looked away for a split second, and I tapped into my Sent folder, just to make sure it had gone through.

> To: sebdel
>
> hows sit going?

"Really?" Zach was back at attention.

"Kind of," I said. Shoot. Shoot shoot *shoot*. *Hows sit going* wasn't even *English*. "I mean, yeah. I'm listening to a lot more music these days."

That part was at least true. Zach nodded at me—or rather, at his phone, which was still in my hands.

"Here. Put on the Flaming Lips. You'll like it."

I hid my phone under my notebook, then swiped through Zach's phone until I found it. Guitar sounds came out of the speakers, but now it sounded less like a jackhammer and more like a rubber band, if that made sense. A spacey-sounding voice started singing about a girl making toast.

It was weird, but not bad.

"Not bad," I said.

"Yeah?" Zach said.

"But not really punk."

"Nope."

"Kind of weird."

"Yeah," Zach said again. "They're like that."

The song kept going, and Zach kept stirring, and I wondered if the girl who used Vaseline instead of jelly on her toast was a real person. Because if I were her, that would be a pretty embarrassing facet of my personality to have immortalized in—

My phone buzzed.

"Shoot!" I yelped.

"Are you okay?" Zach said.

From: Dad

Sure thing NG. Take 5:17 train n I'll pick you up from station on way from work. —Dad

"Fine," I said. Only Dad would sign a text message coming from his own phone. "Just my dad."

Zach nodded. "Hey, can you do me a favor?"

I shoved my phone away, terrified that he'd seen something. "Sure," I said, voice about a dozen octaves too high. "Anything."

*Anything except elaborate the nature of my confusing and ever-evolving feelings about Sebastian Delacroix.*

"Can you add the pumpkin?"

I stared.

"The what?"

"Pumpkin?" he repeated. "The traditional flavor of Halloween-related baked goods."

"I know what pumpkin is," I said. "I just forgot it was almost Halloween."

Zach shook his head in disappointment and dumped a can of pumpkin purée into the bowl.

"I've been busy!" I cried. "I've had treasurer duties and French homework and . . ." I faltered. "Stuff. To do."

Stuff like Pixstagram stalking and listening to "Natalie" obsessively. But whatever.

"You want to do the scooping honors?"

"Do *you* want me to? What if I make them the wrong size, or something?"

"We have ways of making them the right size." He handed me a miniature ice cream scoop, and I rolled my eyes.

"Of course."

Zach grabbed a melon baller and worked in from the opposite side, and in a few minutes we'd filled two sheets. Zach slid them into the oven and clicked a timer shaped like a chicken to the ten-minute mark.

I was about to say something to head off any weird silences from the get-go, but Zach just whistled for Bacon and nodded toward the little set of stairs that led from the kitchen down into the family room, which was on kind of a mezzanine on the way to the basement.

"Lifetime?" Zach said. "While we're waiting?"

"Sure."

I followed him downstairs to the room full of plump leather couches and heavy coffee-table books—the very same venue of the *I Don't Know* Incident—where Zach proceeded to root around for the remote. I sat on the floor, because I assumed Zach would want the sofa, seeing as it was his house and all, but when the TV was on, he sat next to me.

"Let's see," he said. "Heroic suburban mom exacts revenge after her husband's affair with the town yoga teacher, or heroic suburban mom goes undercover to save her son from the grips of video-game addiction?"

I thought about it. "Option two," I said.

"*A Dangerous Game: The Karen Clearwater Story* it is," Zach said.

As the opening credits rolled over shots of a sunny,

cathedral-sized kitchen—Lifetime moms always have *really* big kitchens—I snuck a sideways glance at Zach. He looked relaxed. Not that I *wasn't* relaxed, of course. It was just Zach. We were just hanging out like we always had, sort of. Actually, post–freshman year, most of the time I'd spent with Zach West had been with Tess and Tall Zach, doing stuff like going to the movies en masse or driving around Wister late at night looking for restaurants that were still open. We hadn't had so much as a conversation one-on-one since the fateful night of the *I don't know*. Which, come to think of it, seemed kind of messed up, considering we were supposed to be friends. I could blame it on the fact that he'd until recently been dating Mia and was busy, but really, it was because things were just . . . weird between us.

Well, not *just weird*. Weird because I'd made them that way.

But that was a long time ago. We were more mature now. *I* was more mature now. Sort of.

Zach's hands, also, were right there on the floor. Close to mine again.

*Bzzt.*

"Was that the timer?"

Zach pulled his hand away and checked his phone.

"Oh, um, I think it was the movie." As luck would have it, Karen Clearwater was at that moment picking up her son's pinging phone, but judging by the hum I felt in my pocket, I had *also* gotten a message. But as soon as I saw *who* had messaged me, I shoved the phone even deeper into my jeans.

"I love how no one in Lifetime movies knows how to text like a normal person," Zach said. Without putting his hand back.

"Yeah," I agreed, perhaps too heartily. "Like, we have autocorrect now. It's way more effort to type just the letter u than y-o-u. Who does that?"

Zach grinned. "They might as well be paging each other."

I opened my mouth to respond, but something buzzed again, and this time it *was* the timer. Zach hit Pause and took off for the stairs, and I followed, slowly, unlocking my phone on the stairs on the way up.

> to: nmcullz
>
> in LA. big stuff happening
>
> which i probably shouldnt have mentioned
>
> but i can trust u, right?
>
> ;)

# CHAPTER NINE

The cookies came out perfectly, at least as far as I with my untrained baking skills could tell. Zach even put some in a baggie for me to take on the train, and when I left to head for the station, our good-bye was as not-awkward as it could have been—I just put on my backpack and shoes and Zach walked me to the door and said "Same time next week, I guess?" and we both sort of waved. With Tall Zach, Tess, anyone else, I probably would've gone for a hug, even though I'm the world's most awkward hugger, but with Zach the Anarchist it seemed better not to. Honestly, even thinking about it made my stomach feel a little flippy.

In any case, I arrived at Suburban Station right at five fifteen, and I spent the next twenty minutes reading and rereading Sebastian's messages. The cookies did not last the ride.

"Hey, kiddo!" Dad's tired-looking face turned to a smile as I flopped into the front seat of the Volkswagen.

"Hey, Dad." I tried for the normalest smile I could manage.

"Good day at school?"

"Mhm."

*Big stuff.* And Sebastian thought he could trust me. Except he hadn't actually told me anything. Had he?

I didn't have long in the car to contemplate, because the Wister train station was so close to the McCullough-Schwartz enclave that driving only saved you about thirty seconds of travel time over walking. In the yard, the pile of yurt parts loomed in the back corner, lit up by headlights when we pulled in.

"Hey, Sam." Dad snapped on a light switch and the orangey-red walls of the kitchen perked up immediately. Somewhere in the last two hours, between the sun going down and the bumpy gray clouds that had hovered all day, it had gotten really dark.

"Hi, Robert." Sam Huang waved from his desk. I pulled out my phone and reread all four text bubbles, like I hadn't already committed them to memory.

Maybe I should respond. But literally any response I could formulate would involve me asking a dumb question about what Sebastian meant. And I didn't want to have to ask questions. I wanted to just *know* what he meant. Or at least act like I knew.

"So." Dad dropped his briefcase by the door and pulled off his trench coat. "Whaddya say, kids?"

I dropped my phone on the counter. "Homework?" That would probably forestall any further discussion, because my parents were definitely not the type to request an itemized statement of our assignments. Sometimes they even forgot to send my vaccination forms.

"Yeah. Homework," agreed Sam.

"Ah. The usual mundanities of adolescence." Dad shook his head.

"Sure," said Sam. "If you say so."

"Robert?" Mom's voice glided down to us from somewhere upstairs. "Are you home?"

"Very recently, yes," Dad called back. He loosened his tie and craned his neck out the window. "Hey, NG, do you think it's going to rain?"

The radio was playing softly in the corner. *In LA*. What could possibly happen in LA? All I knew about California was that it was huge and everyone there wore sunglasses all the time. Although Tess had gone to Santa Monica once, and she'd reported that the only major difference was that everyone at Chipotle in California got bowls instead of full burritos to save on bread calories.

"Nattie?"

"Huh?" I whirled around, my train of thought derailed. Dad was down to his shirtsleeves and looking concerned.

"Do you know if it's going to rain?"

"Robert?" Mom's voice echoed again.

"I think it's supposed to," I said, imperceptibly twitching the radio dial from WPHL to the jazz station. "But I don't control the weather."

Dad's eyes widened.

"What?" I frowned.

"Can you start dinner tonight?" Mom called to Dad.

"The yurt is in danger," he said.

I heard footfalls on the back stairs, and Mom entered stage left just as Dad swept up through the dining room, mumbling something about tarps and weights. Mom stepped in, dressed in a more casual old sweater of Dad's, and frowned.

"I could have sworn he was just in here," she said.

"The yurt is in danger," I said.

"The *yurt* is in danger," Mom repeated.

"I think it can't get wet, or something," Sam Huang said. Outside, a rumble of thunder growled in agreement.

Mom took a long, deep breath. And then another. And then Dad reappeared in a beat-up pair of cargo pants and a faded Moby Grape T-shirt, carrying a long roll of scratchy blue plastic under one arm.

"Robert," Mom said, "I was really hoping you could deal with dinner tonight."

"Anne," my dad said, his voice deadly serious. "The yurt is in *danger*."

Mom tried to sigh again, but it kind of morphed into a laugh on the way out.

"I'm sorry," Dad went on, "but I need to get everything covered up before the rain hits or else we'll risk having an unstable foundation."

"That's not already a problem?" I asked. I meant it as a joke, but Mom gave me one of those *not now, Nattie* looks, even though I knew she didn't really care if the yurt rotted away to nothing overnight.

"Why can't it get rained on? Isn't it an outdoor structure?"

The tarp sagged a little under Dad's arm. "I haven't gotten around to weatherproofing it yet. That's the last step."

"Is that what all those are for?" Sam Huang pointed at the corner of the kitchen, where a stack of cans was crowding the shoe basket out of its place by the mail table.

"Robert!" Mom threw up her hands. "That's Epifanes brand varnish."

"I know," Dad said proudly. "I got the good stuff."

"The good stuff is *fifty dollars a can.*"

Probably I didn't want to ask him about the song *right* away. I could ask him how the weather was, except that that is the single dumbest thing that one human being can inquire of another.

Mom was rubbing her forehead now. "Is this yurt going to need any other *good stuff*? A Murano tile floor? A hand-dyed canvas?"

"A generator," Sam Huang suggested. Dad's eyes lit up.

"Now we're talkin'!"

Another growl of thunder sounded. Mom folded her arms.

"Or not," Dad said quickly. "This is it, I promise. Except for the foundation."

"The foundation," Mom said.

"Just a little concrete!" Dad said, backing out toward the door.

"Concrete?!"

"A weekend project! You won't even notice it!"

The door slapped shut behind him, and Mom clutched the countertop with a look that was half frustration, half exhaustion, and half astonishment. I'd seen it many times on Tess after a long OWPALGBTQIA meeting.

I snuck another look at my phone, and realized I still had an unread message—the link to that music blog, from Endsignal.

"Are you mad at Robert, Anne?" Sam Huang asked tentatively.

"Yes. No." Mom shook her head. "I don't know. No, no. I'm not."

My browser opened up to reveal the now-familiar colors and coolness of Vivian Violet's blog, on a post dated a few days ago. I skimmed down past a couple promo shots—Sebastian was standing with a leg up on an amplifier, hands in his pockets, doing his signature expression that made it impossible to tell if he was being serious or messing with you—and looked at what she had to say.

*A little bit poppy, a little bit punky, and every bit the ex-NYU kids they so clearly resemble, it'd be easy to write off the Young Lungs as just the latest widget from the Brooklyn indie-rock industrial complex. And while the title track from last year's five-song EP* Breathe *was a solid, competent entry into the genre, it didn't exactly make waves beyond the New York bubble (full disclosure: I am and will always be a part of said bubble, NO APOLOGIES!) and I was seriously bummed that all the cool teens out in flyover country were going to be deprived of this pretty promising pack of popsters.*

*. . . And that's why I am really freakin' delighted to share the news that my favorite Brooklyn-based boy toys, the Young Lungs, have officially signed to Fort Rox Records in Los Angeles!!! You know what that means: a full-length album, a tour, the works. So claim your indie "I liked them before they were big" cred while you can, because mark my incredibly insightful words—everyone's gonna know about these guys.*

I gasped. I actually gasped.

"Don't worry, kids. No one's getting divorced." Mom rooted around and produced a corkscrew from the silverware drawer. "I just wish I'd known this was all going to be so complicated before I agreed to it."

# CHAPTER TEN

I spent Tuesday morning in silent terror, mind abuzz with questions as I ate oatmeal and subtly changed Dad's car stereo from the radio to Joni Mitchell on my phone, just in case. Was a record deal a bad thing? I mean, objectively, it was a good thing, in the sense that Sebastian et al. had taken the first important step toward launching their careers. But personally, to me, Nattie McCullough-Schwartz, it was *not* a good thing, because a record deal meant there would be a record—or CDs, or MP3s, or whatever—and a record meant that the song would presumably be available to stream or download or even—I shuddered, thinking about it—watch in a music video. Who knew what the Young Lungs had up their artfully rolled flannel sleeves?

Well, one person knew. Sebastian. So after Latin, but before I headed to the cafeteria, I composed a quick message.

To: sebdel

so is this big stuff an album?

Satisfied that I'd hit the right combination of inquisitive and flirtatious, I hit Send, and headed to the inaugural

OWPALGBTQIA bake sale with my mind unburdened. Unfortunately, we only made it exactly four minutes into said inaugural bake sale before Tess presented us with terrible news.

"I have terrible news." Tess collapsed into a chair. "We don't have a venue."

"What?" I said. "How is that possible?" The Wister Prep cafeteria was a basement-y room underneath the main building that smelled like fryer grease and lemon-flavored mop water. Usually, everyone ate outside at the picnic tables, but today we were lucky and had a downpour that forced everyone into cramped quarters and caused a run on chicken tenders. I thought longingly of Zach the Anarchist's cookies and hoped he got there soon.

"Well, okay, we do, but it has to change." Tess narrowed her eyes. "Do you remember where the Winter Formal is held? I'll tell you," she added, before I even could answer. "They rent out a ballroom in the *Wister Racquet Club*."

She paused, probably to let the dreadfulness of her words sink in.

"Come on!" Tess *frappe*-d me on the arm. "The Wister Racquet Club does not allow same-sex couples to become members."

"So?"

Tess gaped at me. "What do you mean, *so*?"

"I mean, does that even matter? It's not like we need memberships. We just need a big room to dance in."

Tess blinked, hard, twice. "I am *not* using our Operation BGDP money to line the pockets of *bigots*. Not that we're going to make any money, by the way, if *this* is the way we're running a bake sale."

Alison looked up from where she was slumped on her elbows behind our station.

"Um, rude. We're working *really hard*."

Chihiro, who was sitting next to her and looking only slightly less bored, twisted a pink strand of bangs between her black-nailed fingers until Alison jabbed her in the ribs.

"Oh. Yeah!" She beamed and spread a hand over the meager array of cookies, cakes, and promised package of Oreos, all of which seemed largely untouched. They hadn't had any customers except maybe themselves.

"Oh no." Tess stuck out a finger. "First of all, this table is a million miles away from the doors, so no one can see us."

I glanced back at the entrance. If anyone *did* come in looking for something sugary of the nonprepackaged variety, they would see the tables of the Nature Club, Pep Squad, Wister Wemembers yearbook kids, and—of course—A Cappella, before ours even registered. I tried to wave over at Sam Huang, but if he saw me, he ignored me. Which, fair enough—standing at a deserted table heaped with everything-free baked goods made me pretty much the epitome of "embarrassing older sister." There was no reason for me to torpedo Sam Huang's social standing with mine.

"Second of all"—Tess stuck out another finger—"you didn't even put up a sign to say *who we are*, and third of all . . ." Here she paused for what I thought was rhetorical effect until the pause kept going.

"Okay, I don't have a third." Tess whipped out her phone, but then seemed to reconsider and shoved it back in a pocket. "And this requires a full-sized keyboard. So here's the deal: I'm going upstairs to send an email to student council, and *then* I am going to track down some chicken fingers."

"They're out," I said. Alison looked smug.

Tess threw up her hands. "Ugh. Okay, some kind of food, or else I'm going to murder everyone. Nattie, you're in charge of fixing everything before I get back."

"Um?" I said, but Tess was already charging past the year-book people with an "Out of my way, nerds!"

"I," Alison said pointedly, "think she needs to *chill*."

I ignored her and stooped down to inspect the baked goods.

"What *are* those?" I prodded the side of a shoe box filled with something puck-like and crumbly-looking.

"They're sugar cookies," Alison said. "I made them last night."

"They look . . . weird." I snuck my phone out of my pocket: no response. Maybe Sebastian was writing a long response. Or maybe he wasn't awake yet. It was only . . . I counted time zones backward in my head. Well, it was definitely earlier in California, whatever time it was.

"I still think they look like macaroons," Chihiro said. "Are you sure they're not gluten-free?"

"For the last time, they're not," Alison snapped. Chihiro looked put out. "They're just a little crispy, is all."

She helped herself to an Oreo out of the box. I stared.

"What?" she said through a defensive mouthful of crumbs.

"They're vegan."

"Good for them."

Zach the Anarchist had appeared at her side, holding a shoe box and wearing a leather jacket that was dripping rainwater onto the tiles.

"Sorry I'm late," he said. "How's it going?"

Alison rolled her eyes by way of response and gave Chihiro a kind of *let's get out of here* head jerk.

"*Fine*," she said, even though no one had said anything to her. "You guys can run things, if you're so smart."

Chihiro handed me the key to the cashbox. "There's only like six bucks in there. Oh, and my cake has to stay covered, or else the carob will get all dry," she said to Zach.

She gestured at a blue plate covered in plastic wrap and what looked like squashed slices of brown, seedy bread.

"Duly noted," Zach said. Behind her bangs, Chihiro's face went a matching shade of pink. I resisted snorting, because that would be hypocritical, given my own borderline romantic feelings for Zach. I mean *former* feelings. And very borderline.

"Nothing worse than dry carob cake," I said instead. Chihiro blushed deeper and then slipped away. Zach didn't seem to want to engage with her either way, which was probably for the best considering she was a fifteen-year-old sophomore.

"How's business?" Zach said.

"I just got here," I said. "But, well, actually, it's . . . bad. And Tess wants me to fix everything."

"What's *everything?*"

"You know . . ." I held out my arm, then let it flop in defeat to my side. "Everything. We're in the middle of cafeteria nowhere."

"Yeah." Zach knocked his knuckles against an unfortunately placed pillar that obscured half of our table from view. "Also, the product we're selling looks barely edible."

"Yup," I agreed. "How'd the rest of our cookies turn out?"

Zach shrugged, which was hardly a satisfactory answer, especially when cookies were involved. "*My* cookies? Probably fine."

Unable to contain my curiosity, I leaned forward and pulled off the top of his shoe box. The cookies were all the same size, and not too brown around the edges like when I bake anything, and—unlike Alison's sawdust sugar cookies—smelled fantastic. I plucked one out.

"You're paying for that," Zach said.

"Quality control."

"I made them," Zach said. "There's nothing wrong with them."

"*We* made them," I said. "And all the more reason for me to eat one."

"All the more reason for you to *pay*."

Zach grabbed the box. I scowled, but Zach did not look like he would budge. Heaving a long-suffering sigh, I fished out my wallet, popped open the cashbox, and put in a crumply single.

"Can you at least make me change?"

"They're a buck each."

"That's ridiculous!"

"That's how we're going to turn a profit." Zach narrowed his eyes at me as I chewed the cookie. It was, of course, really good.

"What kind of treasurer are you, that you don't want us to make money?" he said.

"What kind of anarchist are *you* that you *do*?"

*Touché, me*, I thought. Zach rolled his eyes.

"If you guys knew any *real* anarchists, you wouldn't think I was one. Besides, this bake sale is barely capitalism. At the rate we're selling stuff, anyway."

"Well, I *do* want us to make money," I said, crossing my arms. "I just also want to eat cookies."

"Ooh, brownies."

By some miracle and/or accident, two skinny freshpeople

had skulked over to our table, and Zach gave me a definite *shut up, we have a customer* look.

"What's this bake sale for?" one freshperson asked. She flipped a curtain of shiny hair over her shoulder.

"Don't we have a sign?" Zach said.

"We don't have a sign," I said. To the freshpeople, I said, "It's for the . . ." I took a deep breath and did my best. "Oh-pa-luh-gih-buh-tee-kwee-ah?"

Freshperson two narrowed her eyes. "The *what?*"

It occurred to me that maybe one of the reasons we didn't have many members was that our name was borderline unpronounceable.

"Owen Wister Preparatory Academy Lesbian, Gay, Bisexual, Transgender, Queer, Intersex, Asexual, and Allies," Zach said.

"There's only one *A* at the end," I said. "It can't stand for two things."

"Whatever."

The freshpeople gave no indication of recognition. Tess was right: we probably could stand to improve notice of our public profile in the school community at large.

"Aren't you Sam Huang's host sister?" one of them asked at last.

"Yes," I said. Finally, a shred of acknowledgment! I nodded, probably too enthusiastically, and swept a hand over our spread. "And I'm here to help raise money for the Winter Formal."

"Uh, what?"

"Winter Formal," I said. "It's the dance that happens in December after—"

"We *know* what Winter Formal is," interrupted the one with the hair. The other one eyed Chihiro's carob cake like it was a pile of rotten mulch. "Are you, like, running it now?"

"Kind of," I said, wishing I had Tess's eloquence-slash-forcefulness. "We're reinventing it."

Hair Girl gave her friend an impenetrable, mind-meld stare. "Um, thanks anyway."

"Wait!" Tess would be back any minute, and I was very markedly *not* fixing everything. "Don't you want a cookie? They're vegan!"

Zach shot me a *don't advertise that fact* look and tried to cover up for me. "They're a dollar."

The freshpeople looked from Zach to me like they were trying to figure out what the hell was going on. I seized the opportunity to take the tiniest, most furtive glance at my phone. The last thing I needed was Zach the Anarchist seeing that I was messaging with Sebastian—or worse, finding out about the song. But I still had to check.

"These are really good, too." Zach indicated his pumpkin cookies. "If I do say so myself."

No new messages. The freshpeople shifted their collective weight.

"How much?" one said tentatively.

"A dollar," Zach said. "Everything's a dollar."

The other girl wrinkled her nose. "Why are they orange?"

149

"They have pumpkin in them," I explained. "But not in a weird way."

The girls continued to look uncomfortable, but one reached for her pocket and dropped four quarters into the cashbox. The other one took a brownie, and together they walked away at a speed that suggested they'd only agreed to buy something as the quickest means for escape.

"See?" I rattled the quarters in the cashbox. "Profit."

"That was weird," Zach said. "What do you think their problem was?"

"Maybe they hate dances," I said, rolling a quarter between my fingers. "Or music. Or—"

"Oh yeah. Uh, here." From the pocket of his jacket, Zach produced a CD in a slim case with "Hard Rockin' for Nattie" scribbled on it.

"Oh," I said. "Um, thanks?"

"I mean I wasn't sure if you were serious or not about getting more into music but I had an extra CD so I burned it for you anyway." Zach looked at the ground. His eyelashes were long, for a boy.

"No!" I said, because I did want it—though not so much because I cared about getting a schooling in actual cool music. "I just, uh, forgot to bring in your shirt."

Zach lifted his eyes. "Keep it. If you want it. I have a million like it. It looked nice on you."

What? Did it?

"Oh," I said, again, with characteristic brilliance. "I mean, thanks. For the CD. And the shirt."

But before I could fully compute whether or not Zach the Anarchist had paid me a compliment, he'd taken up fidgeting with the lid of his cookie shoe box and talking about a billion words a minute.

"—sure what you'd like so I tried not to put anything too gross or sexist or anything on there but it was hard to narrow down everything to fit on a CD and still be representative of the evolution of punk in America."

He took a breath.

"Unless you're interested in the UK stuff, too?" Zach smoothed the back of his hair. "Because, look, like, Sid Vicious couldn't sing, and he probably murdered his girlfriend, so—"

"No, I'm . . . just interested in our stuff," I said quickly. "Good old homegrown American rock and/or roll." I laughed, weirdly. "You know me. Joni Mitchell forever!"

Zach was still holding the CD, and I was definitely protest-ething too much, or something, in my enthusiasm for folk music.

"I think Joni Mitchell's Canadian," he said.

*Dang.* "No, I know. I just meant . . . you know, classic stuff. Is what I like. I don't even know any bands that are on the radio right now," I added, for good measure. But just as the words came out of my mouth, my phone buzzed in my pocket.

Zach's face cleared. "Yeah. Right. Of course."

I smiled, in what I hoped was a calm and normal way. Because Zach the Anarchist, who burned custom punk mix CDs and had actual informed opinions about Sid Vicious, who hated corporate *anything*, especially music, and most of all, who I really wanted to think I was, if not cool, at least worth being friends with, could not find out about anything Sebastian-related. Not the messaging, and *definitely* not the song.

But I was still dying to look at my phone.

"Excuse me?!" Tess barged her way through the crowds, holding a paper food boat with something on a stick. "I leave for *two minutes* to go get a corn dog and then work just goes to a standstill?"

"Sorry," I said, and jumped away from Zach a little for no reason.

"What exactly were you expecting us to *do*?" Zach said.

"Ugh." Tess shook her head and took an aggressive bite of corn dog. "You two. Haven't you done enough music-related flirting for this week, Nattie?"

Corn dog on hand, Tess set about re-neatening the stacks of baked goods. My face went brilliantly hot.

"I don't . . . ," I said, just as Zach said, "No, it's cool."

"Right," I said. Another buzz. I flicked the switch on my phone to silent without taking it out of my pocket. "I mean . . . thanks." I held up the CD. "I'm excited to listen to it."

"Cool."

It *was* cool. And I *was* excited to listen to it, I was pretty sure. So why did it feel like I was lying to him?

# CHAPTER ELEVEN

That night, while Mom cut onions and swore as she dabbed at her eyes, I slumped at the kitchen counter, refreshing my Pixstagram feed over and over. Because time zones notwithstanding, in some kind of miracle of modern telecommunications, Sebastian had actually written me back.

> To: nmccullz
>
> so i guess u saw
>
> secrets out haha
>
> nothing gets past u

Nothing *did* get past me, I thought, triumphantly. Even better, the messages came with a black-and-white photograph of what looked like the beach at night. At least, I *thought* it was the beach. There was a dark part at the top and a light-gray part at the bottom, anyway. I guess it could've been anything, an abstract painting or a sandwich taken from really close up and then filtered to oblivion. So maybe that part got past me. But other than that, I was a master at this stuff. Except for the whole "writing a response" part.

Even though I'd gotten the message right after lunch, we were now closing in on dinnertime and I still hadn't responded. Because like any good McCullough-Schwartz, I was procrastinating.

"Shoot." Mom glanced over her shoulder at the calendar. "Is it trash day? I think it's trash day. Would you take the trash to the curb, Nattie?"

"Make Sam Huang do it." I tugged down the stream of pictures on my phone with a little *pop*. Nothing. Just the same picture Tess had taken of her eye makeup forty-five minutes ago, which I had of course obliged with a "TESSICAAAA" and a whole row of fire emojis.

As if on cue, Sam Huang leaped up from his computer, where he seemed to be browsing a website that sold boldly colored neckties.

"No! Fine, I'll do it." I shoved my phone in my pocket and banged out the back door. I didn't *want* to take the trash to the curb, but I also didn't want to look lazy in comparison. Having siblings really keeps you on your chore game, apparently.

"Thank y—Nattie!" Mom clicked her tongue at me as I came back inside. "It's freezing outside!"

"And?" I hopped back up on the stool.

"Why on earth aren't you wearing shoes? Robert, why isn't your daughter wearing shoes?" She shook her onion-chopping knife at Dad, who had just come downstairs after changing out of his work clothes. He glanced down at my feet, which were, admittedly, bare. I just hated having to dig my sneakers out of the shoe basket every time I wanted to go outside. It was such a hassle.

"I didn't feel like it," I said simply. Mom sighed, and Dad shook his head.

"Nattie, you have to wear shoes, for Pete's sake," Dad said.

"Aren't you cold?" Sam Huang said. *He* had on a pair of flip-flops, and not even smooshed-flat, last-summer flip-flops, but nice new ones, untainted by dirt or toe crud.

"*No*," I said. "I'm fine."

"Your feet are going to turn into hooves," Mom said.

"So what? Maybe I'm part hobbit." I pulled my phone back out. It totally didn't count as stalking if I was just refreshing the home feed over and over. That was normal. It only got weird if I went to Sebastian's personal photo stream. If I was just browsing, as one does with social media, any Sebastian-related insights would be totally incidental. Justifiable. Not creepy.

When I looked up, all three of them were staring at me.

"What?" I said.

Mom sighed and went into the pantry for something. Dad chuckled and shook his head.

"You're a rare bird, Nattie G."

"What does that mean?"

"It means you're special." He ruffled my hair, which I hate, and I pulled away.

"*You're special* just means *you're weird*," I said. "It's not a compliment."

"Is too," Dad said. "Trust me. I'm a dad. *You're special* means *you're special*, okay?"

"But that doesn't mean you can go barefoot in October!" Mom called from the pantry, followed by what sounded like an avalanche of cans.

"I'm okay," she said, a moment later. "Dammit."

Sensing a pause in the activity of the evening, Dad rubbed his hands together.

"Well! Anyone want to help with a project while we're waiting for dinner?"

"Nope," I said.

"I'm *already* helping with a project." Mom emerged from the pantry with a box of bow-tie pasta. "It's called *trying to feed our family*. And it's reducing me to tears."

Dad sighed. "Looks like it's just you and me, Sammy."

"Okay." Sam Huang went over to the shoe basket and pulled out a pair of his sneakers and started to lace them up. I gritted my teeth.

"His name's *Sam*, Dad," I said. "I mean, not his *name* name, but—"

"Actually, the name I picked was *Samuel*," Sam Huang said. "But Anne and Robert just started calling me Sam."

"Oh, Sam—Samuel, we're so sorry," Mom said with an oniony sniff.

"Would you like us to call you Samuel?" Dad said.

From the floor by the shoe basket, Sam Huang shrugged.

"I don't really mind," he said. "What do you need to do on the yurt?"

"Guys!" I interrupted. "You can't have a nickname for a nickname."

"That's just how we do it in this family, Nattie Gann. Worked for you." Dad grinned and gave my shoulder a little squeeze. "Come on. Help me and Sam with the yurt."

I ignored him and jabbed at my phone, perhaps accidentally landing on a specific person's account page. "I'm, um, busy."

"Doesn't look like it," Dad said.

Sebastian's feed had not changed since that afternoon: guitar, lime-flavored can of Hypr, a bridge all lit up for the night, guitar again, sunset over a bunch of buildings. Dude was *very* into bridges.

"Well, I am," I said, and idly tapped the most recent photo ("tool of the trade"). "I'm busy being . . . morose."

I wasn't actually feeling morose at all, but it was the first word that came into my head. *Morose* had kept us from bugging Zach about Mia too much. Well, us except for me, I guess. And *morose* seemed quicker than explaining that I was procrastinating writing what could be a life-altering Pixstagram message to a rock star–in–training on the other side of the country. Not that I was going to tell Dad *that*, either.

"Morose?" Dad frowned. "Who are you, and what have you done with Nattie G? Did something happen to you?"

"Ha ha ha," I said dryly. But inside, a shot of panic lanced through my heart, and I clicked my phone screen off as Dad headed past me with Sam Huang in tow. Could he tell? Could *anyone* tell? Maybe I hadn't done as good a job of burying my weird little Sebastian secret within me as I thought. Maybe I should be more careful not to act too different.

I cleared my throat. "What are you doing tonight?" I asked tentatively.

"Tonight," Dad said grandly, "we've gotta bolt together the sections of *khana* into a continuous wall."

That sounded incredibly boring.

"That sounds incredibly boring," I said, at the same time as Sam Huang said, "What should I do?"

I bit my tongue and went back to my phone. Sebastian had a particular fondness for filters that made everything look all jagged and high-contrast, like a photocopy of a ransom note. And he didn't use any capital letters, and he spelled *you* with a single letter, *and* he typed out emoticons instead of using emoji. I made a mental note to do those things in my reply, too.

"You," Dad said, "can help twist the bolts into place. There's over a hundred of 'em! I got 1.25-inch instead of 1-inch, which is a little too long, but it'll work. And—and this is the cool thing—once they're in place inside, we can use them as coat hooks."

"Cool," Sam Huang said, sounding way more interested than any normal person would about bolts. "That's convenient."

"I know!" Dad said, and held open the door for Sam Huang to go out with him. "Hopefully I'll be able to start actual construction before it gets too cold."

"It's almost November," Mom yelled out to the backyard. "It's already too cold."

"All the more reason to have a nice toasty yurt in the backyard, darling wife," Dad called back.

I was only half listening, because I was being fake-morose to cover up some medium-to-heavy pre-message-composition soul-searching. My first instinct, of course, had been to tell Tess, because like any best friend, she was skilled in the art of text-message divination and could squeeze a paragraph's worth of meaning out of a simple "k." But by the time last period had rolled around, and I'd reread those three lines so many times I'd drained my phone battery to 6 percent, I realized I kind of . . . didn't want to show her. Something about the messages felt special, private. Sebastian had sent them *just* to me, after all. He totally could've posted that photograph publicly, too, but he didn't. He was opening up, and inviting someone else to analyze felt like a betrayal.

On the *other* hand, just ignoring something this big would probably cause repressed feelings to squeeze out of me in unfortunate and unusual ways, like volunteering to do anything related to the yurt. I had to say something back to Sebastian eventually. Soon, even. But not too soon. What I *really* needed to do was craft an image. Update my feed. Send out some cool visual/textual hints that, even when Sebastian wasn't around, I was having an interesting life full of meaningful activity.

With a deep, courageous breath, I hit the New Post button.

Unfortunately, there did not seem to be one single thing on my camera roll worth posting: a picture of an extra-long French fry I'd gotten in the cafeteria, a couple accidental screenshots because I didn't know how to turn my phone off, a bunch of unflattering selfies I'd taken in my bedroom when I was attempting to do something interesting with my hair. Just a series of visual testaments to my undying weirdness. I scrolled back further, past the oodles of Acronympho group shots we'd taken over the summer and the picture Tess had taken of me looking uncomfortable in my pre–Meredith White's–party regalia, all the way back to the video from the Talent Show Incident.

My stomach did a little flip. *That* would be something interesting to post, if it wouldn't mean admitting to my total creeperdom. I thought about watching it, but Mom was right there and would have heard everything, and also a six billionth viewing wouldn't reveal anything that I didn't already know about that night. Or Sebastian.

Which was . . . what, exactly?

"Nattie?" Mom blinked and gestured at a cabinet with her shoulder. "Would you get me the big pot?"

"Sure." I opened the door and extracted the pot with one hand while closing Pixstagram with the other. So much for curating my image. Maybe I just needed to do some good, old-fashioned internet stalking first. I typed "Sebastian Delacroix Young Lungs" into Google, and the first result was a fresh, unclicked video link—*Young Lungs live @ Ruby's philly Sebastian Delacroix solo.* I tapped it open just as Sam Huang swung in through the back door.

"Done so soon?" Mom flicked on the tap and wiped her hands on a dish towel. "Is everything okay?"

"I got a splinter." Sam Huang held up a hand. "It's fine, but—"

"Sam!" Mom leaped to his side and yanked his hand into the light. "Oh, God, you're bleeding. And that's your guitar hand!"

"You play the guitar with both hands, Mom," I pointed out.

"It's really fine," Sam Huang said. "I just—"

"Stay right there," Mom commanded. "I'll get disinfectant. Nattie, where's the—"

"Second-floor bathroom cabinet," I said, full-screening the video. "Next to the bath bombs."

"Right." Mom pointed at Sam Huang. "Don't move."

She grabbed the now-full pot, stuck it on the stove, and ran upstairs, muttering something about not dashing Sam's hopes for Julliard.

"Should I tell her I'm not applying to Julliard?" Sam Huang asked.

"Let her have her moment," I said, from behind my phone. Sam Huang peered over my shoulder.

"What are you watching? Guitar?"

"Oh, I . . ." I tried to click off my phone, but it was too late. Sam Huang grabbed it away from me with his nonsplintered hand. The video played on, tinny riffs pushing the limits of my phone's puny speakers, and Sam listened, thoughtfully. Thoughtfully and kind of making a face.

"Is it bad?" I asked, anxious in spite of myself. "Do you not like it?"

"It's not bad," Sam said mildly.

"Sam Huang!" I cried. "You are *lying*."

"It's not! It's just . . . different from what I'm used to."

Sam was not much of a liar. I gave him a hard look. "What's wrong with it?"

"His technique. The way he has his wrist underneath . . ." Sam demonstrated in the air, on an invisible fretboard. "It can give you tendinitis, if you're not careful."

It didn't *look* like there was anything wrong. And it didn't *sound* that way, either.

"Well, not everyone's a classically trained guitarist," I said. "He's self-taught."

"Self-taught? You know him?" Sam tilted my phone in his hand, frowning. "Wait. This is called 'Natalie'?"

"Yes," I said, way too loudly. "I mean, um, *no*, I don't really know . . . but the song, um, I guess I found it by accident when I was Googling myself."

My traitorous face felt hot enough to melt metal. Sam,

meanwhile, did not look at all like he bought it. He just blinked. Then, slowly, he smiled.

"You *like* him."

"What?!" I practically fell off the stool. "No, I don't. I totally don't at all. Shut up!"

Sam grinned. "You like him!"

"Sam!" I cried. "Shut *up*, Sam. Give me that." I grabbed my phone back just as the final chords crashed into place.

"It's good," he said slowly. "For pop."

"Indie rock," I corrected. "And I thought everyone in *A Cappella* had to like pop."

Sam Huang ignored me. "Who is he? Where did you meet him? Can I watch it again?"

He was almost gleeful, trying to get this out of me, and I, having no practice navigating young siblings, wasn't sure how mean I was allowed to be. Fortunately, sort of, Mom chose that exact moment to tumble back into the kitchen, toting a battered-looking first aid kit.

"I think this gauze is from before you were born, Nattie," she said, examining a sealed packet from inside the little plastic chest. "But it's probably still fine, right? How long does gauze stay sterile?"

I gave a noncommittal shrug-grunt just as Sam snatched my phone out of my hand.

"Hey!"

The strains of "Natalie" started again as Mom set about

doctoring Sam's finger, which ended up wrapped in so much gauze it resembled an old-timey cartoon glove.

"Mom," I said. "Stop. You're going to cut off his circulation."

"Is that too much?" Mom frowned at Sam's swaddled hand. "Well, you can be a mummy for Halloween, I guess."

Sam tested his newly bandaged hand, still holding my phone. Which buzzed. I took advantage of Sam's injury and swiped my phone out of his grasp, but when I unlocked it, it was just a text from Tall Zach.

From: Zach Bitterman

SURPRISE HALLOWEEN PLAN!!!! meet downtown at 22nd and fairmount at 9:30. your events chair has something spoooooky planned

p.s. also nattie i already bought you a ticket so you owe me twenty bucks thx

"Oh God." I set down my phone, which was still streaming out the sound of Sebastian's voice, and texted Tall Zach a quick "OK" from the counter.

"What's wrong now?" Sam said.

"My friend's planning some kind of Halloween surprise. And I hate surprises." The song ended again, twanging on the familiar chord, and I jumped. "Especially on Halloween."

"Hm." Mom took the lid off the simmering pot. "You did always cry when I tried to put you in that ladybug suit as a baby. Maybe I traumatized you against costume-related holidays."

"Maybe," I said, still staring at my now-silent phone. When I looked up again, Mom's eyes were fixed on me.

"No, I mean, it's not your fault," I added quickly.

"You like candy," Mom said. "That's a big part of the holiday, if I recall correctly."

"Candy can be scary," I said. "Remember that time I accidentally ate a strawberry lollipop when I was six?" It had been my first—and only, so far—trip to the ER.

But Mom was dumping pasta into the boiling water and looking out the back window, to where Dad was bolting together what looked like two giant baby gates. "Still at it." She shook her head. "Well, Sam, I'm so sorry. We're terrible host parents. If this yurt puts an end to your music career, you have my personal permission to sue my husband for lost wages." She turned to me. "Anyway, sweetheart, just bring your EpiPen. And maybe Sam Huang wants to go, too."

"Thanks," Sam Huang said. "But I actually have plans. With A Cappella. We're doing some new arrangements."

I resisted the urge to sigh. Of *course* A Cappella was too cool to go out on Halloween; they had to polish up their precious repertoire. Taking advantage of my inattention, Sam reached over one-handedly and propped my phone up with the video on-screen like a little TV, but before he could hit Play again, it buzzed.

"I'll take that," I said, and Sam, with only one good hand, was unable to stop me. "Go back to your matching neckties, Sam Huang."

Sam, unscathed, went back to his computer, and I switched apps and stared at the screen: a new message. Several, actually. And not from Tall Zach.

> To: nmccullz
>
> been recording all day actually
>
> adding new songs to the EP

My heart contracted like an accordion, and I immediately flipped my phone facedown on the counter. I glanced at Mom, but she didn't seem to notice that her daughter was in the clutches of a minor cardiac arrest. Trembling, I tapped back into my inbox and reread the message.

He'd responded without my even having to say anything. It was like he *knew* I was thinking about him and messaged me anyway. I chewed my pinky nail, pensive. Now I *had* to reply. I had to reply, I had to come off sophisticated and worldly and like I knew what *EP* stood for, and most of all, I had to avoid at all costs any mention of my actual, weird life. No yurts, no tendinitis warnings, no deadly food allergies. So after long minutes of deliberation, thumb-typing, and procrastination, I sent back a reply.

> To: sebdel
>
> that sounds cool

Okay, not the most original, but maybe it would look like I was being clever instead of stupid. The ball was in Sebastian's court now. After accidentally taking a screenshot, I turned off my phone, for good this time. And waited.

# CHAPTER TWELVE

By Halloween night, I was actually in kind of a good mood, spooky surprise or no. New songs—songs that did not have my name in them—were good news. By the time the Young Lungs' album came out—and that could take *months*, I figured—the old stuff wouldn't be in rotation anymore. They'd write even better stuff and record it in a fancy Los Angeles studio and some guy in sunglasses would push around switches on one of those giant console things to make all of it sound good.

But even better than the promise of new songs was the fact that I, Nattie McCullough-Schwartz, was engaging in clandestine correspondence with Sebastian Delacroix, notable attractive person and soon-to-be rock star. Sure, I hadn't gotten anything new since that last one, but that in itself was kind of exciting. Not knowing when his next message would come was agonizing and thrilling all at once, like in the one Catullus poem where he talks about feeling both love *and* hate. You don't know *why* it's happening, but you can *feel* it, and it's like being on fire. Or so Catullus says. But if that was what it meant to start falling for someone in secret, I think I got it.

Unfortunately, I was not particularly good at keeping secrets.

"Are you mad at me?" Tess said. We were waiting, en masse with the rest of the OWPALGBTQIA, to go to the haunted house at Eastern State Penitentiary, and Tess was wearing a silvery T-shirt dress with a cobwebby-looking pattern over it and dramatic, Elvira-style eyebrows. "Something about you seems weird."

I shivered. The walls were menacingly high and made of charred-looking stones, with actual screams echoing off them. Tall Zach's big holiday surprise couldn't have been candy corn or a hayride. It had to be getting the crap scared out of us by local actors in striped prisoner outfits.

"No," I said automatically.

I wasn't, not really. Mostly I was wondering why Sebastian could respond to my *first* message almost instantaneously and then take a full day and a half to answer my second. Not that he'd answered yet, of course.

Tess wasn't buying it.

"You look like you're a little pissed. Or worried. Are you worried about the dance? Because look, we have to take a breather sometimes." Tess inhaled emphatically. "Activism is exhausting. It's important to relax once in a while."

"I'm not worried, I'm *cold*," I said. The only remotely Halloweeny thing I owned was an orange tank top, which I had worn even though it looked gross next to my hair and wasn't nearly warm enough, even under a (black) hoodie.

And, okay, maybe I *was* worried. A little. If Sebastian had time to go out and take pictures of bridges and give interviews to websites and, like . . . perform shows or whatever, you'd think he'd have time to write one measly Pixstagram message once in a while.

Also, I hated haunted houses.

"And I hate haunted houses," I added. "This does not count as relaxing for me."

"Nattie, don't be such a Halloween pooper," Tall Zach said. He had his hair gelled up straight from his head and was wearing what looked like an orange convict jumpsuit with a giant V neck.

"I'm wearing orange," I pointed out. It was annoying, because everyone else seemed to know exactly what to be for Halloween. I couldn't even figure out how to dress myself *normally*, let alone for a costume-themed holiday.

"Orange alone does not a costume make," Tall Zach said.

"It does for *you*," I pointed out.

"Yeah. What you even supposed to *be*?" Alison had shown up to Eastern State wearing all black, which was pretty much how she seemed to show up anywhere.

"I'm Goku," Tall Zach said.

No one said anything.

"From *Dragon Ball Z*?" He groaned. "The Super Saiyan? Ugh, you guys are the worst."

"I knew who you were," Endsignal said from underneath a pair of light-up devil horns.

"What are *you*?" Tall Zach demanded of Alison.

"We're cats," she said, grabbing Chihiro's elbow and indicating the paper triangles protruding from each of their heads.

"Oh," Tall Zach said politely. "Cute."

"I wanted us to be demons," Chihiro mumbled, looking longingly at Endsignal's horns.

The line shuffled another few people forward. I could hear nervous chatter and the strains of music coming from inside the prison walls. Maybe it *wouldn't* be as horrifically terrifying as I was imagining.

"Can vegans even *go* as animals?" Bryce's voice was muffled by one of those whole-head rubber masks that looked like a cartoony version of Richard Nixon.

Alison gave him a look of withering cattiness.

"We don't eat *cat*, Bryce."

"Not that there's anything wrong with that," Tess said.

Tall Zach burst into a fit of laughter, and Tess smiled her closed-mouth smile. It was hard to tell if Bryce got the joke behind his mask.

"What's so funny?"

Zach the Anarchist appeared next to Tess. Eastern State was downtown, pretty close to his house, so he must have walked. He was dressed completely normal, in a white T-shirt and black jeans, except for a long, rhinestone chain around his neck with a little brown bottle at the end.

"Nothing," Tess said.

"Vulgar innuendo," I said.

"Who are *you*?" Alison said.

"Duh," Zach said, lifting the bottle at the end of his necklace. "Vanilla Ice."

The cat twins stared at him. Tall Zach frowned. Bryce's expression remained unknowable.

"It's vanilla extract," Zach the Anarchist explained. "On the end of a diamond chain. Like ice."

"That's not very scary," Alison said.

"Vanilla Ice ripped off a lot of DJs," Endsignal said.

"I think it's funny," Chihiro said.

Next to me, Zach the Anarchist shrugged, the edge of his T-shirt brushing my shoulder. We were almost at the entrance now, and judging by my rapidly elevating heart rate, my attempts to keep myself calm were totally futile. That, or I was about to have apoplexy.

The line lurched forward again, and a scrawny guy with sunken-eye makeup ushered us into the waiting room. I tried not to think about how this was the same threshold where actual murderers had crossed before serving actual time in prison.

"I'll get the tickets," Tall Zach said. "I booked all of us as a group."

"This is dumb," Alison said. "We should have just gone to *Rocky Horror*."

Tall Zach looked put out. "We've gone like every year. It's a cliché at this point. Besides, *Rocky Horror*'s not even scary! Don't you want to be scared on Halloween?"

"No," I answered, not that anyone listened.

"Hey, shouldn't we be saving money for the dance and

stuff?" Bryce scratched the back of his head. "I thought that was our, like, number one perodidtive."

Zach the Anarchist and I exchanged a look, and I mouthed *don't bother* at him, which made him smile. Which was nice.

Tall Zach sighed. "One, this thing sells out *every year*, so we're lucky we got to go at all, and two, you paid for your own ticket, remember?" He held up a twenty as evidence. "So we're going, and we're going to enjoy ourselves, okay? I'm going to the box office."

"Wait," I said, suddenly desperate to stall. "Is everyone here?"

"I think so?" Tall Zach said. "You can count if you want to, but I told everyone to get here at nine thirty sharp. Snooze, lose, and so forth."

I looked back at the assembled group of OWPALGBT-QIA-ers, which was somewhere between ten and twelve people total, depending on if the knot of girls were actually with us or just trying to get a better look at Tall Zach's sliver of bare chest. The scene would have been totally creeptastic if it weren't for the weirdly upbeat music playing over the PA system. Probably to lure us into a false sense of security.

Apparently Endsignal had the same thought.

"Is this Avicii?" he said, frowning.

"Hey, yeah. Can't we at least hear the 'Monster Mash' or something?" Bryce said in the direction of the college-aged zombie girl manning the door.

"We played that for the first two nights," she said. "Then it started to drive us crazy."

The song faded out, replaced the nasal sound of some Top 40 DJ wishing everyone a spooky-ass Halloween.

Endsignal looked pained, as if to say *and that doesn't?* The zombie girl didn't notice.

"Okay!" Tall Zach had returned from the ticket window with all of our passes and started to hand them out. My hands felt distinctly clammy.

"You okay?"

I whirled around. Zach the Anarchist nodded at me.

"Yeah," I said.

"Are you sure?" Goku-Zach asked. "You're white as a sheet. Or a ghost. A sheet-ghost."

I nodded, but before I could vocally insist I was fine, he had distributed all the tickets and the zombie girl was ushering us forward.

"Ladies and gentlemen, boys and girls, children of all genders!" Tall Zach crowed. "Are you ready to have the pants scared off of you?"

A cheer went up, and the zombie opened the gate.

"Yeah," I said again. "I'm fine."

For about half an hour, I tried to take in as little as possible. There were definitely ghosts, and screams, and very low lighting. But the next *clear* thing I was aware of was a rummy, sweet smell and the sound of my own name. The world was very blurry.

"Nattie!"

I blinked. I was lying down, and Goku-Zach was crouched in front of me, waving something in front of my face. Somehow, even though I vaguely remembered walking past the zombie into the courtyard beyond the gate, I hadn't actually left the room with the ticket window.

"Zach?" I blinked again. My blood felt electrified and unstable as it coursed into my head, but I managed to sit up okay.

"You fainted," he explained. "Just inside the last cell block. But apparently the hook-hand guy with the rotting eyeball is also in charge of taking care of people when they freak out, so he helped us get you back here."

The rotten-eyeball guy. I sort of remembered that. Gross.

"Us?" I said.

"Yeah. Other Zach went to get you some water." Goku-Zach rocked back onto his heels. "And he lent me his vanilla to wake you up."

"I see," I said.

"More like you *smell*," he said. "I thought it would be like in those old-timey movies, when they waved stuff under people's noses or whatever. I figured this was close."

"Did that even work?" It was Zach the Anarchist, holding a bottle of water in one hand and his Vanilla Ice chain in the other.

"I think so," he said. "I mean, Nattie's awake now."

"It does have a very distinct smell," I said. I pressed a hand to my forehead, where things seemed to be slowly recombobulating.

"I've never even fainted before," I said.

"And yet you did it like a pro," Goku-Zach said.

"How long was I out?"

He shrugged. "Not that long. Maybe half a minute or so?"

"*Half a minute?*" I yelped.

"Hey, guys." The zombie girl had come over from the gate. "Your group's almost through. She feeling better?"

"More or less," I answered, even though she hadn't actually addressed me directly.

"Happens all the time," she said.

"Really?" I said.

"Yeah. Last night we had a ten-year-old pee his pants."

"Oh, great," I said.

"Do you want some candy?" she offered.

"Yes!" Goku-Zach handed me the vanilla and followed her back to the gate. Wordlessly, Zach the Anarchist gave me the bottle of water. I put the vanilla in my pocket and twisted open the water. My head was still pounding a little, a fact not helped by the incessant drum line playing over the speakers, and I rubbed my temples.

"Mumford and Sons gives me that feeling, too," Zach the Anarchist said.

"What?" I chugged another gulp of water.

"Never mind."

"Here," Goku-Zach said, pressing a candy into my hand. "Starburst. Your fave."

"Thanks," I said. Sugar would probably help, I reasoned. But before I could unwrap it, Zach the Anarchist bent down and took it from me.

"Hey," I said. "I wanted that."

"No, you didn't," he said. "That one was strawberry. Here." He dropped a yellow square into my palm.

"Oh." I chewed my lip. "Thanks." I barely had a chance to stick the nondeadly candy into my mouth when I heard my name again.

"Nattie!"

It was Tess this time, rushing in through the zombie girl's gate.

"Are you okay?" She looked a little pale herself under her smoky eye makeup, but maybe that was intentional. "I turned around halfway through and you were gone, but we'd already gone around the corner and I couldn't get back. . . ."

"She looks pasty." Alison came in after Tess and sounded much less concerned. "Maybe a vampire got her."

"My aunt's hypoglycemic," Chihiro piped up. "She faints all the time when her blood sugar drops."

"I gave her a Starburst," Goku-Zach said, who was midway through unwrapping one or three for himself.

"It's not blood sugar," I said. "I just . . . got creeped out."

Alison snorted. Tess glared at her, then softened her gaze on me and gave me a little pat on the head.

"Sorry, Nattie," she said. "We probably shouldn't have forced you in there if you were so scared."

"No, it's fine," I said with a glance at Tall Zach. "I mean, I wanted to go in there. Kind of."

"Nattie, don't lie. You would have hated the rest of it," Tess said. "Although it *was* awesome. They had this whole section that was done up like a creepy hospital, and just as you're halfway across the operating room, the lights just go completely out. . . ."

She went on to describe the haunted house in literally gory detail as the rest of the OWPALGBTQIA group reassembled in the foyer. I swallowed the sticky mass of Starburst and felt slightly better, especially now that the kick-drum-heavy song was over. Alison, Chihiro, and Bryce, now sans mask, were discussing whether they could make it to South Street before their curfews were over. A freshman girl with curly hair was asking around to see if anyone could give her a ride. Endsignal was pressing on his horns and getting them to blink in different patterns.

I got to my feet as the noise level rose and found myself facing Zach the Anarchist.

"Sorry you had to miss the haunted house," I said. I was about to reach for the vanilla in my pocket to give it back when Tess's voice jolted me.

"*People!*" she yelled above the din of chatting and music. "Let's start to move out!"

Everyone ignored her.

"Whatever," Zach said. "I go every year. They don't really change it much."

"Oh," I said. "Well, maybe I'll give it—"

My name rang out in the little room again.

"Natalie?"

I whirled around. It was Chihiro, looking confused, and then embarrassed.

"Sorry," she said. "I just thought I heard your name on the radio, but—"

I froze.

"No, that's totally Natalie," Alison agreed. "Listen."

I did, because I couldn't *not* listen, and there it was, invisible and everywhere for everyone to hear.

*"Natalie*
*So fiery from the start*
*Natalie*
*Why'd you break my heart, heart, heart?"*

"Weird," Bryce said.

"I like it," Chihiro said.

"I *love* it." Tess's eyes were gleaming.

"She looks like she's going to faint again," Alison said.

I shook my head.

"I'm not. I'm fine. Let's just go, everyone."

It wasn't until Tess dropped me off at home that I realized Zach's vanilla was still in my pocket.

# CHAPTER THIRTEEN

I spent the time between the haunted house and Monday afternoon fixated on *not* being fixated on hearing the song. The whole fainting incident provided a really convenient cover for my freaked-out-ness in the moment, but the closer I got to my next baking session with Zach the Anarchist, the more I felt a new anxiety welling up in my chest. Because he'd been there, too. He'd definitely heard it; the music was cranked super loud. Despite my best efforts of compartmentalizing, ignoring, and occasionally, debatably lying about stuff, things were starting to overlap.

But, I reasoned, maybe hearing something wasn't the same as listening to it. Plus, I realized with a bone-melting relief, he had no way to know it was the Young Lungs. There hadn't been any DJ announcing who it was or anything. As far as Zach the Anarchist knew, it was just a weird coincidence, a song that happened to have my name in it that happened to come on while I was in the vicinity of a pair of speakers. And he still had no idea that Sebastian and I were messaging.

So when Monday afternoon rolled around, I decided to channel my nervous energy into baking, which by virtue of requiring so much precision would require a lot of concentration, and Latin, which . . . pretty much the same. Failing that, I would distract myself with something pleasant like ingesting enough raw cookie dough to ensure salmonella.

Also, I kind of needed help balancing the budget.

"Don't take this the wrong way," Zach said, "but you're better at making cookies than you are at keeping financial records."

"Thanks?" I took the scoop and started to plop out rounds of snickerdoodle dough in neat rows of four.

"I mean, you're doing okay right now. Keep those farther apart or else they'll spread into each other." He looked down at my notes again. Underneath him, Bacon yawned a languid doggy yawn and sprawled over Zach's stocking feet, belly in the air.

"You know you can set up spreadsheets so they tabulate things automatically, right? Like enter x number of quarters and multiply it out to see how many dollars you have."

"I don't use spreadsheets. I just type everything up in word processing and add it up on my phone."

Zach looked at me like I'd just admitted to using an abacus. I stopped scooping.

"What?"

Zach said nothing, just shook his head, which made me even more irritated.

"It's not, like, inexact or anything," I said. "The numbers are *there*, right? And you can read them?"

"Yeah, but if you use a spreadsheet, you can have it update live and save yourself the trouble of retyping everything each week. And you can make graphs."

"Graphs of *what*?"

Zach didn't answer. I snuck a look at my phone, where, to my horror, my Pixstagram inbox had a tiny *15* on top of it. And all seemed to be from Sebastian. I surreptitiously tapped the first one.

> To: nmccullz
>
> california is so fake
>
> its beautiful dont get me wrong
>
> but its all so NEW

"I can't believe you haven't added the bake sale money to the rest of the money," Zach said. "Addition is literally the first thing you ever learn in math."

I quickly set my phone on the counter, facedown. "I *did* add it up. I'm not stupid. And you didn't answer my question."

"Because you didn't get the same answer twice in all of your Total tallies."

"Why does everything have to be so *exact* all the time?" I said, staring at the first round of perfectly sized snickerdoodles as Zach slid them onto the cooling rack. He stopped, sighed, and handed me one.

"Thank you," I said, and took an eager bite. The snickerdoodle was every bit as delicious as it looked. Zach took one and went back to the sheaf of papers. Under the counter, I went back to my phone.

To: nmccullz

pearl-drop moon on velvet sky

waxwane different every night

le lune est un femme

"Well, it seems like we have somewhere between zero and one hundred dollars," Zach said. "How much do we need to hand over as a deposit again?"

Sebastian really did see poetry in everything, even if his French was still kind of bad—he made all the nouns masculine when they should be feminine, which is literally French 101. I locked my phone and snapped my head up. "Five."

"Dollars?"

"*Hundred*," I said, snorting. "If the buy-in to sponsor a dance was five bucks, even the anticapitalists would go for it."

"Nothing anticapitalists love more than Winter Formal," Zach said.

"Whatever." I forced myself to unhand my phone and nibbled at my cookie instead. "*You're* going, right? So that's one hundred percent of the anticapitalists *I* know."

"I guess."

"What do you mean you *guess*? You can't *not* go."

"I can probably retally these by tomorrow, if you want," Zach said.

"Don't change the subject," I said. For some reason, it bugged me that Zach was going through all this effort when he didn't even care about the dance that much. That didn't seem like him. "Are you thinking about *not* going?"

"Why do you care so much about this dance all of a sudden?" Zach said. He bent down and scratched Bacon behind his ears, which triggered a frenzied leg-scrabbling on the tile floor.

"I mean, doesn't everyone?" I said. "I thought we all did."

"Yeah, everyone who's invested in getting crowned prom king and queen, or whatever."

"Prom isn't until the spring, and I'm pretty sure there will only be a gender-specific court over Tess's dead body." With Zach out of eyesight with Bacon, I took the opportunity to sneak a look down at my phone at message number four.

To: nmccullz

god these tacos are so good

mango salsa is a revelation

It was accompanied with a picture of tacos. What was I supposed to say to that? *Uh, yeah, looks great?* I debated typing it out, then stopped. Sebastian just wanted to talk—talk to *me*, which gave me that familiar melty feeling in the pit of my stomach. And even though I needed—well, wanted badly—to know what the band was doing with the album, especially since the haunted house incident, I couldn't just barge in with some question like *Why is your song suddenly everywhere?* I didn't want to be yet another desperate teenage groupie with no sense of chill like the Meredith Whites of the world; I wanted to be *mysterious*. The kind of girl whose feed is just beachy hairdos, minimalist flower arrangements, and macarons. Because Sebastian had chosen to confide in me for a reason, and I just couldn't let myself screw that up by being lame.

> To: sebdel
>
> looks great

Message sent, I realized the kitchen had been silent for a while, and it was probably my turn to say something to Zach. About the dance.

"It's just supposed to be *fun*," I said. "The dance."

"Yeah," Zach said. "Really fun." He gave Bacon a few belly thumps.

My finger itched to unlock my phone again, but I didn't give in. "What?"

Zach let out a short laugh. "I just *love* dressing up in societally acceptable clothes to take selfies for Pixstagram so everyone can know how great my life is."

I clamped my phone hard in my hand. "Oh please, Zach the Anarchist. You've never taken a Pixstagram selfie in your life."

"You don't know that."

"Um, yeah, I do?" I said. "The only apps on your phone are, like, a guitar tuner and a calculator."

"Well, I've been in them," Zach said. "With other people."

"Oh," I said. Right. Mia. Zach kept petting Bacon, and I

chewed my lip. I knew I had no right to feel this way, especially given the dumb thing I'd said about her, but the fact that Mia was still bothering Zach bothered *me*. I wasn't jealous—there was no way I was jealous—but I guess I didn't like seeing him sad, and especially not about this.

"Are you doing okay?" I said before I could stop myself. "About . . . her?"

Zach kept his gaze fixed on the dog. "I don't know. I guess. I know you didn't like her, Nattie, but—"

"I did!" I squeaked.

Zach ignored me. "—but I did. I mean, past tense. But it wasn't . . . I don't know. She didn't go to our school. She didn't fit in with you guys, so, like . . . how much of a future were we really going to have?" He shrugged. "And we only dated for the summer. It's not like she broke my heart or anything."

A jolt zapped through me. Was he intentionally referencing the song? There was no way. He'd only heard it once; he couldn't have memorized the chorus. And Zach wasn't one to play mind games. Right?

"Oh," was all I could say.

"Yeah." Zach said. "So I'm fine. But, um, thanks for asking."

He stopped petting Bacon and looked up at me. Right up at me, with those very blue eyes. Without even meaning to, I clenched my fingers around my phone.

Bacon made a little *yip* noise, and then, because I had

literally zero idea how to continue *that* conversation, I switched back to a topic I knew even less about than romance: economics. "Well, um, at the rate I've been buying cookies, I think I've single-handedly increased our net income by—"

"Gross."

I bristled. "Um, I am not."

"No," Zach said. "I meant gross income, Nattie."

I stared at him.

"As opposed to net?" he went on. "Gross is the raw amount of what you take in, and net is after you subtract your liabilities."

"Oh," I said. "I knew that."

"Remind me why you're not taking econ again?"

"Because I wanted to take two foreign language courses and they let me out of the requirement." Luckily for me, Owen Wister Preparatory Academy was the kind of place where you could not only take two languages at once, but also avoid something soulless and full of math like econ at the same time. Behind me, the timer dinged on the second round of cookies. "Which, by the way . . ." I took out my Latin notebook.

"Huh?" Zach had sheathed his hand in a frog-shaped mitt and rotated the two hot sheets of cookies from top to bottom. They smelled like cinnamon and vanilla, with little craggy tops and chewy-looking bronzed edges.

"Latin," I said. "Remember?"

"Oh yeah." Zach cranked the kitchen timer to five minutes and shuffled over. I'd put an apron on over my T-shirt, but

Zach was working unprotected, a couple streaks of flour running down the black length of his "Fat Wreck Chords" shirt.

"Do you want to start?" He jumped onto the stool next to me and pulled out his notes.

"Oh," I said. "Um, no. You go and I'll, like, course-correct."

"Okay." Zach pushed a bunch of pages around until he found Catullus 5, the middle of which we'd been assigned for homework. "*Da*. The?"

I gave him a look. "It's imperative."

"Imperative what, that I get this right?"

"An imperative *verb*," I said. "*Da*. From *do, dare, dedi, datum*—give. Like, uh . . ." I tried to think of a cognate. "*Data*, I guess. Next."

"*Mi*," Zach read. "Uh, me?"

"Did you *know* that, or just guess it because it sounds exactly the same?"

Zach shrugged. Our elbows were touching.

"Fine." I licked my lips and didn't move my arm. "Next."

"*Mille* is a thousand," Zach said. "And *centum* is a hundred." He moved his finger to the next line. "*Mille* again—thousand—then another hundred, then another thousand again, then a hundred."

I squinted at the page. He was right.

"You're just getting those right because it's math," I said. Zach didn't meet my eyes, but he did kind of nudge my elbow with his.

"Told you."

"Yup," I said. "I mean, um, nope." I'd looked back at the first line, and started tapping my pencil against the page a bunch of times.

"So what should we write in Themes?"

"You haven't even translated the whole sentence yet," I said.

"Oh." Zach looked back at the page. He scrunched his mouth up when he was thinking. Not that I was looking at his mouth, except normally, as a normal part of his face.

Not that I was looking at his face, either.

"*Basia*," Zach read, "is . . ." He paused, and turned to me so that our heads were practically touching. Our heads, and all the other parts of our faces. "What's *basia* mean?"

I swallowed. "Kisses."

"Oh."

Zach blinked, and I blinked, and we sat there with our heads close and our kissing-obsessed Latin homework between us for what could have been forever but was probably less than five minutes, because just when things were reaching peak awkwardness—

*Ding.*

"The cookies," I practically yelled, and then almost fell off my stool.

"Huh? Oh." Zach put down his pencil. "Right."

As he clambered over to the oven, I attempted to retain a grip on academic seriousness and dispassion, which was made even more difficult by the fact that Sebastian had immediately replied to my last message.

To: nmccullz

thanks ;)

i know ive sent u like a thousand msgs

your so easy to talk to, natalie

you make this shy guy smile

Underneath that was a selfie, or half selfie, of Sebastian's stubbly chin showing a black-and-white grin. I clicked my phone dark as fast as I could, heart thudding. Maybe over Pixstagram message I was easy to talk to, but in real life I was having considerable difficulties.

"So, um." My dumb voice sounded like a squeaky Muppet. Focus. Worksheet. Don't think about Sebastian's mouth. "Themes. I'm just going to write, uh . . ."

"Addition," Zach said.

I ignored him and wrote *romance*. "Okay. Devices."

"Hyperbole."

"What?" I looked up to where Zach was shoveling cookies onto a cooling rack.

"Dude's talking about her kissing her a bajillion times," he said. "That's totally exaggeration."

"It's romantic!"

Zach scrunched up his forehead. "It's . . . kind of annoying."

I pinched my pencil hard between my fingertips. "Maybe he just likes kissing."

"Yeah, but . . ." Zach chipped at a cookie. "So does, like, everybody, pretty much, right?"

At that, my heart thumped against the front of my ribs. I didn't know whether to nod or shrug or say "yeah" or what. Why was everybody obsessed with kissing? Was this even appropriate for high-school students to discuss in a homework-related context?

I took a deep breath, but my heart kept pounding so hard it almost hurt. Because I had this weird feeling that, if I hadn't just been reading messages from Sebastian, if I hadn't been *thinking* about everything so much, this would've been the perfect time to kiss Zach the Anarchist. If I wanted to.

Did I?

"Yeah." I wasn't sure I had anything else to say, so I just wrote *being annoying?* under Devices. It was almost time for the train, anyway. "Well, thanks for the spreadsheets, and everyth—"

"Sorry." Zach stopped moving cookies. "Sorry. In case you can't tell, I'm just not a big, like, kiss-and-tell kind of guy."

"Oh," I said. "I mean, yeah. Me neither. Not at all."

And then it was over, whatever moment we had or hadn't just had. Zach went back to moving cookies, and my phone hummed against my leg.

To: nmccullz

i just feel like i can tell u anything ;)

# CHAPTER FOURTEEN

That Friday night, when I finally got a long chunk of free time, I spent it poring over the internet for anything Young Lungs–related. I looked them up again and saw, to my horror, that the Web results had more than tripled since we saw them on Endsignal's computer. The band was turning up on more and more music blogs, and their record label's YouTube had released a few more concert clips, in which, from what I could tell, Sebastian's wrist position did not seem to have improved. They even got what looked like a feature story in one of the Philadelphia alt-weekly newspapers.

Each new click sent a fresh ripple of fear through my chest. This wasn't like the secretive fun of listening to my song over and over again on the internet behind my bedroom door. This was like a terrifying and ever-widening portal to the Young Lungs' ascent to fame. Sebastian's Pixstagram was full of new comments, mostly from girls and mostly with angular self-portrait profile shots.

pumpkinbaby

Heard you guys on KPLEX this afternoon. CanNOT wait for the album!

xxAnna_bellaxx

new faves! u guys have 2 come back to portland soon!!!

livelifelove228

dancing in my chair!!

He had 11,729 followers. If things kept going at this rate, soon maybe *millions* of people would know my name. Well, they wouldn't know it was *my* name, but still.

I stayed up until it was officially Saturday morning, clicking and searching and watching his Pixstagram rack up more and more fans. As a result, I didn't open my eyes until it was officially Saturday afternoon.

I put my phone in my sweatshirt pocket, clambered out of bed, and headed for the kitchen. The fortunate thing about having one parent who's got early rising in his DNA is that there is always coffee waiting for you by the time you get up, and coffee was definitely the first step to recovering from emotional trauma. Maybe I'd even unfreeze some Eggos while I read the paper. Have a normal Saturday. Act like there wasn't a Sebastian Delacroix–shaped musical bombshell about to get dropped on the unsuspecting radios of the nation.

I could tell something was *not* normal in the kitchen as soon as I walked in. For one thing, Mom, also still in her pajamas, was standing at the counter. For another thing, there appeared to be no coffee in the pot next to her. In fact, she was scooping out coffee beans into the grinder, which she jammed down as soon as I started to say good morning.

"What?" She had to yell over the whine of the blades.

"I said, *good morning*."

The grinder sputtered to a stop. Mom took off the top and dumped it into the awaiting coffeemaker. She looked less than happy.

"I guess it's not really morning anymore," I said.

"It's not really that good, either," Mom said. She sighed and went to the sink to fill the carafe. "Sorry. I'm just in a bad mood because I haven't had caffeine yet."

"I hear that," I said, swinging up onto a stool at the island. Mom jabbed a button on the front of the coffeemaker and turned to me.

"Your father," she said, "decided that he would take the car this morning, and of course, for him, *morning* means seven a.m., and yet he still isn't back, and it's . . ."

She craned her neck at the Kit-Cat clock on the wall, which read just past one p.m., and she shook her head.

"He had time to get up early and leave but not to make more coffee. Oh, and at least he brought the paper in!"

"I'll read the paper," I said, grabbing the stack of newsprint and dragging it toward me. "Why do you need the car on Saturday anyway?"

"The glamorous life of freelance frame-building," Mom said dryly. "I have to get these frames to FedEx by three if they're going to be in Kansas City first thing Monday morning. I spent half the night shellacking and setting gold leaf to get them done on time and now they're just going to be late anyway."

"Why don't you ship them tomorrow?"

"Tomorrow's Sunday. I'm shipping them next-day air as it is, which is going to take a chunk out of my commission."

"I could take them on my bike," Sam Huang said. "How far is the store?"

"That's very sweet, Sam, but these frames weigh more than twice as much as you do." Mom gave him a little smile, and then sighed again. "Honestly. Kids, you know I love your father—host father, whatever—but sometimes I wish he wouldn't get himself so tied up in these stupid projects."

"Maybe he just needs a way to be creative," I said. "It's probably an outlet for him, or something."

"I know. I just wish he could take up . . . I don't know, stamp collecting, or fly-fishing, or something that wouldn't involve massive trips to Home Depot and pseudo-Buddhist philosophy." She sighed. "Do you think he even realizes the irony of spending so much money to learn how to let go of material possessions?"

The coffeemaker beeped and saved me from answering. I

got us mugs from the cabinet over the sink. It wasn't that I didn't see her point, but I also felt like Dad deserved a break. Besides, the yurt seemed kind of cool. It wasn't a hot tub, but it could still be a place to hang out with my friends, and maybe even get enlightened, or something.

I sipped my coffee and dug the last of the frozen waffles out of the freezer.

Mom took a long pull from her own mug, closed her eyes, and let out a slow breath. "All right. I guess I'll call the FedEx guys and see if they can do a last-minute home pickup."

"Okay." I took another sip of coffee and felt a little more heartened. Waves of cinnamony Eggo smell were drifting out of the toaster, the sun was kind of shining, and WPHL was playing something reggae-sounding that was definitely not the Young Lungs.

It was a new day. A new weekend day, actually, I noted as I leafed through the sports and business sections in search of the entertainment news. Maybe there would be a good movie out to go see with the Acronymphomaniacs, or else we could just bum around Wister, drinking Moonpenny's in the nice fall weather. Or I could do homework, but that was more a soul-crushing necessity than a spiritually fulfilling recreation. I yanked a paper towel off the roll to use as a plate and settled back into my seat to nibble at my waffles and read through the boring paper.

And then I froze, my bite of Eggo going tasteless in my mouth.

"What are you reading?" Sam Huang peered over my shoulder. His hair was kind of sticking up from his head.

"Jeez!" I squeaked. "Sam Huang, give me a little space."

"*Nattie*," Mom said. "Be nice to Sam. And why aren't you using a plate?"

"Sorry." I bunched up the newspaper. "I have to, um . . . go."

I sprinted up to my room, abandoning my waffles. Not bothering with a text message this time, I whipped out my phone and speed-dialed Tess. Each successive ring made my heart rate spike a little more.

"Come on," I said out loud. "Pick up. Pick up. *Pickuppick-upickup.*"

"Nattie?" Tess's voice sounded thick. "Whuss up? I was asleep. . . ."

"It's an emergency," I butted in. "A Sebastian-related emergency."

"What, did he call you or something? Is he in town?"

"No," I said. "Look, just go get your newspaper—"

"The newspaper? Nattie, we don't get the newspaper."

"—on page—wait, what?" I stopped. "Who doesn't get the paper?"

"I dunno, everyone who has the internet? This isn't the 1960s. What's with the paper?"

"Okay, well, there's this . . . thing? But if no one gets the newspaper maybe it's not a big deal, but, like, *we* get the newspaper even if my mom doesn't want to read it, but my dad brought it in this morning, and I bet a lot of *other* people get it, and—"

"Nattie," Tess said. "*What* are you talking about? You're babbling."

"There's an ad," I said finally. "Of the Young Lungs. In the paper. And it's huge."

There was a pause, and for a minute I thought the line had gone dead.

"Oh my God," Tess said, her voice utterly serious. "Don't move."

I heard a couple shuffling sounds and then Tess's voice away from the phone, calling up at someone.

"Mom, I'm taking the car. It's an emergency. Nattie? *Do. Not. Move.*"

"I'm in my pajamas," I said, feeling very helpless all of a sudden. "I'm not going anywhere."

"Good. What? No, Mom, no one's dying. Yes, I'll put gas in it. I'll be right there, Nattie."

"Thanks," I said, and then was struck with an idea. "Actually, Tess? Do you think we can run an errand, too?"

Twenty minutes later, Tess and I were waiting in line at the FedEx store, with five giant and apparently "FRAGILE" boxes of frames.

"Okay, *so?*" Tess raised her eyebrows expectantly. I'd refused to show her the ad at my house, mostly because my mom, though grateful, had insisted on closely supervising the loading of her packages into the belly of Tess's dad's BMW.

I looked around us, trying to determine if we were any safer here. Except for the soccer-mom-looking woman behind us and the two old, hat-wearing guys in front of us, the Main Street FedEx store was mostly deserted. The nearest bystander to me was a speaker disguised not-very-convincingly as a ficus plant.

I let out a long breath and pulled out the page from where I'd tucked it into my jeans pocket. Tess snatched it up before I'd even fully unfolded it.

"Well, have a look, then," I muttered. Tess ignored me, studying the ad intently and saying nothing for what felt like forever.

"*Well?*" I said at last.

"Wow," Tess said. "Full color."

"Is that bad?"

"But not full-page."

"Is that good?"

"Next," called the guy at the counter. The first old guy left, and I began to shove each of the packages forward, unaided by Tess, who was still absorbed in the ad.

"I'm not sure," she said. She frowned a second time, and, packages moved, I leaned over her shoulder to peer at the scrap of paper. After the initial shock of recognition, I hadn't been able to look at it alone, just ripped it out and gone upstairs to get away from it and also get dressed. It felt like too much to handle.

"You're not going to like this, Nattie."

"Next," called the guy at the counter again.

"Let me see," I said, my heart pounding. "Let me see. Tess. Let me see."

"That's us," Tess said, nodding at the counter guy. "Maybe we should just send these packages. . . ."

I hefted the packages onto the counter and pushed them forward. "Let me—"

"Kansas City?" the counter guy said.

"What?" I said.

"Yes," Tess said. "Here. I've got this." She handed me the ad in exchange for the credit card my mom had given me to pay for shipping.

I took a deep breath, and with Tess and the counter guy and the annoyed soccer mom as witnesses, I gazed down at the ad and saw for what felt like the hundredth time that same picture of Sebastian with his arms crossed and leg on an amplifier, the rest of the band looking grim and gritty behind him. And then I began to read.

*Sleepmore*—the debut album from Brooklyn's Young
    Lungs
"Vibrant and vivacious"—*Jawharp Magazine*
"14 carats of solid gold alt-rock"—*Grandophone*,
    Editor's Pick
"Your new favorite band"—Vivian Violet

"Do you want these going express, Ms. McCullough?" the counter guy asked.

"Next-day air," Tess said briskly. "Right?"

"Yeah. Whatever." My eyes were still scanning the ad, the headline, the picture of the band, looking for what Tess said I wasn't going to like, and then there it was, scrawled across the bottom corner of the ad.

**Featuring the single "Natalie," available for free download through November 15!**

Oh.

"Nattie?" Tess looked at me with alarm.

"Ms. McCullough? Do you need delivery confirmation?" The counter guy raised a hand, which Tess ignored.

"Are you okay? Are you going to faint again?" She grabbed my shoulders, and I nodded. I swallowed and opened my mouth, knowing that somewhere inside me there was a noncrazy sound that I could make come out. The soccer mom harrumphed again behind us, the counter guy gave up and printed out a receipt, and I made a sound at last, but it wasn't exactly noncrazy. Because I finally realized what was coming out of the plant speaker next to us, garbled and feedbacky but totally unmistakable.

*"Well she's tough and she's cool and she's in command . . ."*

"Is she okay?" Soccer Mom asked.

"Do you want your receipt?" the counter guy asked.

"She's fine," Tess said. "She just has these dizzy spells sometimes, nothing to worry about, just need to get her out of a public area so she can recover." She did a winning, tight-lipped smile, ducked her head politely, and grabbed me and the credit card in one swift motion toward the door, just in time for me to hear my name crackle out over the speaker.

Everything seemed slowed down and saturated, like one of those nightmares where you get stuck naked in the middle of the street and can't make your legs move. It took a full ten minutes for my vision to cartwheel back into place and I realized we were now standing in line at Moonpenny's.

"I got you a hot chocolate," Tess said, handing the cashier my mom's credit card. "It looked like you could stand to take a break from caffeine."

"Yeah," I croaked. "Probably."

Tess bent down, signed my mom's name with a flourish, and then grabbed our order from the end of the counter.

"Come on," she said, nodding toward our usual booth in the very back. "You look like you're about to have an attack of the vapors or something. Again, I mean."

"I do *not*."

Tess smiled. "There's my Nattie!"

I took a deep breath and followed her, trying to take in primary sensations: the warmth of the cup in my hands, the acrid smell of coffee beans, the unexpected relief of the all-franchise mandate that Moonpenny's play jazz and jazz alone over its non-tree-form speakers.

"Okay," Tess said once we were seated. I stared, watching her peeling the paper off a blueberry muffin, and then she stopped. "What, you want some?"

"I can't believe you just used my mom's credit card. You're committing identity theft."

"Fine, I *won't* share," Tess said, breaking the muffin in half.

"I didn't say that," I said. My single bite of Eggo felt like a lifetime ago, and I was pretty sure Mom would understand an emergency pit stop. "Besides, it's not really *her* identity I'm worried about."

"Whoa, whoa," Tess said. "Slow down. Sebastian has not stolen your identity."

"He kind of has!" I cried. "I mean, it's not like he asked my permission to write that song."

Tess frowned. "I thought you thought it was cool, though. I thought *he* thought *you* were cool, and that was cool."

"I mean . . . kind of," I said, staring into my hot chocolate. "When it was just a stupid song that I was pretty much the only one to know about."

"I'm pretty sure some of the people at Ruby's had heard it before you did," Tess pointed out.

"Yeah, but that's different. That was practically nobody. Now it's the people at Ruby's, and the DJ lady on WPHL, and Tall Zach and Endsignal and the zombie girl at the haunted house and the FedEx guy just now—"

"Okay, okay. Whoa. Slow down, greased lightning." Tess put up a hand. "You're going to give yourself an aneurysm."

"Not even eighteen years old and I'm getting aneurysms," I said miserably. "This is the worst."

"It's not," Tess said. "You know what you need?"

"A lobotomy."

"A *plan*," Tess said. "And I am the master of plans."

"What am I supposed to do, hack into their website and stop people from downloading it?"

"Nattie, you don't know *how* to hack," Tess said patiently, as if this would otherwise have been a feasible solution.

"So do *you* have a better idea?"

Tess lifted an eyebrow. "Who do you think you're *talking* to?"

She had a point.

"You've got a point," I said.

"Damn right." Tess nodded. "Even though I think it's kind of ridiculous for you to be throwing away your chance at fame and fortune as international woman of mystery *Natalie*, as your best friend, I will, however grudgingly, act in the best interest of your mental health."

"And?" I was drumming my fingers on the edge of my hot

chocolate, itching for her to just *get to the point.*

"And *here* is the plan for Operation Natalie." Tess took a deep breath. "Just lie low."

"That's it?" I cried.

"Sure," she said. "I mean, first of all, it's not like you ordinarily even *listen* to anything by living recording artists—"

"Joni is not dead, Tess."

"—no one actually calls you Natalie, *and* no one besides me, you, and Sebastian know about the Face-Touching Incident."

"Incident*s*."

"Whatever. Point is, there is literally no reason for anyone to suspect that it's about you."

"You don't think all that red-hair stuff will tip people off that it's me?"

"No offense, Nattie, but I'm not sure that most of Wister Prep even knows you exist."

"None taken, I guess," I said. "I mean, look at Wister Wemembers." I never thought I'd be this grateful to the year-book kids for getting my name wrong.

"*Which*," Tess said, "was in black and white *anyway*. So even if people want to look you up for purposes of cross-referencing, they'll get doubly thrown off your trail."

*Look me up?* That sounded simultaneously creepy and exactly like something Tess and I would do.

"Okay," I said. "So I just play it cool."

"Absolutely," Tess said. "You can't go all Pavlovian when

you hear the song like you did in the FedEx store. Just ignore it like you've ignored every other post-1960 musical act."

"You're really intent on making me sound out of touch," I said.

Tess sighed. "That's the *point*. Or, okay, here. Every time you hear the song, just think something really unsexy, like . . . I don't know, flossing, or getting a colonoscopy—"

"Or the Talent Show Incident," I said, idly locking and unlocking my phone.

Tess shuddered. "Yes. Perfect." She whipped out her phone, which was buzzing. "Ooh! And speaking of good news, here is an email from our brand-new, gay-friendly venue." She tapped up the email. "Dear Ms. Kozlowski, pleased to confirm your blah blah blah, blah blah—oh."

"Oh?" I stopped squishing the Moonpenny's muffin. "What's oh?"

"Shit," Tess said softly, and then much more loudly: "SHIT."

A lady at the table next to us put her hand to her throat, like she was literally clutching invisible pearls.

"Sorry, she's, um . . ." I cast around for a justifiable reason for a seventeen-year-old to swear in public. "College decisions?"

The lady went back to her paperback with a little cough of disgust. Tess, meanwhile, slammed her phone so hard onto the table that my hot chocolate slopped over the side of the mug.

"Shit," she said, emphatically. "Those 'socially progressive' *robber barons* at the hotel say that they have to enforce extra provisions because the nature of our event involves persons under the age of eighteen."

"Meaning?"

Tess eyed my mom's credit card, which was still sitting on the table between us. I snatched it away.

"More money," she said. "A whole freaking *lot* more."

# CHAPTER FIFTEEN

The mood at Tuesday's bake sale was decidedly grim. Tess was silently chiseling oat bars out of a Pyrex, Tall Zach was jiggling his leg under the table, Zach the Anarchist was doodling in his math textbook, and the cafeteria was beginning to drain of potential customers. And me? I was . . . waiting. Watching. I'd been so worked up about the whole thing that I'd last-minute canceled on Zach the Anarchist the day before, leaving him alone to bake and struggle with his Latin and me to listen to Sam Huang play guitar, presumably with proper wrist technique, and stew in my own freaked-out-ness.

Coming to school didn't help things, either. Maybe it was just because I spent my time with a small, semi-insular group of weirdos, or maybe it was because the Wister Prep cafeteria was a miserable place for people-watching, but today it felt mobbed. Had there always been this many people at our school?

"Nobody's going to *buy* these." Tess flung the plastic knife she'd been futilely sawing with onto the congealed mass of oat bars. "Our stuff is gross. We need to make a billion dollars, and our product looks like dog food."

"Not *all* of it is gross." Tall Zach primped the waxed paper around his fruity treats. "I already sold one of these to a guy today."

"Was that guy . . . you?" Zach the Anarchist asked.

Tall Zach said nothing, but brushed at his mouth as a clot of semipopular upperclasspeople squeezed past us—girls and a couple skinny polo-shirt dudes I recognized as cross-country *captians* from last year's Wister Wemembers. Tall Zach threw them a nod of greeting, which they returned—without stopping to make a purchase, of course—but I just stared, laser-focused as they trailed out together. Had anyone in this cafeteria—besides Tall Zach and Tess—heard the song? Did any of them follow Sebastian on Pixstagram? Did any of their parents for some reason still get home delivery of the *Wister Register* and happen to have spotted the ad? I wiped a clammy palm on the front of my jeans. So far I'd been assuming that no one would ever put together that "Natalie" of the song could *possibly* be me, because besides Tess, no one knew about the Face-Touching Incident. Incidents, plural. But with the news of the album very much out there, maybe, terrifyingly, someone would put two and two together.

"Still. These chia-oat-goji bars, or whatever, that the Cruelty-Free twins dropped off?" Tess glowered at the pan. "I'd pay you *not* to have to eat this. No *wonder* we're not getting any business."

She picked the knife back up and stabbed it right into the heart of the pan.

"Guys?" Tall Zach ripped a little square of waxed paper from his box of fruity treats. "Do you ever think that maybe it's *not* the oat bars?"

"Whatcha mean?" I asked, and dropped a dollar into the cashbox, because the fruity treats were calling to me. And then, for the billionth time that day, I checked my phone. Still nothing. No updates, no announcements, not even a picture of a taco.

"I mean, I don't know." Tall Zach tore the square of paper into tinier squares. "I just think people are kind of mad about the dance thing. Like Jake and Max said their girlfriends feel like we're taking over."

"Well, we *are* taking over," Tess said. "Besides, I don't care what a bunch of cross-country bros think."

"I thought this dance was supposed to be for everyone," I said.

"It is! This dance is so that everyone everywhere can show up and have the best time of his, her, their, or zir life." Tess scrunched her lips into a little red circle. "It's not *my* fault if no one understands that."

"See . . . yeah." Tall Zach dropped the little pile of confetti. "I'm not sure anyone outside of this club *does* understand that."

"Wait, wait. Let me get this straight. Oh, it's a figure of speech," Tess said, when Zach the Anarchist chuckled. "Are you saying nobody *likes* us?"

Tall Zach slumped his big shoulders.

"Why wouldn't people like *us*?!" Tess screeched.

"Maybe because you *yell in their ears*." Tall Zach winced and scooched his chair away.

"Or yell in general," I added.

Tess's jaw dropped. "We are an *amazing* presence in this school. *Everyone* should love us."

"Then how come no one's supporting us but us?" Tall Zach had actually leaped up from his chair. "Maybe you need to stop trying so hard to force an agenda on everybody."

Tess gaped. Zach the Anarchist mumbled something about getting tea and disappeared into the crowd. I, meanwhile, nibbled on my fruity treat and was praying for someone, *anyone*, to come by the table at that exact moment and human-shield us out of the blast radius of Tess's fury when a someone arrived.

"Hey hey!"

It was Meredith White, looking as sunny as always in two braids and a bright-blue sweater, one hand securely wrapped around the handle to her rolly backpack.

"Hey," I said generously. Meredith might not be my first choice for emergency interloper, but her cheery annoyingness was infinitely more tolerable than one of my best friends ripping out the throat of another.

"How's the bake sale . . . going?" Meredith's smile dimmed as it went from various picked-over offerings of cupcakes and cookies to Tall Zach with his arms folded to a still-twitchy, knife-clutching Tess.

"Not bad," I said. It was obviously going more than a little bad, but Meredith's arrival was a welcome distraction.

"Yeah," Tess said bitterly. "We've got almost five bucks in nickels alone."

"Cool," Meredith said. "Well, everything looks really yummy!"

"Thanks," I said, just as Tess said, "You don't have to lie."

I silently stomped on Tess's booted toes and grinned, no matter how much it pained me to pretend that *yummy* was a word normal sixteen-year-olds used.

Meredith fussed with the end of her braid. "What's good?"

"The oat bars are gluten-free," Tall Zach said.

"Oh, um . . ." Meredith looked uncomfortable, as if she didn't know whether to praise them or avoid them for this.

"Try a snickerdoodle," I heard a voice say. "They're excellent."

Meredith jumped and dropped the rolly-bag handle as Zach the Anarchist slid by her toward the table, a cup of tea in hand.

"Sorry." Zach picked up the handle of her bag and handed it to her, like rolling backpacks didn't deserve to be abandoned wherever they fell.

"Thanks." She was smiling even wider now. At him. "Okay. Why not?"

She handed me over some change and helped herself to a snickerdoodle.

"Wow." Meredith closed her eyes as she took a bite. "Did you make them?"

"Yeah," Zach said, lowering himself into the chair next to me.

"That's awesome," Meredith said. She made a little humming sound. "Yummy."

"I helped," I said. "By the way."

"Mmph." Meredith spun a *wait a sec* finger by her braids as she polished off her snickerdoodle. "That was great. But actually, I came over to talk to Tess."

"Me?" Tess jerked to attention from where she'd been sulking. "What?"

Meredith rocked on her heels. "Did you guys ever find a venue? Zach told me in econ there was a problem with the old one."

"I did?" said Tall Zach.

"No, Zach West."

I looked at Zach, or the top of Zach's head, because Zach was back to reading about probability theory.

Tess sighed. "As of right now, for a cool extra seven hundred and fifty American dollars over budget, we're having the dance at the ballroom at the Wister Holiday Inn."

Tall Zach wrinkled his nose. "The one by the highway on-ramp?"

"No, the one by the gas station."

"The one where they found a torso in a trash can," muttered Zach the Anarchist.

"That was never corroborated!"

"Okay," Meredith said slowly. "Well, my dad's on the board of the Woodlawn Museum of Art, and they have this kinda big event room." She tugged at one of her braids. "It's got a mural on the wall and everything. It's really great. And I asked him and he said that we could totally have it there, if you want." She paused. "For free."

"Are you serious?" Tess rocketed from her chair and flung her arms around Meredith. "We totally want."

"Um, great!" Meredith squeaked from beneath Tess's leather-jacketed embrace.

"Ugh. I could kiss you right now." Tess let Meredith go. "Not that I will. Because I'm *not* trying to force an agenda on anyone." She threw a pointed look at Tall Zach. He sighed.

"That's awesome." Zach the Anarchist glanced up from his math book, and Meredith bobbed her head. She looked . . . blushy. And she wasn't exactly meeting his eyes.

"Well, I really wanted to help the cause," she said. "Just because I'm not, um, you know—"

"I'm pretty straight, too," Zach the Anarchist said. "So it's fine."

"Yes! See?" Tess pointed wildly from Meredith to Zach. "We're doing it. We're reaching the public."

Meredith grinned. "Well, if there's anything else I can do . . ."

"Great!" Tess cried. "Zach the Anarchist, don't you need help baking all these?"

Zach the Anarchist darted the quickest look at me. "I mean, I had Nattie, but—"

"OMG! Nattie!" Meredith smacked her forehead. "I totally forgot to ask you. Did you know Sebastian's band has an album out? Like, a full one?"

So much for being clueless.

"Um," I said. "No." I wiped my palms on my jeans a few times.

Meredith frowned. "Sebastian didn't, like . . . tell you about it?"

Zach the Anarchist was not looking at his math book anymore. He was looking, just out of the corner of his eye, at me. And I could feel it.

"No," I said, probably too loudly. My traitorous heart was beating like a drum machine in my chest. "Why would he?"

"Oh, um, no reason." Meredith fiddled with the button of her backpack handle. "I thought because—"

"He and I aren't really even friends," I said, maybe a little too loudly. "I mean, I don't know him super well."

I glanced back at Zach the Anarchist, but he'd already gotten out of his chair.

"Oh, okay." Meredith was back to a sunny, if confused, smile. "Well, you should totally listen to it. I can burn you a copy if you want."

"I mean, I haven't listened to them since the show or anything." *Lie.* "It's not really my thing."

Mercifully, the bell rang.

"The bell!" I almost shouted. "Look at that!"

"Or hear that, even," said Zach the Anarchist's voice from behind me. Meredith giggled a very annoying giggle.

"Peace out, dorks," Tess said. "I have to go announce our good news to student council."

She swung her bag on her shoulder and clomped away. Then Tall Zach tucked the remaining fruity treats into his shoe box, gave us a salute, and bounded off. Which left just me, Meredith, and Zach the Anarchist. Well, us, and the rest of the people flooding out of the cafeteria. But I was suddenly a lot less concerned with them.

"Well," Zach said. "Econ?"

"I'm not in econ," I said.

"Not you."

"Sure," Meredith said.

"What about the money?" I said.

"Counted it," Zach said. "And you're the treasurer anyway."

"Well . . . what about all this food?"

Zach looked back at the table. Besides the oat bars, two stalwart cupcakes were the only apparent survivors of the bake sale.

"Here." Zach thrust one of the cupcakes into Meredith's hands.

"Oh, I . . ." Meredith looked like she was about to refuse, but then didn't. Something passed between her and Zach, like a subliminal telegraph, and it made me uncomfortable. "Thanks." Unlike Tess, Meredith seemed to favor showing as many teeth as possible when she smiled.

"There's still stuff left, ahem." I actually said the word *ahem*. "Shouldn't we wrap it up or something?"

Not the oat bars, obviously, but I did feel bad for that poor smudged leftover cupcake. Someone really should've bought it. Gingerly, I picked it up and tipped it around to examine.

Meredith wrinkled her nose. "It looks like someone licked it."

"Nobody *licked* it." I clutched the cupcake to my chest, to the extent that I could without getting frosting on myself. "Someone just smudged the rose on top."

"Don't be gross, Nattie." Zach said. "No one's going to want a week-old cupcake that somebody licked. Just toss it." He went to dump the assorted detritus from our table into the trash, and Meredith crowned it with the fluttering wrapper from her cupcake. They left together, her laughing at some remark I didn't make out.

"Well," I said to the trash can as I hefted the cashbox. "Didn't *that* just work out perfectly."

The smudged cupcake, abandoned on a heap of paper towels, Gatorade bottles, and gluten-free baked goods, did not answer.

From there, it didn't get better. It got much, much worse.

When the word got out that Sebastian Delacroix's band was actually a thing, I had to play it preternaturally cool as what felt like every heterosexual girl and even some of the boys at Wister Prep snapped up a copy of *Sleepmore*. When Ron's Records, quite possibly the only physical music store still in existence, put up a giant poster of the same black-and-white Young Lungs photo I'd practically burned into my eyelids, I had to start averting my eyes every morning as Dad drove me to school down Main Street. When WPHL started playing the single in earnest during their evening music block, I surreptitiously flipped the kitchen radio to NPR and feigned an interest in national politics. I *did* allow myself to skim the *Wister Register* when the paper even ran an article about Sebastian and his small-town roots, only to find it qualified at the end with "Mr. Delacroix could not be reached for comment."

Truer words had never been spoken.

The ironic kicker, the part that really bugged me, was how the threat of being revealed as some kind of sex goddess was making me feel the most ungainly and least attractive I'd ever been in my life. I'd never realized just how *everywhere* music is. The radio at home. The grocery store. The car rolling down the street with its windows open even thought it was November. And even when you're somewhere ostensibly quiet, like the library, everyone is still plugged in to their phones and computers, lost in their own world of music while you stare at them, terrified by the infinite possibilities of their silent listening. Every set of speakers was a ticking time bomb, ready to unleash the four-chord opening at a moment's notice and wail to another unsuspecting group of people about how sexy and mysterious I was.

For almost two weeks, I woke up to the sound of the guitars and went to bed in the glow of my computer, watching their YouTube channel rack up more hits as they went from city to city in a little thread, spidering outward from Los Angeles up to Seattle and then cutting down into the heart of flyover country. And every day, there were more Pixstagram comments to obsess over.

> sammysamsam
>
> great, great show tonight. come back soon. i'll be waiting x
>
> dis_girl_on_fire
>
> YOUNG LUNGS WOW I'M SERIOSLY DIGING IT
>
> caelenorear
>
> any chance u will ever come to Ireland????
>
> _brighteyesbigdreams_
>
> well, it's official . . . i'm jealous of natalie, whoever she is!

And then there was Vivian Violet. Her site seemed to be obsessed with all things Young Lungs, and so I made it my first stop during each day's stalker session. One evening, sitting at the kitchen counter, staring at all the purpleness of it on my laptop, I heard Sam Huang walk in. He was headed for the fridge, singing some a cappella–sounding *da*s and *ba*s, and a few measures in, the syllables started to form a melody, a *familiar* melody, even if all I was hearing was the tenor part. Cold terror clutched my heart.

"What is that?" I snapped my laptop shut. "Sam?"

Sam looked up from the sandwich he was making. "What?"

"That song you were singing just now. What was it?"

"Uh . . ." Sam shrugged. "Nothing? Just something for A Cappella. It's secret. I . . . I've already said too much."

He assembled his sandwich in record time and scampered out of the kitchen.

"Et tu, Sam Huang?" I yelled after him. He either hadn't heard me or *pretended* not to. But if the song had penetrated as far as the Owen Wister Preparatory Academy a cappella group, things were bad.

Heart pounding, I took a deep breath, reopened my laptop, and stared at Vivian Violet's latest #younglungs post. Maybe, as long as I absorbed every scrap of Young Lungs-related information floating out in the ether, I could somehow control it. Maybe.

What is it about a female first name that makes for such catchy songwriting? Dante had Beatrice, Orpheus had Eurydice, and practically every music act since the dawn of recorded music has had at least one single that singles out that one special girl.

So Vivian Violet thought I was in good company. Great.

"Michelle" by the Beatles—Allegedly inspired by students Paul McCartney saw at an art party, this is the song responsible for teaching a whole generation of kids how to fake-speak French.

I vaguely remembered hearing this once, probably accompanied by Dad's commentary on how the Beatles are overrated. I clicked the MP3 link beneath the blurb and listened. The song was pleasant and strummy enough, but the French accents were pretty atrocious.

"Roxanne" by the Police—Leave it to Sting to record probably the most upbeat song ever recorded about unrequited love, and to give it a white-boy reggae beat.

This one sounded jumpy and unsettled, like a cross between a headache and a heart attack, where the singer strained his lyrics so much I couldn't actually hear what he was saying.

"867-5309 (Jenny)" by Tommy Tutone—I can't decide which would be worse, having that phone number, or being named "Jenny" around the time when this song was released.

Another one I kind of recognized. At least Sebastian hadn't released my phone number.

"Hey There Delilah" by the Plain White T's—Ugh, this again. If I never hear this nasal earworm tribute to pathetic love for the rest of my life, it will be too soon. Can you believe this went to number one?

Harsh. I clicked the link, and a few bars in, I sort of saw what she meant, but mostly I felt for poor Delilah. I wondered if the lead singer of this band was into sending cryptic text messages and writing songs instead of actually having conversations.

Anyway, this is all just to say congrats to VV faves the Young Lungs for selling out and cracking into the Billboard

Alternative Songs 200. Whether fact or fiction, Sebastian Delacroix's lost lady love "Natalie" is probably going to be the nation's next mystery girlfriend. Don't believe me? Come out in person to catch the YLs at their East Coast kickoff tour this Thanksgiving weekend at the Knitting Factory in Brooklyn. And who knows? Maybe Natalie herself will show up.

*Oh yeah, maybe she will,* I thought grimly. *Or maybe she'll continue to lie low so that she can survive her junior year of high school.*

"Hey, Nattie."

I jumped, which in turn made Dad look a little alarmed. I was beginning to hate the sound of my own name.

"Hey," I said. I tried for a perky, ordinary Nattie-sounding tone of voice, because I was pretty sure the only thing worse than skyrocketing to national fame for being a heartbreaker was having to explain that fact to your *parents.*

But Dad wasn't so easily fooled.

"Something's up," he said.

"No," I said quickly, locking my phone. "Nothing's up."

"I'm your father," Dad said. "Or, more to the point, you're *my* daughter. I know a worried Schwartz when I see one."

I blew out a breath. There was no getting by him. Maybe I could conjure a reasonable alternative concern to throw him off my trail.

"It's all this . . . uh, college stuff," I lied. "The SATs and stuff are really stressing me out."

"You haven't even taken them yet, Nattie."

"Yeah, well, you know." I gave a noncommittal grimace.

Dad crossed his arms over his Commander Cody T-shirt, a surefire indicator he was flipping into problem-solver mode, and gave me a sage nod.

"I think I do," he said. "Because I know not just what you *mean*, but also what you *need*."

"What?"

"You need a place to clear your head. A place where stress and negative thinking don't exist. A place of emotional detachment."

Oh no.

"Dad," I started, but it was too late. Dad was grinning like a kid on Christmas morning, which didn't seem very emotionally detached to me, and then he nodded toward the yard.

"C'mon, Gann. You need some time in the yurt."

I glanced out the back door at the gray November evening that lay in chilly, foggy wait outside the warmth of the house.

"I think I'm okay," I said.

"Nattie, I'm your father," Dad said. "I know what's good for you. And besides, I just put the canvas over it! You have to check it out."

I heaved the most silent sigh possible and tugged up the zipper of my Wister Prep hoodie. Dad scrambled around to slip on his weekend Crocs and open the back door, letting in a gust of air that was as wet as it was cold.

The muddy ground of the backyard had frozen, the little

pockets of dirt crystals splintering underneath my bare feet as I crossed the yard. Ahead of me, the newly covered yurt structure was a wilting dome of canvas, like a droopy tent for a miniature circus. Dad was taking tripping steps ahead of me, positioning himself right by the entrance so he could usher me in like some kind of yurt butler.

"See, the door is low, so that you can't enter the yurt without bending down and humbling yourself."

"So you've said," I said, not pointing out that it didn't get much humbler than muddy bare feet and an old sweatshirt. Dad pushed open the hobbit-sized door and ducked in, and I humbled myself after him into the yurt.

Inside, it was slightly less cold, appreciably less damp, and smelled like a combination of loamy soil and what must have been Epifanes-brand varnish. It was almost an actual building now, which made sense given that Dad had been spending every waking weekend minute assembling, tethering, post-hole digging, and shellacking. I couldn't stand up fully unless I stood right in the center, which was more or less impossible thanks to a stout support beam in the middle. At one side, there was a little platform that Dad had furnished lavishly with my old beanbag chair and a couple scented candles.

"Canvas," Dad said, tapping his knuckles against the material protecting us from the elements. "Now, this is just up temporarily until I get it water-treated, so that it'll be suitable for use in all seasons."

"Assuming you can make it out here without freezing,"

I said. I slumped over to the beanbag chair, which made a plastic rustling sound when I sat in it.

"Just you wait. Once I get the Franklin stove in here, it'll be nice and toasty. You could even spend the night with your friends out here, if you want. Maybe over the long weekend coming up."

I tried to imagine the Acronymphos crammed into the yurt, Tall Zach practically bent double and Tess complaining loudly about getting dirt on her jeans. Zach the Anarchist might like it if it was sufficiently warmed.

"I think they're all leaving Wister for Thanksgiving," I said. Technically, this was true: Zach Bitterman was going to Boston, "out of town" for Tess meant spending the day forty minutes away in Media, and Zach West didn't live in Wister to begin with.

"What about that big party you guys always do?"

"Friendsgiving happens the Tuesday of Thanksgiving week. And it's always at school. That's kind of the point. Actually," I said, seeing a chance for a yurt-scape, "I should go call Tess about it. She probably wants to get some details worked out before the weekend's over."

"Oh, okay." Dad seemed only the tiniest bit bummed that I didn't want to stay out and freeze in the yurt with him. And I felt a little bad about it, too, but the fact was that no matter how relaxing and humbling the yurt was, it was still a ridiculous thing to have squatting outside our house where our backyard neighbors could see it.

"It's great, Dad," I reassured him.

"Do you feel a little better? Like you have a newfound clarity?"

I looked around at the beige, canvas-y glow of the walls, the tons of screws that could act as coat hooks, the admittedly humble dirt floor, and weirdly, I *did* feel a little better. In the yurt, there was no stereo in constant danger of blaring the Young Lungs news or computer stuffed with new blog posts about Sebastian. In the yurt, there was barely anything at all, and that was nice.

"Yeah," I said, and shivered again. Even with all the internet stalking I'd been doing, I still couldn't control where the song was going. I still didn't have a clear read on Sebastian and whatever relationship he and I had, or were having, or might have. In fact, I still didn't have *anything* from Sebastian besides a string of stream-of-consciousness messages. And even those had stopped when the album news had come out.

"Could use a little light, though," Dad said thoughtfully. I only nodded, because with my newfound clarity, I realized I had to stop playing it cool, at least a little. If I wanted to know what Sebastian really thought about me, if he really *liked* me or wanted me or whatever, I was going to have to ask him. So, with trembling fingers, I composed a Pixstagram message:

> to: sebdel
>
> hey, can we talk?

# CHAPTER SIXTEEN

"I think she's a junior. I took her yearbook picture last year. Natasha Something or Other."

"No way. It can't be her."

"Why not? She has red hair."

I was late to the rescheduled OWPALGBTQIA meeting, and I was only getting later. Since we had a half day Tuesday, the cafeteria would be closed, thereby killing our chance to have a bake sale and giving us a good excuse to celebrate Friendsgiving in Dr. Frobisher's room instead. Still, bake sale or no bake sale, I knew today was likely to include a few solid minutes of Tess grilling me over budget details, and just because I *hadn't* ever taken an econ class didn't mean I couldn't be as good as someone who did, so I had swung by the computer lab after bio to print out my new and improved spreadsheets. I was hovering at the print station, where the black-and-white was chugging out slow copies of my documents, when it occurred to me that the conversation I was overhearing was about me.

"Okay, I'm ordering tickets. December fourth at the TLA in Center City."

"It says it's twenty-one-plus."

"God, Celeste, so bring your fake."

As another sheet spat out of the printer, I took a slow, stealthy look behind me. Two senior girls with matching flat-iron-straight hair were casting twin, hard-eyed glances across the room, partially veiled by the giant screens of iMacs but definitely in my direction. I swallowed hard, squared my shoulders, and *acted* like I couldn't hear them, while in actuality I had never listened to anything more intently in my life. If they could see me, I didn't want them to know I could see *them*.

"I knew Sebastian was going to get famous," the first one said. "He's always had *such* a good voice."

"I know, right?"

I refrained from rolling my eyes, even though they couldn't see me. Apparently they had not been present during the Talent Show Incident.

The first looked at her reflection in her phone. "I have red hair, too. Maybe *I'm* the one Sebastian's in love with."

The other girl snorted, which made the first one pout.

"Come on! Like it's really that rando junior. I see her hanging out in the cafeteria with all the gay club kids. She's probably a—"

And then she called me a very not-okay word for gay people, a word that was so not-okay that my face burned as I took my sheets out of the printer. If I were Tess, I'd jump over there and threaten to tear out their jugulars for using a slur. If I were Tall Zach, I'd explain to them, politely but firmly, how hurtful it is to say things like that. If I were Zach the Anarchist, I'd flip them off.

But I wasn't. I was just plain old Nattie. Too inconsequential to even get the right name in the yearbook.

"God, that freakin' club." The first one groaned a horrible nasal groan. "That one girl is suddenly *everywhere*."

"Like being on a billboard wasn't enough?"

"Omigod, I forgot about that. Of *course* it's her."

They laughed. I cringed. Between the blatant bigotry and the mention of her past as an orthodontic model, Tess would be *furious* if she were here.

"But yeah, like, I'm not homophobic or anything?" the first one went on. "But they're turning Winter Formal into a protest. It's supposed to just be a dance. I don't even, like, want to *go* now."

"Dude, didn't you hear?" The second girl dropped her voice. "*No one's* going."

The final page was finally stuttering out of the printer's mouth, but I hit Cancel to make it shut up.

"Everyone's going to Brian's carriage house instead. We're throwing our *own* party."

But that was the last I heard, because they were leaving, and I only had four and a half of my five pages. I hit Resume, then grabbed the sheaf of papers and made a beeline for the OWPALGBTQIA meeting, my heartbeat clogging up my throat the whole way.

People were guessing. Not guessing especially well, but they were homing in on me. And once they did, there was no amount of lies or dumb nonanswers that could keep everyone fooled, especially someone as not-dumb as Zach the Anarchist. Everyone was going to know about my hips and thighs and—ugh—breasts, like I was some kind of dissection project.

And even worse, Sebastian still hadn't answered my message.

By the time I pulled back the door into Dr. Frobisher's room, I felt like I was going to tremble away into a puddle, right in the middle of the floor.

Of course, there was no space for me to do such a thing.

"Well, *I'm* just saying that we shouldn't even be celebrating this holiday."

To no one's surprise, Alison was dominating the discussion. I slunk into a desk at the back of the room and tried to catch my breath. Tess was at the blackboard in front of a half-finished list of potluck contributions and looking like she'd rather stuff Alison instead of a turkey.

"That's why it's called *Friendsgiving*," Tall Zach said with his characteristic patience. "We just get together with our friends and eat a lot of food."

"Exactly," Tess said, nodding. "It's firmly anticolonialist."

Alison glowered in her seat.

"Well, *I'm* not going to bring anything," she said.

"That's fine," Tess said, "since I sincerely doubt anyone else wants vegan food."

"I like that fake sausage stuff," Bryce piped up.

"Shut up, Bryce," Alison said.

"Why do you have to be so negative, Alison?" Chihiro said, fiddling with the edge of her sweatshirt sleeve.

"Yeah," Bryce said, as if slowly realizing that Alison *wasn't* an outgoing cheerleader type. "I was just trying to pay a compliment to the food of your people."

"I can make one of my pies with shortening instead of butter," Zach the Anarchist said.

Everyone stared.

"So it's vegan," he explained.

"Seriously?" Tess looked incredulous, but Zach did a kind of affirmative shrug, so she chalked the word *vegan* in parentheses next to Zach's entry for *two pies* on the blackboard.

"Okay. Anyone else? Have we covered all of our dietary bases?" Tess stared down the rest of the club in a way that was hardly inviting to further contributions.

"Corn bread," Endsignal said without raising his hand.

"*Mashedpotatoes?*" whispered the freshperson in their hoodie.

"Gyoza," Chihiro said. "They're dumplings."

"Fake sausage," Bryce said.

Tess said nothing, just raised her eyebrows and took it all

down onto the board. It was certainly going to be an unusual holiday spread, that was for sure.

"Okay. Good. We should be fine, then. I'll bring paper plates and stuff. Dr. Frobisher says we can use her room again as long as we clean everything up, so . . . same time tomorrow, I guess." Tess slapped the desk in front of her, making Bryce jump in his seat.

"Adjourned! Until Friendsgiving, anyway."

The room stirred and began getting to its feet. I barely had time to slide the rest of the way out of my jacket when Tess was at the other side of my desk.

"Nattie, I really need—"

"Listen, Tess," I said, "I need to talk to you."

"I'm not canceling Friendsgiving, if that's what you want," Tess said. "It's a tradition. People *love* Friendsgiving."

"Alison doesn't," I pointed out.

"Alison doesn't like *anything*," Tess said. "And she'll warm up to it if Zach makes her her own special pie." She nodded over my shoulder, to where Zach the Anarchist was standing in his leather jacket with his backpack over his shoulder and his eyebrows up.

"Everything okay?"

I looked from Tess, who was looking limp and very un-Tess-like, to Zach, who was standing practically at my elbow and whose eyes were, I couldn't help but notice, *very* blue today. Now did not seem like the time to abandon my *play it cool* strategy.

"Yup," I lied, putting on the most cheerful front I could muster.

"How's the budget?"

I made a face. "Well . . ."

I went to hand him my printouts, but Tess snatched them away.

"It doesn't matter," she said. "We've already paid the student council."

Zach frowned. "Wait, what?"

"Paid? How?" I said.

Tall Zach, who'd been at the blackboard drawing a pilgrim riding a unicorn, turned around but didn't say anything.

"We were seven hundred dollars short of the total last week," Zach the Anarchist said. "There's no way we made that up yesterday."

"We didn't," Tess said.

"Then where did the money come from?"

Tess folded the spreadsheets in half again, which was getting tricky because there were so many sheets. "If you must know, I paid it. With my own money."

"Tess!" My mouth actually hung open. "Are you serious? Seven hundred dollars?"

"Yes, I'm *serious*," Tess said, and rapped the folded spreadsheets against her palm. "This dance *has* to happen, Nattie. It *has* to. Besides, what was I even going to spend that money on?"

"College?" I said.

"A car?" Zach the Anarchist said.

"Clothes with little spikes on them?" said Tall Zach.

"Seriously, Tess," I said. "It's not worth it. We'll just figure some other way to—"

"It *will* be worth it," Tess said. She was looking kind of ferocious, actually, with her eyes big and bright and her jaw so tight it was almost hard to understand her. "It *will*. And none of you get to tell me how to spend my money. If I have to get personally invested, then so be it." She took a short, hard inhale through the nose. "So if what you needed to tell me was that the money issue is over, then yes, I already know. Case closed."

Everyone looked at me.

"I, um," I said, thinking back to the computer room. "I just said I had to tell you *something*, actually."

"If it's about tomorrow, uh . . ." Zach the Anarchist shrugged. "Do you want to help with the pies? I mean, if you want."

"Excuse *you*, interrupter." Tess barged in front of Zach the Anarchist. "What did you need to tell me, Nattie?"

I looked from Tess's face to Zach's.

"Oh, it's, um . . ." I swallowed. "Just that a bunch of people aren't, uh, actually going. To the Winter Formal, I mean."

Tess's face went ashen. "What?" she breathed.

"I just heard them in the computer room," I said. "Two seniors. Celeste and, uh—"

"Celeste Franklin and Brooke Lieberman?" Tall Zach bailed on his drawing. "I know them. They're dating some guys on the team. They're—"

"They're in *A Cappella*," Tess said shortly. "And they probably can't stand something not being about them, for once. What are they trying to do?"

"They said something about not going to the dance. About throwing their own party," I said. "I guess so—"

"So they don't have to go to ours," Tess said. She put a fist to her mouth, and then slammed it against the bookshelf. "Dammit! Dammit dammit *dammit!*"

On top of the bookshelf, some eighth grader's model of the Acropolis rattled forlornly.

"It's okay, Tess," Tall Zach said. "We don't even want them there, right?"

"No!" Tess cried. "Of course I want them there! I want everyone there! That's the whole point! You think I cashed in all my savings bonds from my grandma just so *we* could have a party *by ourselves?*"

"Savings bonds?" I said. "You didn't say it was *savings bonds.*"

"What, you think I just *have* seven hundred dollars lying around? No, this was a big deal." Tess sank into a desk chair, defeated. I sat next to her and petted her back, which was kind of hard with all the zippers in her T-shirt.

"This blows," Tess muttered from her hands. "Or sucks. Or

whatever expression doesn't malign some kind of sexual activity. Dammit!" She kicked the leg of the desk and rubbed at her face. "Hey, Mom and Dad, I secretly spent all my christening money to throw this giant party to show you how normal gay kids are, and nobody from the rest of the school wanted to come because we're such *freaks*. Oh, and, by the way, I'm a lesbian. Ta-da!"

"Tess. Hey. Come on." I plopped into the desk next to her, Tess didn't move, so I gave her a knee-to-knee bump. "*Tessica*."

That got her attention. "What?"

"Remember how we met?"

"What, in second grade? No offense, Nattie, but who cares?"

I reached across the desk for Tess's shoulder and sort of squeeze-pinched it with my fingers to show I wasn't, in fact, offended. This was just how Tess worked.

"It was at lunch, remember? The yogurt?"

Tess sniffed, but less loudly. "Oh. Yeah." She cracked a tiny smile. "I forgot about that. You were *so* excited to finally eat that yogurt."

"Because you showed me the lid trick!"

"Can . . . someone fill me in here?" Zach the Anarchist asked.

"The lid trick," Tess explained, "is when you fold the foil yogurt top thing into a little scoop and eat with it."

"That's . . ." Tall Zach wrinkled his nose. "Okay. You do you."

"It was second grade!"

"*Anyway*," I said. "I had forgotten my spoon, and I was *really* disappointed about not getting to eat my yogurt—shut up," I added, when Zach the Anarchist smiled. "Yogurt was my dessert." I took a deep breath. "The point is, Tess, that I saw you were the kind of person who wouldn't just throw away her yogurt if she didn't have a spoon. You figured stuff out. And that's when I was like, wow, I need to be friends with this girl."

"Really?"

"Really." I leaned out of my desk so I could stretch my arm over her shoulders. "So, like, if anyone can fix this, it's you. The Tessica Kozlowski *I* know doesn't just give up."

"For the last time, my name is not—" Tess sighed, but she was smiling now—a real, big, lips-together smile. She smashed her face into my shoulder and then looked back up. "Okay. Okay, fine. We're going to figure this out."

"So . . . what do we do?" Zach the Anarchist asked.

Tess sniffled one last time and wiped a streak of eyeliner off her cheek. "Make everyone in this school want to come to our dance," she said resolutely. "Or *die trying*."

# CHAPTER SEVENTEEN

"Some of these?"

Nothing felt less useful to the cause than a trip to the supermarket, but since Friendsgiving was tomorrow, Zach the Anarchist and I were in the frozen foods section of the Round Earth Gourmet Grocery, shopping. While Zach was grabbing bags of blueberries, I had located a box of pie crusts—efficiently, or so I thought. Zach looked at the box in my hand like it had rat poison in it.

"No way."

I crossed my arms, which kind of forced the pie crusts into my armpit.

"What's wrong with them? They're even organic," I said.

"Organic has nothing to do with it," Zach said.

"Those berries are organic," I said, pointing at the bag in his hands. "*J'accuse!*"

"Calm down." Zach looked around the aisle, where the only other shopper was a woman in a long coat evaluating two packages of sweet potato fries. "There's no need to have a meltdown in the middle of the store."

"I am *not* melting down," I said, and realized too late how much the words made me sound like a three-year-old having a temper tantrum.

Zach raised an eyebrow and I shifted my weight.

"It's too cold here for *anything* to melt," I said.

"Give me that." Zach took the package of pie crusts and replaced them inside the giant glass freezer.

"The reason I got frozen blueberries," he said, leading us toward the baking section, "is that they're frozen when they're still in season, so they won't taste as bad as the fresh ones they ship in from Argentina this time of year. The organic thing is just a bonus."

"Oh," I said.

"And pie crust," Zach said, "is just flour, salt, water, and butter. Or in this case, shortening."

We stopped in front of a wall of brick-shaped packages promising "No Trans Fat" and "You'll Assume It's Butter"!

I made a face as Zach selected an appropriately cruelty-free chunk of shortening and headed for the checkout.

"I can't believe you're buying this stuff just so one person can eat your pies," I said.

To our left, the woman with sweet potato fries was now arguing with the cashier over an expired two-for-one coupon as Zach swiped the groceries one by one across the self-scanner.

"I guess. I mean, I bought these, too," he said, zipping the blueberries over the little red beam.

"Yeah, and? Everybody likes blueberries."

"Right. But usually I'd use strawberries."

It took me a minute to realize what he meant. Not using strawberries, so that I could eat the pies. Which probably meant something.

Didn't it?

*It means you're friends*, I told myself, before I could even articulate the question in my mind. *He bought shortening for Alison, for crying out loud, and* nobody *likes her, except for maybe all the animals whose lives she's saved.*

"Thanks," I said. It seemed like a good start.

"You're welcome," Zach said. "I mean, it would suck if you died."

"Nattie!"

I spun around at the sound of my name, to see Meredith White, of all people, bouncing over to us from the doors.

"Hey . . . Meredith," I said. "What are you doing here?"

It must've come out a little too accusatory, because Zach the Anarchist gave me a look. Meredith, however, didn't seem to notice.

"Zach invited me to come help," she said. She was wearing actual earmuffs.

"Oh," I said. "Great."

"Yup," Meredith agreed, and for a moment we just stood

there at the end of the checkout lane, listening to the woman harrumph over her coupon and the checkout girl's voice cutting out over the PA system.

And that was when I heard it.

*"Well she's tough and she's cool and she's in command."*

"Wow!" I said, loudly, to hopefully to cover up the sound of the radio. Meredith frowned.

"Hey, isn't this—"

"A *crazy* amount of butter?" I said, crazily. "Zach, why are you buying so much butter? That's an awful lot of butter for one Friendsgiving."

I sounded insane, but talking too much had successfully covered up the chorus.

"I'm in charge of pies for the family Thanksgiving, too," he said. "So I need a lot of butter."

"Oh," I said, trying to sound normal despite the fact that my sex anthem was blaring out in the middle of Zach's rich-person grocery store. "Is Bethany coming home?"

"Who's Bethany?" Meredith asked.

"My sister," Zach said, and shook his head. "She and her boyfriend are staying in New York. His family's there."

"Oh," I said. "Well, more pie for you guys, I guess!"

I laughed, hopefully loud enough over the music. Zach, being Zach, said nothing.

"*I* usually end up having to make the stuffing, because otherwise no one remembers," I went on. "My mom and my aunt are turkey fanatics and my dad is content eating nothing but cranberry sauce and celery with peanut butter on it. But as you may recall, I'm not the greatest cook, so sometimes it ends up kind of crunchy."

"The stuffing or the peanut butter?" Meredith asked.

"Both, actually." I shook my head. "I have no idea why he does that. I think it's a Schwartz thing? Or maybe just a my-dad thing."

"Oh," Meredith said politely. "I see."

Without a word, Zach punched the Finish and Pay button, fed in two twenties, and went to bag our stuff. I stayed totally still, Sebastian's voice echoing from the tile floors to the display cases of probiotic sodas, as the song ended.

"Well," he said. "Let's go, I guess."

Laden with butter-filled bags, the three of us walked back to Zach's house, me in awkward silence and Meredith contentedly chattering away about something.

"And so I was thinking of making one of the freshmen an editor next year, but usually it's just rising juniors, so—hey, buddy!" She stooped as we came into the kitchen, where an overjoyed Bacon was yipping and jumping in circles at the arrival of humans.

"That's Bacon," I said. "Named for Francis Bacon, who was a philosopher."

"Hey, buddy!" Meredith said again, clearly not concerned with what dogs were actually properly called. I tried to give Bacon an affectionate nudge with my knee since my hands were full, but he was too busy weaving in between Meredith's puffy boots.

"Wow, he really likes me."

I dumped my armful of butter on the counter. "You probably smell weird."

"He's just hyper from being cooped up all day." Zach plugged his phone into the stereo and turned up the volume to its usual crash and crunch, then grabbed all the boxes I'd just put on the counter and swept them into the freezer.

"Aren't we going to use that?" I said, tugging off my sneakers and jamming them in the shoe rack by the door.

"Keeping the fat cold makes the crust flakier," Meredith said.

"Yeah," Zach said. "Exactly."

"I love baking," Meredith said. "I do it all the time with my mom."

She smiled, as if she had no idea how weird it was to still require adult supervision for food preparation at our age, and Zach reached up into a cabinet and pulled down a squat machine with a removable bowl and a bunch of clanking plastic parts on top.

"It's a food processor," he said, to my stare.

"I knew that," I said. Bacon nuzzled my leg, and I hunkered

down on the floor to scratch his belly. He stretched out as far as his stout doggy legs could and let out a floppy-mouthed sigh. "I'm just not that into cooking."

"Oh man, we have the same scale at my house," Meredith said.

"What *are* the odds?" I said. From my prone position, I could only see the bottom of the counter, the fridge, and Zach's ankles. He was wearing black jeans, of course, but one of his socks was red.

"Cool," I heard Zach say.

"Is Nattie just going to lie there?" I heard Meredith say.

"I'm right here." I ran my hand diligently over Bacon's belly. "Besides, it's comfortable here." I lay back and stared at the ceiling, the chandelier of pots and pans, and listened to the soft sounds of flour getting measured.

"'Scuse me." Zach's red-socked foot was nudging my bare one.

"Excuse *you*," I said, and gave him a little kick back.

"Ow," Zach said, even though there was no way I had actually hurt him. "Jeez, Nattie, keep your hooves to yourself."

"I do not have *hooves*," I said indignantly.

"Your feet are gross," Zach said. "What are you, part hobbit?"

I glanced down at my feet, which were admittedly not the nicest part of my body. All the going barefoot was catching up with me.

"Maybe. Shoes are boring."

"We usually wear slippers in my house," said Meredith, who was wearing two matching socks with hearts on them. I crossed my arms, which was not as easy to do on the floor, and looked back at Bacon, who was yawning. I followed suit. "Mmph. Can you just wake me when the pie is done?"

Instead of answering, Zach started the food processor.

*Fine*, I thought. *You and your new girlfriend, Meredith, can make the pies all by yourself.* Maybe Zach was some kind of serial monogamist who targeted girls whose names start with *M*. Not that I cared, because I totally didn't care. *I* was the one with an inbox full of messages from Sebastian Delacroix. Even if I hadn't gotten a new one in weeks.

After a good thirty seconds of grinding, pulsing noises, I decided I'd had enough and righted myself from the floor.

"Just kidding. I want to help."

Meredith, who was holding a measuring cup, looked at Zach, who was filling cold water from the tap.

"It's kind of a two-person job," Meredith said at last. Zach just kept filling ice water.

"Okay," I said. "Well, Zach and I, when we bake together, usually also do Latin homework. So if you don't mind—"

I insinuated myself in the stool between where Meredith was measuring flour and where Zach was now cubing butter and hefted my backpack onto my knees.

"Catullus Eight," I said out loud, to no one in particular.

"*Valē puella. Iam Catullus obdūrat, nec tē requīret nec—*"

"Nattie," Zach said. "Can you maybe just read in English?" He glanced significantly at Meredith. "And not so loud?"

"We're supposed to read the Latin before doing the translation."

"I know, but . . ." Zach threw another significant glance at Meredith, who was humming tunelessly as she scooped out flour. I tensed my jaw and started again.

"Good-bye, girl. Now Catullus is firm, he will not seek you out, nor will he ask one who is unwilling, but you will be said, when you are . . . no one not asked?" I scribbled a note to refine my translation and kept going. "Woe to you, evil woman! What life stays for you? Who now will come to you? To whom will you seem beautiful? Whom now will you love? Whose will you be said to be? Whom will you ki—"

"Wow," Meredith interrupted, and dusted her hands off. "What is this, again?"

"Catullus," I said shortly.

"Roman poet," Zach said.

"Whose girlfriend must've done something slutty," I said, "because apparently he's determined not to see her anymore and says no one will love her."

"Harsh," Zach said.

"I mean, it's not as bad as *some* of his stuff," I said. "In one poem he says this guy brushes his teeth with pee."

"What? Gross. No, I meant you." He plopped out a chunk of dough. "Calling someone slutty, I mean."

Meredith winced. "Yeah, I try not to use words like that against other girls."

My face got hot. "I mean, me neither, but, like, in this poem, you can tell—"

"He called her evil," Zach said. "He's name-calling and being pissy."

"Whatever." I put away my notebook and looked across the counter.

"Did you guys get pie plates?" Meredith asked. Zach looked at me.

"Oh," I said. "I . . . may have forgotten."

"Dammit." Zach groaned. "I mean, my parents have, like, two, but if we're making six pies—"

"Ooh," Meredith said. "What if we just did pie pockets? Like homemade Pop-Tarts." She smiled. "That way everyone can get what they want."

Zach nodded. "Yeah. Totally. Good idea." He stacked the plastic-wrapped hunks of dough onto one another and put them in the fridge.

"Ten minutes chilling?" Meredith said.

"Yup."

"Cool," she said. "This is fun."

"If you're *doing* something," I said. "Speaking of which, can I do something?"

"I thought you said you weren't into cooking?" Meredith said. I ignored her.

"Here." He tossed me a lemon, which I almost didn't catch, from the bowl by his elbow. "Can you juice that?"

Zach hit the Preheat button on the oven and went back to the island. By way of response, I sliced the lemon in half, pulled down a cereal bowl from a cabinet, and squeezed. I handed it to Zach, who promptly handed it back.

"Without the seeds?"

"Oh."

I fished around the bowl, which was less than easy, while Zach dumped a bag of frozen berries into a saucepan, and Meredith, like she'd read his mind or something, hovered over his shoulder to add sugar and a few pinches of some spices.

"This is hard," I said loudly, as another seed slithered from my grasp.

"You should have squeezed it into your hand," Meredith said. "Then you could catch the seeds in your fingers."

"Oh well. You'll have to forgive me for not knowing all the secret kitchen tips. Raised on microwave lasagna, remember?"

Zach made a noncommittal noise and stirred the pot. Last seed retrieved, I handed him the cereal bowl.

"Thanks." He dumped the juice in and gave it another stir. There was a long pause, the kitchen silent except for the bubbling of the filling and the soft snuffling sounds of Bacon hunting for food scraps.

"I'm glad I could come help you guys," Meredith said. "This is *so* fun."

"Yup," I said, wiping my lemony hand on my jeans. "Tons of fun."

"You hate baking." Zach snapped off the burner and moved the filling to a hot pad on the counter.

"I . . ." I didn't really have an answer to that. Meredith didn't seem to notice.

"I think it's totally lame that there's that other party happening," she said. "It's so rude of them! I would never go to a party instead of Winter Formal."

*Probably because you wouldn't be invited*, I thought meanly. Outwardly, I just smiled—also kind of meanly.

"Anyway, I know I'm not in your club, but I totally support you guys in this," Meredith went on. "Also, can I use your bathroom?"

"Front hallway, first door on the left," I answered for Zach. She disappeared, and Zach went back into the fridge for the dough.

"Rolling pin," he said. It took me a moment to realize that the tool in question lived in the canister I was sitting next to.

"Oh, sure." I withdrew it and brought it over. "Can I roll?"

"You can try."

I took that as a yes and peeled out a circle of dough. Zach threw some flour on the counter, and I set the crust in the middle and began to work the pin over it.

It was like rolling over a rock.

"Maybe you can take this one," I said after thirty seconds of ache-inducing effort. Zach said nothing, just took the pin and rolled it over the dough like it was marshmallow. I could see the muscles in his arms moving a little under the edge of his T-shirt sleeves.

"Um," I said, because I needed a distraction. Zach looked up, and I tried to remember what we had been talking about.

"Cooking is *kind of* fun," I said. "I mean, when it's not backbreakingly difficult. Plus, it's practically a science lesson when *you're* doing it."

"Mm." Dough rolled, Zach moved to a second piece, which flattened obediently under his quick motions. I felt Bacon's fuzzy nose sniffing around my bare foot and stooped down to acknowledge him.

"Though it really is kind of a two-person job," I added, picking at a flake of dough on my fingernail.

"I didn't think . . ." From the countertop above, Zach's voice came out quickly, then stopped, as if he'd thought better of it. Slowly, I rose to my feet, hefting Bacon up in my arms and wondering if I was missing something. Zach slapped aside the second round of dough, looked up at me for a split second, then shook his head and started in on a third.

"Nothing," he said. "I mean, yeah. Science, cooking, et cetera."

"And talking and stuff, too. Hanging out," I said, since it

seemed rude not to acknowledge that aspect. I mean, we *were* friends, after all.

"Yeah." Zach sort of smiled to himself. "You're being *real* social right now."

"What?"

"Oh. Nothing." The problem with Zach, I realized, was that sometimes he was so deadpan it was hard to tell if he was even being sarcastic. Either way, I had a rising feeling of anxiety in my chest that I ought to change the subject.

"This music is great," I said loudly as Meredith reentered from the bathroom. "Zach's made me a whole mix, so I know lots about punk music." Total lie. "Do you like punk, too, Mer?"

"Me?" Meredith shook her head. "No, not really. Actually, I'm pretty into folk music. Have you ever heard of Joni Mitchell?"

I narrowed my eyes at her. "Of course I've heard of Joni Mitchell."

I pulled out my phone as a signal that I did not want to discuss my favorite musician with someone like Meredith, and Meredith went amiably over to Zach's side and started filling in the pies. Over the edge of my phone screen, I watched them work—a perfect little team. Whatever. I was probably moments away from receiving a message from a literal rock star. A literal rock star who thought I was attractive. I aggressively refreshed my Pixstagram feed.

"Hey, Nattie?" Meredith held up a trayful of little pies. "Could you please get the oven door?"

"Sure." I climbed off the seat and pulled open the door with one hand. Meredith bent over with the tray, and I scrolled down on my phone. Something flashed and vibrated on the screen, and I almost dropped my phone in surprise.

"Ow!"

The oven door snapped shut. Meredith sprang back, clutching her hand to her chest. Zach leaped from the food processor to her side.

"Jesus. Are you okay?"

"I'm fine," Meredith hiccupped. "The door just hit me. . . ."

Slowly, she uncurled her hand, which now had an angry red welt across the top.

"I'm sorry," I said quickly. "Meredith, I'm so sorry." My heart had started beating sickeningly fast, like I'd downed six cups of coffee. "Are you okay?"

But Meredith was being led to the sink, where Zach flicked on a cold tap and stuck her hand under the water.

"It was an accident." My voice was annoyingly high again. "I didn't mean to."

Meredith winced as the water rushed over her hand. Zach fixed me with a hard look, the kind of look you give someone who's really, really dumb.

"It doesn't matter if you *meant it*, Nattie. You still hurt her."

"I—"

"Go get some bandages." Zach wasn't looking at me now. "Since you know where the bathroom is."

I slipped into the hall, hating myself with every step, and hating myself even more once I'd gotten the bandages but stopped to read what was on my phone.

from: sebdel

hey sry this really isnt a gud time

# CHAPTER EIGHTEEN

Needless to say, I had totally lost my appetite for pie by Friendsgiving.

"Fake sausage, Nattie?" Tall Zach held out a pan that smelled nauseously savory. I shook my head.

"Suit yourself." He helped himself to a fourth link. "This stuff is delicious."

"I know, right? It's even precooked. You'd totally never know they make it with tofu," Bryce said.

Endsignal, who was sitting on Bryce's other side, glanced to where an excited banner proclaimed "Made with 100% Wheat Protein!!!" across the box of sausage, but said nothing. Next to him, Zach the Anarchist was doing his best to carry on a conversation with Meredith, who had showed up for some reason, against the background of Alison and Chihiro arguing about imperialism or socialism or something. Not that I was looking, or even cared. Zach could talk to whoever he wanted. Despite whatever his anarchist philosophy wanted to decry about the US, it *was* a free country.

Tess and I were sitting next to Dr. Frobisher's desk, which had become our impromptu feast table, and she was doing a great job encouraging people to take more food than they probably wanted and welcoming stragglers as they came in. I, on the other hand, was barely able to eat. Besides my frustration at Sebastian personally, there was also the small matter of my identity hovering millimeters away from public knowledge, and being at school only refreshed my anxiety about it. If people like Celeste Franklin and Brooke Lieberman were guessing, it was only a matter of time before the OWPALGBTQIA found, or figured, it out, too.

I looked around the room, eyes narrow. These people were my friends—well, all except Meredith—and yet every one of them was a potential backstabber. Tess and Tall Zach—and Endsignal, I guess—already knew, and I had no choice but to assume they were trustworthy. Everyone else, I wasn't sure. I'd like to assume that they'd sympathize and understand my need for privacy, and that they would never stoop so low as to spread gossip about their beloved, if incompetent, replacement treasurer.

Then again, I thought, as I watched Meredith snort-laugh at something Zach the Anarchist had said, you could never be too careful.

"The corn bread is effing *delicious.*" Tess stuffed a hunk in her mouth, which made Endsignal perk up a little. "And Nattie, you need to eat more."

"I *am* eating." I was picking at—but not really eating—some mashed potatoes, my mind still trying to work through the cognitive dissonance. Because despite the insane fight-or-flight response about getting discovered that had taken up residence in my nervous system, I still hadn't been able to bring myself to respond to Sebastian's message.

hey sry this really isnt a gud time

What did he *want* with me, anyway? When exactly *would* it be a "gud" time to talk to him? It's not like he ever asked if *I* was available before rapid-firing his thoughts on California and the moon and mango salsa. And now, just because I'd had the audacity to address something more serious than his feelings on Mexican food, he was cutting me off? I took an angry bite of mashed potatoes.

"These taste like wallpaper paste," I said to no one in particular. The freshperson in the hoodie froze, midrefill on potatoes, and looked like they were going to cry.

"They're *great*, Kennedy!" Tess gave her the biggest closed-mouth smile possible and whirled on me as soon as Kennedy turned around.

"Nattie. What the hell is wrong with you? You *love* Friendsgiving."

I gave my mashed potatoes a very morose stab.

"Look," Tess went on. "I know we're all upset about this bullshit boycott of Operation Big Gay Dance Party. It's completely ridiculous and insulting that a bunch of heteronormative seniors think they can have their own party just to make us look bad. But trust me, we *are* going to figure out some way to force everyone in the school to come—I mean, *want* to come. Of their own free w—"

"It's not Operation BGDP," I said. "It's"—I lowered my voice to the barest whisper—"*Sebastian.*"

"Right. Of course." Tess cast a glance around the room, where everyone seemed to be either in the process of eating or in the process of getting more food *to* eat. Classic Friendsgiving. And usually, I did love it. But not now.

"Did you text him again? I thought we agreed it was best if you just ignored him from now on."

"I *was*," I said. "There've just been . . . some developments."

Across the room, Meredith was getting up for a second helping of Zach the Anarchist's pie. Because of *course* that would be her favorite.

"Developments?" Tess chewed furiously at her corn bread. "What have you been keeping from me?"

I took a big breath in, let an even bigger breath out, and started to explain, everything from the Pixstagram messages to the girls in the computer room to my suspicion that Sam Huang was in the process of arranging it for the a cappella group to perform. When I was finally done, I looked from my plate of potatoes up to Tess. Her gray eyes were positively flinty with resolution, and she was doing a slow, solemn nod.

"I know what we have to do."

"You do?" I said. By this point, I was totally, utterly at a loss. Even for someone with Tess's interpersonal experience, this was a capital-*s* Situation.

"I'll take care of it," she said, and then said something I *really* wished she hadn't.

"Hey, Zach!"

"What?" Tall Zach popped his head up from his umpteenth vegan sausage.

"Not you. Anarchist Zach."

Meredith nudged Zach the Anarchist, who was in the middle of telling her some story and looking unusually animated—which, for him, was barely animated at all, really.

"Do you think Nattie and I can stay with your sister on Friday? We're going to New York on an emergency shopping mission and I don't want to have to take the late train back because we'll get killed."

"Tess," I said, but Zach the Anarchist answered her like I hadn't even said anything.

"Sure, I guess," he said. "I mean, I can ask."

"Excellent." Tess waved her hands at the room, which had quieted considerably under her yell.

"As you were, everyone."

She settled back into her desk and picked up a homemade Pop-Tart. I gaped for a minute and then started in.

"Shopping mission?"

"Yup." She grabbed my hand and stared into my eyes. "It's

a cover, although we may end up doing that, too. Because you, Nattie M-S, are going to confront Sebastian in person at his show in New York this weekend."

"What?" I yelped. "Why? How?"

Tess bit into the tart and actually rolled her eyes back into her head.

"Have you *tried* these? They're amazing."

"Are you serious?"

"Yeah. Zach is really talented."

I shook my head. "No. I mean about going to New York."

It didn't seem possible. But then again, it seemed *equally* impossible that I would be the subject of a chart-topping anthem of indie-rock sexiness, and look what happened with *that*.

"As a heart attack. What are best friends for?"

"And what exactly am I supposed to say when I get there?"

Tess squared her shoulders. "You are going to march up to him, look at him with all your smoldering hotness and fury, and demand that he explain himself. And then"—she sucked in a dramatic breath—"you are going to demand that he and his band play the Owen Wister Preparatory Academy Winter Formal."

"What?!"

"It's *brilliant*, Nattie!" Tess cried. "I can't believe I didn't think of it earlier. We haven't even found a DJ yet, and this way we won't have to. Plus, no one will be able to resist coming to a dance if hometown hero Sebastian Delacroix and his band are playing. And you're our secret weapon. You're going to use your fame to single-handedly save OBGDP. You'll be a gay-rights legend for years to come."

"But I'm not even gay," I said. "Liking a boy is kind of how I got into this whole mess."

"Well, right," Tess said airily, "and like I said, you'll sort that out while you're up there, too. But—hey!" She spun in her chair. "Be careful with tha—"

But it was too late. There was a *crack*, and then a *plop*, as the dish of mashed potatoes slipped through Bryce's fake-sausage-greased fingers and smashed on the floor. Tess groaned.

"Don't go anywhere," she said, as if I was about to leap up and help. "Everyone, clear the area!" She lunged forward to herd everyone out of harm's way. "No, Bryce, it's fine, just go get a vacuum or something from the janitor's closet."

I half expected Zach the Anarchist to make some crack about vacuuming mashed potatoes, but he was still . . . occupied talking to Meredith. So I chewed noncommittally on a string bean and stared at the "CAVE CANEM" poster, which unfortunately was right above Alison's head as she took a bite of her second vegan pie two desks away. She narrowed her eyes at me.

"These are good," she said, defensively. "Do you mind?"

"Um . . . yeah," I said, since I couldn't really take credit. "I mean, no. Zach's a good baker."

"Ugh." Alison broke off a corner of crust and chomped it with relish. "Do you know how hard it is to find good dessert when you have a restricted diet?"

"Actually . . . yeah," I said. "I've, um, had to pass up a lot of shortcake, I guess. No one gets that I can't just scrape the strawberries off. And then I feel rude."

Alison smacked her hand against the desk. "I know! People get *so mad*. 'It's just butter, the cow's still alive.' Like, that's not the point. Just let me live, okay?"

She chewed a moment longer, looking like she was sizing me up.

"You don't like me, do you?"

I blinked. "Um?" It took a full two seconds for my white-lie instincts to kick in. "No! You're, um, I just . . ."

She sighed. "Look, don't think I don't know I'm loud and stuff. But I'm not going to apologize."

"I . . . okay." I looked at my soggy paper plate.

"If you're not loud, people don't hear you, let alone *listen*. And if other people are afraid to speak up, then I have to be twice as loud for them. This"—Alison whipped out her phone and held it two inches from the end of my nose—"is my motto. Or one of my mottos."

I squinted at the screen, at what seemed to be a tiny blog post with a bunch of swoopy, handwritten text. "I . . . can't really read that."

"Don't you take Latin? God." Alison yanked back her

phone. "*Fortuna audaces iuvat.* Fortune favors the bold. So I try to always be bold."

"What *is* that?" Tess, mashed potato crisis over, appeared at Alison's elbow and snatched away her phone. "Did you *draw* this?"

"*Yes?*" Alison rolled her eyes. "It's called hand-lettering, duh."

"This is amazing," Tess said. "I've been making cruddy clip-art posters this whole time. Why didn't you *tell* us you were good for something?"

Alison pursed her lips. "I tell you *lots* of things. You just don't *listen.*"

"Fair point. Okay, Alison, I'm sorry for ignoring you, and from now on, you're on official poster duty. *Nattie.*" Tess turned to me, her voice notionally softer. "Are we doing this, or what?"

"I . . ." I swallowed. "What about, like, train tickets? Or *concert* tickets, for that matter? And what am I supposed to tell my *parents*? I don't even know how to take the subway."

"Leave it all to me," Tess said. "Well, except the part with your parents. Come *on*, Nattie! This is your chance!"

My heart was banging against the front of my chest—not in an anxious way, but in an adrenaline-y, *let's do this* kind of way. Maybe, crazily, Alison was right.

"Okay," I said. "We're on."

261

# CHAPTER NINETEEN

It turned out the secret to lying was to use a really boring excuse, and also to spring it on your victims while they were in a tryptophan haze. When I asked on Friday morning, my parents were happy to let me sleep over at Tess's house for the evening, because I'd been doing it for practically half my life, and because apparently they wanted to do some really boring parent things that night anyway.

"The Brandywine River Museum is *fascinating*," Mom told me. "All these American illustrators are on display."

"Yup," I said, only half listening, because I could not find my phone among the jumble of newspapers and nonfunctional pens on the kitchen counter.

"*And* the Carters invited us to come stay over for the night," Dad said. "Gonna make a whole getaway of it."

"Nattie?"

I looked up from a pile of old *Wister Register*s to where Sam Huang was holding my phone. "Did you forget this?"

He glanced at the screen, where I could read a text from

Tess: JAMBA ALERT train leaves in twenty!!!

"Train?" Sam Huang frowned. I snatched my phone away and clutched it to my chest.

"Sam Huang," I hissed. "Swear to me that you won't say anything."

"But . . ." Sam Huang looked to where my parents were reading an actual road atlas, like they were pioneers or something. "Robert and Anne . . ."

"Come on, Sam Huang," I said. "Brothers and sisters do this for each other all the time."

"They do?"

"Sure," I said, assuming this was true. "Look, swear to me you won't say anything and I'll take your dishwasher duty for the next two weeks."

I gave him a thumbs-up that he dubiously returned, then ran out the door as Mom called the Phone Responsibility and the Privilege of the Family Plan litany after me, and two and a half hours later, I was on the outskirts of America's cultural capital.

Something thumped into my arm.

"*Je frappe toi.* Are you alive, Nattie?" Tess jabbed me a second time, just as the conductor on the commuter train started announcing New York as the next stop. "Quit looking so *pale.*"

"*Je frappe toi* more," I said weakly, and brushed my knuckles against her sleeve in a faux-punch. "And I would, but it's not exactly something I can *control.* I'm white and I haven't seen full sunlight since September." Not to mention that I was feeling less than ready to shop for a Winter Formal outfit and *intensely* less than ready to see Sebastian in the flesh.

Tess rolled her eyes. She was in full-on city gear: leather pants, long black trench coat, and lipstick the purpley-red color of a day-old bruise. She looked awesome. And I, based on a quick glance in the greasy train window, looked scared. Weird. And more than a little pale.

"You know what I mean," Tess said. "We have a very exciting day of fancy-dance-outfit shopping ahead of us. And then a very exciting night of—" The train car lurched forward, squealed, and then slammed to a stop.

"Penn Station," the conductor said.

"This is us," Tess said, and got to her feet, as if there was even the possibility of further stops on a one-way commuter train between Trenton, where we'd transferred from the SEPTA train from Philadelphia, and New York. Somehow, she'd managed to pack all of her overnight essentials into a small messenger bag slung on her hip. Not having a small messenger bag, I had to bring a WPHL tote bag, which wasn't exactly the wieldiest thing to navigate up to the subway level of the world's busiest train station. I followed Tess to a wall map as what felt like the entire population of New York City streamed past us.

"Okay, so we just have to take the A, C, or E down to the L and then we can hit the East Village," Tess said. "I need something to wear to this dance, and the Plymouth Meeting

Mall isn't going to cut it, so while we're there I want to investigate some vintage stores. Then we can just hop back on the train at Union Square and get to Bethany's place."

"Sure," I said. Tess was one of those people who, despite never having lived in New York, seemed to know the names, locations, and characters of all the neighborhoods in the city. As for me, I'd seen Times Square once and kind of hated it.

The first subway car we got onto was way warmer than it needed to be, and the second was practically an oven. I loosened my scarf to let out some body heat.

"So, did you bring anything else to wear, or is that it?"

"This is it, I guess," I said. Under my peacoat, I had on a black, tunic-type top with three-quarter-length sleeves and the one pair of jeans that didn't gap at the back when I sat down. I'd even worn a pair of peacock-feather earrings my aunt had given me the day before as an early Christmas present, which I thought looked pretty good against my hair.

"Mm." Tess lifted her eyebrows. "Well, good thing we're going shopping."

"Hey," I said, but before I could adequately berate her for slighting what I thought was a pretty cool, New York–y outfit, she was up and slipping out the doors onto a platform and toward the exit stairs.

I caught up with her just as she stepped out onto the street, where I was struck instantly by competing odors of Lysol, pizza, and bus exhaust.

"This is great," Tess said.

"If you say so," I said.

"New York!" Tess yelled.

"Uh, Tess . . . ," I said.

"Shut up, lady!" some guy passing us said.

Tess shrugged, as if strangers told her to shut up all the time, and jerked her head to the left.

"This way. Come on."

I followed obediently, picking my way past soggy newspapers and what looked like an entire carton of french fries spilled on the sidewalk. Even though I'd grown up in the suburbs, I'd spent a decent amount of time in Center City Philadelphia, and I'd always thought I liked the slightly gritty character of cityscapes. But the shiny skyscrapers of Walnut Street and the colonial-age buildings around the Liberty Bell looked like a model train set compared to New York, where everything seemed to be squat, dirty, and crowded, with stores selling anything from sunglasses to sandwiches spilling their wares out into the path of pedestrians who all seemed to look angry at just having to exist. For the rest of the ten-minute walk, I tried to strike a balance between clutching my tote bag to my side and not *looking* like I was clutching whatsoever. And trying not to look so pale, if that was even possible.

"Here," Tess declared, yanking my wrist and pulling me across a crosswalk mere seconds before a taxi whizzed into our path.

"Asshole," she called after him, and then turned to me.

"Ta-da! Vintage heaven. Weirdos galore. I guarantee you that none of those prepster prom queens in Wister will have duds like these."

The mannequin in the store nearest us was wearing a curly blue wig and a fishnet bodysuit.

"To say the least," I said.

We picked through that store, which turned out to be mostly novelty costumes that were mostly *really* skimpy, and then the next one, which was all *real* vintage stuff with designer labels, where Tess insisted on trying on a fur stole, complete with dead mink head at one end, until she noticed it cost six hundred dollars.

"We'll have better luck here," she said, picking another store at random and charging in.

Surprisingly, we did. Despite a square footage rivaling that of the yurt, the place was jam-packed with all kinds of awesome stuff: sequins and shoulder pads and taffeta in tropical colors.

"This is amazing," Tess said. She'd found an old 1940s-style suit with a neat little blazer and skirt. "Check it out. It's like a flight attendant became a dominatrix, or vice versa."

"Cool." I was more into the place's business cards, which had nifty scalloped edges and read "Va-Voom Vintage" in sparkly letters. I slipped two into my pocket as souvenirs.

"Freaking fantastic." She yanked something spangly off

the hangers and shoved it into my hands. "Here. You try this."

I obeyed, and two minutes and a lot of struggling with zippers later, I had on a blue-green gown that pinned my legs together and rustled when I walked.

"It's great," Tess said. "You look killer."

"I look like a landlocked mermaid," I said, examining my butt in the mirror. "And I can't walk."

"Beauty is pain," Tess said. "You have to get it."

She brushed her palms over the front of her skirt. The girl behind the counter, who had cool rockabilly bangs and lipstick to rival Tess's, paused in the middle of filing a boxful of receipts to give Tess a short nod of approval.

"Looks pretty good," she said.

"Oh," Tess said. "Yeah. Thanks."

The girl went back to her receipts, and Tess slumped.

"Well, there goes *this* outfit." She started shoving off the blazer.

"What?" I said. "Why? I thought you liked it."

Tess stopped, one arm still in the jacket. "Yeah, because it screams *girl-on-girl*. Ten bucks says Bye Bye Birdie over there is writing down her phone number so she can ask me to a sock hop later."

I glanced over at the counter, where the shopgirl was indeed writing *something* down.

"I thought the whole point of this dance was being ourselves," I said.

"Not anymore," Tess said, yanking at the zipper. "The point of this dance is for everyone *else* to be themselves. The point of this dance for *me* is to not terrify my parents when I tell them where all my savings went. I need to look like Tess Kozlowski, all-American girl. Not Tess Kozlowski, radical and attention-seeking cliché."

"But . . ." I shuffled around in my mermaid dress. "Isn't that—"

"And now I have this whole stupid A Cappella party to compete with," Tess went on. "We're losing our chance to reach new people because they're afraid we're changing things too much. And I can't let that happen. I have to *show* them. I have to . . ." She sighed. "It's complicated, okay, Nattie? And it's my life, and it's my decision." She looked at my outfit and jerked her head at the cash register. "Get changed and pay and we'll go."

"No," I said. "I'm not buying this."

"What? But it's so *seductive*."

"I don't want to be *seductive*!" I put my hands on my hips, which was not easy given my current constricted state. "I want something . . . I don't know."

I waddled back to the racks of clothes. What *did* I want? My usual fashion prerogative of *don't look weird* didn't really work in formalwear situations. I couldn't just fall back on jeans and a T-shirt. For this dance, I'd actually have to commit to a *look*. And seductive was not it.

I pushed dresses aside. Nothing sparkly. Nothing with a plunging neckline. Just something ordinary, but pretty. Something Nattie-y. Something like . . .

"Oh." I stopped pushing. "I like this."

Tess appeared over my shoulder. "What? But it's *yellow*."

"So what?" Carefully, I dislodged a bunch of banana-colored taffeta from the rack and held it to my shoulders.

"So you can't wear yellow with red hair," Tess said. "You'll look like a stoplight."

But I wasn't listening. The color was more gold than canary, with elbow-length sleeves and a high-cut bodice, and the skirt *poofed* more than *flowed*. It just looked *nice*, like a grown-up version of the party dresses you wore as a kid, or the sort of thing you'd see in the dance from *Back to the Future*. Classic high-school formal wear. Not seductive in the least.

"I'm trying it on."

Inside the dressing stall, I pulled it on and tugged it into place on top of my hips, doing a few seconds of awkward back-and-forth for the zipper before I came outside for help.

"Zip me?"

Tess obliged, then steered me in front of the scarf-draped mirror, squinting like the color clash was going to burn her eyes, but I didn't care. It was perfect.

"Well, at least it's only thirty bucks," Tess said, ignoring the zipper and going straight for the tag in my armpit. "Which means you can totally go for something for tonight, too."

*Right.* For some reason, the dress had made me forget the actual reason we'd gone to New York. The one that involved confronting Sebastian and, apparently, a different wardrobe. I stepped back into the changing room and began to shimmy out of the dress.

"How do you feel about backless tops?" Tess's voice came from outside.

"How does it stay *on?*"

"Okay, *mostly* backless."

I folded the yellow dress with a sigh and gave it a fond little pat.

"I'll think about it."

Somehow, "thinking about it" turned into "actually purchasing it," and so I ended up with my first mostly backless top. It was only twenty bucks, which seemed an order of magnitude less than what I'd expected clothes to cost in New York, and something about being out in a big city, unsupervised, made me feel okay with making spontaneous sartorial decisions. Tess, on the other hand, rejected the rest of everything we found: too old, too new, too expensive, too polyester, too eerily similar to something her mom had definitely worn in the nineties. After a brief pause for black coffee—"sorry, that's all we have"—in a wood-paneled place that was about the size of the Moonpenny's bathroom, Tess declared the shopping portion of the day over and led me to the subway once again.

Forty minutes later, we emerged from the ground in what was presumably Brooklyn, and followed Tess's phone to where Bethany West lived. I'd only met Zach's sister a few times before—school potlucks, occasionally glimpsing her when she was home from college—so I really only knew things about her I'd absorbed by osmosis. She was twenty-five, a grad student in psychology, lived in New York Actual City, and yet was somehow still willing to put up two of her little brother's friends for a night.

"I'm sorry I have to just . . . leave you guys here." Bethany yanked off her chunky orange scarf and dropped her backpack to the ground with a single, swift *thud*. After clomping up five flights of stairs, Tess and I had taken a seat at Bethany's postage stamp of a table, which was in the middle of the kitchen-slash-dining-room-slash-living-room. The apartment itself was on the sixth floor of a brownstone, in a neighborhood that was less like the mess of Manhattan and more like the area around Zach's house: residential and even a little calm.

Bethany pulled off her jacket and boots in quick succession and then tramped off back down a narrow hallway.

"It's just that I've got the first shift at the restaurant, and I got out of class late, so I'm basically only coming home to ditch one set of clothes and put on another before I hop back on the train to SoHo."

She reappeared, clothed in head-to-toe black and winding

an elastic around the tail of a hasty blond braid. She *looked* a lot like Zach, too, right down to the blue eyes. Which made sense, of course, but also made me feel another twinge of guilt.

"Don't worry about it," Tess said quickly. "I mean, you're doing us a huge favor by putting us up for the night, considering you, ah, barely know us."

Bethany paused, shrugged, and then went back to pulling her boots on. "You're Zach's best friends. He's told me all about you."

"He has?" I said, my voice suddenly asserting itself.

"Oh yeah. Tess is the one who runs the club with all the letters—sorry, I can't remember them, I know that's a big deal—"

"Not at all," Tess said, and sounded like she meant it even though I knew it *was*.

"And Nattie's the one he likes . . ." Bethany stopped, mid-zip in replacing her coat, and did a microcough.

"To talk to," she finished. "Likes to talk to."

Oh. Huh. I'd thought she'd go with *Nattie's the one who makes fun of his ex-girlfriend and whines every time she comes over to bake*, but this was fine, too.

"Well, it's still awesome of you," Tess cut in.

"Like I said, no problem. My roommate's back in Cleveland for Thanksgiving, and she said you guys are welcome to crash on her bed. Our couch is kind of Tuna's home base, so . . ." She waved at hand at the "living" portion of the room, where an otherwise comfortable-looking brown love seat was jammed into a corner and covered with tiny feline hairs.

"Anyway. Here's Taylor's keys." She plunked down a key chain with a tag that read "No Sleep till Brooklyn." "Bathroom's back by my room, Taylor's room is by the front"—she nodded forward—"and those cookies are going stale, so eat as many as you want."

Bethany swiveled her head to the clock on the stove, swore softly, and then turned back to us.

"I really have to go. You guys are good? Know how to use the subway and all that?"

"Totally," Tess said, just as I said, "Not really."

"Great. I'll be back around midnight. Zach said you were here to go shopping or something?"

"And to see a concert," Tess said. "The Young Lungs."

Bethany frowned. "Never heard of them. But that's Brooklyn, I guess."

"Speaking of, are they super strict about IDs here?" Tess asked. "Because this show is *technically* twenty-one-plus."

My mouth fell open.

"Tess!"

"Oh, um, hm." Bethany frowned. "I mean, you guys aren't going to drink or anything, right?"

"No, ma'am," Tess said.

"Here." Bethany rummaged around in the mail-table drawer and handed us each a laminated card: a PA license for me, what looked like a college ID for Tess.

"Wow," Tess said, examining the Columbia ID. "Thanks."

"Are you sure?" I looked at the tiny Bethany photo in my hand. If you squinted, you could maybe convince yourself that she had auburn hair, which was close to red. Kind of.

"I think they were supposed to punch through this when I got my New York license, but it wasn't the most organized day at the DMV. Just go in separate doors and you'll probably be fine." Bethany stooped to pick up her bag. "Oh, and if you want to get food, the falafel place on the corner is great." With that, she swung out of the room, her "Bye!" getting clipped by the door shutting.

"Well," I said. "She's, um, busy."

"I think it's a New York thing," Tess said. "Everyone here is rushing to stuff. It's the lifestyle."

"Yeah." I took a cookie and a long look around the kitchiving room. It was a tiny space, maybe a fifth of the size of the Wests' kitchen in Philadelphia, but it was still impressively tidy. There was even a tiny box of herbs growing on the very skinny windowsill. "Besides, we did just kind of *appear* here at the last minute."

"Whatever. I knew Zach would come through."

"Yeah," I said, even though I hadn't known that at all. I figured Zach had been telling Bethany I was either a Mia-hating bully or a pop-music poser. Or both.

"I can't believe she just gave us IDs like that. And this

place is so legit, too," Tess said, getting up to investigate the chunk of room around the corner, where the cat-condo couch faced a small TV flanked by two orderly bookcases. "They have a rug and everything."

"Yeah," I said. It *was* legit, and that was kind of weird. Bethany West, who I'd always just sort of mentally rounded down to around our age, was already settling into an actual apartment. I finished my biscotti and looked down at my new driver's license: Bethany West, age twenty-five. Not terrible.

As Tess nosed through their DVD collection, I stuck to perusing pictures in their frames: another blond girl who was presumably Taylor of Having Gone to Cleveland fame, Bethany and a guy with a dark beard who was presumably her boyfriend, the Wests on vacation in the Poconos from back when Bethany was at Wister and Zach's hair was still blue. I'd forgotten how goofy it made him look.

"They have like a zillion old movies," Tess said, shaking her head. "On VHS. It's like they're my *parents* or something." She straightened and put her hands on her hips.

"Anyway. Operation Confrontation time. What are you going to *do*?"

"Do we have to call it that?"

"Nonnegotiable."

I suppressed a sigh and nodded, a weird heavy feeling in my chest. Just *getting* to New York was exhausting, and outside Bethany's window, everything seemed dark, loud, ominous, and unfriendly. So calling the whole thing "Operation Confrontation" wasn't really reassuring.

"Fine, fine. I'll start." Tess ticked off actions on her fingers. "We get dressed, get falafel, and then hop on the G train for Williamsburg."

"Okay." I swallowed. "And then, um, we'll go to the show."

She nodded briskly. "It'll probably be hard for you to find him beforehand, since they won't even open the doors until a half hour before the show starts. Unless you want to creep around the backstage entrance and wait for him to show up—"

A sudden, terrible vision of me attempting to scale a chainlink fence in my fancy new top popped into my head. "No way. Let's . . . wait until after the show."

"Good plan." Tess tapped the side of her nose. "I'll obviously be at your side every step of the way, as your incognito associate. Then what?"

"Uh . . ." I scrunched up my mouth, thinking hard. "I go up to the stage, and—"

"Right, good," Tess interrupted. "Act like you're going to grab the set list off the mic stand, or something."

"Yeah. And then I'll . . . talk my way backstage." I winced. That sounded impossible, or, at least, impossible for someone like me. Tess must've had the same thought, because she shook her head furiously.

"Yeah, no. You're never going to be able to." She snapped

her fingers. "I'll come with you. Create a distraction so that whoever's guarding the door leaves his or her post."

"A distraction?" This was starting to sound less like a feasible plan and more like sitcom-level hijinks. "Like what?"

"Oh, you know. Someone snatches my purse, or I fall and twist my ankle, or I rip my shirt off and indecently expose myself." Tess waved a hand. "Leave it to me. The *real* question is: what are *you* going to say to Sebastian once you're in?"

"Well, I . . ."

"Wait." Tess grabbed my shoulders and squared me to her. "Pretend I'm him." She slouched and lowered her eyelids, clearly doing what she thought was a good Sebastian impression.

"Hey," she growled. "Nattie. How are ya?"

Actually, it wasn't half bad. I stood up straight and tried not to laugh.

"Sebastian, I need you to do me a favor."

"No, no, no." Tess snapped back to herself. "You have to lead *into* it. Seductively. Like, *hey, Sebastian, how are you? Funny seeing you here.*"

"If I'm backstage at his own show, it's not going to be funny seeing him there at all," I pointed out. Tess groaned.

"Fine, fine. But you know what I mean. Start casual, *then* mention that you want a favor."

"Okay." I chewed my lip. "But what if he says no?"

"Then you move from carrot to stick." Tess pounded a fist into her hand.

"What? Like, beat him up?"

"No, dummy. Bring out the big guns. Your secret weapon." She nodded at the phone in my hand.

"What, texting him?" I said. I noticed I had a text message from Dad—hey kiddo can you make sure yurt has tarp on? love Dad—but before I could forward it to Sam Huang, Tess grabbed it out of my hands.

"No! The Talent Show Incident!" She held my phone up like a beacon. "Mention you have footage and he'll *have* to do what you say. There's no *way* he'd want that going public."

She had a point. I swallowed and looked from my phone in Tess's hand to the wall above the TV, where there were twin posters: one with an alien, for a long-past Green Day concert, and one of a guy bowling that I was pretty sure was Richard Nixon. They looked totally out of place in the otherwise dignified setting of the living room, but for some reason, that made me feel way better.

"Okay," I said. "It's on."

"Excellent." Tess grinned, closemouthedly, and dropped my phone on the couch. "Now let's make ourselves beautiful."

And we did, sort of, crowding into Bethany's closet-sized bathroom so Tess could attack her hair with a straightener and I could mess up my eyeliner three times in a row. Outfitted and made-up, Tess grabbed her purse and I grabbed Bethany's keys and ID and tucked them into the pockets of my jacket. I was ready, or as ready as I would ever be. And Sebastian had no idea what he was in for.

# CHAPTER TWENTY

The Young Lungs were playing somewhere called the Knitting Factory, which was only a couple subway stops away from where Bethany lived. From the looks of it, the Knitting Factory had nothing to do with actual knitting, though it probably could have been a factory at one point in time. As in: it was huge. And noisy. And very, very full.

"This is great," Tess said. "Look at all these people!"

"My field of vision is a little limited," I said from my position millimeters away from a patch of flannel covering the shoulder of a hipster girl with a side-mullet. I was getting jostled from behind as more and more people poured from the bar area into the part with the stage, which was less than comfortable for the swath of skin exposed by the not-quite-backless top I'd gotten at the vintage store.

"Here."

I felt a firm tug on my wrist and sort of *fell* sideways, emerging with Tess into a little clearing that had appeared like an oasis in the middle of the crowd.

"Better?" she asked. In her red T-shirt and dramatic eyeliner, she looked completely at home—actually, she *was* completely at home. Me, I was taking a little while. But I still nodded.

Tess squinted a cat-lined eye at me. "I don't believe you."

"Everyone here is very cool," I said.

"Yeah, *you included*," she replied. "Hello? You're *Natalie*. As in, from the *song* 'Natalie.' And you look *incredible*. And, coming from a lady-liking lady, that opinion is solid gold."

I smiled. It might be flattery, but then again, Tess never *didn't* speak her mind. Besides, she wasn't wrong: I'd seen myself before we left, and the drapey dark blue of the backless top did look solidly decent with my earrings and my hair.

"When do you think the first opener is going on?" Tess asked, just as the house lights went off.

"Guess that answers it," she said, yelling to make herself heard over the cheer that rose from the darkened crowd. "I'm getting a drink. Do you want one?"

"What?" I yelled back, because I wasn't sure I'd heard her right and also because I wasn't sure if she meant a Diet Coke or a *drink* drink.

"I'm getting us some beers," Tess called back, answering both of my questions at once and then disappearing.

From what I could see from my relatively unobstructed position, the first band was a guy on drums, a guy on keyboard, and a girl with a guitar. The drummer counted them in with a couple clicks of his drumsticks and they launched into something electronic and spacey-sounding, not fast enough to dance to but not slow enough to stand still, either. Around me, the crowd was doing a kind of collective sway as the girl onstage stepped up to the microphone and started making bluesy vowel sounds of words I couldn't quite understand.

I had just begun a kind of slow-motion shuffle when the song cracked open and sped up, the guitar whirling and the girl shouting something about *love love love.*

*That* made people dance. The bodies around me ebbed and flowed and I bobbed around like a buoy in a tidal wave. The anonymous sea of people was caught up in the band's performance, the music was loud and pulsing, and I remembered that I really didn't care. I didn't care about the music because I wasn't here to hear it, and I didn't care about the people because I wasn't here to impress them. I was here to confront. I was here to . . .

"Nattie!"

Somewhere on the banks of the dance floor, Tess was calling for me, but I couldn't see her. Another chorus of *love, love, love* had started onstage, which, weirdly enough, reminded me of Dad's text-message sign-off. I went for my phone so I could send the yurt alert to Sam Huang, but when I slid my hand into my jeans pocket, it was empty.

My phone. I'd left it on Bethany's couch.

Panicked, I started to push my way back to the bar, where Tess was waiting.

"*There* you are," she shouted. She was clutching two plastic cups that seemed to be mostly foam and stuck one out to me. I shook my head *no thanks* and Tess rolled her eyes.

"You're no fun," she yelled, taking a healthy swig from each of them.

"Tess," I said, voice rising. "I forgot my phone. It's at Bethany's."

Tess sucked her teeth. "Ooh. Yikes."

"Is it that bad?" The song was ending, and the crowd dissolved into applause that was just low enough on the decibel scale to let me get a word in.

Tess immediately shook her head. "No. No way. It just means you have to be extra-persuasive. But you can do that, right? Especially with the entirety of the OWPALGBTQIA counting on you?"

It took her a few tries to get all the letters right. She batted her eyelashes and went for another swig of beer. "Sure you don't want some?"

"I'm sure." I didn't like the idea of not having my faculties around Sebastian, because as much as I hated to admit it, he had a kind of alcoholic effect on me. I needed to stay as sharp as possible.

The guitars started up again, and the rest of the opening band's set passed in a blur of husky voice, angular instrument sounds, and flashing lights. It was all making my head hurt a little. I would bet that Joni Mitchell never had lighting effects at any of *her* shows.

And just like that, it was over.

"Thank you, Brooklyn," the lead singer said. "We're Plain and Tall, and we're psyched for the Young Lungs!"

"Woo!" Tess lowered one now-empty plastic cup and raised the second in a toast, which kind of annoyed me. We weren't here to be excited about the band, after all. For all her talk about Operation Confrontation, she didn't appear to be taking it very seriously now that we were actually moving forward.

We stood like that, my feathery earrings practically swatting Tess in the face, as a couple roadies hustled onstage to swap out guitars and clear away the first drum set to reveal the second.

"This is fun," Tess said after a while, and took a long pull of her second beer. I crossed my arms.

"You know," I said, "we didn't even have to *go* to this concert. I could've just . . . had Sebastian meet up with me somewhere in New York."

Tess wrinkled her nose. "You think he would've gone for that?"

"No," I admitted. *This really isnt a gud time* was not the kind of message you sent to someone you'd be happy to go out for coffee with. But now that we *were* here, the boredom of band-watching was making me antsy.

"Plus"—Tess had a little blob of beer foam on her nose, which I didn't bother pointing out—"this is *fun*."

"You said that already."

"And this way," Tess went on, like I hadn't said anything at all, "you get to look at *that*."

She did a kind of vague wild-armed gesture in the opposite direction, but there was no mistaking who she was pointing at. My heart started up like I'd been defibrillated and my back felt a chill that had nothing to do with the absence of shirt: it was Sebastian, and he was smiling.

"Hey," he said into the microphone. "We're the Young Lungs and we make music."

From the first notes of the guitar, the volume was louder than before—one of the roadies must have cranked up the amplifier—but it wasn't coming through to my ears. All of my senses were occupied with Sebastian: his broad shoulders and green T-shirt, his new, long hair swinging around his chin, the occasional pause he made midlyric to lift his eyebrows or bite his lip. His movements were as fluid and relaxed as his stare into the crowd was intense. He was performing *perfectly*, and I was buying it completely. This wasn't Sebastian from high school or the Almost Kiss or even Ruby's Rock Club: this was an actual, bona fide rock star, and he was really, *intensely* hot.

Right then, I wanted more than anything for my heart rate to slow down. I couldn't focus on the plan for Operation Confrontation at all, because my hormones were chasing any nonimmediate, non–Sebastian-related thought from my head. The visions I'd had of me storming up, indignant but cool, and telling Sebastian to knock it off were replaced with scenes of him laughing, touching me, and looking into my eyes. The songs kept going, one after another, but never quite the one I recognized. I wasn't dancing, but I wasn't holding still, either. Onstage, Sebastian lowered his guitar and treated us to a little half smirk.

"For a job that doesn't pay much, this has got some truly excellent perks," he said. "You are one good-looking audience."

A communal laugh bubbled up. I looked back at Tess, who was now leaning on the bar and giggling along with everyone else.

"So, this one is for you guys. Girls. Or really just one."

Sebastian picked up an acoustic guitar from the stand next to his microphone and shouldered the strap. My heart leaped into my throat, because as soon as his fingers touched the strings I knew what was going to happen.

*"Well, there's curves like madness in her hips*
*And red like sin painted on her lips."*

But it was different this time, the instruments quieter and more organic and the words sounding like Sebastian was just thinking of them, right there, right then.

Somehow, I'd come to the middle of the crowd. Somehow,

I was staring right at Sebastian. And somehow, I knew he was staring back at me.

*"Natalie—"*

I tore my eyes off the stage, looking into the crowd as a way to reset. I flicked from one strange face to the next. It seemed like everyone had their eyes front, faces lit up, and hands in the air. A girl in a jean jacket put her hand to her heart. Another one with a short crop of black hair was mouthing the words as they came out in Sebastian's voice. A few were even jumping up and down in time. And all of them, I realized were female.

I turned around, doing a full one-eighty of the space behind me. It was like a real-life version of Sebastian's Pixstagram page, everyone entranced, enraptured, and capturing the moment on their cell phones. All those faces, all lit up and all looking at Sebastian. Like they knew him. Like they *wanted* him.

*"Why'd you break my heart, heart, heart . . ."*

Maybe I just had to forget what anyone else thought. Forget about this audience. Forget about the senior girls at school. Forget about everything except the Almost Kiss and the Face-Touching Incident and Sebastian and me.

He'd written me a song. He'd been messaging with me for

weeks. And he was, after all, kind of a sensitive guy.

Maybe the heartbreak was real. But the song was over.

"Thanks, Brooklyn." Sebastian put down his guitar and ran a hand through his hair, like he was a little embarrassed at having to sing for all of us. Claps and cheers burst out all around me, and he leaned forward into the microphone.

"You're beautiful."

Maybe I was crazy, but I felt like his eyes were dead on me. And then he was gone.

"Tess!"

I yelled out her name even though it was useless in the confusion of rising conversations and piped-in music as the lights came up. I needed to find her because I needed to get Operation Confrontation going before I lost my nerve.

"Natalie!"

Tess was over by the bar, arm waving wildly like she was drowning. I hurried over, or *tried* to hurry over, which was basically impossible in the crush of people, and tried to formulate some plan of attack for Tess to perform an adequate distraction so that I could get backstage.

"There you are," I said, when I finally made it over. "Okay, so, um, I guess we should—"

"Nattie," Tess interrupted. "It's fine. You don't need a distraction. Because"—she singsonged—"look what *I haaaave*!"

She held up something dangling on a lanyard—a big card with "Backstage Privileges" printed on one side.

"What?" I snatched it out of the air. "Seriously? Where did you—"

"Shh. Shh." Tess put a finger first to my lips, then to hers, then to mine again. "I made a *friend*. It doesn't *matter*." She turned back to the bar area, where a girl with a mess of deep-purple hair gave her a little wave.

"Not really my type," Tess said, "but then again, I'm not going to reject the kindness of strangers. Now put it on. Ready?"

"Yeah." I slipped the lanyard over my neck, heart thrumming. The song still felt like it was *in* me, somehow, fizzing in my veins and sending little sparks of energy down my limbs. Phone or no phone, Tess or no Tess, I was the girl in the song. I wasn't scared. I *wanted* to see Sebastian. Wanted to do more than see him, maybe. A shiver went down my bare spine.

"Okay. Okay." Tess smiled as wide as it was possible to smile without showing a single tooth and gave me a hug. "Good luck! Remember: the dance is December third. Two days after they play Atlantic City and the day before their Philadelphia gig. It'd barely be any time out of their schedule."

"Right," I said.

"Got it?"

"Got it."

"Are you—"

"*Tess*," I interrupted, or else this pep talk could go on for hours. "I'm fine. I know what I'm doing."

And for the first time, I think I actually believed myself.

The murmur in the room crescendoed, and as Tess headed back to the bar, I pushed myself through the crowd toward the stage. I had no idea where the backstage door would be, but logic seemed to dictate that it'd be *back*, somewhere. At the lip of the stage, two guys in black T-shirts were standing like human pillars, arms crossed. I fingered the pass around my neck and went up to them.

"Excuse me," I said, forcing my voice to sound as Tess-like as possible. "Where's the stage door?"

"You're joking, right?" said the one who was bald.

"No," I said. "I'm, um, with the band."

I held up the pass. The bald guy grabbed it, inspected it, and dropped it. For a moment, I thought I'd totally screwed it up, but then he nodded toward the back and motioned for me to follow. I did, weightlessly, my whole body feeling lit up with excitement.

"Here you are." The bald guy stopped by a peeling door in the wall and tugged it open. "Hope you get a good interview, Miss, uh—"

He squinted at the pass, and I jerked it out of sight as soon as I realized he was looking for a name.

"Thanks," I said coolly, and stepped in, trying not to freak out. I had just effectively smuggled myself not only into a twenty-one-plus show at a New York City venue, but *backstage*. Who did I think I *was*?

Then, of course, I remembered. I was *Natalie*. And Natalie was going to get what she wanted.

Backstage was a lot less glamorous than I thought it'd be. It was dark, and smelled like a basement, and had extremely inadequate signage. After a little fumbling around and wishing I had my phone to use as a flashlight, I located a door marked Green Room and, before I could think too much about it, pushed it open.

Inside, the greenroom was not actually green, but a chipped beigeish color and stuffed with battered furniture and a greasy-looking light-up mirror. The air was chilly and tasted like cigarettes. A few guys—the other Young Lungs—were flopped on the deflated sofas, drinking beers, and it wasn't until the door swung all the way open and hit the cinder-block wall that they looked up.

"And you are?" one of them said.

"Uh," I said, immediately forgetting I was supposed to be cool. Somehow I'd forgotten to prepare myself for the fact that *other people* were in the band, and would obviously be backstage. "I'm, um . . . Natalie."

The bassist and the drummer didn't move. Only the other guitarist, a skinny black guy with a knit hat and goatee, seemed to catch on.

"No shit," he said, and stubbed out his cigarette. "*The* Natalie?"

"Uh . . ." No point in lying here. "Yup."

"No shit." He rubbed his jaw. "You're a real girl."

"Is that a surprise?" The words just popped out of my mouth. I resisted the urge to cringe. But the guitarist guy laughed.

"A funny girl, too," the guitarist sad. "I'm Ed. Hey, guys, check it—Natalie's here."

Not knowing what else to do, I gave the single dorkiest wave I think I've ever done in my life. The other two guys gave me a look from behind their beards. Then they smiled. Then laughed.

"Welcome, Natalie!" one boomed, fake-regally.

"Yeah," said the other one. "All hail Natalie."

"Guys, leave her alone." Ed gestured at an upended crate. "Wanna sit?"

"Oh, um, sure." I sat. Ed cleared his throat.

"Sebastian's . . . out. With, ah, this . . . another—" He cleared his throat, frowning. "You know what? Let me just text him and tell him you're here."

"Sure." I could only imagine what it was like coming off-stage after a show. Sebastian was probably exhausted, and right about now would be when he'd probably go outside for some alone time, take some pictures, send some Pixstagram messages. But I was *here* now, and we were going to talk.

"You want anything to drink?" Ed asked, pocketing his phone. "There's shitty beer and Seb's shitty sugar water.

And Pop-Tarts if you're hungry and share our lead singer's childlike eating habits."

"Oh, um," I said. "No thanks."

"Is she even *old* enough to drink?" said the bassist, who had those expander things in the lobes of his ears. He elbowed the drummer, who exhaled a plume of smoke and laughed. "When's her curfew?"

"Can it," Ed said.

"No, seriously," said the drummer. "What's the age of consent in New York? Google it. Just in case."

"Seb's probably gonna take her to senior prom or something," said the bassist with a snort. "Bet he looks great in a tux."

In fact, Sebastian had gone to senior prom with Kirsten Fisher, a hippie girl with blond hair down to her waist who'd left Wister and gone to teach yoga in Spain. And he *had* looked really great in a tux—powder blue—at least according to his Pixstagram. I opened my mouth to make a joke about it when I realized that, besides Ed, no one had actually spoken *to* me since I'd gotten there.

"Actually, I think I will take a beer," I said, more loudly than I meant to. Ed leaned forward and fished a Budweiser out of the bucket.

"Cheers." He twisted off the top and handed it to me.

"Thanks." I took a tiny, terrible sip and held it between my knees.

"So what brings you here, Natalie?" Ed said. "Surely it can't be the company."

"Music's not that great either," the bassist said. "Tonight sucked."

"My monitor was all messed up," Ed said. "I couldn't hear myself."

"Could you not hear the *rest* of us, either?" the drummer said. "Because—"

"Can we not do this now?" Ed said, and glanced at me. "Save that shit for the bus."

"Whatever," the bassist said, and flopped back onto the couch. Next to him, the drummer was snapping a lighter under a cigarette. Noticing me staring, he lifted his eyebrows.

"You want, baby doll?"

"Don't give the kid cigs, Colin," said Ed. "That's irresponsible."

*Kid.* That was what I was to them. A kid in a too-big sparkly top whose biggest concerns were curfews and—I cringed, thinking of what I'd come here to ask Sebastian about—*school dances.* If I was going to go through with Operation Confrontation, I needed to talk to Sebastian away from these guys. Actually, first, I needed to find Sebastian, period.

"Excuse me," I said, so loudly that the drummer stopped snapping his lighter. "Um, where exactly *is* Sebastian? I need to talk to him."

They looked at one another.

"He, uh, he says he's coming," Ed said quickly, looking at his phone. "Just, uh . . . busy with someone. Something."

Behind his cigarette, Drummer Colin was staring at me. "What'd you say your name was again?"

"Natalie," I said for the second time. But this time it felt like it might be the wrong answer. Drummer Colin just looked at the bassist, who grunt-laughed.

"Yeah, sorry," Drummer Colin said, on a puff of smoke. "It's just, like . . . we thought it was just a song, you know?"

Heart pounding, I turned to Ed, who was the closest thing to an ally I had in this whole room. He shrugged.

"Hence my surprise," he explained. "No idea that you were a real person. Let alone one who'd show up backstage and—"

"There she is!"

The greenroom door flew open. The bald-headed bouncer was back, and he did not look happy.

"Miss," he panted. "You are not authorized to be back here."

"What?" I looked around the room, as if anyone there was going to help me. "I mean, um, yes I am, I have this—"

I held out the backstage pass, and the bouncer grabbed it from my hands so hard it unclipped from the lanyard.

"What did you say your name was?" he said, studying the pass.

"Natalie," Ed said. "That's Natalie. We were just chatting."

"Natalie," the bouncer repeated, looking at the badge. "That's not what it says here."

My heart plummeted to my stomach. "I can explain," I said hastily. "It's just . . . I'm not . . ."

The bouncer crossed his arms. "You wouldn't happen to have ID on you, would you, *Natalie*?"

"I . . ." *Shoot! Shoot shoot shoot.* I should have said Bethany, or at least looked to see what name was on the backstage pass.

"Miss, are you aware that this is a twenty-one-and-over event?"

"I'm—" I started to say, but the bouncer snapped his fingers at me.

"Your blond friend's about to get her ass thrown out by the bartender, so now is *not* the time for you to lie to me."

"Tess?" I said, voice cracking. I looked around—at the band, at the beer bottles, at the room that was totally empty of the one person I'd come all the way to the greenroom of a twenty-one-and-over show in New York City to find.

"Go get her," bald guy said. "*Now.* Or I'm calling the cops on both of you."

"But—"

But there were no *but*s. The bald guy clamped a hand on my shoulder and yanked me up from the crate, and none of the band guys moved to stop him.

"Bye, Natalie!" Ed's voice called after me. "Cool to meet you!"

I didn't even get a chance to answer. The bouncer steered

me down the hallway, through the peeling-paint door, and back into the big concert room, which was now down to a few clumps of people and gave me a clear view over to the bar. As soon as she saw me, Tess rushed forward and threw her arms around my neck.

"Natalie!" she cried. "Natalie. Natalie. Natalieeeeee—"

"Shh!" I pried her off me, on high alert again. "We're still very much in public, you know."

I tried to look behind us, back to the door, but there wasn't really anything to see. The greenroom was locked away again, and the bald guy was blocking my view, anyway. And it had all been over so fast.

"You the friend?" A bartender with a handlebar mustache glared at us. "Get her out of here."

"I'm so sorry," I said. "She's just, uh—"

"She's drunk," he finished for me.

"Show's over, ladies," bald guy said. "Time to get out of here and go back to Jersey."

Tess's black-rimmed eyes went wide.

"Excuse *me*." She jabbed in the general direction of the bald guy's chest. "We are *not* from *Jersey*, I will have you know, Mr. . . . Man. We are from *Phil-uh-del-fee-uh, PEE-AY*! Do you *know* who we *are*? This girl . . ."

She grabbed for me, but I ducked.

"Tess," I said, through gritted teeth. "Shut. Up."

Only a handful of people were left now. The lights onstage

were off, too. The band was probably done drinking their stupid beers and was already packing up all their stuff into the trunk of whoever's car. Or maybe they had a tour bus now. And Sebastian was . . . I didn't even know. Operation Confrontation was a total failure. But even worse than that—and I hated that I cared so much—was what the band had said. That to them, I wasn't even real. To Sebastian, even.

"Come on," I said, and wedged myself under Tess to help her stop weaving everywhere. "Let's go."

"But what about Sebassssstian?" Tess said, clomping along next to me. She whipped her head around to look back at the stage, but I gave her a pointed shove in the small of her back. "Did you taaaalk to him?"

I didn't want to get into it, and Tess was not in a state to understand what had happened backstage. *I* barely understood it, and I was dead sober.

"Shut up," I said. "I mean, let's just go. I'll explain later."

Outside, Brooklyn was dark and sleety and orange from the streetlights. A few people were standing around, waiting for cars or shivering around cigarettes.

"Sorry," Tess said, and lowered her voice. "*Natalie*. It really is a great name, you know."

She laughed, and wiped her sweaty bangs off her forehead, which took a couple of tries. I dropped her arm.

"Tess, how did you get this drunk?"

"Pff." She shrugged, and almost missed her hip when she

went to strike an indignant pose. "I am not *drunk*, Nata—Nattie." She gave me a sweet smile. "I *may* have had a couple of beers. From my new friend V. Remember?"

As if on cue, the purple-haired girl from before appeared from the shadows.

"V," Tess explained, "is the one who gave you that backstage pass. And she likes buying drinks. And she is *also* a lesbian. What are the odds?"

"One in four, maybe more," V said in a raspy alto, and the two of them collapsed into giggles. V started poking Tess in the ribs, and Tess started laughing so hard she wobbled and almost fell. V, who was wearing only a T-shirt and fishnets under shorts, pulled a pack of cigarettes from her pocket.

"You guys want?" she said.

"No thanks," I said.

"Don't do that!" Tess gasped. "Smoking kills!"

Apparently being drunk brought out Tess's self-righteous streak. V just laughed and clicked her lighter.

"Did you get the interview?" she asked.

It took me a moment to realize she was talking to me. "What?"

V nodded at Tess. "Your friend said you were on deadline. Had to get in with the Lungs to file by nine a.m."

"Oh," I said. "I, uh . . ."

"That was a lie," Tess blurted out. "I lied to you about that. Sorry."

V laughed again on a puff of smoke. "No big. I've seen them, like, five times now. Where are you ladies headed?"

"Uh . . ." I realized I had no idea. I had Bethany's address saved in my phone, but my phone was at Bethany's. And Tess was the one who knew where all the subways were. Did the trains even run this late?

"Crown Heights," I said at last.

"Cool. I'm in Bushwick. Want to split a cab?" V said.

I had never taken a taxi before, not even in Philadelphia. But this was New York, and I was stuck, and presumably the presence of a driver as a potential witness would prevent V from murdering us and turning us into fodder for a new episode of *Law & Order*.

"Sure," I said, as if I split cabs every day and knew what that meant.

"Cool." V exhaled twin streams of smoke and lifted her arm into the air. Almost instantly, headlights appeared out of the mist and a cab heaved to a stop at the curb.

"Ladies." V ground out her cigarette and opened the door. "Your chariot awaits."

We piled into the backseat, V and I at the windows and Tess in the middle. V gave the driver her address and we lurched off into the night.

"So what brings you cuties to the big city?" V said.

"The concert," I said.

"The concert," Tess said, "and vintage shopping. Oh, and Nattie's true love."

V arched an eyebrow. Unlike her hair, her eyebrows were just regular black, although it looked like she'd drawn them on with charcoal.

"You don't say?"

"Uh, not exactly," I said. "I mean, it's kind of complicated. I think it's more lust than love, actually."

"Even worse," V said. "Or better. Who's the dude or lady?"

I thought about Sebastian onstage, singing, and tried to imagine Sebastian backstage now, drinking a tall can of something sugary and caffeinated, running his hands through his hair, drumming his fingers on his jeans. In another world, I was still there, with him, kissing him, or touching him, or something more—

The cab hit a bump.

"Dang!" Tess lolled onto V with more force than necessary. "This car is crazy."

"Totally." V gave her a kittenish smile. Tess grinned, and together they laughed a secret laugh I didn't quite get.

I folded my arms and stared out the window. Maybe if Tess hadn't been such an idiot, I could've gone through with Operation Confrontation. I *would* have. I just needed more time. Now I'd missed my only freaking chance.

"Sorry," Tess said, righting herself with my shoulder as an anchor. "Sorry, Natalie. Nattie. Sorry."

"Natalie like the song 'Natalie'?" V said.

"*Egg-zactly* like the song 'Natalie,'" Tess answered for me. "*Too cool to leave, too tough to tease.* Boop."

She tapped me on the nose. I rolled my eyes, not that she could see me in the dark.

"No way," V rasped. "Wait. No way. You're here to see your true love because it's Sebastian Delacroix."

"I didn't say that," I said, finally tearing my eyes away from the endless parade of bleak row houses and bright bodega awnings.

"She didn't *say* it, but it's *true*," Tess said helpfully. "We are here for Operation Confrontation! Fighting the good fight!"

"That is crazy, dudes," V said. Even in the dark, I could tell her eyes were lighting up. "How *old* are you guys, anyway, like . . . high school?"

"We are juniors. Juniors at the Owen Wister—"

"*Tess.*" I elbowed her.

"Sorry, sorreeeee," she said. "Anyway, we're both seventeen. But *my* birthday is in March, so."

She gave a meaningful wink to V, who was ignoring her and tapping at her phone.

"Great idea!" Tess said, and grabbed V's phone. "Let's take a selfie!"

Before either of us could answer, Tess had pulled open Pixstagram, thrown out her arm, and tapped the shutter button.

"Smile!"

"Here."

The cab stopped hard, and we all smacked into the plastic divider.

"Here," the cab driver said again, in an accent I didn't recognize. "DeKalb Avenue."

"Thanks." V popped open her door and slid out—she hadn't even been wearing a seat belt—and handed a few crumpled bills to Tess, who dumped them into my lap.

"Text me!" Tess said, and threw V's phone back at her.

"You bet. Great to meet you, too, Natalie."

V winked, slammed the door, and disappeared.

"Where to now, please?" the cab driver said.

"Uh," I said.

"Kingston and Pacific," Tess said. "And step on it!"

"How did you remember that?" I said. Tess shrugged.

"I have very good information recall when I'm drunk," she said, and tapped the side of her head. "Frees up the unused ninety percent of my brain."

"That's not even real," I said. The cab pulled out, and I suddenly felt very, very tired. My legs hurt from standing up and my feet hurt from my shoes and my head hurt from, well, everything. Mostly the music. Right then I didn't want to be Natalie or "Natalie" or anyone.

And, I realized, to Sebastian, that's just who I was. Nobody.

# CHAPTER TWENTY-ONE

If Bethany had noticed us looking particularly forlorn that morning, she didn't say anything. Even though it was technically a Saturday, we had to get up at the disgustingly early hour of seven thirty in order to catch a train to a train to the transit train that would get us home by a nonsuspicious morning time, and all around us the flower shops and bodegas and liquor stores of Brooklyn were cold and blue-colored and shaking off their padlocks for the morning. Tess was pale and slumpy on the too-bright subway car, clutching her head the whole way and only looking up to tell me when to get off and stand on another platform until we got to Penn Station.

"Blech." Tess made a face at her coffee. "This is terrible."

"Do you want me to throw it out?" I was sitting with my tote bag crammed under me as a cushion, since we apparently weren't allowed into the waiting area with seats unless we had Amtrak tickets, and picking at the penitential bagel Tess had bought me for the train ride home.

"No." Tess grimaced and slugged back another gulp. "I need the electrolytes."

Now, I knew, was not the time to point out that coffee did not have electrolytes. Instead, I rubbed the back of Tess's leather jacket, which squeaked a little under my fingers.

"Muhh," she moaned. "I feel like rotten death. I feel like I'm going to puke into this dishwater coffee."

I withdrew my comforting arm as a precaution, but Tess just burped and took another sip.

"What even *happened* last night?" she croaked.

"Uh . . ." I wondered where to begin. "Well, we ate some falafel—"

"Ugh. *That* I remember," Tess said. "Did not taste as good the second time."

I winced and pushed on, eager to move off the topic of falafel barf. "So the Young Lungs played, and—"

"That's *right!*" Tess's eyes lit up, as much as they could behind their bleariness. "You talked to him. You nailed him down for the dance."

I squashed a pinched bit of bagel into a bready pulp and exhaled hard. "No."

"No?!" Tess said it so loudly a nearby one-legged pigeon squawked and flapped into a See Something? Say Something poster. "What do you mean, *no*, Nattie? That was the whole point of this mission!"

"I was a little busy making sure *someone* didn't get *arrested*,"

I said, but Tess was already up and off.

"We came here for *one reason*," she said. "*One* very important thing we needed for OBGDP, and you screwed it up."

I stood up and threw the bagel into the trash. "Oh, *that*
was our one reason? Because it looked to me like we were just
here to get wasted."

Tess narrowed her eyes and slurped her coffee insidiously.
Then, with a dramatic sniff, she closed her eyes and pressed a
hand to her forehead.

"I can't deal with this right now. I'm too hungover."

"Yeah." Having nothing to counter with, and having
thrown my butter-covered prop in the trash can, I instead
pulled out my phone. I had no reception, so I couldn't text
Sam Huang to tell him we were on our way back. But I could
get Pixstagram, even if it took a while to load on the station
Wi-Fi. And still, there was nothing. Nothing. Nothing new
from the show, not anything. Sebastian's latest posts were
the same as they'd been last night: an untitled, artsy-looking
shot of the underside of a suspension bridge and a picture of
a single can of blue-raspberry flavored Hypr ("tour fuel for
a poor fool #younglungs"). Idly, somewhat bitterly, I clicked
on the hashtag—maybe someone had posted pictures from
the show.

My butt was starting to hurt from sitting on my lumpy tote
bag as I scrolled through grainy shots of the crowd. I knew
Tess was looking over my shoulder because she was breathing her coffee breath in my ear, and so I scrolled as angrily

and as slowly as I could scroll, lingering over every picture in fake-y consideration before double-tapping it to make the heart appear, until—

"Hey," Tess coffee-breathed into my ear. "Is that . . . us? Who took that picture?"

It was—the selfie Tess had taken in the taxi. Tess looked amazing, even while completely drunk, the purple-haired girl looked impossibly cool, her nose ring just barely glinting, and I looked . . . awful. Supremely weird. To the extent that I was even visible in the dark taxi backseat, anyway. If I squinted, I could see my hair, all puffy from the humid concert air, and my eyeshadow melting down my face.

"*You* did," I said shortly. I went to scroll away—*not* giving this one a heart—when I saw the caption beneath it.

literally actually ran into #NATALIE last night!!! freakin out y'all #younglungs #vivianviolet

"What?!" I said, loud enough to scare the pigeon again. Tess screwed up one eye.

"Jesus, Nattie, don't yell, my head is—"

"That girl from last night." My heart was skittering in my chest. "With the purple hair. Did she tell you what her name was?"

"What? No. I barely even remember her. Why?"

I held the phone half an inch from Tess's nose. "Look at her username."

"I can't freaking see—oh."

"Oh?!" *Oh* was an infinite understatement. The picture

was posted by *vivianviolet*, and it had 1,893 likes. And the little hearts kept on coming.

"New Jersey Transit train to Trenton, now arriving on track seven west."

"That's us." Tess grabbed my elbow, but I didn't get up. I double-tapped into my browser and thumb-typed in Vivian Violet's blog address as fast as my shaking fingers would let me, frantically paged down, and there it was.

> BREAKING FREAKING NEWS
>
> Posted by V. Violet at 1:24 a.m. EST
>
> Are you sitting down, kittens? Auntie VV has THRILLING gossip. As we're all aware, I and the rest of Cool America have a massive aural hard-on for precious hipster rockers the Young Lungs and have been dying to know WHO the heartless heartbreaker behind their infectious earworm "Natalie" could be. I'd just about written off Natalie as a figment of studly singer/guitarist Sebastian Delacroix's imagination when I LITERALLY MET HER IN PERSON.

There in the middle was our photo again, which I skipped over.

> Now, obviously I didn't get a *huge* interview in with Miss N., but we did talk enough to confirm that she and SebDel were high-school sweethearts—in fact, she's still in

high-school. #Jailbait much? Still, a source close to Natalie describes her relationship with Mr. Delacroix as "true love." No word yet on why she broke his heart, heart, heart, though. Hopefully she'll come forward soon with a statement and put an end to our misery!!

"Nattie," Tess said. "The train?"

I shook her off. My heart was beating so fast it felt like it had whirred right out of my chest. It was like I was empty, floating a few inches above my backpack, and not in a dreamy, romantic way. In a ghost way. A dead way. A way that made me feel like I might barf up my bits of bagel.

"This is bad," I said robotically. "This is very bad."

Tess squinted at my screen for two seconds as people started streaming around us. "Okay, so what. So there's a girl out there named Natalie who Sebastian wrote a song about? That's the same as before." She shrugged. "You're making a big deal out of nothing."

"It's not *nothing*." I tapped back to Pixstagram. "It's at over two thousand likes."

"So? It's a terrible picture of you."

She was right, ish: between the low light levels and the weird Pixsta filter, you could barely tell I was *human*, let alone *me*.

"Come on." Tess held out one hand to me, and used her other hand to root around for her phone, which was in her pocket and now buzzing. "You're not mad at me, right?"

"*No.*" I gritted my teeth.

"Good. And don't cry, Nattie. We're in the middle of New York."

I wasn't going to cry. If anything, I was going to scream. I clenched my phone in my hand. Then I set it down again. Then I picked it up again. Then I looked at Tess, who was *not* running for the train but instead yelling into her phone.

"What? No. I don't even *know*—"

And then she went pale, a pale that was paler even than hungover or pissed off about bad coffee.

"Shut up," she said into her phone, and jammed it back into her pocket.

"Now boarding, track seven west, train eight thirty-seven to Trenton."

"Um, let's go," said Tess. She sounded nervous, which was not something Tess often sounded like.

"What?" I didn't move. "Who was that on the phone?"

"Remember how you said you weren't mad?"

"I'm not," I said. "I mean, I don't think I am."

"Remember how I'm your loyal best friend who shepherded you around New York and took you to find an awesome dress to wear to the Big Gay Dance Party and supported you after the Almost Kiss and—"

"I remember, Tess," I said. "What happened?"

"I think I kind of, um, gave Vivian Violet my phone number."

"You *what*?"

A woman pulling a rolly bag glared at me from under a beret. Tess didn't even blink.

"Look, when she finds you, just—"

"*When* she finds me?" I cried. "Why would she be able to find me?"

"Don't be dumb," Tess said. "There aren't a lot of Tess Kozlowskis with a two-six-seven area code. One Whitepages search and a cross-reference with the schools in the area—"

"You put your *last name* in her phone?" I was still catching up. "How did you even manage to *spell* it?"

"It's a Polish thing," Tess said. "I guess I did it before I found you. Back when I was still at the bar."

"Of course," I said. "Of *course* you were at the bar."

"What is *that* supposed to mean?"

"It means that you abandoned me to get drunk!" I threw my hands into the air. "And now all this stuff is happening."

"I didn't *abandon you to get drunk*," Tess spat. "*You* told *me* you wanted to go by yourself, remember? And I didn't know who she was. I just thought she was some cute Brooklyn girl. Do you know how often I get to talk to cute girls outside of OWPA? Outside of a place where everyone knows who I am? Not very fucking often."

"Now boarding, track seven west—"

"Let's just go," Tess said. "We'll deal with this later."

"Deal with this? How can we possibly *deal* with this?"

"We'll make a plan. Operation—"

"No. No way." I buried my face in my arms. "I don't want to make a plan right now. Honestly, I just kind of want to scream."

"Don't scream." Tess glanced around at the crowd of commuters. "God, do *not* scream."

"Well, I sure as hell don't have anything to say!" I looked up. "I can't believe this. You sold me out to the press."

"V is not 'the press,'" Tess said hotly.

"Oh, so she's still V, huh? So should I start calling you the *source close to Natalie*?"

"Come on, Nattie." Tess tugged on my arm. "It's not like there's going to be paparazzi hiding in your dad's woodshed—"

"Yurt." I didn't move. Tess let go.

"Okay." Her voice was a little higher now. "Okay, Nattie, I get that—"

"No."

But Tess didn't even listen and blew right on by.

"I get that you're feeling bitter. And that's understandable. But listen to yourself—"

"I *am* listening to myself," I said. "Actually, for the first time, I'm listening to *myself*, and not *you*."

"Oh, so this is *my* fault? Please." Tess fluttered her eyelashes, which irritated me for some reason. "*You're* the one who broke Sebastian's heart."

"But I didn't!" I was almost yelling now. "I drove around

with him one night, one time, and he touched my face, and that was it. Then *you* made me dress up for that show at Ruby's, and you dragged me to New York, and now—"

"Nattie, look, I get it, okay?" Tess interrupted. "I know better than anyone what it's like to be made famous for something you're not proud of, but—"

"Are you serious?" I couldn't believe it. "That stupid billboard? News flash, Tess: that was *six years ago*. And *nobody cares*. Nobody *ever* cared. You just can't see that because you think the whole stupid world revolves around *you* and your *plans* and your *dumb dance*."

Tess's mouth fell open. Then she shut it and pressed her lips tightly together.

"That's great." She laughed mirthlessly. "*I'm* the selfish one."

I should've said I was sorry. But I *wasn't* sorry. I hadn't realized that was the truth until I'd barfed it out like that, but now that I had, it felt like the first thing to make sense in weeks.

"Let me ask you something," Tess went on. "Did you even *ask* Sebastian about the dance last night? Or were you just trying to grab a piece of his indie-rock ass?"

The image of the band guys in the greenroom came flooding back. *Seb's probably gonna take her to senior prom or something.* My stomach twisted. I looked at the ground, but Tess was still talking.

"You know, I'm not just your quirky lesbian sidekick,

Nattie. I don't exist just to make you feel better about all the dumb mistakes you make. I have stuff I want, too. And I'm actually working hard at something over here, for—*yes*, for myself. And yeah, I made you come up here for one thing, one stupid small favor. I guess I'm sorry that I relied on you. I'm sorry that I thought my friend could support me. God, I should've known better."

I looked back up, and she gave me a shove. That was it— just a real shove.

"Good luck, *Natalie*."

Tess turned and pushed away, and the train-station crowd surged into the space where my best friend used to be.

# CHAPTER TWENTY-TWO

Tess was gone. Tess, who knew how to take the subway and who wasn't afraid to shoulder-check people to get on an escalator and who thought I was a terrible friend, was gone. Very gone. I immediately broke out in panic sweat. I had missed the train, and the next one wasn't for an hour because apparently no one wanted to go to Trenton on a Saturday, which meant I wouldn't get back until three—and that was before I took the train from Center City to Wister. Penn Station was filling with people coming back from Thanksgiving, pulling industrial-sized suitcases, looking bleary or angry or both. The overhead voice echoed against the tiles with a reminder not to approach or pet police dogs. In my stomach, the bagel felt like a hunk of lead.

Okay. If I was going to barf up bagel bits, I at least didn't want to do it onto a leather-jacketed New Yorker with fancy luggage. I gripped the strap of my tote bag and pushed through to the side of one of the staircases, next to an Amtrak touchscreen. For $104, I could get to Philadelphia by 11:20 a.m. Except that

I did not have $104. I had seventeen crumpled dollars and a concert ticket stub and—shoot—Bethany West's old ID. I ran my finger along the edge of her PA driver's license and contemplated my wallet. Technically, in there, I had a credit card, but Mom and Dad had said it was strictly For Emergencies Only.

The bagel-block lurched within me.

Right. What was this if not an emergency? If swiping away that $104 into this touchscreen swiper-thing meant I would return on time and my parents would never suspect I'd been on a stealth trip to the cultural capital of the eastern seaboard, well . . .

I ran the card before I had a chance to reconsider, took my printout ticket to the track, and fell asleep in a train seat.

An hour and a half of trundling through New Jersey later, I bolted up the stairs at 30th Street Station, ignoring the siren call of the cinnamon-scented pretzel booths, and dashed for the regional rail platforms. I made it onto the 11:23 local to Wister with literal seconds to spare. The train was eerily quiet, with everyone else plugged into earbuds, but I turned my phone off, terrified that I'd be tempted to look at Pixstagram otherwise. Once I'd finally found a seat, I allowed myself to catch my breath. The fizziness in my stomach had spread to my chest, and I hadn't even had anything to drink the night before. And Tess was gone and mad at me and I was alone and mad at Tess and I wasn't even trying to do anything wrong. It was all so unfair.

I put my head between my knees and started to cry, right there on the 11:23 local.

If there was one thing I was good at (besides being weird), it was self-flagellation, and in between tears I berated myself with gusto. I'd been a terrible friend. No, even worse, I'd been selfish, when all Tess was doing was trying to help. I hadn't done anything to help Operation Big Gay Dance Party. But worst of all, and worst that this was still what I cared about the most, I hadn't gotten to ask Sebastian anything about me. About us.

God. I couldn't even get the pronouns right in my head. I let out a sob and smeared my face on the knee of my jeans.

"Miss?"

I jerked my head up. A white-shirted SEPTA conductor was peering down at me, his hand on the back of my seat.

"I'm sorry, miss, but this is the quiet car." He pointed to a sign by the window. "No, uh, noise."

"Right." I sniffled and scrubbed at my face. Quiet car notwithstanding, I shouldn't have been crying on the 11:23 local to Wister anyway. This poor nice conductor in his little round hat shouldn't have to deal with me. The only really acceptable place to cry is home.

So I held it together until the Wister stop, and then climbed up the rickety wooden steps from the platform to Evergreen Street. I could already see the roof of the McCullough-Schwartz enclave, which made the fizzing in my chest settle a little. The house was still there, and somewhere inside, so was my family. I rubbed my eyes, smoothed my hair, and practically ran for it.

"Hello?" I called as I creaked through the squeaky front door and into the hallway. "Is anyone—"

"*Natalie McCullough-Schwartz.*"

The sound of my full name sent an electric shiver down my spine. Mom and Dad leaped up from the kitchen table at once, Mom livid and still in her pajamas and Dad just quiet and sad. Behind them, Sam Huang peered out from his desk, ashen-faced.

"What?" I stopped short, so short that the kitchen door slapped me on the butt. "Ow."

"Where," Mom said, "*where* have you been?"

Oh no.

"Tess's?" It was more of a squeak than a confident answer. Mom folded her bathrobed arms.

"Don't lie to us, Nattie. We know you weren't at Tess's."

"I was," I insisted, pathetically. "We just, um—"

"New York, Nattie G?" Dad shook his head. "What were you thinking?"

My heart plunged into my stomach. For two agonizing seconds, no one said anything.

"I'm sorry," I said, at last. "I know the card is just for emergencies. . . ."

But something about my words wasn't registering. Dad

frowned at Mom. Mom clicked her tongue. Sam Huang quietly got up from his desk chair.

"Never mind," I finished.

"You weren't answering our texts," Dad said. "We got worried."

"I'm sorry. My phone . . ." I pulled it out of my pocket. "I left it behind, and then it was off—"

Mom made a *tzzp* noise and snapped her fingers in the air. "We're not interested in any more lies, Nattie."

"But I'm not lying!" The phone part had been the truth, at least.

"Aren't you? I'm not sure I can trust you, Nattie." She closed her eyes for a long moment, then breathed out, hard. "No answer to our texts. No one answering at the Kozlowskis' house. Do you know how scary that is, Nattie? Not to know where your baby is?" She swallowed. "If we hadn't seen evidence that you were still alive . . ."

"Evidence?"

Silence, except for the sound of Sam Huang shutting his computer. And then I realized.

"Sam Huang?" I cried. "How could you?"

Sam Huang shifted in his desk chair. "Anne and Robert asked me where you went, and I said I thought you were out with Tess, and then . . ."

"He showed us that picture someone posted," Mom said. "You and Tess."

"Blitztograph, or whatever." Dad nodded somberly.

I clenched my hands into fists.

"How could you, Sam Huang? You know, if you hadn't said anything, I would've come back and everything would've been fine."

"I'm sorry, Nattie," said Sam Huang.

"No, Sam, don't apologize," Mom said. "You did the right thing. Sam told us the truth because he was *worried* about you, Nattie. Because he wanted you to be safe. And thank God he did."

"I wasn't not *safe*. I was *fine*. So yeah, thank *God* he got me in trouble when I wasn't even in danger or anything." I threw my tote onto the ground and jabbed my phone into the charger by the toaster, suddenly feeling very, very ugly.

"That's it, young lady," Dad said. "You're grounded. No dance whatsoever."

"Fine." I threw my hands in the air. "Great. Thanks, Sam Huang. You know, I'm *so* glad you came to live with us."

The words tumbled out before I even realized what I'd said. Sam Huang blinked, once, twice, and then grabbed his sweatshirt from his chair and slipped up the back stairs. Mom gaped, her face flushed, but before she could say anything my phone started to buzz.

"I'm sorry," I said quickly. "I'm sorry. I'm—"

My phone wouldn't shut up. The call was an unknown number, and when I fumbled for the switch to silence it I noticed I had something like fifteen missed calls since last night—none of them numbers I recognized. Then I stood there, phone in hand and heart pounding queasily hard.

"I'm sorry," I said again, my voice preschooler-tiny. Mom got up and shoved her chair back in place a little too hard.

"Grounded," she said. "And I hope you think a little harder about how you treat your family, Nattie. Sam, your father, all of us."

"I—"

Dad, tight-lipped above his Haverford sweatshirt, stood and came over, presumably to give me a squeeze on the shoulder, but I shrugged out of his grasp. He sighed.

"Well," he said. "Well. I'm disappointed, Natalie."

And then he was gone, leaving me alone with my phone in my hand and a stomachache. I stood for a minute, two, overwhelmed, until a single memory started pushing its way to the front of my mind. The texts. From Dad. From last night. When they'd been out of town and so, of course, had I.

I picked my phone up again and tapped over to my texts.

Hey NG can you gimme a call? xo D

NG it's Dad, you at Tess's? Looks like rain . . .

from Mr. Yurt

please call . . . SH at A Cappella & says you're not

home?? v important . . . need someone 2 tarp

yurt before big storm! love Dad

The yurt.

The bottom fell out of my stomach. *No.* I shoved on a pair of Mom's clogs, flew out the screen door into the muddy backyard, and gasped. In the corner of the yard stood a pile of splintered, soggy wooden slats and a soaked, dirt-covered heap of canvas.

"No," I said out loud. But I was too stupidly late. The yurt was destroyed.

If I'd felt guilt heartburn on the train before, I was now utterly immolated. Carefully, awfully, I stepped over to the corner of the pile and crouched—maybe the damage wasn't so bad—but when I picked up a slat, it split right in half.

"Shit." I threw the slat back into the mud, and then, because swearing didn't seem to do anything the first time, I increased the volume. "Shit!"

Everything was broken. Every stupid thing was broken. And my phone was buzzing with another call—a New York area code. *Bethany,* I thought. *Shit.* I took a deep breath and answered.

"Hello?" I said. "Hi, Bethany, I'm really sorry about your ID. I totally—"

"Hello?" The voice was deep and male and definitely not Bethany. "Hey, hi. Are you—is this Natalie?"

"I . . ." My *wrong number* died in my throat. "Yeah?"

"Awesome," he said quietly. "I mean, hi there. This is Carter Murasaki at *Jawharp* magazine. Can I ask you a couple of questions about Sebastian Delacroix?"

# CHAPTER TWENTY-THREE

I turned off my phone for the rest of the weekend, which was like being a ghost, or living without a soul. When I did go back to school, for the first time in my entire high-school life, even though it was a special emergency last-minute Monday damage-control session, I skipped an OWPALGBTQIA meeting. Or tried to, anyway.

"Excuse me?" A tiny freshperson girl with severe eyebrows cornered me just outside Dr. Frobisher's room, as I was attempting to skulk past. "Um, are you Natalie?"

"Um," I said. "What?"

She threw a look back at the double doors of the Alumni Building, where her friends were clearly waiting.

"Um, sorry. I was just wondering. Because you're kind of . . ."

I braced myself for her to say something nasty.

". . . famous."

She giggled, and her eyes went wide. And even though I knew it didn't matter, and that I shouldn't have cared, I felt a tiny glow in my chest. No freshperson had ever thought I was cool before.

"I was just wondering if you, um, knew Sebastian Delacroix?"

"Everyone at Wister knows him," Tall Zach, my savior, my excellent sugar-fueled, long-legged friend, had bounded up to me in the hallway and insinuated himself between the freshperson and me. "I mean, everyone who was here when he went here, anyway. *I* know him."

"Yeah, but, like . . . she *kissed* him, right?"

"Question time is over!" Tall Zach shouted, and he gave the girl a few emphatic shooing gestures with his bag of candy until she finally scurried off.

"Thanks," I said.

"No problem." Tall Zach held open the door. "I guess you're a celebrity now."

My stomach gave a nauseous wiggle. "Don't say that."

"Sorry, sorry. For the record, though, I always thought the song was kind of . . . never mind," he finished, seeing my look of anguish. "Anyway, I hope you're ready for intense problem-solving mode. That *party* is becoming, like, a thing."

"Party?"

"The A Cappella party?" Tall Zach said. "Well, A Cappella slash cross-country, I guess. The guys are sort of polite about it in front of me, but basically *no one* is planning to go to the dance. Except us, I guess. And now that A Cappella is going to the party, too, Tess is trying to get some major firepower on our side, and . . ." He sighed and rubbed his temples. "This whole thing is really becoming a thing, huh?"

"I mean . . . yeah." I swallowed, thinking about the weekend. "Would you expect any less from Tess? Go big or go home."

"Yeah. It's just, like . . ." Tall Zach's lips twitched, and he folded his long arms. "Okay, remember my bar mitzvah?"

"Um, of course? You became a man. And also crushed my hopes of us getting married."

"Nattie." His eyes went wide. "Really?"

"You . . . have good bone structure," I said, feeling myself blush. "I couldn't *help* but have a crush on—actually, never mind. I don't want to talk about it."

Zach laughed. "God, and we'd have had such beautiful children! But, anyway, so . . . yeah." He fiddled with the strap of his fancy digital watch. "*That* was a whole thing, too. I mean, the party and stuff was fun, and all of you guys were great after I pulled the whole 'hey, I'm gay' declaration. But my family wasn't . . ." He exhaled. "My parents were fine, more or less. But my grandparents and stuff . . . they didn't think it was 'appropriate' for that occasion. And we kinda didn't talk for a while?"

"Oh," I said. "God. I had no idea."

Zach shrugged. "I mean, I don't regret doing it, but sometimes I wish I hadn't, like, gone in so hard. Like maybe I should've gone easier on it, for everyone else? So when I see this whole thing with Tess and the dance getting bigger and bigger . . ." He sighed. "It's not that I don't support this thing. You *know* I do. I just . . . I worry about her. I can't help it. We kind of *have* to worry about each other, you know?"

"I mean . . ." I couldn't finish. I worried about Tess, too, but it was different. I hadn't even thought about it, but of course it was different for Zach.

"Hey, it's okay." He swept an arm toward the classroom. "Shall we?"

I didn't move.

"I, um, I have to go." I held my backpack straps tight and shuffled my feet sort of toward the door.

"Go?" Tall Zach frowned. "Where are you going?"

"Somewhere else," I said. "I . . . um, I can't today."

"Can't?" Tall Zach looked aghast, or as aghast as one can look while biting the head off a gummy shark. "But we need you, Nattie."

"Yeah? For what?"

Tall Zach chewed his gummy. Saying nothing. Of course.

"Yeah, so." I started to go, but Tall Zach jumped in front of me and grabbed my elbow.

"Wait! Um, for treasuring?"

I gave him a look. Tall Zach let go of my elbow.

"Okay . . . well, then, as our token straight girl?"

"Hey, Nattie!"

Meredith White, chipper as ever, was rolling her backpack right for us. "Did you hear about the song that—"

"*Yes*," I said, so sharply that Tall Zach almost dropped his candy. Meredith actually gasped a little.

"Oh," she said. "Um, okay. Is this where the OWPALGB—"

"Yup!" Zach said, and jerked his head toward the room. "Why don't you just go . . . on . . . in."

Meredith kicked her backpack from off its haunches and hurried inside. I, meanwhile, folded my arms over my stomach, wishing I could fold up entirely and disappear.

"So, yeah," I said to Tall Zach. "I think you're fine on that front."

"But Nattie—"

"Just . . . go, okay?" I said. "Your boyfriend's probably waiting."

"What do—oh." Tall Zach made a face like the gummies had suddenly gone sour. "Endsignal? We're not a thing. He's just way too young for me."

"Oh."

"I mean, he's nice and all, but it'd be creepy, you know? I don't want to be that older guy who takes advantage."

I looked at my sneakers to hide how furiously embarrassed I was. Because of course—only an interloper would make a mistake like that.

"Yeah," I said at last, my voice whispery. "I really don't think I belong here."

And with that, I pushed through the Alumni Building doors and into the freezing-cold rest of the world.

After school, I sat on the Donut, forlornly, my phone still off. I had spent the rest of the day fighting off heart-stuttering panic and the weird shimmery feeling you get in your eyeballs right before you erupt into sobs, but because being seventeen meant alternating between life-melting emotional disaster and intense academic boredom, I *also* had Dr. Frobisher's Latin test to study for, which I had forgotten about until she'd mentioned it at the end of class.

The main building door banged, and Zach the Anarchist came out, backpack over one shoulder and no jacket on even though it was only like forty degrees. His T-shirt today was blank—just black.

"Hey! Wait up!"

Zach kept walking fast toward his Volvo. He must not have seen me on the Donut, so I had to jog to reach him, and my breath was coming in puffs by the time I got to his car. "Can I have a ride?"

"Why?"

"So . . . I can get to your house?" I said. "To do Latin stuff?"

"Oh." He bit his lip. "Yeah. Sure."

The whole drive there, Zach the Anarchist was weirdly silent. The *drive* wasn't silent, because as soon as we'd gotten in, he'd jacked in his phone and started blasting something angry and anticapitalist, before even turning the heat on. Also, it seemed like he was driving way faster than usual. Either way, we were pulling into the West abode like twenty minutes later.

"Hey, Bacon. Hey, buddy." I fell to the ground as soon as we got in, but Bacon just sort of lolled on his doggie bed.

"He's been having megaesophagus problems," Zach said. "He just got back from the vet."

Bacon waggled his tail-stub, but didn't get up.

"Oh." I got up and kicked off my shoes. "Well . . . should we get started?"

Zach put his backpack on the counter and just kind of looked at the floor.

"Whatever. I'm gonna bake something."

I got out my Latin notebook and hopped onto my stool. "I thought we were done with bake sales."

"We are. Which you would've known if you'd come to the meeting."

Zach unfolded the little cupboard door and started getting stuff out. I stood there, stupidly, unable to help and unable to play with Bacon, which was my fallback activity whenever my help was not needed.

"Oh." I swallowed. "Okay. Well, do you want to read, or—"

"I have notes. Just check them."

"Okay."

I flipped open Zach's notebook to Catullus 58, where he'd done a translation in pointy boy handwriting on Dr. Frobisher's worksheet.

| | |
|---|---|
| *Caeli, Lesbia nostra, Lesbia illa.* | *O Caelius, our Lesbia, that Lesbia.* |
| *illa Lesbia, quam Catullus unam plus quam se atque suos amavit omnes,* | *That Lesbia, whom Catullus alone Loved more than himself and all his own* |
| *nunc in quadriviis et angiportis glubit magnanimi Remi nepotes.* | *Now in the crossroads and alleyways, She jerks off the descendants of magnanimous Remus.* |

"*Ew,*" I whispered. Zach didn't even look up. I flipped incredulously to the *G*s of my student's abridged Latin dictionary for *glubo, glubere*: "to deprive of its bark, to peel, to husk. In obscene sense, to service manually (Roman men being uncircumcised)."

I slammed the dictionary shut, still grossed out, and went back to the worksheet. Under Themes, Zach had written *righteous indignation*.

"What do you mean, *righteous indignation?*" I asked. Zach shrugged.

"You're the one who's so good at Latin."

"Your translation is totally perfect," I pointed out. Zach pulled a cookbook off the shelf.

"She did something gross and so he's mad that he wasted his time." He flipped through pages. "Pretty simple."

I pushed away my notebook and rubbed my arms. The West kitchen, which was usually so cheerful and warm and full of the good kind of organic snacks, now felt chilly. I looked from the countertop up to the refrigerator, which was papered over with pictures: Pat and Trish hiking up some mountain, little Zach playing a guitar twice his size, Bethany grinning a mouth full of braces at her Wister Prep graduation.

"It was cool to see your sister this weekend," I said. "Thanks for asking her to let us stay there."

"Mm."

"Tess found this awesome suit to wear to the dance," I said, with a weird twinge of guilt. I hadn't spoken to Tess since our fight. It was the longest time we'd gone without speaking in possibly ever. "Except, um, she didn't actually buy it. But I got this yellow dress, which I thought was going to look horrible with my hair, but it actually looks pretty great."

"Mm." Zach was measuring out chocolate chips and didn't look me in the eye.

"Can I help?" I asked.

"I've got it."

I stood and watched for another few minutes as he melted butter and chocolate in a small saucepan, then started to stir in some sugar. It smelled divine.

"I should really say thanks," I said, to break the silence. "You really pulled all those bake sales and stuff together. We never would've gotten any customers without your stuff."

"Mm."

He grabbed the guitar spatula and began to scrape the melted chocolate into a bowl. I folded my arms. Zach's silence was the opposite of Tess's overtalkativeness, but it was just as annoying. Maybe worse.

"You know, most people say *you're welcome* when someone thanks them for something."

"Mm."

"Zach!" I actually banged my hand on the counter. "Come on. You're being really weird."

Zach stopped scraping.

"You didn't tell me you were going to New York to see *him*."

"What?"

"Bethany told me about the concert," he said. "The Young Lungs? Seriously? You told me you didn't like him."

"I *don't* like him," I said. "For your information, it was *Tess's* idea. She wanted me to ask him to get the band to play at the dance. So more people would come."

"Yeah? So now we're having them at Winter Formal?"

"Well . . ." I looked at the ground. "It didn't exactly go as planned."

At that, Zach rolled his eyes. "Of course not. Good going, Natalie. Way to think of someone other than yourself."

I clenched my hands into fists. "No, actually, you know what? So what if I liked him? What's the big"—even in the heat of anger, I couldn't make myself swear—"*freaking* deal?"

"Sebastian Delacroix is a tourist, Nattie. He's a shitty musician and he's a total tourist. He only goes places so he can take pictures of them and use them to make himself seem more interesting."

"Yeah, well . . ." I struggled to figure out what I wanted to say. "We can't all be cool, anti-*social media* types like you."

Zach stopped stirring and looked me right in the eyes.

"Did you really date him?"

"What?" My heart thudded against my rib cage. "Who told you that?"

"The song, Nattie. The one that's *named after you?*" Zach shook his head. "Seriously, Nattie, how dumb do you think I am? I may not be on Pixstagram or whatever, but I'm not *dead*. Everyone at school's talking about it. Did you actually think I wasn't ever going to hear about it? Or did you just *happen* to forget to tell *me* in particular? Because I know you told everyone else."

He'd heard it. He'd heard it. My heart sank. I had to act fast—deflect. No, deny.

"Oh, 'Natalie'?" I tried to fake a laugh. "For one thing,

that's the thirtieth most popular name in the US right now." I knew this because I had checked. "For another, the song's not about me." I knew *this* because Sebastian's bandmates had all but confirmed it in New York. I'd never been anything to him.

"That's not what the interview says."

I snapped my head up. "What interview?"

"The one on BuzzKlik?" Zach's cheeks were a little pink. "Everyone's seen it. He's calling you his ex-girlfriend. Says he wishes you could still talk. Is that true?"

"I . . . what?" None of this was making sense. "But we talk all the time!"

Zach looked away.

"God, this is stupid," he said. "You're better than this."

"Better than *what*?" Suddenly, I was mad. Zach was supposed to talk to me, make me feel better, not berate me.

"Better than being a *groupie*, Nattie." Zach made a disgusted noise. "You don't like his music. You don't even like *him* that much. You just like being famous."

"For your information," I said, "I spent last night really messed up about this whole situation. I had to lie to my parents because magazines wouldn't stop calling my house. I had a huge fight with Tess about it."

"Yeah. Well, I bet she was probably right."

"You have no idea what you're talking about!"

The oven beeped, finally preheated. Zach ignored it.

"You're just jealous," I said.

"That's great." Zach gave a short laugh. "I'm jealous of a guy with a man-bun who writes bad hipster lyrics."

"You're jealous because Sebastian Delacroix wasn't too *afraid* to say he likes me."

Zach went very, very red.

"Afraid? Are you—do you not even . . ." He picked up the mixing bowl, then set it down again and knocked over the bag of sugar. "You know what? Forget it. Because you're clearly really good at forgetting things."

My heart plummeted to my stomach. Zach was right. If anything, *I* was the one afraid to say anything. *I* was the one who said *I don't know*. But what right did he have to attack me? If we were supposed to be friends, he was still treating me pretty terribly. And I hated to admit it, but I wanted to be terrible back.

"I don't need to stay here and be judged, you know," I said. I'd been mean, and I knew I had, but I still didn't want to give in. I was done letting stuff like this upset me.

"Fine. I didn't invite you in the first place."

"Fine."

I shoved my shoes back on, grabbed my backpack, and stomped out the back door and onto the street. Maybe it was my imagination, but as I marched toward Center City, I thought I could hear Bacon howling.

# CHAPTER TWENTY-FOUR

I pulled up the interview with Sebastian as soon as I got on the train back to Wister—well, as soon as I got on the train and as soon as the train got out from Suburban Station and my cell reception came back. The article had only gone live that morning, but seven hours was a long time on the internet.

**WE FOUND OUT WHO "NATALIE" REALLY IS—**
**AND THE ANSWER WILL SHOCK YOU!**

*By Brigid McBride, BuzzKlik Music*

It's heartbreak, not happiness, that has inspired some of the best and most enduring pop music of all time. But while most power ballads and breakup songs stay general as they relate these universal themes, Brooklyn indie rockers the Young Lungs have had all of America guessing about "Natalie," the love-'em-and-leave-'em lady who inspired lead singer Sebastian Delacroix to write their chart-topping single—until now.

"She's an ex-girlfriend," said Delacroix, in an exclusive

interview with BuzzKlik. "I felt really strongly about her, which you don't need me to tell you if you've listened to the song."

Delacroix, who grew up in suburban Philadelphia, says he met Natalie in high school, although "I wouldn't call us high-school sweethearts exactly," he was quick to add. "But yeah, sometimes I wish we could still talk."

Although he refused to elaborate further on Natalie's identity, Delacroix coyly fueled further speculation that a woman pictured with music blogger Vivian Violet after a recent Young Lungs show in Brooklyn is, in fact, the girl who broke his heart.

"It's a pretty blurry photo," Delacroix said. "Next you're going to ask me to ID the Loch Ness Monster."

Regardless, he says that if Natalie's listening out there—and with the all the airplay the single's been getting, odds are pretty good—he has no hard feelings.

"As long as people are getting enjoyment out of our song, well—that's the most important thing. Not whoever it's about. Or," he added, "whatever heartbreak might have inspired it."

Catch the Young Lungs next at the TLA in Philadelphia this Saturday night. More tour details are on their website.

I did some quick mental calendaring. If Sebastian was playing Philadelphia this Saturday, and had just played New York City last Friday, then he had to be in Wister.

As the train trundled out of the city and toward the

suburbs, I pulled Pixstagram back open. The latest picture in my feed wasn't Sebastian's, thank God, but Tess's: a selfie with all her makeup done up. *Dance looks!!!* was the caption, followed by a string of tiny cartoon balloons and hearts and then *PLEASE COME EVERYBODY!*

I swallowed hard and tapped into my message inbox. Maybe I couldn't go to the dance, but I could make everyone else want to go. Because if Sebastian really wished we could still talk, who was I not to grant him that?

With quivering thumbs, I typed out a message.

> to: sebdel
>
> hey, i know you're in town. i saw the article. we
> need to talk.

No sooner had I pressed Send than my heart started to squish hotly inside my rib cage. What if he didn't see it in time? What if he did see it in time and just ignored me? How was I, Nattie McCullough-Schwartz, supposed to get Sebastian Delacroix to realize that I was worth talking to?

As I clenched my phone, it started to buzz with an unknown number—New York again—as the train squealed to a stop.

"Wister!" yelled the lady conductor. "Wister, this stop."

I immediately hit Decline and then realized the answer was literally in the palm of my hand.

As the train pulled away, I ran up the station steps two at a time and furiously typed out a string of new messages.

> to: sebdel

> reporters have been calling me for days
>
> and I haven't been answering
>
> but if you don't talk to me TODAY
>
> i'm giving the next one that calls a video of the
>
> talent show
>
> you know which one

I walked the rest of the way home trembling but triumphant.

"Hi, Nattie." Sam Huang waved from his computer. "Where were you?"

"Um," I said, doing my best to conceal the fact that I was undergoing a blackmail-related blood-pressure spike. "Just . . . out. Studying. At Zach's house."

"I thought you were grounded," Sam Huang said.

"Studying doesn't count," I said, and then wondered if this was true. No one had really laid out the parameters. But I didn't have long to wonder, because two seconds later my phone buzzed almost right off the counter and I pounced on it.

> to: nmcullz
>
> ok

Okay. Okay! Sebastian was going to talk to me! I threw my phone back on the counter in terror and began to pace the kitchen. Having never blackmailed someone before, I wasn't exactly sure of the procedure. I had vague notions of offshore bank accounts and escrow, whatever that was, from movies, but I was pretty sure those only applied in situations where the currency was literally currency and not a poorly shot phone video of a teenage boy making a fool of himself in a school auditorium.

I was midway through my mental composition of a threatening opening statement when my phone buzzed again.

to: nmcullz

be at yr house in 2

"Holy—" I started, and then clapped a hand over my mouth. I had to act, and I had to act fast. I didn't even have time to consider all the stupid possibilities spinning through my mind.

"Sam?" I yelled into the recesses of the kitchen. "I'm going . . . out. I mean, not *out* out, but . . . outside."

Yes. Good. Keep Sebastian from infiltrating the property. Definitely don't let Sam Huang see him.

I had barely banged out the screen door when Sebastian's Crown Vic pulled up to the curb. In the bright afternoon light, I could see all the patchy spots of rust covering its snout and sides. It looked as tired as I felt. It looked . . . kind of gross, actually.

Sebastian swung out of the driver's seat. He was at peak Sebastian today, face scruffy, half smiling, half . . . chewing.

"Hey." He crumpled something shiny and foil-y into his pocket, swallowed, and smiled.

I should've felt shivers. Or at the very least, stomach butterflies. But what I really felt was . . . annoyed. Annoyed at his stupid tight pink T-shirt. Annoyed that he didn't even bother to finish eating whatever he was eating before he showed up, and annoyed that he was drumming on the thigh of his jeans even as he was staring me down. And most of all, annoyed that he'd ignored me, gone totally silent after all those messages, and then suddenly decided he could call me his "ex-girlfriend" just because it would make an interview sound interesting.

He swallowed whatever he was eating and rubbed his chin. "So, listen—"

"Hey. Wait. Hey." My words were stumbling and mushing together. "Can we not talk here? Not inside, either," I added, thinking of Sam Huang on his computer. "Let's go . . . here."

I swept my arm toward the yurt. Sebastian frowned.

"What *is* that?"

"It's a yurt," I said. After a few evenings of work from Dad and Sam, it was more or less back to its yurtly shape.

Sebastian laughed softly, which, honestly, made me want to smack him.

"Well, it *is*," I said. "My dad's been working on it for weeks. Just go in, okay?"

I held up my phone as a tacit warning. Sebastian stopped laughing.

I marched over and pulled open the yurt flap to usher Sebastian in, casting a careful eye around the yard. No one on the street, no Sam Huang emerging from the house, no Mom coming home from the art supply store—

*Clonk.*

"Ow!"

Sebastian straightened up, a hand to his forehead. "Damn. What the hell?"

"It's a low door," I said. "Just get in, okay?"

Since Sebastian seemed to be challenged in the art of humbling himself, I demonstrated. Inside, the yurt was warm and pleasantly glowy, and smelled like the inside of an L.L.Bean tote bag. Unfortunately, the canvas ceiling was so low that the only place we could stand straight was right in the center. Right next to each other. Inches apart.

"Hey."

When he spoke, I could *feel* it—the words, his breath, the hum of someone else's body so close to mine. Closer than any male person had ever been, maybe.

"Um," I said. "Hey."

I wished I could close my eyes, but Sebastian's face was too close to mine. The yurt air was pressing up on every inch of my skin, particularly my feet, which were bare.

"Natalie." Sebastian bit his lip and cocked his head. "So."

We were not having an actual conversation, let alone a confrontation. I squinched my eyes shut for half of a half of a second and plunged in.

"Bring your band to the dance." I practically shouted it. "That's it. I just need you to have the Young Lungs show up on Friday night and play and then I won't post the video or . . . or anything."

Sebastian shifted his weight, considering me. Then he chuckled.

"Natalie," he said again. "This isn't like you."

"Like me?" I blinked. "How would you even *know*?"

"Because we've been talking for so long," Sebastian said. "We have a *connection*."

He cocked his hip out, coming even closer toward me in the already very small space. But I refused to flinch. Because now that he was here, now that we were actually talking, I realized something about all those Pixstagram messages.

"First of all," I said, "it's Nattie. Second of all, *we* haven't been talking. *You've* been talking *at* me. You just sent me tons and tons of random stuff about beauty and the moon and tacos, or whatever, but when *I* actually asked you a question, you ignored me. Remember? Even when I came all the way to New York."

Sebastian didn't seem to be listening.

"God, you're so tough," he said, his voice annoyingly soft. "And yet . . . kinda delicate."

His eyes settled on the only available exposed part of my body, which was the triangle of skin where I'd cut the elastic out of my Wister Prep hoodie because it had been choking me. But the way he looked at it did make it seem . . . sexy. Sort of. Just a little.

And then he kissed my neck.

I froze. I had never had anyone kiss my neck before. It was warm and suctiony and kind of wet, like how I imagine a sea slug might feel if it cuddled up to you. I didn't know what to do, especially with my hands, so I just stood there, and tried to . . . well, to enjoy it.

No. No. Focus, Nattie.

"Haven't you been wondering," Sebastian mumbled into the space behind my earlobe, "why I wrote a song about you?"

He mashed his lips into my neck a second time, and right then, I *did* wonder. Wonder whether it mattered. Wondered whether Sebastian was even going to have a good reason, and if I cared. If it would make any difference.

"Uh, Sebastian, um—" I remembered I had hands, and pushed him in the chest, which was surprisingly firm. "Stop."

Sebastian looked confused, as if no one had ever pushed him away before, which I realized might be true. I sucked in a deep breath and went for it.

"Look," I said, words tumbling out faster than I could control them, "I know the song's about me. I know you're telling people I was your ex-girlfriend when I wasn't. And I know you never really liked me, because . . . because you never even *knew* me. But, um, I don't care. I mean . . . okay, actually, I care a lot, and if this weren't an emergency I'd be super pissed. I mean"—shoot, this was not going well—"I *am* super pissed, but if you just get your band to play this one dance so that everyone at school will show up, then the rest of it doesn't matter. One show and you can keep singing about me as long as your career lasts."

Sebastian's mouth hung open a little, which was not a great look for him. Then, as if he remembered what he was trying to do, he slipped back into seductive mode.

"Didn't really like you?" He chuckled. Sebastian never *laugh* laughed, I noticed, just made a low rumble, almost like he was clearing his throat. "Would I being doing this if I didn't like you?"

Then he put a hand behind my neck and kissed me. On the mouth.

It was the strangest thing that had ever happened to me. I felt every molecule in my body seize up with my own weirdness, and stay seized, even as Sebastian kept opening his mouth on top of mine. The weirdness wasn't going away. If anything, I was starting to feel weirder. Whatever the opposite of melting was, that's what I was doing. Solidifying. Hardening up.

"Stop!" I pushed Sebastian away, right in his stupid gym-chiseled pecs. "Sebastian, no offense, but gross. I don't even li—"

"Nattie?"

Crouching at the yurt flap, bent over so he wouldn't hit his head, was Zach the Anarchist.

"Shoot!" I jumped, actually jumped, and would've fallen

backward if there had been space in the yurt to support it. "Zach? What are you *doing* here?"

Zach silently held up my Latin notebook. The notebook I'd forgotten at his house.

"This isn't what it looks like," I said quickly. My face was burning up. "I mean, no, it is, but trust me, I did not think *that* was going to—"

"Hey, man, how's it going?" Sebastian, who was irritatingly not reacting to anything, put his hands in his pockets and nodded at Zach the Anarchist. Zach did not nod back.

"We're kinda—hah—*busy*," Sebastian went on, "so if you could—"

"Yeah, okay." Zach the Anarchist dropped the yurt flap.

"*Zach!*" I swallowed a lump in my throat and leaped out after him. Even outside of the yurt, I still felt like I was burning up. Somewhere behind me, I heard the yurt flap flop shut again.

"It's because of the *dance*," I called across the yard. "To get the band to play."

"*Him?*" Zach stopped, halfway to his car. "Seriously? The guy who sang 'A Medley from Andrew Lloyd Webber' in a literal Technicolor dreamcoat? Or was I the only one watching that talent show?"

All Sebastian's coolness dropped away.

"You said nobody knew!" he squealed at me. "Did you *tell* people?"

"Shut up," I explained. Clearly, my suspicions were correct: for indie rockers, an earnest performance of musical theater was the kiss of death. Especially when it was wickedly off-key. "Zach, it's for Tess. For everyone. So people will come."

But Zach was focused on Sebastian.

"You know what, Sebastian? I listened to your album."

Zach took a step toward Sebastian, my Latin notebook still in hand. Sebastian kind of flinched. I rolled up the sleeves of my sweatshirt, desperate to calm down.

"Yeah?" Sebastian folded his arms. Zach took another step.

"Yeah." Zach shook his head. "You stole riffs from the Stiff Little Fingers, drum lines from Dave Grohl's early stuff, and most of your shitty lyrics from, I don't know, the Maroon 4."

"Maroon 5," I said, and itched the inside of my elbow, which was amazingly itchy all of a sudden.

"Whatever."

Sebastian gave a one-shouldered shrug. "What can I say? Artists steal."

"Oh my God, seriously?" The words barged right out of my mouth. "Sebastian, you're *not* an artist."

Zach the Anarchist smiled a tiny smile. "Yeah. Yeah, that's not making art. That's making money."

Instead of being angry, or even ruffled, Sebastian just shook his head and looked at me from under his bangs.

"Really?" he said. To me. "You're really going to let this guy tell you what to think?"

I couldn't answer. The weirdness was coalescing. My entire body felt like it was getting stabbed with tiny pins. I was kind of having trouble breathing. I was literally speechless.

"See, man?" Sebastian said. "She doesn't agree with you."

"Don't tell Nattie what she thinks."

It was too much. My lungs hurt, and my itchy elbow had become my itchy entire torso.

"Shut up!" I wheezed in the deepest breath I could. "Both of you! I . . . I . . ."

I started to cough, and grabbed onto the side of the yurt for support. I barely had time to see Zach the Anarchist's eyes get very wide before he sprinted across the yard.

"Nattie? What's up? Are you okay?"

Behind us, Sebastian hovered. "Uh, is she, like . . . dying, or something?"

My throat felt like a straw that someone was pinching shut. I tried to shake my head, but everything was getting kind of one-dimensional.

"Holy shit, Nattie, are you having an allergic reaction?"

"Yeah," I wheezed. "I just decided to *eat a strawberry*."

"Right," Zach the Anarchist said. "You're not dumb. But then how . . ."

"What's going on?" It was Sam Huang, standing at the screen door and looking perplexed. "I heard yelling."

"We've got to get her to the hospital," Zach the Anarchist called back. "Go get Nattie's EpiPen. It should be in her backpack. And call her parents."

"Thanks," I gasped.

"Don't worry about it," Zach the Anarchist said. "Let's get you in my car. The hospital's only five minutes away."

He yanked me to my feet. Sam Huang remerged with my EpiPen, which Zach the Anarchist uncapped.

"Close your eyes," he said. "This is going to hurt, and you don't want to see—"

"Holy shit," Sebastian said, "you're going to stab her with that?"

Zach the Anarchist gave him a dirty look.

"It's fine, it's fine," I said. "Less talking, more stabb—ow!"

It *did* hurt. And as soon as I was adrenalined, my heart started beating in quintuple time.

"You okay?" Zach asked. I barely had time to nod before he shoved me into the backseat of the Volvo. And before I could shut the door, he shoved Sebastian in, too.

"Keep an eye on her until we get to the hospital," Zach said, and flew to the driver's seat. "Do you think you can manage that?"

"Hospital?" Sebastian blinked. "Is this, like . . . serious?"

"That's why they call them *life-threatening allergies*," I said through chattering teeth. "Idiot."

"You're allergic to something?"

In unison, Zach and I both turned to Sebastian.

"What?" said Sebastian.

"What's in your pocket?" I said. "What were you eating?"

Sebastian frowned, but produced the crumpled something

he'd stuffed in there: the wrapper for a Pop-Tart. Strawberry.

My dizziness got even dizzier.

"Are you serious?" Zach yelled as he threw the car into reverse. "That's like the *one thing* you need to know about Nattie."

I had never heard Zach the Anarchist raise his voice like that. Maybe it was the epinephrine talking, but it was kind of exciting to hear.

Sebastian looked paler than his pastel T-shirt.

"Wow," he said. "You're, uh . . . you're going to be okay, right?"

"If we get to the hospital in time," I said. Which, considering that Zach the Anarchist had just taken an illegal U-turn to run a red light, we probably would.

Sebastian gripped the edge of the seat. "I . . . wow. I'm sorry?"

"Of course you're *sorry*," said Zach the Anarchist from the front seat. "Think of how bad it'll look if you *killed* the girl you wrote a song about."

Houses and stores careened past the windows at a Tilt-A-Whirl clip, and I couldn't tell if I was nauseous from Zach's emergency driving or because my body was violently rejecting the genuine strawberry filling of a breakfast product. We spun into the Emergency entrance for Wister General Hospital so hard that I slammed straight into Sebastian's chest. Two weeks ago—okay, maybe even two *hours* ago—I would've freaked out from being that close to him. Now, though, I just wanted him out of the way.

Zach the Anarchist spun out of the driver's seat, leaving the Volvo idling crosswise in the driveway loop, and pulled me out of the car. With Sebastian loping behind, we tumbled through the automatic doors.

"Hey!" he shouted. "Emergency!"

Instantly, a nurse was at our side.

"Please don't shout, sir," she said, and looked at me. "What's happened?"

"Strawberry reaction," Zach the Anarchist said.

"First kiss," I gasped.

"Disaster?" Sebastian offered.

The nurse gave us all a look.

"Right this way."

# CHAPTER TWENTY-FIVE

Apparently, going through triage for a severe allergic reaction involves getting whisked away on a rolling bed with little oxygen tubes stuck up your nose so a doctor can poke you with enough needles to make a Nattie pincushion.

"Just so you know, I'm not a doctor, I'm a nurse," said the not-doctor man, who was poking around the crook of my arm with purple-gloved fingers for a suitable vein to skewer. "And yes, men can be nurses, and I am going to take excellent care of you. I'm Brett."

"Oh," I said. I got the sense that he gave that little speech a lot. The IV needle in his hand was very big. My forehead went clammy.

"This'll get you steroids and an antihistamine," Nurse Brett said. "You might want to look away."

I not only looked away, I scrunched my eyes shut for good measure.

"Agh!"

I winced and tried my very hardest not to flail out of the

crispy-sheeted bed they'd put me on when they'd yanked me away from Zach the Anarchist and Sebastian. I'd at least gotten my own private recovery room, probably because it would be traumatizing to give someone a roommate who could choke to death on her own swollen throat tissue at any moment. It smelled like Listerine and barf.

"All done." Nurse Brett straightened and gave my shoulder a little pat, which should've felt patronizing but actually reassured me, like I was still a sentient being in a body, not yet dead, even if I was covered in fist-sized red blotches. "Are you in pain? Is something wrong?"

"No, no," I said, and rearranged my face to look as pleasant as I could, given the circumstances. Out there, somewhere, beyond the mouthwash-and-vomit-scented hallway, were one of my best friends on the planet and the lead singer of a moderately successful indie-rock band. What were they doing? Sitting on plastic waiting-room chairs? Reading old issues of *Town & Country*? Watching the dumb CCTV thing about eating low-fat foods to prevent heart disease?

Another nurse jogged in with a clipboard, which Nurse Brett took.

"Okay"—he glanced at my chart—"Natalie. That's a beautiful name. How are you—"

"Actually," I said. "It's Nattie. If you don't mind."

Nurse Brett grinned. "Not at all. Nattie, how are you breathing? Are you feeling nauseated? Dizzy?"

I took a slow, steady test breath. Then another.

"I think I can breathe," I said. "I think."

"Good." He lowered the clipboard. "The steroids ought to help you look less like a lobster, and the Benadryl will bring down the swelling, okay? We're going to let you hang out here for a while and see how those are working."

I nodded. Nurse Brett glanced out the door, to the hallway.

"Do you want me to get your boyfriend?"

"Uh," I mumbled, too medicated to explain the intricacies of my waiting-room situation. "Sure."

Nurse Brett smiled and disappeared, only to return a minute later.

"Uh . . . which one *is* your boyfriend?"

"Neither?" I shook my head and sat up on the scratchy pillows, desperately trying to well up enough spit for a longer answer. "Uh, both, I guess? It's kind of . . . complicated."

Nurse Brett winked. "I'll get them both."

I settled uneasily back onto my pillows and prayed that if I was going to die from this allergic reaction, that it happen in the next thirty seconds so I did not have to face Zach and Sebastian together again.

"Nattie?"

My eyes flew open. Zach the Anarchist was hovering at the door, looking pale.

"I, uh, got you some ice chips," he said, and held out a cup. "The nurse guy said you can't have anything to drink yet."

"Cool," I croaked. "You can come in, if you want."

"I thought I'd just throw the ice at you from here."

I laughed, which kind of hurt my throat, and Zach came to my bedside with the cup. When he was standing next to me, I couldn't smell the barf smell. Just Zach.

"Here. I . . . oh." He drew the cup back when he saw the pulse monitor clipped to one hand and the blood oxygen monitor clipped to the other. "Can you open your mouth?"

I swallowed. Painfully. "Sure."

Zach rooted around in the cup and dug out an ice chip with his long fingers. I opened my mouth, and he touched it to my lips, where it was deliciously cool and gone in an instant.

"Thanks," I said, wondering if it was possible to blush underneath hives. Zach's face was brilliantly pink.

"You're welcome." Zach looked at the floor. His now-ice-free hand was inches from mine on the nubbly hospital blanket. "Nattie, I—"

"What's going on? Is she okay?"

Sebastian swung into the room, nose wrinkled against the barf smell, and widened his eyes when he saw me.

"Shit," he said, his face sagging under his man-bun. "She doesn't *look* okay."

"Thanks," I said dryly. Zach retracted his hand and stared hard out the window, a strangely murderous look in his eye. "Also, I'm right here."

"Right, yeah." Sebastian shook his head and sank into a chair. "Are you okay? I didn't . . . kill you?"

Zach the Anarchist put down the cup of ice chips. "Why are you even still *here?*"

"Yo, chill out, man." Sebastian leaned back in the chair, palms up. "I just wanted to make sure she—"

"I'm not your *man*, dude." Zach got up and actually almost got in Sebastian's face. "You're bothering her. Leave."

"Hey, come on, I'm just trying to—"

"Everything okay here?" Nurse Brett popped his head back in.

Zach looked at Sebastian. Sebastian looked at me. I lay back across my pillows and pretended I'd fallen into a catatonic state.

"Nattie!"

My eyes flew back open.

"Mom?"

It *was* Mom, frantic and dressed in a sweatshirt and polar-bear pajama pants that were her standard on-a-deadline outfit. She vaulted to my bedside and flung her arms around me. "Oh my God, Nattie! We thought you were dead!"

"She's not dead, ma'am," said Nurse Brett, a firm hand on her shoulder, "but she has suffered a minor anaphylactic reaction. You're going to have to give her a little space."

"Right. Right. Of course." Mom backed away, but I could see that there were tears in her eyes. Tears that dried up as soon as she laid eyes on Sebastian.

"Excuse me. I don't believe we've met," she said coolly, and stuck out a hand. "Anne McCullough. Nattie's mother."

"Oh." Sebastian didn't get up from his chair. "Yeah."

Mom waited barely half a second. "And you are?"

"Hey," said Sebastian, as if that were enough of an explanation. "I'm friends with Natalie."

"Mom," I started. "The thing is—"

"Man, I'll tell you, trying to validate parking here is— Nattie G!"

Dad rushed to my bedside, with Sam Huang trailing. "Hey, kiddo." He planted a kiss on my forehead, stood up, and realized that no one else in the room was moving. "What's going on?"

"Um, hey, guys," I said weakly, and gave a tiny wave with my pulse-monitored hand. "I . . . am in the hospital."

"What happened?" Dad asked.

"Do you need more ice chips?" Zach asked.

"Who is *he*?" Mom looked less concerned with the fact that I was lying, blotchy, in a hospital bed, and more with the slouchy hipster leaning next to a Pepto-Bismol-colored curtain.

"I . . . hi? Uh, Sebastian, I . . ." Sebastian raised a hand, but stuck it out too high for Mom to shake, and she didn't look at *all* like she wanted to shake hands anymore, so he deflected and went to his pocket for his phone, which he started nervously locking and unlocking.

There was a tense silence. Silence except for all the beeping machines and the click, click of Sebastian unlocking his phone.

"I'll give you all a moment," Nurse Brett said, and sidestepped gracefully out of the room.

"I think," Dad said loudly, "*I* think we could all stand to hear what's going on. Right, Nattie?"

I nodded as vigorously as I could, although the combined effects of Benadryl, steroids, and an intramuscular shot of adrenaline were making me feel seriously zonked. "Well, I'm fine. And I'm sorry, everybody."

"Sweetheart." Mom fell back to my side and ran her fingers through my hair, which I now realized was both unwashed and severely overrun with split ends. Dad gathered us both in an awkward bed hug that lasted about three seconds. "What on *earth* happened to you? How did you end up in the *hospital*? And what . . . *else* is going on?"

She glanced over at Sebastian, who had gone practically bug-eyed in addition to looking pale.

"Please tell me it's not drugs, Nattie Gann," Dad said. "You're too smart for that, right?"

"It's not drugs, Dad," I said. "I just, um, had an allergic reaction, and—"

"An allergic reaction to *what*?" Mom interruped. "You didn't just eat a strawberry, did you?"

Across the room, Zach's murdery glance flicked to

Sebastian. Sebastian, looking chastened, unlocked his phone again and ducked into the hall.

"Right," I said. "About that. The thing is, um—" I coughed and glanced at my cup, which was now full of melted water. "Can I have some more ice chips, please?"

My throat was still recovering from being swollen practically shut, and I also wanted to take every opportunity to stall.

"Sure thing, NG." Dad saluted and started for the door, but Zach the Anarchist was already off and down the hall, in the opposite direction of Sebastian.

"Thanks." I lay back on my pillows and tried to look forlorn. "So, the thing is, I didn't exactly *eat* a strawberry, but, um—" I faked a cough. "God, almost dying takes a lot out of you, let me tell you."

"That's not funny," Mom said, but Dad was smiling.

"Nattie, I swear, if you hadn't almost died, I would kill you."

"Did someone say Nattie?" A female voice rang out in the hallway. "I think I heard someone say Nattie."

"Maybe they were talking about the beer," said another voice. A boy.

"Tall Zach, this is a *hospital*."

"No place for drinking," said a third voice, another boy's. "Or jokes."

"No place f—OH MY GOD."

Tess's blond head popped in from the hallway and screamed. "She's alive!"

Tess launched herself at the bed and wrapped herself around my neck.

"God *damn* it, Nattie! We thought you were—oh my God." When she pulled back, I could see that she was crying, too.

"Hi," I said. "Um, we?"

Tess looked back at the door, where Tall Zach, Endsignal, and Zach the Anarchist were hovering—Tall Zach in his running shorts, Endsignal looking a little confused as to why he was there, and Zach the Anarchist smiling, just a bit.

"Hey," I said, and gave a little wave. Somehow, only Zach the Anarchist knew to wave back.

"Hey," he said. "I found them wandering around, and—"

"Hey!" Tall Zach bounded over and gave me a kiss on the forehead. "Hello, Mr. and Mrs. Nattie's Parents, it's lovely to see you again. I'm very glad your daughter is alive, and I am going to go raid the vending machines, *and* does anyone have any requests?"

"Peanut M&M's," said Mom.

"Triscuits," said Dad. "Ooh, no, Wheat Thins."

"Vodka," Tess said. "Just kidding."

"Ice chips," I said.

Zach the Anarchist pushed through my sudden crowd of bedside visitors bearing a small, cold, deliciously wet paper cup.

"Thank you," I said, and awkwardly dumped them into my mouth as Tall Zach took off down the hall with Endsignal in tow.

Six pairs of eyes watched as I carefully clicked the ice around with my tongue until it had melted. No sooner had I swallowed than Mom launched back in.

"Okay," she said. "Explain. Strawberry."

"One second." I went to put the cup down, but Zach the Anarchist took it for me. Our fingers brushed a little.

"Um, actually, if it's okay?" I licked my lips and looked at Tess. "What are *you* doing here?"

Tess looked at Sam Huang, then at me. "I got an emergency Jamba alert from your brother here."

"Sam?" I croaked. Sam Huang blushed.

"Thank you," I said.

"He told me you were dying or something, and that it had something to do with, uh, Sebastian," Tess went on. "And I *freaked out*, because I thought maybe he'd kidnapped you or something—"

"*Kidnapped?*" Mom pressed a hand to her forehead and sank into the chair formerly occupied by Sebastian.

"So *then*," Tess said, irritated at being interrupted, "I alerted the team and borrowed the BMW to drive over here, because it was an emergency, fully expecting to find your corpse in a gutter along the way or something."

I smiled weakly. "Well, I'm alive now. Alive and kind of tired. I think I might try to slee—"

"*Natalie McCullough-Schwartz*," Mom thundered from her chair. "You owe us an explanation *five minutes ago*."

I swallowed.

"You're way too smart to eat strawberries, NG," Dad said. "Was someone trying to poison you?"

Mom glared. Sam Huang looked alarmed. Tess squeezed my shoulder. I took a deep breath, which I would never again take for granted in my life, and went for it.

"I didn't eat a strawberry. I . . ." I squeezed my eyes shut. "I *may* have"—the word felt lodged in my throat—"*kissed* someone who had strawberry Pop-Tart in his spit."

"What?" said more or less everyone at the same time.

"Ugh." I buried my face in my hands, which was kind of tricky given the oxygen tubes in my nose and the plastic pulse monitor clamped on my right index finger. "This is all so stupid."

"Nothing you ever do could be stupid, Nattie Gann," Dad's voice said.

"You know you can tell us anything," added Mom's voice.

I lifted my head and took a shaky breath.

"Mom. Dad. For the past two months, your daughter has been the subject of America's number-twenty-three alternative-rock single."

"Number *twelve* in Germany," Tess said. "What? I looked it up."

Mom shook her head. "I don't understand."

"Me neither," I said. "I mean, I'm joking. Here's the thing."

So I explained the whole stupid story, starting with the show at Ruby's and going through the single on the radio, the single *everywhere*, the show in New York and our selfie with Vivian Violet, and ending with the disastrous confrontation in the yurt.

Silence, except for the beeping of my various monitors. Sam Huang laughed. So did Tess.

"Are you serious?" she crowed. "That dumb-dumb Delacroix doesn't even know the *most important basic fact of Nattie safety?*"

"Delacroix?" Mom was on high alert. "Wait. Who is Delacroix?"

"Sounds like a Napoleonic duke," Dad said. "A Napoleonic duke who got a lot of swirlies in middle school."

"Uh." Sebastian was back at the door. "That's me. Sebastian Delacroix. Hey."

"Who," Mom said, voice quavering with rage, "*are* you?"

"Sebastian," said Sebastian. "Look, I'm, uh, really sorry about all this. I swear I didn't do it on purpose."

"Eat the Pop-Tart?" Mom asked.

"Kiss my daughter?" Dad asked.

"Write that song?" Tess asked.

"Uh . . ." Sebastian looked genuinely lost. Every part of him had gone limp, even his hair. Especially his hair. And weirdly, even though I was the one hooked up to all the monitors, *I* felt kind of bad for *him*. He scratched the back of his head with his phone. "I just texted the guys. We can totally play the dance if we really have to."

I looked at Tess hopefully, but she just pursed her lips hard.

"After all this bullshit? No *way*."

"But Tess." I tried to sit up on my cardboard pillows. "What if nobody comes? What if everyone goes to that party?"

"Oh, but they won't." She smiled the prim, contented smile of someone who has an ace up her sleeve. "Sam, would you like to explain?"

All eyes went to Sam Huang, who stepped over to my bedside and held out his phone. It was a screenshot of someone's Pixstagram feed—*cfranxx00*. The top picture was a bunch of bottles: *cant wait for friday!!! #therealwinterformal #acappellalife.* *36 likes*

"It's Celeste," Sam Huang said. "Soprano section. She was going to bring them to the party. I was invited, but—"

"Sam's being *modest*," Tess said, and clapped him on the shoulder so hard it must've hurt. "He turned them in! Everyone who RSVP'd to their party is *bus-ted*."

"Really?"

Sam Huang nodded. "Suspended. For a week."

"Sam!" I tried to hug him, but ended up just kind of wrapping an arm around his neck due to my many machine tethers. "You're the best."

"So . . . does that mean you don't need us to play?"

Everyone swiveled to where Sebastian was just kind of holding his phone aloft. Then everyone swiveled to me. I took a deep breath, or as deep a breath as I could.

"No," I said. "No, we don't."

Tess folded her arms. Zach the Anarchist pressed his lips

together in what was almost a smile. Sebastian just looked blank. Blank and a little hurt. Chunks of hair were falling out of his man-bun. And he was clenching and unclenching his hand again.

"Wrist pain?" Sam Huang asked. Sebastian frowned.

"How did you—"

Sam Huang said nothing, but shot a look in my direction. Dad stepped forward, a very Dad-like sympathetic expression on his face. "I think you'd better go, son. Good luck with your band."

Sebastian put his phone in his pocket. "I . . . is that what you want?" He was looking at me, with those eyes I had once thought were, I don't know, dark depths of artistic meaning. Clearly, he was desperate for me to forgive him. And strangely, I found I could.

"Yeah," I said. "But don't worry. I'm not mad. About, um, any of it. You're fine."

Sebastian looked a little relieved, probably because he realized that even if I *did* die, my family wouldn't sue. "Okay. Well, get better soon, Natalie."

"It's Nattie," I said.

"Oh," he said. "Right."

And with that, Sebastian left, finally, finally gone for good from my life.

As soon as he'd disappeared, Mom clucked her tongue at me.

"Him, Nattie? You kissed *him*?"

"Sort of." I twisted the pulse monitor around my finger. "He kinda kissed me first. I don't, um, actually think I like him that much."

"Thank God," Dad muttered. "I don't think I'd be able to trust him with you."

"Dad," I said, with a look at Tess. "I'm a human being, not a piece of chattel."

"A very *cute* human being," Tess said, and kissed my temple. "I'm so glad you're not dead."

"Thanks," I said. "Me too."

"Me too," said Sam Huang.

"Us too," said my parents.

"Me too," Zach the Anarchist said. "For sure," he added softly.

"Snacks!"

The door banged open and Tall Zach and Endsignal returned, arms full of bright packages that they dumped onto my blanket-covered legs.

"They didn't have Triscuits *or* Wheat Thins, but—" Tall Zach looked up from where he was spreading out the bounty. "Nattie! Are you okay?"

"We can go look for Wheat Thins," Endsignal offered.

I shook my head, scrubbing at my eyes. Silently, Sam Huang took my empty ice-chips cup and started for the hallway.

"Wait," I said. Sam waited. "Sam, I'm sorry I said that to you. Before. I'm glad you're my not-exactly brother."

I hiccupped. "Tess, I'm sorry for . . . well, everything. And Zach and Other Zach and Mom and Dad . . . I'm sorry, everyone. I'm just . . . I don't know." The Benadryl was really starting to kick in, and I felt like I was trying to talk underwater. "I'm gross and blotchy and this is so weird and embarrassing. *I'm* so weird and embarrassing. I'm just . . . I don't know why I'm lucky enough to have you."

A tear trickled down my cheek.

"Hey! Hey," Zach the Anarchist said. "It's not weird."

I sniffled and gave him a look. "I'm in the hospital, covered in snacks, because I don't know how to kiss right."

"Okay, it's a little weird." His pink cheeks were back. "But it's not embarrassing."

"We're glad we have you, too, Nattie," said Tess.

"Really glad," said Sam Huang.

"You could never embarrass us," said Dad.

"Sebastian doesn't know what he's missing," said Tall Zach.

I laughed, and then cried a little bit more, and then everyone started tearing into the snacks. Sam Huang brought me more ice chips, Tess ate an entire package of Butterscotch Krimpets, and Endsignal and Dad got into a long conversation about the history of sound engineering. Also, at some point, Zach the Anarchist slipped his hand into mine.

"Everything okay?" It was Nurse Brett, back at the door. "Whoa. Hi, everybody."

Nurse Brett did some nurse-ly things and told me that as long as I kept up the good work, I would probably be good to go home in a couple hours. Everyone cheered.

"Somebody's popular," Nurse Brett said. "Glad I could deliver good news."

He left, and everyone started throwing things out and deciding who was getting a ride home with whom. Except Zach the Anarchist, who wasn't moving from my bedside, and Mom, who was hovering by the window, her sweatshirted arms folded and another round of tears twinkling at the corner of her eye.

"See? Look at this." Dad wrapped his arm around Mom's waist and nodded at the packed room. "You bring people together, Nattie Gann."

He kissed Mom, and she smiled.

"It's true," she said. "You're our star, Nattie."

Zach the Anarchist gave my hand a squeeze.

By the time my skin went back to its normal Nattie color and I was declared fit to be discharged, it was almost ten at night. Tess and Tall Zach and Endsignal had all left an hour or two before, so it was just Dad and Mom and Sam Huang and Zach the Anarchist and me who headed out to the waiting room. My parents went up to the counter to deal with the paperwork, and Sam Huang took a seat in the corner so that Zach and I could pretend that we were alone together. Which was actually kind of nice.

"Do you need these?" Zach handed me the stack of printed-out aftercare instructions Nurse Brett had given me after he'd unhooked me from all the machines.

"Gross." I folded them up and gave them back to Zach. "I can't even think about it. I'm still too traumatized."

Zach rolled his eyes and reopened the handout. "You know, when hospitals give you things to read, they're usually pretty important."

"What's to know? Just don't eat strawberries again," I said. Then, after a second, I added, "Or, um, you know, get them near my mouth in any way. Which I'm not going to. Again."

Zach was busy reading the handout. "The steroids can give you a flush, but it's perfectly normal. And apparently you can also have something called a biphasic reaction."

"What's that?"

"A recurrence of symptoms within seventy-two hours. So, uh, watch out." Zach handed me back the papers, and this time, I kept them. The CCTV above Sam Huang kept blaring something about the importance of whole grains and the other waiting people rustled their magazines and the two of us just sat next to each other for a minute. And I have to say, sitting next to Zach West was very reassuring, even when he wasn't reading to me from my own medical literature.

"Zach," I said. "I'm sorry."

His head jerked up. "What?"

"About everything I said at your house. And . . .

everything." I chewed my lip. It wasn't the world's most articulate apology. But Zach didn't seem to mind.

"It's okay." He smiled. "I'm just glad you're alive. Dying with that on your conscience would've probably doomed you to becoming a ghost or something."

"Ugh, I'd be the *worst* ghost," I said. "I look terrible in white."

Zach chuckled, and we sat there a moment longer, listening to the whole-grains lady on the CCTV struggle to pronounce *quinoa*.

"So there's this dance coming up," Zach said suddenly.

"I think I heard about that."

"Do you want to go?"

"I am going. I mean, I guess I'm grounded, but I'll have to figure something out. Because Tess will kill me if I don't."

"Yeah." The corner of Zach's mouth twitched. "I meant do you want to go *with me*?"

Oh God. Duh. My skin got hot, and my mouth went terrifically dry, and I briefly wondered if I was indeed having a biphasic reaction.

"Are you okay?" Zach asked. Nurse Brett, who just happened to be passing by with a clipboard, skidded to a stop. I waved him off.

"I'm fine!" I said cheerily. "Still breathing just great!" I took a few healthy inhales to show him. To Zach, I said, "Sorry. Um. Yes. I would. Like to. That would be great."

"Yeah?" Zach smiled, and I noticed that he'd been

fidgeting with the hem of his T-shirt.

"Of course," I said. "What did you think I was going to say? You're one of my best friends."

Zach stopped fidgeting, and instantly my heart sank. Shoot. SHOOT. I'd blown it. I'd said the thing I didn't mean to say and didn't even mean, period. I turned in my little plastic seat, trying to read Zach's expression, trying to think of anything to say that would counteract what I'd just said or just make sense already.

"I mean," I started. "What I meant was—"

"Nattie, do you like me?"

I opened my mouth, but he wasn't done.

"Because I like you. And I'm sorry I'm not great about saying it. I guess . . ." He blew out a breath. "I guess I was figuring you'd catch on, which was stupid of me, but—"

"Wait." I put up a hand. "Catch on? Catch on to what?"

Zach stared. "Latin? You don't really think I'm that bad at class, do you?"

My face flushed, in a nonanaphylactic kind of way. Zach laughed.

"Wow. Well, so much for my reputation as an academic all-star."

"You were really bad at some of those translations," I said. "I hope you didn't fail any tests for me."

He shrugged. "It all worked out. I got to see you a lot more. And that was pretty cool, so . . ."

Over at the desk area, my parents appeared to be wrapping

up, by which I mean Mom was putting her hat back on and Dad was tugging at the zipper on his polar fleece. I looked back at Zach.

"So . . . is that a yes?" he said quietly.

"Yes," I said.

"Yes, you'll go, or yes, you actually . . ."

"Yes," I said. "Yes and yes."

Zach smiled, and I smiled back. That was it—stupid and simple and right. It was kind of incredible, what could happen when you finally came out and just told the truth. Fortune did actually favor the bold.

Which gave me an idea. As soon as my skin had lost its last trace of steroid-induced flush, I had a Pixstagram selfie to take.

@nmccullz

11:37 p.m.

Hi, people of the internet and of the world. I'm Natalie and you may have heard of me.

For the past few weeks, everyone's been trying to figure out who the Real Natalie is. Well, using the power of social media, I'm here to tell you. The real Natalie is 17, allergic to strawberries, loves her friends so much she'd die for them as long as it wasn't a particularly painful method of death, and has a Latin test this week. What she is not is Sebastian Delacroix's ex-girlfriend.

So there's your answer. I know it's anticlimactic. You probably wanted some cool drama, or epic heartbreak, or even a lawsuit, but really, that's all there is to my side of the story.

Well, sort of.

See, the thing I've realized about songs is that they can be about anything—cute girls, cute boys, making toast, whatever. What really matters is what they do to you. How they make you feel. About that stuff, Sebastian's totally right. And over the past few weeks I've seen so many people freak out and go crazy and clap and cheer over "Natalie"—not me, Natalie the person, but "Natalie" the song. So if you like the song, you have my official permission to keep liking it. I don't want anything out of it other than for everyone to just leave me alone for the rest of forever. That's it. Enjoy.

—Natalie, alias Nattie

#Natalie #music #indie #pop #rock #younglungs #YLs #sebastiandelacroix #sebdel #sleepmore #fortroxrecords #vivianviolet #buzzklik #jawharpmag

PS. Okay, I lied. There's a link in my profile to support my awesome best friend, who spent seven hundred dollars of her own money to stage our school's first officially queer-friendly dance. If there's one thing I want out of this, it's for that dance to just rock.

# CHAPTER TWENTY-SIX

"Okay. Time." Tess patted the side of the tub. "Let's rinse."

She flicked on the water and gave the shower wand a few test pulses. I unwrapped the towel, bent over obediently, and watched as Clairol Raven Black 001 swirled down the Kozlowskis' drain.

"All done. I think," Tess said. I heaved my head out of the tub and shook it like a dog.

"Hey!" Tess threw a clean towel over my head. "Watch it."

"It looks weird," I said. "Does it? Does it look weird?"

Tess ignored me and scrubbed a bit roughly at my head. "It looks fine. Dry yourself off and let's get you in hot rollers."

The last three days had been . . . eventful, to say the least. Mom let me stay home from school on Tuesday and sleep in. I came back to school on Wednesday, and if people were talking, I didn't care. I had more important things to worry about, like my Latin test.

*Odi et amo. Quare id*
*faciam, fortasse requiris.*
*nescio, sed fieri sentio et*
*excrucior.*

*Translate:*

*I hate and I love. Why I do this,*
*by chance you ask.*
*I don't know, but I feel it*
*happening and I am tormented.*

*Catullus 70:*

*Nulli se dicit mulier mea nubere malle*
*quam mihi, non si se Iuppiter ipse petat.*
*dicit: sed mulier cupido quod dicit amanti,*
*in vento et rapida scribere oportet aqua.*

*Translate:*

*To no one ~~herself~~ my woman says that she prefers to marry*
*than me, not even if Jupiter himself might seek her.*
*She says [this ??]: but what a woman says to her desirous lover*
*Is fitting to write on the wind and the fast water.*

*Theme analysis:*

*This whole semester, we've been studying Catullus. And that's*
*great—he is a poet, he did write a lot. He talks all about how*
*torturous art is, and I'm sure making poetry was difficult. But*
*right now, I'm honestly much more sympathetic toward Lesbia.*
*She was smart, too, and she was probably a perfectly normal*
*person—flawed, maybe, but who isn't? But we can't know for*

375

*sure. We can't know because all we do know about her is what a man tells us about her, which is a little—for lack of a more academic term—creepy. Catullus says he loves her and wants to give her literal millions of kisses, but then he turns around and he writes poems about her giving sexual favors in the back alleys of Rome. At best, he's mercurial; at worst, completely inconsistent— he literally says he hates her and loves her at the same time— and yet somehow he attempts to claim that women are the ones whose opinions change with the wind and water. Everyone says women are crazy, but reading Catullus makes you realize that everyone who says that is just a bunch of angry dudes.*

When I got my test back, I'd aced it: A– for the translation, A+ for the analysis. *Spoken like a true feminist*, Dr. Frobisher had scribbled on the bottom of the sheet. *You should read some Sappho.*

"Five minutes." Tess came into her bedroom, hands on hips, looking absolutely dynamite in her vintage suit and red lipstick. "Make that four."

"Wow." I stopped unwinding a chunk of my now-raven hair from Mrs. Kozlowski's hot rollers and attempted a wolf whistle. "Damn girl, ya look good."

"Flattery will get you nowhere," Tess said, but she was grinning. "It's pretty boss, right?"

She curtseyed, to the extent that she could in the skintight skirt. The package from Va-Voom Vintage had arrived yesterday, along with a number scribbled on the invoice that was now programmed into Tess's phone as Hot NYC Vintage Girl.

"Totally boss," I agreed. "Also, you're welcome for saving those business cards."

"Yeah, yeah," she said. "I mean . . . um. Thanks. By the way." She nodded at the phone in my hand, where I was checking the GoFundYourself I'd set up for the OWPALGBTQIA on my phone. "What's the latest?"

The Pixstagram post had been an instant viral success. Within hours, my face and statement were all over the internet, and although I sort of wished I had taken my selfie somewhere other than my aggressively pink bedroom, I knew the end result was worth it.

"Five," I said.

"Dollars?"

"*Thousand.*"

"What?" Tess whooped. "Holy *crud*, Nattie! You're amazing! You're the best treasurer we've ever had."

"Hardly." I twisted a dark strand of hair nervously. "I still feel bad I didn't, like . . . treasure very well. And about everything in New York."

Tess gave me a little *frappe* on the shoulder. "It's okay, Nattie."

I waited. Tess rolled her eyes.

"Okay, and I'm sorry, too. About everything. And especially about not talking you into buying that mermaid dress, even though I was totally righter than you about it."

"Pushy," I said. "You were pushy."

"Fine, fine," Tess said, and waved her silver-manicured hand in the air. "We both know I'm working on not bossing people around, okay? And I mean it when I say I'm sorry, because honestly, there is no way I could've done this without you. Money or no money."

"Really?" I was genuinely shocked, because besides taking terrible care of the spreadsheets, and literally almost dying in order to get Sebastian to play the dance, what *had* I done to help?

"Really. You're my best friend, Nattie, and I don't give out superlatives lightly. You are literally the best at being my friend." She *frappe*-d me again, but in an affectionate way this time, then straightened the hem of her jacket.

"Now, are you ready for this?"

I shook my head. "Doesn't matter. Are you?"

Tess gave herself one last look in the mirror. "In the words of honorary lesbian Joan of Arc, I was *born* to do this."

Downstairs, after taking a few pictures in our dance outfits, Tess squared her shoulders and ordered Dr. and Ms. Kozlowski to stand still.

"Actually, sit. You'll want to be sitting for this." She waved her hands, and they sat, looking a little confused. Tess took a deep breath, or as deep a breath as her tightly tailored jacket would allow, and when she glanced back at me, I gave her a tiny thumbs-up.

"Mom," she said. "Dad. I'm a lesbian. I've known pretty

much my whole life, but I wanted you to know, and I wanted you to know today, because this dance is very important to me, and I've been working very hard to make it not just an inclusive event for every student at Wister Prep but also a celebration of my own orientation."

It was amazing. She said it all in one breath, like she'd written it down beforehand, which she probably had. There were a few long seconds of silence, and even though I desperately wanted to rush in and stop it from being so, well, *quiet*, I knew I couldn't. This was Tess's time.

Her parents looked at each other, then back at Tess. Then they got up off the couch and hugged her.

"You're not . . . mad?" From inside her parental embrace, Tess's voice sounded extraordinarily thin. "Or disappointed?"

"Shh," her mom ordered, in a very Tess-like way. "No. Honestly, we did suspect, honey."

"You *did*?" Tess cried, back at full volume. "Then why did you keep asking me stuff about boys?"

"We were trying to give you the opportunity." Her dad—who was basically a male, middle-aged version of Tess, especially around the eyebrows—smiled, with a full set of impressively white orthodontist teeth. "A chance to correct us, maybe. But we didn't want to push."

"We knew that if you wanted to tell us, you'd find a way. A very big way," said her mom. "And we could never not be proud of you, Teresa."

Then there was some crying and some head-patting and lots of whispery Kozlowski things I couldn't hear until Tess finally pushed her way out of her parent sandwich.

"Okay, okay, let's not mess up my makeup." She dabbed at the corner of her eye with an elegant finger, sniffing, and took a deep breath. "Phew. Okay. You guys can take tonight to figure out how involved you want to get in the advocacy side of my life. No pressure or anything, but I've left some PFLAG literature with the takeout menus." She turned to me. "What time is your heterosexual Prince Charming going to arrive with our carriage?"

"He said six thirty," I said. "And it's—"

"Six thirty," Tess said.

She fluffed my curls with her fingers.

"Gorgeous," she said. "You're going to give that nice West boy a heart attack."

"I don't know about that," I said, but looking in the mirror over the mantel, I had to admit, I did look pretty great.

I was still totally, utterly grounded for the whole New York incident. But Mom and Dad had made an exception for Operation Big Gay Dance Party, partially because Tess had reminded them that, the events of this week notwithstanding, I had been a very responsible if slightly incompetent treasurer of the OWPALGBTQIA, and partially because, on the way back from the hospital, Zach the Anarchist had very politely asked their permission to take me.

The doorbell rang, and Tess stomped off.

"It's for you," she called. I followed, slowly, trying not to wobble on my heels.

"Hi, Nattie."

Zach West was wearing a suit. Zach West looked very nice in a suit.

"You changed your hair," he said.

"Oh," I said. "Um, yeah. I just wanted to be . . . different. A little. From all the . . . stuff that happened."

"It looks fantastic."

"Thanks."

Zach West was smiling. Zach West was holding something out.

"This is for you. It's a corsage. I don't know why, but they put it in a plastic box like it's a tuna sandwich or something."

"Thanks," I said. "Though a tuna sandwich would've been fine, too."

"Beep beep!" Tess had already marched herself to the Volvo and had stuck her head out of the backseat window. "Some of us need to be there, like, now!"

"We're coming," Zach yelled over his shoulder. "Do you need help putting it on?" he said to me.

But I'd already popped open the box and slid the flowers over my wrist. "It looks great."

"Great."

"It is great." I pursed my lips and fished around for my

phone. "Can . . . Do you mind if we take a quick picture? I promised my parents. And Sam. I won't put it online or anything, if you don't want."

"It's okay," Zach said. "You can, if you want."

"Okay," I said. "Well, smile."

We smiled, and the picture looked pretty great. Zach didn't even make a face. We got into the Volvo, and as Zach backed us out into the direction of the Woodlawn Museum of Art, I realized I was actually incredibly excited about this dance. And I didn't care if that was lame.

I never heard from Sebastian again. I mean, maybe it was premature to say I *never* heard from him again, but I was fairly confident that after nearly killing me with his poison-strawberry spit on our second date—if you can even call it a date—he probably wasn't coming back for more. And that was perfectly fine with me. Yes, I'd listened to their new single—which was, without a hint of irony, called "Déjà Vu"—but it was just okay. Nothing really special. And the Young Lungs *was* a really dumb name for a band.

"It's here!" Tess clapped her hands to her chest and spun around. The museum ballroom was bedecked with shiny streamers and a gaggle of balloons and little light-up center-pieces on every white-clothed table. On the back wall was a giant banner that said "OWPA WINTER FORMAL" in a distinctly Alison-y script.

"Yup," I said.

"I mean, technically, *we're* here," Zach said. "The museum hasn't gone anywhere."

"You guys." Tess stopped spinning and looked at us. She blinked a few dozen times, then started to fan herself. "Sorry. Sorry. I'm not going to cry and ruin my makeup. But you guys. We did it."

"Yup," I said. "Powered by sugar cookies."

"And pumpkin chocolate chip."

"And vegan pies."

"Gross." Zach made a face.

"Shh," I said, and pointed out to the dance floor, where Chihiro, in a beautiful sequined black dress, and Alison, in jeans, were already slow dancing. Bryce was standing off to the side, looking confused as always, and drinking a cup of punch. Cross-country guys clustered and chatted around the table with the drinks—probably so they could hydrate efficiently— and a gaggle of terrified-looking freshperson girls giggled and whispered under matching flower crowns. The theater tech kids were all wearing black tops and black pants, irrespective of gender, and the girls of knitting club all seemed to be in matching scarves. There were even some A Cappella kids—the ones who hadn't gotten busted, anyway—and when Sam Huang spotted me, he actually broke rank to come over.

"Hi, Sam," I said. "Nice tie."

"Oh, thanks." Sam held up the tie, which had a music-note print and which I was pretty sure was actually Dad's.

It definitely did not match perfectly with the rest of the group's ties, that's for sure. "This dance is really cool."

"Yeah," I said. "It is. I'm glad I'm ungrounded for it."

Sam Huang stared at the middle of his tie.

"No, no, I mean . . ." I shook my head. "I'm not mad. About you telling on me. I would've done the same thing, if I thought *you* were going to get hurt."

Sam smiled. "Cool. Um, well, there's one thing. . . ." He glanced back over his shoulder, to where the A Cappella kids were huddled in a perfect circle. It was like they couldn't *not* stand in formation. "That song you heard me singing? We're not doing it."

"You mean 'Na—'" I caught myself. "That one song?"

"Yeah." Sam leaned in closer. "I cut it from the list. We're doing a *Hamilton* medley instead."

My jaw actually dropped. "Sam Huang. Did you just break the embargo on A Cappella repertoire reveal? For *me*?"

Sam raised his eyebrows and shrugged in that Sam way of his, and I *frappe*-d him on the arm, because that's what sisters do. I think.

"Thanks, Sam."

Sam headed back to his place in the A Cappella cadre just as Zach My Date sidled back up to me. It was weird: I'd stood next to Zach West probably a thousand times in my life, from picture day to the cafeteria line, but this felt different, like there was a little spark crackling in between us. And not in a bad way, either.

"So," Zach said. "Do you—"

"Friends!" Tall Zach jumped in between us. "Nattie! Your hair! Zach! Your . . . shirt that's not a T-shirt!" He beamed, then frowned. "Oops. Wait. Did I ruin a magic moment?"

"This whole *dance* is a magic moment," Tess said rapturously. "Look! The balloons are all rainbowy!"

"You're fine," I told Tall Zach, but he wasn't listening. He and Tess had put their heads together, having some quiet conversation I didn't need to hear. When it was over, Tall Zach threw his arms around her neck and whispered something in her ear. Zach the Anarchist gave me the tiniest smile.

I cleared my throat. "So, um, not to be the absentee OWPALGBTQIA member, but, uh, how did we end up pulling all of this together? How'd we get music without . . . you know?"

Tess nodded to the front of the ballroom, where Endsignal was bopping between two speakers, pushing buttons and holding half of a pair of headphones to his ear. "We couldn't exactly book anyone on short notice, but fortunately our dear mop-topped freshman friend stepped in and offered to spin for us."

I wasn't really listening, though, because I had noticed someone off in the corner. Meredith White was in a floor-length blue gown, alone, holding a cup of punch and nodding to the music. While everyone was busy discussing the successful details of the dance, I slipped away.

"Hey! Nattie!" Meredith brightened as soon as she saw me. "You look freakin' *amazeballs*."

"Thanks," I said, trying very hard not to care that she'd just said *amazeballs*. "So do you."

"Thanks!" Meredith fingered a lock of hair, which was falling everywhere in frizzy ringlets. "I did the hot rollers myself."

And even though her hair didn't look super great, and you could kind of see her underwear line, and her lipstick was a totally mismatched shade of pink, the thing I noticed most about Meredith at that moment was that she was smiling. And if she liked the way she looked, then so could I.

"I just wanted to say that, um," I said, almost shouting over the music, "we should definitely hang out more."

Meredith beamed. "That'd be awesome! By the way," she added, "you and Zach make a really cute couple. I totally knew you were going to end up dating."

"You . . . we . . . what?" How come *I* couldn't have figured that out? But before I could say anything else, someone had grabbed me by the shoulders.

"There you are!" Tall Zach said. "Okay, get excited, becaaaaaause . . . I have a surprise for you!"

"I hate surprises," said Zach the Anarchist, who had trailed after him.

"Not *you*, Other Zach. You, *Nattie*."

"Uh, ditto," I said. "I've had enough surprises to last me until college at least."

"You'll like this one," Tall Zach said. He turned to the DJ stand and gave Endsignal a thumbs-up, which he returned.

"So . . . do you want to dance?"

Zach barely had a chance to get the words out when the familiar, cringe-inducing chords started up out of the speakers. I could practically feel the blood drain from my face.

"Tall Zach," I yelled. "Zachary Bitterman! Please don't do this!"

"What?" Tall Zach held a hand to his ear. "I can't *heeeear* you!"

Recognition dawned slowly over Zach My Date's face.

"Do you want to go outside?" he said.

"I . . ."

But instead of cutting to the verse, the opening chords of "Natalie" kept playing. Then, after a few measures, they started to stretch, and sound a little more . . . funky, like they'd been run through a weird filter or something. Then a beat kicked in—not the ordinary drums from the song, but something electronic and syncopated. Then the words started.

> "She's too tough.
> She's too cool.
> She's too tough.
> She's too cool."

The voice didn't sound like Sebastian's at all. It sounded angular and robotic and totally different.

"What *is* this?" I said.

"No idea," Zach My Date said.

Tess, who had somehow insinuated herself into the center of the dance floor, waved wildly for us to join her.

"You wanna?" Zach asked.

"Yeah," I said. "Let's."

We slipped past a bunch of people in long skirts and shiny dress shoes and started to move: me kind of awkwardly, and involving a lot of elbows, Zach My Date with a lot of head-bobbing, and Tess shimmying like crazy. The song crescendoed to a chorus, but not any chorus that I'd ever heard.

*"Oh Na-a-a-a-a-ttie.*

*Oh Na-a-a-a-a-ttie."*

"This is amazing!" I said.

"I know," Tess said, and grabbed my hand to spin me. "How'd he do this?"

Tall Zach reappeared and shrugged his giant shoulders. "He's always up to something on his laptop. Who knew?"

"Not me," I said. "Not me at all."

We grooved and shimmied and spun, and when the song finished, we burst into applause. At first it was just us, the Acronymphomaniacs, but slowly the rest of the room got into it, and the sound of claps and cheers was deafening. Louder than it had ever felt at a Young Lungs show, that's for sure.

"Thank you!" I yelled over the din.

"That was awesome!" yelled Tess.

"Nice drum line!" yelled Zach My Date.

"Why are we clapping?" yelled someone from behind us—Bryce, I saw.

"We're clapping because Nattie McCullough-Schwartz is amazing," said Tess, "and so is Endsignal. So is everyone. So is this whole party! Dance, you beautiful people! Dance!"

And we did—for what felt like hours. I jumped around with Tess and attempted to jitterbug with Tall Zach and, when a slow song came on, held hands with Zach My Date and swayed quietly against him.

"Ahem." Tess came up to us, hands on hips. "As Nattie's best friend, I think I deserve to cut in."

"Yeah, well, as Nattie's date, I think I deserve to not let you," Zach My Date said, and tightened his hand around my waist a little.

"As Nattie *herself*," I said, "I think I deserve to make my own decisions. And I will dance with you, Tess, later."

I thought she'd be pissed, but Tess didn't even flinch.

"Oh, Nattie. I love you. Not in a gay way. Well, yes in a gay way, because I love everything in a gay way. But you know what I mean." She pinched my cheek. "You're my best friend."

And then Tess did something extraordinary: she smiled with her teeth. They were beautiful teeth, of course, thanks to all the free orthodontia, but it was more the gesture that counted. And it counted a lot.

By the night's end, we were exhausted. Zach My Date had loosened his tie, Tess had kicked off her heels, and my corsage had wilted against my arm. We had to stay late, of course, for Tess to boss around some underlings vis-à-vis cleanup and Endsignal to pack up all his DJ stuff into Tall Zach's car, but that didn't take forever, and soon we found ourselves slumped around one of the tables, too tired to move.

"Stoplight Diner?" Tall Zach said. "They have fried Tastykakes."

"No offense, but ew, gross." Tess made a face. "I say we go down to the pavilion by the creek. I bet we could see stars."

"We'll get arrested for loitering," Zach the Anarchist said.

"And it's, like, two degrees out," Tall Zach said.

"Says the guy who always wears shorts," Tess said, and rolled her eyes.

"So let's go to Wawa," Tall Zach countered. "We can just get sandwiches."

"And then what?" Tess said. "I don't want to just loaf around my living room. I've got an hour left in my curfew and I intend to *use* it."

"You can use it getting sandwiches!"

"Or a fried Tastykake!"

"What do *you* want to do, Nattie?" Zach My Date said. When I said my feet hurt, he had very chivalrously allowed me to put them in his lap, which might have been weird with someone else, but with Zach West, it was fine. Nice, even. I was about to say I didn't know and would be fine just eating a fried Tastykake when an idea hit me.

"Hey!" I slammed a hand onto the table, making the light-up centerpiece fall over and everyone snap to attention. "Let's all go over to my house. I've got a place we can hang out."

The yard was dark when we got there, and the ground was really cold. Tall Zach sprinted right over, with Endsignal trailing, and Tess followed in leaps and bounds facilitated by hitching her skirt almost all the way up to her butt.

"And don't anyone dare look at my underwear," she said, "or I will murder you and use your organs for snowshoes."

"That doesn't even make sense," Zach My Date muttered. He was holding my hand again.

"That's Tess," I said. He started to walk over, but I stayed back.

"What?"

"This is such a weird thing to be doing after a dance," I said.

"Nattie," Zach said, "after the events of this week, this is by far one of the most normal things we've done. And also, who the hell cares if it's weird? Where would you rather be, off drinking wine coolers and having premarital sex?"

"As long as they're not strawberry wine coolers," I said, and even in the darkness, I think I could see Zach blush. "I'm kidding," I said quickly. "I meant it's weird in a good way. Like, look at me here, with my weird little life and my weird, awesome friends."

"Yeah," Zach said. Now I could tell he was blushing, because he was standing very close to me. Close enough for us to kiss.

I stood on my tiptoes and pressed my lips into his.

"This isn't weird, is it?" Zach said, as soon as I pulled away. I had to laugh.

"Well, *now* it is!"

"Hey! Nattie!" Tess poked her head out of the flap. "How do you turn on this heater thing? I'm freezing."

"Wrap yourself in a blanket," I said. "I'm coming."

Tess rolled her eyes and went back in.

"Should we go?" Zach said.

"In a second," I said, and kissed him again. "Okay. Now we can go."

Zach held my hand and helped me step over the frozen dirt, and together we followed our weird friends into the yurt.

# ACKNOWLEDGMENTS

Writing a book is a lot like building a yurt, in that it's hard, it takes a long time, and it makes people think you are crazy for even trying. Fortunately, I had lots of help, for which I am supremely grateful. First, thank you to Uwe Stender, the most unflappable and indefatigable of agents, and to Brent Taylor and all of TriadaUS. To Alexandra Cooper, my fantastic editor, thank you for championing, guiding, and pushing by turns: I could not have done this without you. At HarperCollins, thanks also to Alyssa Miele for all your help, to Bethany Reis, Emily Rader, and Megan Gendell for sharp-eyed copy edits, and to the publicity team for truly impressive levels of enthusiasm.

Thanks to Kate Brauning and Alex Yuschik for early reads and years (!) of creative friendship. Thanks also to V. Arrow, Kate Hattemer, Julie Leung, and Naseem Jamnia for your invaluable feedback on this book, and to Katie Locke, Eric Smith, and Chris Urie for all the moral support/writing dates/Gchats. Eli Sentman and Kirsten Madsen: thanks for all the Jamba alerts. Ari Kaplan, *je suis* indebted to *toi pour* having coined "*je frappe toi*." To the Under the Stairs Club, thanks for all the Friendsgivings of breaking bread with the math department.

To Germantown Friends School, where I first learned Catullus, and to Hamline University's MFA in writing for children and young adults program, where I learned almost everything else that matters: thank you for teaching me. Special shouts to my amazing advisors and my lovely Hamlettes.

Finally, endless thanks to my family: Alice, Sam, and my parents Rebecca and David (the real-life McCullough-Schwartzes) who knew I would be a writer before I did. I love you; please be my family forever.